Deliverance
from Evil

Deliverance from Evil

FRANCES HILL

DUCKWORTH OVERLOOK
London and New York

This paperback edition first published in the UK in 2011
First published in hardback in the USA in 2011 by
DUCKWORTH OVERLOOK

LONDON
90-93 Cowcross Street,
London EC1M 6BF
Tel: 020 7490 7300
Fax: 020 7490 0080
info@duckworth-publishers.co.uk
www.ducknet.co.uk

NEW YORK
141 Wooster Street
New York, NY 10012
www.overlookpress.com
For bulk and special sales, please contact sales@overlookny.com

A catalogue record for this book is available
from the British Library
Library of Congress Cataloging-in-Publication Data
is available from The Library of Congress

ISBN 978 0 7156 4087 6

Design and typeformatting by Bernard Schleifer
Printed in the United Kingdom by
CPI Bookmarque, Croydon, Surrey

for Leon
again, and always

PART
ONE

Chapter One

Maine
January 1692

THE SNOW GAVE THE REVEREND BURROUGHS THE ADVANTAGE OF silence. The minister had set out as soon as the blizzard stopped and a yellow moon sliding from clouds revealed glimmers of whiteness on the ground and in the trees. In normal conditions it was an hour's ride to York but the snow was powdery and deep, full of drifts and buried undergrowth, and he kept his horse to a walk. Following, in single file, so quietly he would not have known they were there, were ten soldiers and eight settlers, all the men Burroughs had been able to persuade to come with him. The rest believed the expedition ill-judged.

The ruddy light appeared to be the first streaks of dawn but it was ahead, not to the east. A flame leaped like a serpent's tongue and the snowdrifts on either side glowed. A rumbling noise seemed at first distant thunder but soon grew into crackling fire and gunshots. Indentations mounting the drifts appeared too big to be footprints till another tall flame showed the crisscross markings of snowshoe tracks. Banked against the palisade, the snow had given entry to Indians. The gate stood open; the snow piled against it had collapsed and been worn flat by feet. Burroughs climbed off his horse and led him to a tree, its branches sloped with snow. After tethering the animal he untied the sling that held his gun from the saddle. The rest of the men were tying up their mounts, horse rumps almost touching, legs knee-high in snow.

"We will be outnumbered." Captain Peter White, Burroughs's second in command, spoke to him softly so no one else could hear, tugging the black woolen hat under his helmet down over his unusually small ears, their little lobes almost as transparent as his breath. Burroughs fitted the sling cradling the six-foot gun across his body. He glanced round at the men, the soldiers' uniforms distinguishable only by their helmets, belts, and buckles from the settlers' long leather or wool jackets over breeches and boots. The minister commanded them because he had lived in these parts longer and fought in more battles than any of the army men. He was also a natural-born leader.

"We have come too late," said a settler with a deeply lined face, one of the oldest of the party. Burroughs wondered for an instant if they should turn back but a woman's piercing scream sent him running through the gate.

White flesh and white linen were rosy in fire glow; dark flesh gleamed; spears and gun barrels glinted; red and blue paint shone on ferocious high-boned faces. The houses were ablaze, not only the large garrison building on the snow-covered rise but also the smaller dwellings beneath. Burroughs felt almost overpowered by the heat. The Indians were stabbing, spearing, and axing; the whites fought as best as they could with weapons seized when they had been woken by the roar and crackle of flames, sometimes guns but more often kitchen knives, fire tongs, or pokers. They were inflicting few injuries and falling with terrible groans, turning white snow crimson. Burroughs saw a hatchet split a small boy's head like a fruit. He sprang forward but a howl made him spin round to see a man in his nightshirt drop on the ground. The minister leveled his gun at the Indian standing over him but the native bent down and thrust a dagger through the man's heart; when Burroughs pulled the trigger the Indian fell on his victim, their English and native blood merging. In the doorway of a house spurting flames an elderly settler was struggling with an Indian, hardly more than a boy, for his ax. Shoving his gun back in its sling, Burroughs leaped forward, lifted the native, and threw him at the house, whose front crumbled on the impact, revealing as on a stage a blazing table and spinning wheel of fire. Another Indian clubbed the white-haired settler to the ground as a woman in an ankle-length shift and unbuttoned boots ran from the flames. She screamed and fell on her knees. The Indian who had killed the man strode toward her but Burroughs swung his gun at his skull. With the sound of metal cracking bone, the native staggered but stayed on his feet. Burroughs dropped the gun and seized his throat.

"Forgive me, brother," he said, as dark eyes bulged in a red and blue mask.

"Gate's closing!"

The cry was Peter White's. It was taken up by others. Burroughs let go and the limp, heavy form collapsed. He picked up his weapon, grasped the woman by the arm, and pulled her past the dead and wounded to the gate, where soldiers were struggling with Indians trying to shut it. Burroughs felled one of the natives with the butt of his gun and pushed the woman through; another Indian seized him from behind and a third ran out through the gate and dragged the woman back in. Burroughs got free, turned, felled his attacker with a punch, ducked as another Indian lunged with a knife, wrenched the woman from her captor, and raced with her for the gate. He pushed it further open and as she ran through yelled to his men. Fending off the natives still standing, he got through after Peter and the rest, pulling the gate shut.

"To the horses!" He held his gun ready at shoulder height in case the gate reopened. "Everyone here?"

Everyone was.

"Fit to ride?"

They were, if in some cases only barely. Removing his jacket, Burroughs threw it round the woman's shoulders. She was shaking.

"Pull up your shift."

"What?"

"You can't sit sidesaddle. There isn't room."

He lifted her over the horse to sit in the front of the saddle, untied the horse, handed her the reins, put his foot in a stirrup, sprang up, and landed behind her. He reached round her to take the reins; as he held them loosely, she got his jacket on and buttoned it up. He glanced behind. All the horses were mounted.

"Let's go."

They trotted at first, following their own tracks. But, when Burroughs felt certain they weren't being pursued, he slowed his horse to a walk. As they left the burning village behind, the way ahead was dark. Only the trees on each side kept them to the path. Their hoofbeats muffled by snow, the only sound was the ever fainter crackling of flames.

Soon the lingering glow in the sky was shot with streaks that seemed to be blood. But Burroughs remembered that always after killing he was beset by strange fancies. The streaks were the dawn.

"We are going to Wells," he said, to try to occupy his mind, to the woman in his arms. There was a movement against his groin and he became aware for the first time that she was slender and young. She had pulled her dark brown hair out from under the jacket and it hung down her back to the saddle, as long as his own. He tried to see her face but could only glimpse dark lashes. She held the horse's mane as though used to riding without reins. She gave a sudden wail, then another that led to slow, deep, body-shaking sobs.

"Was that your father who was killed?"

"Aye."

"I could not save him."

"You saved *me*."

"By God's grace."

"That was better."

He said nothing.

"For him, I mean."

"To be spared your loss?"

"I was everything to him."

The horse, weighed down by the two bodies, sank with each step even in the well-trodden snow. The path ahead was faintly lit now by the first morning light but the snow-laden trees on either side were still dark except for gleams in the top branches.

"Once the light is better we will trot," Burroughs said. After a while he asked, "What's your name?"

"Mary Cheever." Her voice, though flat and low, carried clearly in the chilled air.

"Mine is George Burroughs."

"I know."

"How?"

"I have heard about you."

"Did you lose others in your family?"

"There was just father and me. Mother died five years ago. My sisters are married and gone."

"You can stay in Wells. I am the pastor there."

"Why did you come? How did you know?"

"An Indian warned me."

"An *Indian*?"

"He's a friend."

"A *friend?*"

"I have many Indian friends."

"They are savages!"

"Some English are more savage."

"Aren't you English?" Mary asked with surprise.

"Of course. But the Indians only attack us when we break our promises and steal their lands."

"Yet you rode here to kill them!"

"It is not the fault of women and children that men do what they do."

"Is that why your Indian friend warned you?"

"Aye."

"He saved my life. I wish I could thank him. I have not even thanked you." She twisted round toward him, showing a sweet face with big dark eyes.

"The best thanks will be keeping still and facing forwards. Easier on the horse."

The lingering glow and red streaks were dissolving in daylight. The trees and path ahead were becoming more visible, revealing forked dents made by robins' claws and the paw prints of rabbits and raccoons and twigs and bark strewn by squirrels. Burroughs's horse carefully stepped over a pile of pinecones. This steed was the most dependable and good-natured Burroughs had ever possessed, named by him Waramaug after an Indian he had once known with the same easygoing nature. Physically, the horse resembled himself, being dark, short of stature, lithe, and muscular.

"I remember hearing about you when you first came to Wells," Mary said. "They said how strong you were. What a fighter. It was amazing, how you lifted me."

"You weigh nothing."

"They said you were the only minister who dared stay in Maine, apart from ours." Her tone changed. "He must be dead! Our dear Parson Dummer! Dead for sure! Oh, I hope it was quick!"

"Indians always kill quickly." He paused. "Your father died instantly."

"You saw?"

"Aye."

She was silent, then again started crying, her sobs wrenched from deep inside her.

"He is at peace," Burroughs said.

"No, no, it's not that!"

"What then?"

"I hurt him so!"

Burroughs tightened his arms round her. She exclaimed again, "I hurt him so!"

"How?"

"If only I could have said I was sorry!"

"For what?"

"I would take the horse without telling him and go riding in the forest and I knew he would be worried to death. But I did not want to think about it and when I got back he'd look white and strained, but he'd just tell me not to do it again. Yet I did, and one day some Indians chased me and I got back just in time, and Father had almost died with fear."

"You gave him more joy than pain."

"How do you know?"

"I have a daughter."

"I did good things too. I looked after him when he was sick. Oh, I wish I could look after him now. He is lying where he fell. I must get back to bury him!"

"In good time. When 'tis safe."

Rounding a bend in the path, they saw ahead of them a woman with bloodied arms, holding a baby, and several children clothed in shifts, feet bare in the snow. All were looking round at them, eyes huge with terror. Burroughs stopped Waramaug, handed Mary the reins, and jumped off.

"Is anyone left alive?" called the woman, running toward him, distraught.

"Unlikely. I am very sorry."

"God rest his soul."

"Your husband?"

"He said he had to stay and fight. I got the children up a ladder and over the fence."

Peter White, riding up, called to her, "Get on my horse. Tell your children."

But the little ones were already running toward the horses he pointed to. Burroughs reached out for the baby. In his arms, the infant screamed as though speared.

"Give him me," Mary said.

Burroughs did so but the child's screaming did not lessen; the horse whinnied and shifted. Mary kept hold of the reins with one hand as she cradled the baby. Peter leaned down, grasped the woman under her arms, and tried to lift her to his saddle but could not. Burroughs seized her by the waist from behind and lifted her easily. Then he took back the screaming baby and handed him to his mother, in whose arms he gulped and snuffled to quietness. Peter opened his saddlebag, took out cloths, wrapped one round the infant, and gave the rest to Burroughs.

"Give these to the men to tie round the children's feet."

They were soon on their way again. A pale sun appeared above the horizon between the trees; a light breeze shook flutters of snow from the branches. The riders made their way up an incline where, beyond a steep drop to the right, they caught a glimpse of the ocean, its gray waters ridged like metal slats. Despite the full daylight Burroughs did not urge their horses to trot, weighed down as they now were with vulnerable burdens.

"Where will I go?" Mary said suddenly. "One of my sisters went back to England. I do not know where the other is."

"You can stay with us," Burroughs said. "I have seven children with no mother. The eldest's eighteen and looks after the others but there is too much work for her. You can help."

Mary said nothing and Burroughs wondered if she found the offer demeaning or if she suspected him of bad motives. He considered what to say to reassure her. But she spoke first.

"I have no experience with children."

"Rebecca would show you what to do."

"You must take me on trial. If I am no good I will leave."

"A bargain!"

"Thank you. This is very kind. Thank you so much."

"I have a strong feeling you and Rebecca will like each other." Burroughs peeped again at the dark lashes. "You must be about the same age as her."

"A year older."

They rode on for a little, then Mary said quietly, "I am very sorry your wife died. When did it happen?"

"Last spring."

"In the attack?"

There had been an assault on Wells the previous June.

"No. Before."

"Was that attack as bad as this?"

"Yes, except that we won."

"Thanks to you, I heard."

"Not just me. But there has been no safety since. We cannot plant or harvest."

"Why do you stay in Maine? You could go anywhere."

"I like it."

"Because you have always lived here?"

"No. I grew up in Massachusetts and went to Harvard and for a time was pastor in Salem Village."

"Why did you leave?"

Burroughs did not answer at once, then said, "It did not suit me."

"I heard Salem's a grand town."

"It is. I was not in the town. Salem Village is three hours' walk from Salem Town. A quite different place."

"At least your life wasn't in danger."

"No, but at times it hardly seemed worth living."

She turned to look at him. Her smile, curious despite its sadness, was the most captivating he had ever seen.

"What was wrong with it?"

"Felt like a prison."

Chapter Two

Salem Village
January 1692

HER GLOVE CAPTURED DIAMONDS, THE ONLY DIAMONDS SHE'D SEEN. She had heard people tell how they gleamed. Closing and opening her hands, she smudged the jewels into paste. Never before had she stood in the snow as it was filling the air, hiding the sky. This feeling of rapture made her afraid. It was wrong, except when praying or listening to sermons. God would punish her. She hoisted a foot from the blanket growing deeper each moment, to run back to the house, but saw nothing but whiteness and did not know which way to go.

"Betteeeeeee!"

The scream gave her her direction. She ran, diamond shards hitting her face, at once turning to water.

"Betteeeeeee!"

This was closer. Betty's shoulder collided with substance. She kept next to the wall, her shoulder pushing along it. A bare hand grasped her arm and hauled her into faint firelight.

"They'll whip me for lettin' you out!" Abigail's eyes were furious. She slammed shut the door and pushed Betty through another one to where the fire was. The snow on Betty's shoes was turning the threshing to mud.

"Get new straw, I'm not goin' to." Abigail pulled Betty's cloak off her shoulders, dropping snow in great clumps, and threw it on a peg next to the hearth meant for Reverend Parris's hat, sending up great clouds of steam.

"Your cap's off." Roughly Abigail pulled it back up on her head. Betty stepped into the huge fireplace, inches from the flames.

"You'll burn yourself!"

Betty stepped back.

"No one's here." Abigail's shoulders twitched in a way that showed she knew what she was doing or planned to do was wicked. She was tall for eleven, ungainly, her legs long for her body, her rear end prominent, her shoulders narrow and hunched. Betty, two years younger and several inches shorter, had a neater, prettier appearance, with a face of great sweetness. Abigail had lived with the family ever since the younger child could remember. Her parents were dead, slaughtered by Indians. Her mother had been Betty's mother's sister. Betty pointed at the fireplace, a great, lit cave, the tips of flames disappearing up the chimney. Abigail knew she was inquiring with this gesture about the occupant of the next room.

"*She's* here," said the older girl.

"In bed?"

"Of course."

Betty peered round as though someone might be lurking behind the table or wooden chest or one of the four spinning wheels. "Where's Tituba?"

"Fetchin' a rabbit from Ingersoll's. She'll keep there till this snowin' stops."

"I got lost."

"I was waitin' and waitin'. Now's our chance."

"For what?"

Abigail hurried into a corner, where shadows cast by the fire soared and ducked.

"What you doin'?"

Abigail came back, holding something in each hand.

"You made me play that stupid game, pretendin' to be Pharaoh's daughter findin' Moses in the bulrushes. This'll be much better sport."

The object in Abigail's right hand gleamed and sparkled.

"That's Father's glass!"

"He's at Mister Putnam's. You know how they gab. He won't be back now till dinnertime. Fetch a stool."

Betty brought one from the table, carrying it by two of its four legs, the seat higher than her head. With the glass, Abigail scooped water from the pail on the hearth, kept next to the fire to keep the liquid from freezing.

"Are we going to drink that?"

"Course not." Abigail put the glass on the stool and opened her other hand to reveal a small brown egg with a wisp of straw stuck to it.

"What's that for?"

"You'll see."

"She'll notice it's missing!"

"Who cares?"

"She'll be in trouble if there's none left tomorrow."

"You and her, makes me sick, slave's pet, that's you."

"No I'm not!"

"They're devils, all them Indians, they're not human. I grabbed it from under old Sarah, she squawked terrible." With a fingernail she flicked off the straw. "If you ask if we eat it I'll clout you."

Betty stared into Abigail's gray eyes, which wore the frightened yet resolute look that often accompanied the shoulder twitching.

"What do we do with it?"

"I break the egg in the glass an' ask it a question an' the white settles an' answers."

"Answers?"

"With shapes."

"Shapes?" Betty stared from Abigail to the egg and back again.

"I ask what my husband's callin' will be an' it goes to the shape of a hoe or a pulpit."

"That's dabblin' with spirits!" Betty glanced round. The shadows in the corners danced on small hooves. The orange and blue flames among the logs were imps cackling and hissing.

"Watch!" Abigail bent over the stool, cracked the egg on the side of the glass, and, with the expertise of an experienced pie maker, held the pieces close together to let the white flow into the water without losing the yolk. Betty squatted, her breath coming fast, till her face was on a level with the glass. Abigail threw the shell and yolk in the fire and squatted beside her. They watched as separate strands, faintly lit from behind by the flames, shifted and turned, as slowly as though nothing would follow from this, as though fate would continue its course determined at the beginning of time.

Betty screamed. Abigail smacked a hand over her mouth but Betty tore it away, digging in her fingernails.

"It's a *coffin*!"

Several strands had merged and settled in the form of a rectangle with wisps at each end curling upward like handles. Abigail tried to gag Betty with both hands but the smaller girl fought her off, scrambling to her feet, moving away from the stool and the glass, staring round. She backed into a corner, Abigail following.

"All it means is my husband might be a coffin maker," Abigail hissed at her.

"Someone's goin' to die!"

Betty's terror was dissolving the world around her.

"What's wrong?"

Betty opened her mouth but no sounds came.

"Your eyes have gone funny! You're shakin'!"

Though still conscious Betty did not know where she was. Or who she was.

After an hour, day, or a lifetime thin arms enveloped her.

"Come, Betty, come now, Tituba's here, Tituba's holding you."

The smell of mustiness and spices was as familiar as the angular contours. She felt warmth and smelled smoldering logs as she realized she was being lowered onto the floor. The fire still glowed. Abigail appeared from the shadows, her shoulders still, eyes blank. Betty tried to speak but again no sounds came. Her arms were jerking of themselves. Abigail stood behind Tituba; Abigail's arms began jerking too. Sounds of the outer door opening were followed by the appearance of a tall black-garbed man in a high buckled hat.

"Oh, Mister Parris, Betty's sick!"

The Reverend Parris moved quickly toward her. Cold emanated from him as though his body were sculpted from ice. A shorter man entered behind him with a young, skinny girl with a shark fin of a nose and small, close-set eyes.

"What ails her?" Samuel Parris stared at his daughter. Abigail jerked her arms again. "What ails Abigail?" His voice was high-pitched.

"Abigail?" Tituba saw the older girl's arms and body jerking just as Betty's were. "Oh, master, it were only Betty before . . ."

"What in God's name has happened here?"

"Nothin', master, nothin', I was out fetchin' a rabbit from Ingersoll's, gone just a minute, when I come back Betty was wild and sick. Now Abigail too, but only just now."

Betty's arms were still twitching and her head turned from side to side. The reverend's underlip stuck out, a sure sign he was angry or fearful. Betty still could not speak. Her father made a motion as though to seize Abigail, then changed his mind. For Betty everything again began to grow distant. She clung to Tituba to try to stay in the everyday world.

"Is my wife in the bedroom?" asked the pastor.

"Aye, sir, same as always."

"Something mighty strange has happened while you have been away, Mister Parris," said the man who had come in with him. His voice grated and his round face, framed by tightly curled hair, wore the smallest of smiles. His daughter stepped forward, staring from Betty to Abigail. After her first look of amazement her eyes had narrowed to the same calculating expression as the man's.

"I shall get to the bottom of it soon enough, Thomas," said Parris. "Slave, fetch Dr. Griggs. No, I shall go myself, 'tis quicker on horseback. Get these girls up to bed. Thomas, stay here till I come back. Ann, help Tituba."

"Never fear, Pastor," said Thomas Putnam. "We will take good care of everything."

Once the reverend was gone, he came closer, gazing down at Tituba as she held Betty in her arms.

"Slave magic, eh? Who taught it you? John Indian? Powwows in the woods? The old boy?"

Ann Putnam ran to Abigail and clutched her arm, peering into the narrow eyes, their expression frightened but not resolute. Though a year older than Abigail, Ann was the same height but skinnier. The tight curls escaping from her white linen cap were just like her father's but her close-set gray eyes were quite different from his widely spaced brown ones except in their expression. Her eyes and curved nose were her mother's.

"Stop shakin,' Abby," she whispered. "Come upstairs, come on." She pulled at her friend and suddenly the two girls ran from the room and up the stairs.

"No slave magic, Mister Putnam," said Tituba, rocking Betty. "See how Abigail run. But Betty's sick, I don' know why, as the Lord above is my witness."

Her father gone, Betty felt herself returning from the edge of the void. Sleepiness overwhelmed her as completely as if she'd drunk a whole cupful of cider.

"Ti . . . Titu . . ."

"She's speakin'! Lord be thanked!"

"So sleepy."

"I'm takin' you to bed, sweeting."

Putnam grinned, showing a gap in the middle of his teeth. "When you come down, fetch a pitcher of ale. An' this fire needs buildin'. Where's John Indian? What's the use of a husband if he don' build a fire? Even an Indian husband, who never made vows."

"He made vows!"

"Oojie goojie, in front of a powwow!"

"Christian vows, in front of Mister Parris!"

"I beg pardon, Goodwife Indian." Putnam leered. "All the more reason for his stoking your fire."

Tituba looked away. "He's workin' at Ingersoll's."

"Get upstairs."

As Tituba and Betty entered the girls' bedchamber, Abigail and Ann, whispering together in Abigail's bed, shifted apart and fell silent. In the freezing air Tituba helped Betty off with her woolen bodice and long outer skirt and three layers of petticoats. In her shift, the small girl climbed into bed, lay her head on the pillow, and almost at once was breathing the long slow breaths of sleep. Tituba stared across at Abigail.

"Why you causin' more mischief?"

"What mischief? I was sick same as Betty."

Tituba went on staring but Abigail stared back with such insolence that she said nothing more but turned to leave the room. Pausing in the doorway, she said, "You'd better both come downstairs, we don' wan' more trouble."

When Tituba reentered, Parris had returned not only with the doctor but also the doctor's wife's niece, a girl so undersized she looked closer to ten than her true age of seventeen. Elizabeth Hubbard helped her aunt and uncle with the housework in return for board, lodging, and clothes. Tituba saw with alarm she was pouring cider into mugs, filling them full. The barrel the liquid had come from was empty and she knew she hadn't the physical strength to prize the bung out of the hole of another one, let alone hammer in the tap, roll the barrel over, and hoist it onto its cradle. She needed John Indian for those things. But would the cider last till he came home? What would Samuel Parris do to her if it didn't? Beat her? Make her go without dinner? As for dinner, she should start cooking it now. Weariness almost overwhelmed her. Instead of skinning a rabbit, she felt more like going outside, lying down in the snow, and never getting up again.

"Are my daughter and niece in their beds?" Parris demanded.

"Betty's sleepin' like a baby. Abigail's better, she'll be comin' on down."

"Dr. Griggs is here to discover what ails them. Tell him how it all started."

"I don' know how it all started!"

Dr. Griggs, whose sparse white hair covered only small portions of his narrow, bony skull and whose elderly, lined face showed an irritation he was trying unsuccessfully to make look like concern, was seated on the room's only chair, by the fire, staring at Tituba. Addressing him, not her master, the slave explained what had happened. She did not dare say she thought Abigail had copied Betty out of mischief. As Tituba finished speaking, the door opened and the girl in question appeared, Ann behind her. Parris asked his niece how she was.

"Well, thank you, Uncle." Abigail spoke almost in a whisper. "My arms and legs ache. I'd be glad to sit down."

Parris pulled a stool up to the fire next to the doctor. Abigail perched on it, hunched. Ann stood beside her, smiling slightly, eyes darting to and fro. Everyone gathered round them except Tituba, who headed for the door with the pitcher.

"Stay here!" shouted Parris.

"I was gettin' more cider from the lean-to, Mister Parris." In truth she was removing the cider to save it.

"Time enough for that. I want to find out what mischief or worse has been occurring here in my house." He turned to Abigail. "What happened, niece?"

"I don' know, uncle." Abigail still spoke softly. "Tituba and Betty were here by themselves. When I came in, Betty was shakin.' Then I felt myself shakin' too."

"That's not true!" Tituba cried. "I was out, when Betty's fit started,

Mister Parris! What you playin' at, Abigail? I bin close to a mother."

"You say Abigail is lying?" shrieked Parris.

"I'm not saying anythin', Mister Parris, 'cept I'd gone to Inger-soll's for the rabbit for dinner and when I got back Betty was wild and shakin'."

"Where was Abigail?"

"Goin' out the door to the lean-to, but I didn' take no notice, I was carin' for Betty. Then Abigail come back in and Betty was quietin' and then you got here, Mister Parris."

"Pardon me," exclaimed the doctor, trying to mask his exasperation with a smile of solicitude. He cleared his throat. "May I suggest we go back to this later? I should go see Betty, and Tituba should start making the dinner. Ye need nourishment, all of ye."

If Dr. Griggs expected to be allowed to see Betty by himself he was wrong. As Parris led him out of the room into the entranceway and up the narrow wooden stairs, everyone followed except Tituba, who again made for the lean-to with the almost empty jug of cider.

"Walk quietly," Parris warned them. "My wife is sleeping."

Soon six people were gathered round Betty's bed. Dr. Griggs leaned over, took the girl's arm out from under the blankets, and placed his bony fingers on her pulse. She did not stir. He lifted up her eyelid. Still she did not stir. But when he hoisted the second eyelid she gave a cry and sat up.

"'Tis only Dr. Griggs, child," cried Parris.

Betty started shaking.

"Are you in pain?"

Betty opened her mouth but was unable to speak.

"Be still, child!" shouted Parris, gripping her arm. The shaking got worse. At the foot of the bed, Abigail started to shake too. Ann Putnam followed suit, then Elizabeth Hubbard.

Chapter Three

Wells, Maine
January 1692

THE PALISADE GATES OPENED AHEAD OF THEM AS THEY RODE PAST THE remains of the houses destroyed by Indians a year ago. Inside, the waiting townsfolk surrounded them. Burroughs's daughter Rebecca ran forward, her blue eyes and bucktoothed smile showing her joy and relief as she shouted, "Welcome back!" She took the reins from her father as he lifted Mary from the horse.

"Are you hurt, Pa?"

"Nay, thanks be to God."

Mary was shivering.

"This is Mary Cheever. Get her indoors."

"Come with me," Rebecca said. "I'll get you some clothes. We're about the same size."

All around them womenfolk were greeting their men, taking care of the women and children who'd been rescued, and getting news of what had passed. Burroughs's younger children surrounded him, the smallest hugging his legs.

"Take the little 'uns with you, Rebecca," Burroughs called after her. "I have not time for them now."

As Burroughs led Waramaug to the barn, there flowed through him a relief at being alive he had not dared feel before. The horse stood patiently while Burroughs unsaddled him.

"Good boy. You did not like the fires and noise. But you kept calm." Burroughs patted his neck, then carried the saddle to its hook in a corner of the barn and fetched an armful of hay. Waramaug pushed his nose into it and ate noisily. Burroughs was closing the door of his stall when Peter White came in with his mare, who at once, seeing

Waramaug, whinnied joyfully. Peter took her into the next stall and the two animals nuzzled over the partition. Burroughs and Peter exchanged smiles of amusement that also expressed the gratitude they felt for each other's comradeship.

"They have forgotten the horrors already," Burroughs said, waving toward the horses.

"Spared the worst of them, outside the fence."

As Burroughs walked back across the rough grass to the house, phrases for his next sermon began forming in his mind.

"We live each day for God . . . 'Consider the lilies of the field . . . They toil not, neither do they spin . . .' We toil and we spin but we are as much in God's hands as the lilies. . . . We live for him, not for ourselves, as he lives for us."

In the house he made for the stairs to go up to his study but, passing through the main room used for cooking, eating, working, and most other indoor activities, came across his daughter peeling carrots. He looked around and, failing to see Mary, asked where she was.

"I put her in my bed after she'd warmed up by the fire. I think she's got a fever."

"Have you given her water?"

"Aye. And gruel."

Burroughs climbed the first flight of stairs but, instead of continuing up, turned and headed for the bedchamber where he and his family slept. A mound under the blankets in his daughter's narrow bed showed, on closer inspection, the upper half of a white face with large, wide-awake eyes. He felt the forehead. Hot but not burning. He squatted down.

"How are you?"

"Aching." Her voice was faint.

"I shall send Peter White. He's our doctor."

"I do not need him." She managed a small smile.

"I shall send him anyway."

"I dreamed I saw my father and asked his forgiveness but he could not hear me."

"Your *Heavenly* Father can hear you. Ask *his* forgiveness."

Her eyes were green, flexed with brown.

"Will I see him when I die?"

Burroughs knew she was talking of her earthly father.

"God willing. I hope that will not be for years yet. When you meet him you can ask him to forgive you but he will not need to. He loved you too much to have anything to forgive."

"Is that true?"

"You have my word for it."

"Will you pray with me, to help me ask *God's* forgiveness?"

"We will say the Lord's Prayer together." He bent his head and closed his eyes. "Our father . . ."

She recited it with him, her soft voice becoming almost a whisper when they reached the "forgive us our trespasses." Afterward, she said, "I am sorry to be a burden on you."

"You will soon be better."

"Where will I sleep tonight?"

"Here."

"But this is Rebecca's bed."

"We will put another one next to it."

"I keep thinking about Father lying in the snow."

"We'll go back there soon."

"Do not go without telling me."

"I will not, I promise. Sleep now."

"Yesterday Ann climbed into a corner of the cellar and stayed there for two hours." Thomas Putnam spoke in the tone of someone whom nothing ever surprised. Raising a slice of dark bread topped with cheese, he sank his teeth in.

"They grow worse every day." Parris put down his mug on the low table beside him.

"Ann is no use for anything." Putnam spoke indistinctly, his cheeks ballooning like a hamster's. He chewed for a while, then said more clearly, "Her mother had to bake all the bread herself yesterday. Luckily our little maid Mercy has still got her wits, such as she had."

"My girls have not done the baking since my wife took to her bed. John Indian does it now. They do not do any spinning either; maybe that's what has led to this; they have been idle. When I tried to talk to Abigail this morning she just babbled. As for Betty . . . " He shook his head, his underlip jutting. Fingering the mug handle, his voice sinking, he said, "I fear for her life."

"Bad as that, Mister Parris?"

"Where will it end?"

"Aye, aye, where?"

"Griggs tells me Elizabeth's no better."

"My step-niece Mary Walcott is as bad as any of them now."

"So I have heard."

"She is a fine well-grown girl, seventeen years old, makes a sight to behold with her writhings and rollings."

"I have not been to Walcott's house lately. Too busy in my own."

"My poor sister's beside herself. She has had trouble with the girl ever since she married her father. Now she has no control of her at all."

"There are other females too starting to act strangely. Dr. Griggs has ruled out epilepsy."

"There seems only one answer."

"Our enemies would use it against us."

"Let them try!" Putnam washed down his food with a large gulp of ale.

"You forget, Thomas, they are more powerful now, they control the committee, they are threatening to stop paying my wages, they are refusing to deliver any more firewood, as our contract obliges them."

"That is a moot point, Reverend Parris."

"It was made perfectly clear in my demands of April '89, I have the copy in my study."

"That business about firewood was never accepted. You cannot complain, Pastor. You own the ministry house. Few thought we would ever achieve that, though I never myself doubted it. If the will is there, the way can always be found."

Anyone looking at Putnam, seeing his round face, curly hair, and beneficent smile, might think he was a man of goodwill. Some people still thought this, even after getting to know him, if their interests tallied with his. He had that ability to ingratiate himself that depends on an acute though contemptuous understanding of others' obsessions, and his enjoyment of making egotists love him was as precious to him as were all other exercises of power. Samuel Parris's interests certainly tallied with his: he would not be here as the ordained pastor of Salem Village were it not for this ally.

"There is money needed now for more weapons," Putnam observed.

"That is not my concern."

"You might change your mind about that if there was an Indian attack."

"My task is to defend Salem Village from deadlier enemies than Indians."

"Too bad George Burroughs escaped with his life."

"What?"

"Talking of deadlier enemies. The Reverend George Burroughs. In that attack on York."

The news of the massacre that had taken place a week earlier had reached Salem Village only yesterday.

"He is not *in* York."

"He was. He rode there. Did you not hear? Too late to be of any use to anyone, of course, despite the strength he's so famous for."

"How did he know the attack was going to happen?"

"Told by an Indian." Putnam grinned, showing the gap in his teeth. "But maybe it was not an Indian but one of those spiritual enemies you talk of, if they are not one and the same."

"Can I fetch you anything, friends?"

Despite the large white apron tied round his waist, hanging just below his knees, the man standing beside them had an air of confidence and authority wonderfully combined with warmth and understanding. The confidence was partly based on his large frame, straight back, full head of hair, and resonant voice. But it was also due to his knowing himself to be one of the wealthiest and most influential men in the village, the wealth stemming from his monopoly of the catering trade and an estate he'd inherited, the influence from his posts as a lieutenant in the village militia and deacon in the church. The appearance of warmth and understanding came from his soft but serious brown eyes, kindly smile, and wide salt-and-pepper beard. It in truth revealed a somewhat readier human sympathy than was usual in this strictest of Puritan regions but did not arise from any deep wisdom. Nathaniel Ingersoll's apparent love of mankind stemmed purely from his desire for others to share his love of himself. People often came to him for advice, having failed to realize his standing was the result of good fortune and his compelling demeanor purely of the surface. Had he lived anywhere but here, where entertainments were forbidden, he would have been an actor. Had he a sharper mind and more energy, he might have entered the ministry.

"'Tis your wisdom we have come for, even more than your excellent ale," said Parris. "Pray sit with us."

Ingersoll stroked his beard first with one finger, then two, then his whole hand, as though the more he felt it, the more he admired it.

"The doctor is at a loss, I believe." The innkeeper obliterated a stool, letting go of the beard and resting his hands on his white aproned knees.

"An utter loss," said Parris.

"If Abigail and Betty do not grow better, it might be wise to part them."

Hannah Ingersoll had said this to Nathaniel yesterday, after visiting the Parrises to tend Samuel's wife. If Nathaniel loved anyone almost as much as himself it was Hannah. She provided him with utter devotion, excellent meals, and almost all his ideas. He maintained the devotion by detailed attention to and enjoyment of her charms, which he regarded as more than part of his property, as part of his being. When he chose to marry this woman his self-love encompassed her and he and she became "one flesh" beyond what was meant in the Bible. This state of affairs was upheld by Hannah's being subtle and patient enough to quell her annoyance at Nathaniel's overweening vanity and thus avoid provoking his temper, which, once unleashed, was ferocious.

"Part them?" exclaimed Parris. "How can I do *that*? There are not enough rooms in my house as it is, with my wife on her sickbed."

"Have they been meeting Ann and Elizabeth?"

Hannah had asked this of Nathaniel, who had not known.

"I believe Abigail has. Betty has not stirred from the parsonage since these horrors began. Only Tituba can calm her. I fear the slave has some unnatural power over the child."

"The power of love," said Ingersoll, softly. "Not unnatural." This thought, for once, was his own. He knew a great deal about the power of love.

"You are saying my daughter loves an Indian and slave?" Parris gave an incredulous laugh. "I have summoned two physicians and the Reverends John Hale and Nicholas Noyes to talk to the children and give their opinions and pray with them."

Putnam looked surprised, then thoughtful. "I would request my daughter Ann may be with them for that visit."

"By all means."

"We must all pray," Ingersoll said. "Hannah and I mention the children in our prayers morning, noon, and night." As he smiled, the creases round his eyes enhanced his misleading appearance of kindness and wisdom.

When Parris got back to the parsonage he found his ailing wife in the living room in her shift, eyes wild, with Tituba hanging on to Abigail, who was straining forward toward the fire, struggling to escape, apparently trying to run into the flames. Betty sat in a corner, staring sightlessly, her head and limbs jerking.

"Help us!" shrieked his wife.

Parris ran and gripped Abigail's arm, which was stiff as a branch. The girl almost twisted free but he managed to hang on.

"Tituba! Fetch Dr. Griggs! *Now!*"

The slave let go of Abigail and ran, while Parris grasped Abigail in his arms as his wife lost her hold and slid to the floor. Abigail pushed her hand under the sleeve of his coat and dug her fingernails through his thick linen shirtsleeve.

"Stop that!" He pulled her wrist away. The girl gave a weird laugh. He was tempted to get his hands round her throat but instead pushed her face forward to the floor and sat on her rump, thrusting down her head till her nose was in the threshing. Only her muffled screams persuaded him to lessen the pressure. His wife lay moaning.

"Elizabeth, get upstairs if you can."

"Betty . . ."

Parris looked at the girl, still staring vacantly, limbs jerking like a puppet's.

"You cannot aid me here, wife. Try and get up to bed."

Mistress Parris crawled to the door, sticklike arms protruding from unbuttoned sleeves, hauling herself through the straw, panting, her cap off, gray hair hanging round her face. Abigail's arms and legs still thrashed but Parris stayed on her rump, holding her head down.

"The doctor's coming. For God's sake, lie still."

After another few minutes, Abigail *did* lie still, though Parris dared not get up in case she revived.

When Dr. Griggs arrived the minister gave a breathless but clear enough account of what had passed.

"What is happening to them?" Parris implored. "What ails them?"

"I have not wished to say it before but now I feel certain. There can be no natural cause of this. They are bewitched."

Chapter Five

Maine
February 1692

THE SURVIVORS KEPT COMING. THERE WERE FAR MORE THAN BURROUGHS had dared hope. Some had hidden in cellars, one under an overturned tub, another in a pile of flax. A young couple and their baby were asleep in a house so small as to be completely covered in snow. One woman was spared when a wounded Indian cried out for water and she gave it him. The rest of her family was slaughtered. All the new arrivals had seen terrible sights: heads axed from bodies; a child with a hatchet still in its skull; strewn limbs; ripped stomachs; people in their death throes; worst of all, children burning alive.

"I thought I saw Reverend Dummer," gasped one man, tears streaming down his face. "Then I realized it was an Indian dressed in his clothes. The reverend lay next to him, naked, his limbs hacked from his body."

The survivors told of the injured, unable to walk and too heavy to be carried: one man with a bullet through his thigh, another whose foot had been shattered, a woman who had broken her ankle jumping from a second-story window. Later that day, Burroughs decided to lead a party of soldiers and settlers, as many as there were horses to carry, to fetch out the wounded and bury the dead. He knew the ways of the Indians well enough to feel sure they would not attack again. They had destroyed York completely. A year ago they had attacked Wells and the settlers fought them off but then they had returned until most of their number were dead and only then retreated. But they had no reason for further fighting now. Pulling on his boots, he remembered his promise to Mary and told Rebecca to inform her they were going. As he was getting his gun in its sling across his chest Mary ran into the room,

Rebecca's skirt and bodice hanging on her loosely, her expression distraught.

"I'm coming!"

"She's still got a fever!" shouted Rebecca, running in behind her.

"Get back up!" Burroughs barked.

"I want to bury my father!"

"We could not take you even if you were not sick! We need all the horses for the men."

"Come, Mary." Rebecca tugged at her arm. "Father's right. Come back to bed."

Bursting into tears, Mary ran from the room, Rebecca following. Minutes later, as Burroughs was going out the door, Rebecca hurried back in.

"Mary wants me to tell you she's sorry."

Burroughs grunted

"She's feeling very foolish."

"So she should be." Burroughs left the room.

"Shall I say anything else to her?" Rebecca called after him.

"Apology accepted."

The journey to York was much quicker by daylight and over well-trodden snow than the one the night before. But the sight that greeted them was as terrible. Walking through the open-air charnel house of rubble, ash, and snow strewn with bodies, Burroughs prayed silently for strength. Reaching the spot where he had killed the Indian with his hands, and not finding him, he looked about him again and realized there were no dead Indians anywhere. They must have been carried off by their kin to be buried in the forest's sacred places.

Burroughs and his men began the long, arduous task of burying their own dead. It would have been foolhardy to carry them to the York cemetery, outside the palisade, or to Wells, in case against expectations the Indians returned. So they broke through the frozen earth to dig a pit large enough for a mass burial, having not time or numbers to give each victim his or her own grave. Burroughs made one exception. For now, he left one body lying where it had fallen.

Later, as he again axed the frozen earth, he felt glad Mary was not with them. Her father's corpse was frozen in its posture of death, arms spread, legs twisted, eyes and mouth open. When it was covered with ice-marbled soil, Burroughs recited a short burial prayer, then silently, head still bowed, added another, asking God to guard and help this dead man's daughter.

Some of the men had brought little wooden crosses. Burroughs chose the sturdiest and dug a hole for it at Mary's father's head. If there was no more heavy snow it stood a chance of staying there until, with God's grace, York was retaken and the bodies could be buried in consecrated ground.

At last the remaining survivors were helped onto horses and the rescue party made the weary journey home. By the time they reached it, night had fallen.

Chapter Six

Salem Village
February 1692

THOMAS PUTNAM CALLED HIS DAUGHTER ANN INTO HIS OFFICE, A
partitioned nook at the end of the living room, itself small. He walked
back behind the little table that served as his desk, past a pitchfork
propped against a workbench covered in saws, hammers, nails, and screws.

"Are you going into your fits today?" he asked as she entered.

"How can I tell?" The little, close-set eyes stared at him, curious
but also anxious. Putnam came round the desk, carrying a stool. He put
it down and sat on it, his face level with his daughter's. She jigged her
right heel so hard her skirt vibrated.

"Did you really see Tituba when she was out of the room, when
the Reverends Hale and Nicholas Noyes were visiting the parsonage?"

Ann stopped jigging.

"Did you?"

"Yes!"

"You saw her *through the wall*?"

"Do you think me a liar?"

"I do not think anything. That is why I am asking you."

Ann crossed her arms. "I *did* see her."

"Through the *wall*?"

She opened her arms, holding her hands out. "It was as though the
wall wasn't there. I saw her standing in front of Ingersoll's, just like
Betty said she saw her."

Father and daughter gazed at one another. Putnam leaned forward, hands on knees. "Will you see her again?"

"I don't know."

"You could if you wanted to."

"I didn't lie! Reverend Parris can't say I lied!"

"Course he can't. You're the best girl in the village, my pigeon. Here, sit down." He swung round on his stool and with one sweep of his arm sent tools, screws, and nails to the floor. Ann inspected the table and then hoisted herself up on it.

"Lean back against the wall. Make yourself comfortable."

Ann obeyed the first of these instructions and did her unsuccessful best to follow the second. Putnam leaned forward a little.

"I am going to talk to you now in a way you won't understand but I have very good reasons for it. Pour all thoughts from your mind like cider from a jug. As I talk listen hard to my voice so no thoughts creep back in. If you find your eyes growing heavy let them close."

"Why are you doing this?"

"Do not question me." He spoke these words with a hint of asperity but sounded soothing again as he said, "Just listen, chuck, listen. Night follows day and blood flows when there's murder and wives appear in their winding-sheets and he'll take you up on the mountain and promise you the kingdoms of the earth."

"What on earth are you talking about, Pa?" Ann whispered.

"Sshh, just listen, think of nothing. There's sleep coming, breathe slow and deep, let your eyelids close slowly, there's sleep coming, and something else is coming, the witch is coming, breathe slow and deep."

Ann closed her eyes and, as Putnam's voice continued its incantation, began breathing rhythmically, her head drooping. After continuing his strange words for some time Putnam said, very gently, "When you open your eyes again you will see her." He paused. "Open your eyes now."

Ann raised her head, stared past her father, and said, "She's standing next to you."

"Good girl!" He smiled, showing the gap in his teeth. "When you want her to go, breathe out, and tell her to."

Ann exhaled, then shouted, "Go!"

"Gone now," said Putnam. "Breathe out again. Everything's as it was."

"I saw her," said Ann, now staring at *him*.

"I hear the rattling of plates and mugs, chicken. You will be wanting your breakfast." But he stayed on his stool. "I expect you will be seeing other witches soon."

Ann's blank stare filled with calculation. "When you tell me I will?"

"No, when *you* tell me you will. When you close your eyes and breathe deep and say to yourself she will be there when you open them."

"And she'll be there?"

"If she's a witch. Only witches can send out their spirits."

"Who will she be? Sarah Good? Everyone knows *she's* a witch."

"The whole village knows."

"Old bed-rid Sarah Osborne?"

"A devil's accomplice if ever there was one."

"Who else?"

"Maybe some no one ever even suspected. Maybe *church members*. Maybe some who have been saying there aren't any witches."

"Martha Cory?"

"She's been saying you ought to be whipped."

"*She* ought to be whipped! She had a baby before she was married!"

"That she did."

"John Proctor says we witched girls ought to be hanged."

"People are more likely to believe a man is a witch when he is married to a witch."

"Elizabeth Proctor's been giving us strange looks."

Putnam showed the gap in his teeth.

"Mother hates her," Ann added.

"There may be others, who have never given us Putnams proper respect, who thought they were better than we are . . ."

"Such as . . ."

"Not yet, not yet. First we must have a confession, to silence the doubters."

Putnam lifted Ann off the table. She stood before him, looking in his face with frank awe.

"How did you do it, Pa?"

Again Thomas Putnam showed the gap in his teeth.

"I have watched and listened when men of no account steal away women's souls. . . . But you need know nothing of that, my dear, suffice it to say that my voice and your thoughts together can find out invisible evil." He took her in his arms. The strange sound she emitted could have been a gasp of bliss or a sob.

Chapter Seven

Maine
February 1692

THERE WAS A SHORTAGE OF BEDS IN THE THREE TWO-STORIED, SMALL-windowed garrison houses, with their thick bulletproof timber walls, but rather than make use of the smaller, less well fortified dwellings, men and women crammed in on palliasses or just blankets.

Burroughs thought of taking his rope bed to his little study under the eaves. But it was as cold up there as in the night air outside. So he slept in his usual place in the family room, at the other end from Mary, with his seven children and several new occupants in between. There was no immodesty in this sleeping arrangement since, with the temperature well below freezing and not enough blankets, everyone slept in their clothes.

Amid the cacophony of snores, gasps, mumbles, and quick and slow breathing, he thought he could recognize sounds made by Mary. His last thought before falling asleep was that it was strange a snore could sound musical.

Though his dreams were full of dreadful sights he woke refreshed and full of vigor, ready to lead his followers through whatever new hardships awaited them.

However, over breakfast and during the rest of the morning it became clear, as people talked about the future, that half the town, knowing the Indians might attack Wells again next, wanted to leave at once for Massachusetts. Burroughs, though disappointed, could understand their fearfulness. But many injured and wounded were immobile, or virtually so, as were those who had fallen sick with fever or suffered from frostbite or simply exposure and exhaustion. Besides, as Burroughs argued to any who would listen, there was nowhere to go. Who would want them? Where would they be truly safer than here? He surmised another full-scale war with the Indians might be starting, with the French providing arms and equipment. Even settlements around Boston and Salem might be in peril.

Peter White agreed with him. As Wells's unofficial doctor he feared for the lives of his patients if they traveled. He was tending them as best he could, washing frostbitten fingers and toes with tinctures of beech leaves, dressing wounds with poultices made of star moss, giving people with fevers tea brewed from sassafras. Everyone, he hoped, would recover, but only with care. Like Burroughs, he doubted life would in any case be easier anywhere else. For the Anglicans, Baptists, and Quakers, it might be harder.

Burroughs organized a meeting, hoping to convince his whole flock that Wells would be safer and stronger the greater its numbers, and that no one should leave.

In the late afternoon all the town's adults not too sick to get out of bed or caring for children, crammed into the main room of the garrison house Burroughs lived in. He preferred not to take them to the meetinghouse, which was inside the palisade but flimsier in structure and far less safe from attack. As everyone found chairs, stools, or places to stand he, refusing offers of help, pushed the long maplewood table against the wall and climbed onto it. More than a hundred people, including the forty soldiers stationed in the town, stood, or sat facing him. Peter was near the table and Burroughs called to him to come up. As he did so, he bumped his head on the ceiling and had to crouch. Someone handed up a stool for him to sit on.

It occurred to more than one of the women in that crowd that between them these two men possessed every aspect of masculine beauty. Burroughs was short but lithe and well-muscled, with a swarthy complexion, expressive dark brown eyes, and black hair hanging to his waist, smartly dressed in the coat, kerchief, and breeches of a minister; Peter White was unusually tall with a strikingly handsome, fine-boned face, his light brown hair tucked behind his tiny, pink-lobed ears and his slender frame draped in an elegantly threadbare military uniform. However, to *one* woman, standing near the back, it was Burroughs who exerted a force that stirred feelings quite new to her.

"Friends! Can you all hear me?"

"Aye!" the room responded.

"As I think you all know I have called this meeting because some of you want to abandon our town and go to Massachusetts. I wish to urge you to stay. Together we can fend off any attack, as we did before, nearly a year ago now though it seems a far shorter time. We are better prepared than York was, and more vigilant. Some survivors have told us their watchmen failed in their duties that night. It was when they slept that the Indians attacked. That would never happen here! We would never stop patrolling. Our watchmen would never sleep."

There were shouts of agreement and some murmurs of dissent.

"We have not enough soldiers or arms!" a man called. "We need reinforcements!"

"We have only food enough for a few months!" someone else said.

"I shall write again to the Council in Boston to send soldiers, guns, and grain."

"They did not respond last time!"

"Or the time before that!"

"This attack on York will prove the extent of the need we are in."

A woman's voice carried forward, making everyone turn.

"If we all went to the Council in Boston they would have to help us or send us back with reinforcements."

Burroughs had been aware of Mary's presence from as soon as he got on the table, though she was so far to the back. Two days of rest and many cups of sassafras tea had cured her fever. Everyone craned their necks, trying to see her. For once in his life, the minister found himself speechless. Peter, his instincts as a gentleman overwhelming his memory, rose and bumped his head again; crouching, he shifted his stool closer to Burroughs and perched, long legs tucked under it.

"I apologize for sitting while addressing a lady who is standing."

There was good-natured laughter.

"Miss Cheever, if only what you just said were true. But we can have no confidence the Council would take either action you mention. It is unclear whether we are even ruled by Massachusetts now that the old charter is gone and Mather is not yet back from England with the new one."

"What's the charter?" asked someone, causing more laughter.

"Who's Mather?" called someone else, causing groans.

"I will not go into any of that now but what matters is that Maine may now no longer be part of Massachusetts. In that case, the Council might take no pity on us, specially since so many are not Puritans."

Mary pushed forward, the throng giving way.

"In that case we cannot rely on them for reinforcements either! Every one of us has seen horrors we never want to see again. I would leave today by myself if I had anywhere to go."

There were shouts that she must not think of that. Burroughs at last found his voice.

"Miss Cheever, I have a proposal." He drew a paper from his pocket but, as he continued to speak, did not look at it. "Firstly, I will write to the Council with an urgency and eloquence beyond anything I have accomplished before, and send soldiers to carry the letter to Boston tomorrow by first light. Secondly, I shall set about organizing parties of men to strengthen the palisade. I shall ensure four men will always be on guard, even at night, and also have men strengthen the timbers of the garrison houses and meetinghouse. Thirdly, I shall arrange for armed parties to collect wood, game, and fish for the stores and patrol the country around for signs of the Indians. And, lastly, I shall declare a special day of prayer, devoted to begging God's forgiveness for the sins that have brought these calamities down on us. I make a promise that if all our attempts fail and no reinforcements arrive within three months, by which time spring will have come, everyone who still wishes to leave shall be welcome to do so, with the help and blessing of the rest of us. I ask you, Miss Cheever, and everyone here, may we agree to that?"

"Yes!" said many, though not all.

"Miss Cheever?"

"I do not know."

"May I speak to you after the meeting?"

"Aye." She turned away.

"Is everyone else in agreement?"

Some said "aye"; some shook their heads but no one said "no."

"May I take that as a unanimous yes?"

"Yes!" many called. Burroughs bowed his head.

"Let us pray."

Mary's heartbeat, in her own ears, drowned Burroughs's mellifluous voice intoning the prayer. She had taken herself by surprise when she spoke. Altogether these days she felt she hardly knew herself. At times thoughts of her father froze her in place and almost made her scream. She kept forgetting things people asked her to do, such as fetching something from the storerooms or taking a pot off the fire. She had let the stew almost boil dry a couple of times. The other women were usually kind to her but many had suffered their own losses and there was always too much to do. Some were impatient, even sharp. Last night under the blankets she had felt a desolation she could never have guessed at, deeper than during that first night after the massacre. She was at last fully aware, as she had not been till now, that she would never see her father again in this earthly existence. Her only consolation lay in the conversations she'd had with Rebecca, who had keenly felt the loss of her stepmother just over a year ago, and of her own mother, Burroughs's first wife, ten years before.

The two women had less time to talk than they wanted but Rebecca had managed to tell Mary a considerable amount about Burroughs's two wives. Rebecca's mother had been a simple girl from Roxbury but her stepmother the daughter of a rich Salem merchant and the widow of an officer from the old, established family of Hathorne. Though often high-handed, even with her husband, she had always been gentle and kind with Rebecca. The girl could not recall her birth mother's face or voice but could well remember her kisses and hugs and the overwhelming grief she had felt when she died.

Mary waited for Burroughs to approach with excitement and fear but resolve. She could see him talking to others on his way down the room, even when he was half-hidden, since every part of him was so distinctive, from his dark complexion and long black hair to his short, muscled body. He seemed almost of some other race from everyone else. Rebecca had told her he had often been taken for an Indian and there were people who persisted in believing, despite his denials, he really *was* half Indian. But this was not so: he had been born in England, of a high-class Anglican family, and brought to Virginia as a baby. His parents had separated when his mother had converted to Puritanism and she had taken him with her to Roxbury. He had attended an excellent grammar school there, been received into Roxbury's Puritan church, and gone to Harvard.

He was now talking with a woman Rebecca knew to be recently widowed and an excellent pie-maker. She was reasonably good-looking and Mary was glad to see him nod good-bye to her with no apparent reluctance. He then vanished from view.

When he reappeared he was in front of her, his face inches from hers. He smiled, his eyes the darkest brown she had ever seen in the face of a white man. She had first noticed how dark they were when she had looked round at him on his horse and then again when he had talked to her when she was ill. She found now to her discomfiture his muscled body under his minister's garments exuded the extraordinary power she had felt even down the length of the room but many times more strongly. She said at once, before losing the ability to speak, "I know I cannot leave here alone and I understand your reasons for wanting everyone to stay, but I think you are making a mistake and we will be attacked again and most of us will die."

The dark brown eyes gazed into hers.

"Nothing is more important to me than preserving your life." He took a quick breath. "What a waste of effort saving you would have been if we lost you!" He smiled what seemed to Mary a rather fatuous smile. She felt a rush of defiance at being patronized.

"I am serious."

"So am I. I wish I could add to the arguments I used before but I can only assure you again I know we will fare better by staying."

"I wish you could add to them too! They do not convince me!"

"I have lived nearly forty years in New England, Miss Cheever, fifteen of them in Maine. I know the ways of the Indians better than anyone. They may attack again but we can rebuff them again. The dangers are less than if we left here."

"There are so many things we do not know. Such as whether the Council will send reinforcements."

"The Council *will* send reinforcements. I shall show you my letter. I mean . . . that is . . . I will read it to you."

"I can read!"

"Can you?" He was surprised.

"My father taught me. I have read the Bible and all the books my father brought from England."

"What books?"

"Shakespeare. Milton."

"Your father cannot have been a Puritan!"

"He was not. He was an Anglican. As am I."

"*My* father was an Anglican."

"I know."

"How?"

"Rebecca told me."

He frowned. Perhaps he was annoyed, Mary thought, that they had been talking about him. Why should not they talk about him? However, he said nothing about that but continued, "Out here those differences count for nothing but in Massachusetts they are dangerous. That is another reason for not going there, as Captain White said."

"I see your mind is made up."

"Aye, it is. Promise me you will not leave on your own."

"How can I leave? I have no horse. I do not know the way."

In bed that night Mary as always thought about her father and how much she had loved him. She remembered how when he was alive she had sometimes wished he had been something more than a homesteader but felt that now, if she could have him again, she would want him just as he was. She felt her loneliness without him as physical pain.

She did not let herself think about Burroughs. There was nothing to hope for: he was out of her realm. Besides, she had done nothing in the short time she had known him but cause him annoyance and trouble. He disliked her, she believed, perhaps even despised her. She must endure her hard, comfortless life as best she could. She had no choice.

Chapter Eight

Salem Village
February 1692

WHEN SHE HAD BEEN NO MORE THAN FIVE, BETTY PARRIS HAD ASKED her father to teach her to read. He had ordered a primer from Boston, given it to her to look at, and forgotten the matter. Betty kept the book under her pillow and, whenever she could, stared at the squiggles, wondering by what mysterious means they signified words. She did not dare remind her father about the reading lessons and then her mother became ill, her father more preoccupied than ever, and reminding him impossible.

Betty's time was mostly her own, since her mother could no longer supervise spinning or sewing. But no amount of staring at the squiggles brought knowledge, only harassment from Abigail. When it was warm enough Betty escaped from the living room, climbing down to the cellar or up to the loft, where she lay among barrels of cider or sacks of grain, looking at the words with pictures next to them, searching for clues to their meanings. But most of the pictures were as mysterious as the letters. One little drawing showed a blob with four sticks, one stick touching a bubble or ball. Other pictures were less puzzling, such as one of an hourglass like that in the meetinghouse, which she stared at while her father's voice rose and fell, from as loudly as when he was shouting at Tituba or Abigail to as softly as when he was talking to her mother. Yet the accompanying words remained indecipherable. Betty's thoughts wandered to her attempts in the meetinghouse to catch sight of a grain of sand dropping but never quite doing so. Yet the bottom half of the hourglass always filled before her father finished his sermon.

Near the end of the book was a large picture of a man with a round face, curly hair, and a superior expression. He reminded her of

Mr. Thomas Putnam. Standing with one hand on his hip, the other holding an ax, he loomed above a smaller man next to a pile of logs. Betty wondered if Mr. Putnam was about to chop firewood while the other man stood ready to help him.

Wherever she hid, Abigail always found her. Then she would make her go outdoors to chase hens or shout at cows or race up the field, despite or perhaps because Betty hated doing these things. If Betty tried to refuse Abigail faced her, seized her shoulders, and squeezed her thumbs into her collarbone. She would not let go, however hard Betty screamed, till Betty agreed. Sometimes Abigail went into rages that so frightened her, she would curl up in a ball with her eyes shut and her fingers in her ears. The rages would blow up because of something Betty had said or done with no intention to hurt. Once she thrust a doll against Abigail's chest to give her a turn with it and Abigail shouted she was pushing her. She was deaf to Betty's explanation and her face went dark red. Once by accident Betty let the thorny branch of a hedge snap on Abigail's hand, drawing blood, and Abigail screamed that she was trying to kill her. That time Betty ran away without trying to explain.

The younger girl never told anyone about any of these or other incidents; she knew no one wished to know.

Her favorite times were when she was alone or Abigail was sleeping. She loved waking at first light and lying silently, listening to a bird that repeatedly sang one quick uprising note followed by three longer, lower ones, as though it were saying "Oh, one, two, three. Oh, one, two, three." Betty could count now and sometimes whispered the numbers along with the bird. Other birds would start to sing cheerier, though equally unvarying, tunes. When there was no light at all she would hear the long swooping call of an owl, and often the croaking of a toad, that sometimes reminded her of Dr. Griggs's throat-clearing and sometimes of John Indian sawing logs. It seemed so strange, lying there in darkness, hearing noises made by invisible creatures. Sometimes she wondered if the birds or frogs really existed or if God was making the noises and if *anything* really existed beyond the meetinghouse and tavern and watch-tower and forest and, if it did, if she'd ever see it. She wondered where the forest ended, and if the devil truly roamed in it.

The leaves had fallen from the trees again, and the cellar and loft were too cold to retreat to, when Reverend Parris told the girls to come to his study for the long-deferred reading lesson. What had caused this was Thomas Putnam's telling him Mistress Putnam had succeeded in teaching his eldest daughter, Ann, who now delighted in reading long sections of the Bible in family prayers.

The girls entered Mr. Parris's study to find the reverend searching his bookshelf; Betty silently gave him the book she'd been treasuring. His underlip jutted; he walked to his desk and told them to sit on the stools placed on either side of his chair.

An hour later Betty knew all the letters of the alphabet and was reading her first syllables. Abigail was sitting with her hands clenched in her lap, her shoulders hunched, staring alternately at Betty and the page, looking as though she wanted to spit.

Mister Parris said he would summon them again soon but never did. However, he let Betty keep the book and soon she had figured out for herself how to read. She learned from the rhyme on its right that the small pictures of sticks and a bubble showed Eve plucking the apple from the tree. The rhyme said, "In Adam's fall / We sinned All." She had understood enough of her father's sermons by this time to grasp the implications of this, including her own possible future eternity in hell unless she found grace.

The text beneath it now told her that the big picture of the two men with dogs was of an English martyr called John Rogers about to go to the stake.

She found a moment at the end of the meal to ask her father what a stake was. He explained.

"He was burned alive?" she asked in horror, thinking of the time she had forgotten to use a potholder when taking a pot off the fire.

"Yes."

"It must have hurt so!"

"Not as much as the fires of hell. That is where those who murdered him went."

There was much on this subject Betty wanted to ask without knowing quite what the questions were. She switched to something less pressing but simpler.

"Were all Puritans burned alive, when they were in England?"

Her father paused for a moment before answering, "Not all. But many. That is why they came to Massachusetts."

"Were other people burned alive?"

"Witches. They deserved to be. They would overthrow God's church if they could."

"Are they still burned alive, if they're caught?"

"Not here in New England. Here they are hanged."

"Have any been hanged in the village?"

"No. Nor in Salem Town. The last was in Boston, thirty years ago. But that does not mean we can let down our guard. There may be witches in our midst even now, without our knowing."

Betty had a nightmare that night that left her when she woke with an image of her father's hat resting on a pile of ashes.

Now Betty had nightmares every night, worse nightmares, and nightmares in the day too, seeing Tituba when she was not there, and Sarah Good and Sarah Osborne, and feeling them stabbing and pinching her. She could not call for the flesh-and-blood Tituba to comfort her because she was always sad and distracted, sometimes sobbing from Mister Parris's thrashings, and besides she was a witch. Betty heard her father shouting to her, over and over, to confess she was.

Abigail was more horrible to her than ever and behaving strangely and running wild or closeting herself with Ann Putnam, Elizabeth Hubbard, or Mary Walcott or all of them at once.

Sometimes Betty wished she could die, if only she could be sure she'd go to heaven, not hell.

Chapter Nine

Maine
February 1692

"HERE'S THE LETTER."

Mary spun round, her hands sticky with carrot juice.

"What letter? What letter?" shouted Burroughs's second youngest son, at her side. The youngest sat on the floor, surrounded by wooden bricks, looking up at his father. Burroughs ignored both, gazing straight at Mary.

"I promised I would show it to you."

"I need to wash my hands."

"What letter?" shouted the elder boy again.

As Mary put the carrot back in the bowl and the knife on a board, Burroughs ruffled his son's hair, saying, "Haven't you got anything better to do than pester Miss Cheever?"

Her back to him, Mary noticed yet again how deep and attractive his voice was. It was a voice that could reach to the back of the meetinghouse and enthrall the entire congregation but was equally compelling when used quietly.

"I was playing English and Indians but it's started to snow again," the boy said.

"Ask Mr. Digby over there if you can polish his gun for him."

"Will he let me?" the boy asked with awe.

"Hey, Rob," Burroughs called across to a man readying his fowling piece on his knee, with a piece of leather and polish at his side. "Can my boy help with that? No bullets there, I trust?"

"Not a one. Come here, lad. I'd be glad of some help."

The boy ran forward eagerly.

Mary was dipping her fingers in the bowl of water kept on the table and wiping them on a cloth. As she turned and took the letter, Burroughs let go of it before their fingers touched. She read, "We doubt not but your honors before now have received the sorrowful tidings of the death and captivity of above an hundred persons at York."

The letter went on to describe the burning of York with its "pillars of smoke and raging of merciless flames."

It should surely persuade the authorities, if anything could, to send the reinforcements they so desperately needed, Mary thought. But could *anything* persuade them? She handed it back, feeling presumptuous at making a judgment on a piece of writing by a man twice her age, the leader of the town, yet perceiving that strangely enough he truly wanted her view. She said sincerely, "It is a wonderful letter."

"I believe it will produce the desired effect." There was the barest hint in his voice and eyes of asking for her agreement.

"I hope so."

"You are not sure?"

"I do not know." She turned away. "They may never get it."

He moved a fraction closer and she did not trust herself to speak further. He took her resumption of carrot peeling as dismissal, caused by continued resentment. Clutching his letter, he strode off.

The weeks following were arduous in the extreme. All the refugees from York, as well as the inhabitants of Wells, stayed in the garrison houses, cramped though they were; no one dared move to the less well fortified dwellings. Mary spent all day every day washing, dressing, and feeding the smallest children and then keeping them in sight while helping prepare meals, bake bread, wash dishes, make beds, mend clothes, and gather eggs from the lean-to. She was used to working hard, having been responsible after her mother died for all the chores in her home as well as for eking out food supplies, foraging for fruits and berries, gathering nuts, and, with other women, digging for clams in the clam flats. But the overcrowded conditions here made every task tougher. As did loneliness and constant fear.

Now and then smoke rose from the trees no more than a mile off or a gunshot pierced the air. When the second of these things happened the settlers knew a rabbit or deer was lying dead. But one day they knew by his screams the slain creature was no animal but a boy who had gone out past the palisade to fetch wood. Burroughs led an armed band to find and bring back his body and bury him; the whole town attended the short, stark funeral in the meetinghouse. The boy's grave, just inside the palisade, was marked with a stone levered out of the earth and carved with his name, together with dates fourteen years apart.

Many of the townspeople talked again of leaving but Burroughs once more persuaded them to stay.

The pastor avoided Mary as far as he could. He believed she saw him as wrongheaded, stubborn, and tyrannical. Accused of these faults by both his wives, he now felt he possessed them, which he rarely had before. He found himself ashamed of refusing to go to Massachusetts, though both he and Peter were sure the decision was the right one.

He should not try to make her like him, he told himself. She should find someone younger than he, unburdened by children, willing and able to take her to Boston or Salem and support her in safety and comfort.

And how could he be sure, if he married again, he would not find as many faults in this wife as the others, adorable as she was? Mary had shown herself to be both hotheaded and proficient in argument. Neither trait promised married tranquillity.

Chapter Ten
Salem Village
March 1692

THE SNOW HAD MELTED AT LAST. THE CROWD GATHERING OUTSIDE Ingersoll's tavern buzzed with fear, partly genuine, partly feigned. It was just past nine in the morning; people were filling the street right across to the watchtower. On the platform a man and a boy in his teens, supposedly keeping a lookout for Indians, were staring down at the throng.

"I pity Constable Herrick," said pockmarked Samuel Sibley, nervously rubbing his hands. His wife, Jemima, had, unbeknownst to him, ordered Tituba and John Indian to bake a witch cake, with Betty and Abigail's urine in it, to feed to the family dog to see if it would run mad. This, according to Jemima, was an old English method of testing for witches. The dog, a venerable beast with a cast-iron stomach, had slept particularly well after this unexpected treat. Samuel Sibley had not known about it until afterward; Jemima rarely told him of her occasional boredom-killing projects. When he had learned of it from the furious Parris, who had found the remains of the cake on the parsonage living-room table, almost eaten a slice, and been stopped just in time by John Indian, he was shocked and impressed in equal measure. He forgave his wife fully when he realized he and she were now seen all through the village as experts on witchcraft.

"Herrick?" asked William Allen, leaning on his musket, a lock of hair flopping over his eyes. "Why pity him in particular?"

"Having to bring the witch Tituba."

"I pity whichever constable's bringing Sarah Good."

"No, Tituba's worse. She's not just a witch but a devil. All them Indians are."

"She won't resist though. Mister Parris would thrash her."

"Herrick will have to bring Sarah Osborne too."

"She's so sick she can hardly walk."

"The devil will give her strength!"

"Well, I wouldn't be either of them constables." Allen pushed back his hair. "I'd rather make a barrel in a day, hoops and all."

"I'd double your wages!" Sibley punched the younger man's shoulder. He was a cooper, Allen his apprentice.

"I'd want a day's rest after!"

"Herrick'll need one, after fetching Tituba. She's bin pinchin' those children half to death."

"How could they tell it was her?"

Sibley stared at him. "Why, they could see her!"

"I thought she was invisible!"

"They saw her specter! Her invisible specter!"

"How could she see it, bein' invisible?"

Sibley rubbed his hands, then crossed his arms.

"Spectral sight."

"What's that?"

"Why, the gift of seeing specters."

"How'd they get it?"

"From Tituba."

"Why'd she give it them? Then they'd know it was her as was hurtin' them."

Sibley rubbed his nose, then crossed his arms again.

"She needs them to see her so she can tempt them to write in her book."

"What book?"

"The devil's book."

"How'd she get it?"

"Made a pact."

"With the devil?"

"Aye."

"What do they write?"

"Why, their names, to show they belong to him."

"*Can* they write?"

Sibley stared at him a while, then said, "They make their mark."

He added, as an afterthought, "With their blood."

"Do they cut themselves to do it?"

Another pause.

"She cuts 'em."

"They should put her in irons," said Allen with feeling.

"Sarah Good and Osborne too," Sibley agreed. "Two year ago Goody Good set loose all Haycroft's cattle. She's been a witch these ten year. But Sarah Osborne's pinchin' the girls bad as them other two now. She's the wickedest woman in the village, apart from them two of course."

"Married her servant."

"After living in sin with him."

"Now she's bed-rid."

"Easy prey."

"For burglars?"

"For the devil."

The noise of the crowd lessened. Reverend Parris, in his tall, buckled hat and black coat and trousers, was leading his daughter and niece toward the inn, ordering people out of the way. The girls were not the screaming creatures Sibley had expected but quiet and docile. Behind them came curly-haired Thomas Putnam and his wan-looking wife with their daughter Ann and, behind *them*, Elizabeth Hubbard with her uncle and aunt, Mary Walcott following, plump and voluptuous.

"What you smilin' at?" Sibley asked.

"That Walcott girl."

Sibley looked at him sideways. "What you're thinkin', that's a sin."

Allen shifted his gaze to Mary's ragged-jawed stepmother, Deliverance Walcott, Thomas Putnam's sister.

"There's Tituba!" cried Sibley.

The slave was walking, head bent, arms clutched across her thin chest. Her ruddy, high-cheekboned face filled Sibley with a hatred he'd never felt before but would now swear was long-standing. Constable Herrick gripped the slave's arm as though she might try to escape, which seemed unlikely. Where could she go? Who would help her? Another constable was leading a horse carrying a bundle of old clothes.

"Sarah Osborne!" exclaimed Allen, whose eyes were sharper than

the older man's. A head rose from the clothes, cap askew, hair straggling, as the bundle heaved. People ran toward it. The crowd was growing noisier again.

"What's happening?" asked Sibley.

"She's vomiting."

A commotion at the other end of the throng drew both men's eyes
to some constables trying to push a ragged, skinny woman back on her
horse. She was punching, kicking, and biting. The constable who had
been riding behind her on the same horse leaned over, trying to pull her
back up, but she fell further, hitting the ground. He fell off the horse;
the horse reared. The woman punched, kicked, and bit the constable
now on top of her. This was Sarah Good.

"I wouldn't give ha'pence for that constable's cows," Sibley said.

Looking back the other way, they saw Parris reach the steps of the
tavern to be greeted by large-bodied Nathaniel Ingersoll and a pastor
whom Sibley told Allen was the Reverend John Hale of Beverly.
Another pastor, even portlier than Ingersoll, was, Allen told Sibley,
Salem's Nicholas Noyes. Next to Parris was a marshal bearing a gold-
headed, six-foot-long staff. All the men conferred and Parris mounted
to the top step and turned to face the crowd.

"Brethren!" His preacher's voice was carrying enough to be heard
even by Allen and Sibley at the top of the watchtower. Tituba, her arm
still held by the constable, and Sarah Good, twitching in the grip of
several men, stared up at him. Only the bundle on the horse showed no
interest.

"Beloved friends and neighbors!" Parris turned to right and left to
include everyone, then, facing forward, drew himself up to his full
height.

"The Lord hath brought us together this day to witness the doing
of his work by his good and faithful servants, the honored magistrates
John Hathorne and Bartholomew Gedney. It is such work, alas, as we
never thought to see in our village. But our great and blessed God, for
His wise and holy ends, hath lengthened Satan's chain, that he may
tempt vile and wicked persons amongst us to perform his devilish tasks.
'Tis well that a complaint has been made by four of our good yeomen,
including excellent Thomas Putnam, to the civil authority to examine
these persons and, if the Lord in His mercy and goodness should will

it, hear their confessions. And 'tis well so many are gathered to witness this work. But so great is our number that Captain Ingersoll tells me he cannot accommodate us and we have resolved to remove to the meetinghouse. I invite you now to walk there and take your customary places."

The crowd began to move down the road. Sarah Good could be heard screeching as she was dragged along by several constables.

"What happens now?" Allen asked.

"Like Mister Parris said, the magistrates examine the prisoners to find out if they're witches. If they are, they'll be sent to prison and tried. They'll examine Sarah Good first, I'll be bound, 'cause she's causing the most trouble."

"I wish I could watch!"

Sibley hesitated, then said, "Go. For ten minutes. If the Indians attack, all the men are here in the village."

By the time he finished speaking Allen was halfway down the ladder.

Because he was only a boy, Allen sat for services in the gallery reserved for male children, servants, and slaves. Everyone else sat below. On the benches men were on one side and women on the other, but in the enclosed pews family groups sat together. The most important families were at the front. Two pews, on opposite sides of the meetinghouse, were unoccupied but everywhere else all the seats were taken. Yet people were still noisily pouring in, going quiet and still when they found places to stand.

The Salem village meetinghouse was used for community events as well as services but, despite its plain wooden walls, small, barred windows, and a high ceiling crisscrossed with beams, it always inspired reverence. On this occasion, despite the intense excitement, even the riffraff in the galleries were hushed. Allen's heart raced. Three witches were about to come in, as were the girls they had been torturing. The witches might fly out again through the roof or turn people to pigs. The girls might go into fits, faint, or even die.

Shushing noises heralded the marshal, carrying his staff. Behind him, walking slowly and deliberately as though his precise method of placing one foot before the other were an outward sign of faultlessness, came the chief magistrate, Captain John Hathorne. His girth spanned the aisle; he wore a white wig long enough to rest on gargantuan shoulders. His bulk seemed a lifetime's store of certainty. This prime lawgiver was followed at a distance, with an air of respect, by lesser magistrate Bartholomew Gedney, then pastors Parris, Hale, and Noyes and another man whom Allen recognized as, puzzlingly, the Salem Village tailor, Ezekiel Cheever. John Hathorne walked round the table at the foot of the pulpit and faced the crowd, his heavy eyes expressionless. Gedney ran forward to pull out a chair, half-bowing while backing away, and Hathorne majestically sat down. Gedney seated himself, taking up half the space Hathorne did. John Hale sat on the other side, smiling charmingly, and Nicholas Noyes next to him, at the end of the table, a bulging calf and fat ankle in full view. With a cringing air, the tailor perched on a stool. As he placed pens and sheets of paper in front of him, Allen realized why he was there. His tailor's nimble fingers had gained him the prize job of scribe. The Reverend Parris mounted the pulpit and, underlip jutting, stared around. When the murmuring ceased, he announced he would deliver a short prayer.

"An hour at least," Allen thought. But Parris was as keen to get down to business as anyone and restricted himself to five minutes of asking God to aid the magistrates in their holy endeavors. Then he descended and took a seat in the empty pew on the right. This belonged to the Putnams, who had not yet arrived.

There was a stir at the back. Down the aisle walked an ungainly child followed by a girl of the same height but skinnier, glancing around, her close-set eyes and curved nose giving her the look of a bird hunting prey. Behind these two came little Betty Parris and the older but equally little Elizabeth Hubbard, and then plump Mary Walcott, who had had such a regrettable effect on young Allen. She did not do so now; he was too awed by the occasion. All five girls looked highly respectable, with their hair tucked under ironed caps, faces agleam. Allen noticed how young they seemed, even younger than he, except perhaps for Walcott. As they drew near the table, the fathers and uncles who followed them exchanged nods with the magistrates and they and their wives walked to their pews. The girls stood facing the table till Hathorne, in deep, measured tones, ordered them to move, two to one side, three to the other. He told them to lower their eyes till he ordered them to raise them, then turned to the marshal.

"Bring in Sarah Good."

Allen felt the hair rise on his head. He did not know what might come in. A witch can change into bird or beast or a cross between the two. And, indeed, as Sarah walked down the aisle, her quick, half-controlled movements, dirty face, and tiny, darting eyes made her seem more a captured wild creature than a woman. Behind her, followed by a constable, came an emaciated man leading a ragged child by the hand. The marshal who had preceded them ushered Sarah into the pew remaining empty. This belonged to the family headed by Israel Porter, Thomas Putnam's chief economic and political rival and, in Putnam's mind, enemy. The authorities had known he and his kin would stay away and commandeered their pew to serve as the dock. Sarah clutched at the partition, staring round at Parris and the Putnams, the girls with bowed heads and the magistrates. Hathorne rose, giantlike. He cleared his throat; his small eyes under heavy lids darted to the accusers before focusing on the prisoner.

"Sarah Good, what evil spirit have you known?"

She flinched as though struck. There was murmuring all through the meetinghouse, quickly shushed. Hathorne repeated the question, more loudly.

"None!" Sarah Good shouted, her voice high-pitched, her head again jerking.

"Have you made no contract with the devil?"

"No!" The word was almost a scream.

"Why do you hurt these children?" Hathorne raised his huge arm to point with a thick finger at the girls with bowed heads.

"I do not hurt them!" Good sounded incredulous, outraged, and terrified at once.

"Who do you use then?"

"Nobody!" Her head jerked again.

"What creature do you use to hurt them?"

"No creature! I am falsely accused!"

"Why did you go away muttering from Mr. Parris's house?"

For a while Sarah Good could not answer this and looked up and down and all around as though desperately searching a way to escape. At last she said, now so quietly as to be almost inaudible, "I did not mutter. I thanked him for what he gave my child."

"Have you made no contract with the devil?"

"No!" Again the word was a screech.

Hathorne turned his eyes to the girls on one side of him, then the other. "Children! Look at this woman! Is she one of the witches that torments you?"

Betty, Abigail, and the rest looked up at the desperate figure in the dock, who stared wildly back at them. Ann spoke first, murmuring, "Aye, she hath oft times tormented me." The others echoed her, bar Betty, who stayed silent, looking down. Then Ann shuddered. The rest shuddered just as she had, again except for Betty. Ann began clutching herself, giving shouts of pain. The others did so too. The congregation was gasping and calling out in fear. Then Ann, followed by the rest except Betty, fell to the ground and began rolling around. Betty started crying. The congregation was in uproar; people rose to their feet.

They must be convincing, Thomas Putnam had made clear to them. If they were not, they would be suspected of being witches themselves. Betty collapsed without volition, lying motionless and silent. Several women rushed to her.

"Has she fainted?"

"Is she dead?"

"Poor, poor child!"

John Hathorne shouted, "Sarah Good, do you not see now what you have done! Why do you not tell us the truth? Why do you torment these poor children?"

"I do not torment them!" Sarah, clutching the partition, glanced from the marshal's staff on her right to the constable's bulk on her left and all round the meetinghouse. Ann and the rest were up on their feet again and seizing different parts of themselves as though being stabbed. Betty still lay senseless. The emaciated man who had come in behind Sarah Good called out, "My wife's a witch! She's the enemy of everything good!"

"She's *his* enemy!" someone shouted, with delight at his own wit. "He's Good!"

There was cackling, with some groans. The man's small daughter started sobbing.

"What evil spirit do you use?" Hathorne bellowed at Sarah. "Here you see, your own husband condemns you!"

"None! None!"

"How come the girls are tormented?"

"How do I know?" Sarah's expression changed to one of cunning. "Maybe others are doing it! You accuse others too!"

Ann went silent and still. So did the other girls. So did the crowd. William Good hushed his daughter, who clung to his leg. Hathorne asked, "Why, who are they, these others we accuse?"

"The others you brought in the meetinghouse."

"Who was it tormented the children?"

"It was Osborne."

Hathorne, giving a small smile, lowered himself into his seat. From a jug he poured water into a glass and took a sip. Cheever laid down his pen and shook his wrist. Hathorne asked a few further questions but everyone knew the interrogation was over. By accusing someone else of being a witch, Sarah was admitting *she* was a witch. Otherwise, how could she know? Of course the accusing girls knew, but they had special God-given powers. Not long afterward Good was escorted from the meetinghouse. Reluctantly, Allen left too. He had stayed too long already.

During the next few hours the village stayed empty. All human life, apart from the men on the watchtower, was concentrated in the little wooden building with barred windows. When the doors opened at last and Sibley and Allen saw the constables come out with Tituba and Sarah Osborne, the older man said, "Run and find out what's happened. Come straight back."

Five minutes later Allen was climbing back onto the platform, shouting, "Tituba confessed! Tituba confessed! She said she'd seen the devil! She said she'd flown on a stick! She said Sarah Good and Sarah Osborne were witches as well, and there are others she's been with, and she's been tormenting the children! They're holding her at Constable Herrick's house! She'll be brought back tomorrow!"

When he had calmed down he told Sibley how Sarah Osborne, like Sarah Good, had refused to confess but everyone knew they were witches because Tituba had said so. They too would be brought back for more questioning.

Betty came to consciousness to find Hannah Ingersoll sitting on the end of her bed. She at once started crying.

"Sshhh, ssshhh, the witches cannot hurt you anymore, they are locked up, they can't reach you."

"They can!" Betty sat up. "There's Tituba!" She pointed at emptiness.

"No, no, there's no one there."

"I can see her!"

"She is locked up, sweeting. You only think you see her."

Abigail appeared through the door.

"I can see her too," Abigail said.

"Get your uncle!" Hannah shouted at her. But before she could move Parris strode through the door.

"Betty must not go to the examination tomorrow," Hannah told him.

Abigail said again, "I can see her too!"

Parris and Hannah both ignored her.

Later it occurred to the older girl that Betty would have to stay home the next day while she went to the meetinghouse with the others to stand in pride of place next to the magistrates to help convict witches. When Abigail woke in the night and saw Tituba standing, grinning, by the light of the moon sliding through the edge of the shutters, she buried herself under the blankets, curled into a ball, and said nothing, then or later. She must admit to seeing witches only when her uncle and Mr. Putnam wanted her to, even when they weren't there.

But Elizabeth Hubbard, seeing Sarah Good standing on the table when she got home, did not hesitate to say so. Dr. and Mrs. Griggs sent for Samuel Sibley, now the village expert on witchcraft, and Elizabeth shouted to him to hit the witch with his staff. He thrust where she pointed and she cried out that he'd hit Sarah on the back.

The next day Herrick's wife told everyone that when she had gone to wake Sarah Good in the morning she had seen blood on her arm.

When William Allen heard this he was puzzled.

"Why did she have blood on her arm when you struck her on her back?" he asked his master, as they took out their tools to work on a barrel due last week. Sibley carefully placed his hammer down next to his lathe.

"Goodwife Herrick must have mistook."

"Mistook a back for an arm?"

Sibley considered.

"I didn't strike *Sarah Good*, I struck her *specter*."

"I thought that was the same as the person, every way, only invisible."

"We don't know." Sibley paused. "After all, 'tis invisible."

"So the back might be where an arm is?"

After a moment of silence Sibley said, "Pass me the nails."

That evening, as dusk blurred the landscape, young William Allen and another boy hurried along the path leading over the hill rising from the land behind Sibley's house, set back from Hobart Street, to their parents' farms, next to each other. Sibley and Allen and their assistant had worked late to make up for lost time. Each boy had separately wondered whether to go by this dark, lonely route or take the longer one along well-traveled tracks, but neither wanted to admit this to the other. So they walked off together up the desolate hill, covered with bracken and fern and scattered with rocks. Even before the present alarm there had been tales of witch meetings here. Reaching the brow, the boys looked down through dimness. Allen saw something move.

"What's that?

"What?" His friend stared round. Allen pointed.

"Can't see aught.

"Behind that rock."

"Oh! I saw it!"

They clutched each other. A shape like no animal or bird Allen had ever seen before flew up in the air. Both boys screamed. More shapes followed.

"The witches!" Allen gasped. "On sticks!"

The boys turned and ran. When they got home, much later than usual since they had to start their journey again, this time by road, they told their horrified families they had seen Sarah Good, Sarah Osborne, and Tituba rise from the earth and scud through the sky. William's mother gave him extra helpings of dinner and refilled his cider mug and made him tell the story again. His little sister started crying and his father said they would all be seeing witches soon unless the magistrates put them in dungeons or, better still, hanged them.

In the morning William wondered if what they'd seen might have been crows but by then the story had spread round the village and he couldn't retract it.

That day at the second examination Tituba suggested there were nine other witches in league with the devil besides Osborne, Good, and herself. The hearings continued till the end of the week, with all the girls present, screaming and shouting as needed, except for Betty, who stayed home.

On Saturday the three accused witches were sent the hour's ride to Salem Town jail and Betty was told she was to go to Salem too, to stay in the house of a distant relative of her father, once they had arranged for someone to take her.

Chapter Eleven
Salem Village
March 1692

AT THE SABBATH MORNING SERVICE, THE DAY AFTER THE EXAMINATIONS had finished, the size of the congregation surpassed anything anyone remembered even though the Porter pew stayed empty. The girls were all present but for Betty and, most people believed, so were the additional witches talked of by Tituba. The sense of expectation was intense and it was not long before it was gratified. Ann Putnam, in her usual place in the front pew with her mother and father, soon started glancing behind her as though searching for someone. With her close-set eyes she once again had the look of a bird hunting prey. She tried to stand up but her mother and Mercy, the Putnams' pretty seventeen-year-old maid, clung onto her. She muttered that she saw the woman who had tortured her for days and was afflicting her even now, pointing at an elderly farmer's wife several rows behind.

"Martha Cory," said Ann's mother loud enough to be heard. Her father said nothing, just watched calmly, as though these were mere women's affairs. Martha Cory stared back at Ann defiantly.

No one had told Abigail that Ann was going to do this. She too began to rise but Hannah pulled her down. Her uncle mounted the pulpit and Ann Putnam went quiet and still, bowing her head.

Young William Allen, peering down from the gallery, felt pleasure that such a doubter of the existence of witches was now shown to be one. Perhaps he could persuade Sibley to let him have time off to watch her whole examination.

The rest of the service passed without incident. Afterward, in Ingersoll's tavern, the crowd jostled and bickered till calmed by Nathaniel's warm greetings and cider and cake. By the time they had left, the Ingersolls were exhausted. However, as a deacon and wife, they dared not doze off during the afternoon sermon, like some of the boys in the galleries and even adults in the pews. Constable Herrick was kept busy patrolling the aisles, waking the sleepers by prodding them with his stick. Though he would have preferred to sleep too, this was easier work than guarding Sarah Good. None of the girls caused any trouble; they too were sleepy.

The congregation emerged to air so bright after rain that everything shone. Nathaniel and Hannah at once crossed to the tavern, hoping to get to their chairs as soon as possible and stay put till bedtime. As the shadows lengthened, the congregation dispersed, some past Ingersoll's on the walk toward Boxford, some toward Topsfield and Ipswich, some down past the Francis Nurse homestead toward Beverly. A more assiduous deacon than Ingersoll, one of Thomas Putnam's brothers, cleared away rubbish and collected forgotten belongings and at last went home to his farm. The meetinghouse, with its closed shutters, roof in the shape of an upside-down V, and dark wood walls black in the thickening dusk, had a sealed-off appearance, impenetrable even to specters.

Martha Cory walked at speed down the hill toward her farm and Thomas Putnam, following her, caught up only at the bottom. They talked briefly, then Putnam walked back up, the smile on his face broad enough to show the gap in his teeth.

A little later the shadow of the watchtower fell over Ingersoll's tavern and down the road that ran off to the parsonage, reaching the edge of the field where Betty and Abigail were playing in the last of the light. Betty searched for flowers in the grass while Abigail took quick runs and jumps, tripping and falling, and climbed onto a low branch of the dead oak at the end of the field. There she sat, swinging her legs, then jumped off and threw herself down, lying on her back, gazing at the darkening sky. There was no reason for going indoors now that Tituba was in prison and there was no one to make supper. John Indian was still working in the kitchens at Ingersoll's, as he did every Sunday.

Abigail's momentary contentment drained like the color overhead. She closed her eyes; Martha Cory was waiting for her. Abigail kept her eyes closed, fearing that even if she opened them the image would remain. She stretched out her arms to each side, palms down, clutching grass.

"Abby!" Martha scolded. But when Abigail opened her eyes her little cousin was above her, holding out a small bunch of snowdrops. Abigail sat up and reached out but Betty clasped them to her chest.

"They're for Tituba."

"*Tituba!* Flowers for a *witch*?"

"She must be so sad."

"She tortured us!"

"It was the devil made her do it."

"She could have said no!"

"She doesn't know how, she wasn't brought up a Christian. She told me when she was little she hadn't even heard of Lord Jesus."

"Has she made *you* a witch now?"

"How could she? She doesn't torture me anymore. She can't now that she's in prison."

"'Tisn't being in prison as stops her. Her specter could fly through the wall easy as anything."

"Why doesn't it then?"

"'Cos she's in irons."

"Irons?"

"Chains. Round her legs."

"Oh!"

No one had told Betty this before. Abigail jumped to her feet. "She deserves them!"

"Poor Tituba!"

"Poor Tituba! Poor Tituba!" Abigail mocked, leaping about till she tripped on her skirt and fell over. Betty clutched her own calf, near the ankle, under her dress.

"Are the chains tight as this?"

"Tighter!"

"Oh, they must hurt!"

"Course they hurt!"

"Oh, poor Tituba!"

"I hope her ankles are bleeding, I hope they get weals, I hope she's crying like she did when Uncle Samuel beat her!"

"Will he let me give her these flowers?"

"Course not, stupid baby."

Betty dropped the bouquet and ran to the house.

Samuel Parris sat with his wife. Her condition had become worse; he knew she might die. But the knowledge was too frightening to hold in his mind for very long at any one time, though not nearly as frightening as the possibility that his daughter and niece might be branded as frauds. Or as witches. There was a fine line between accusers and accused. Parris mostly refused to let these thoughts enter his mind, with the result that they settled over it like a miasma, dampening his spirits. Life had never been quite as bad as this, not even when his business failed.

He was glad to sit quietly by the fire with his loyal companion, for once sleeping peacefully. In better times he had been constantly fraught with annoyance at her limited capacities, both mental and physical, but now he only remembered that she never contradicted or questioned him and did everything he asked her to. Trying not to think about how he would manage without her, he stood up and looked through the window giving onto the track that led north to Putnam's farmhouse. The image came into his mind of a pair of close-set eyes and curved nose. When Ann had risen from her seat, pointing, he had wondered if she would make the accusation right there, loudly and clearly. He was both relieved and disappointed when she did not.

The light was gone. The minister closed the shutters he had opened half an hour ago to let air in the sickroom and the only illumination now was the firelight. His wife stirred and he sat down again.

"How do you feel, my dear?"

"Prithee, some water."

Supporting her with his arm, he brought the mug to her lips. When she had taken a few sips and her head was back on the pillow, she whispered, "Pray with me."

Bowing his head, Parris recited the Lord's Prayer. His wife moved her lips as far as "thy kingdom come" but then drifted into sleep again. He stayed sitting a while, then tucked a limp gray lock behind her ear and walked quietly from the room.

As he reached the bottom stair there was a knock on the door. He opened it an inch but when he saw Thomas Putnam, his round face smiling in the light of his lantern, he pulled it all the way. Putnam stepped in, the men exchanged greetings, and Parris ushered him into the living room.

"I have invited Martha Cory to visit my daughter." Putnam put the lantern on the table. It was the only light in the room apart from the glow from smoldering embers. He waited for Parris to ask why he had made this invitation, but he did not. Putnam said, "You preached a splendid sermon today."

"I hope I was persuasive about Satan's threats to our village." Parris glanced around, as though some of the specters he had been warning of might be here.

"'Tis a shame there are people who still need persuading," said Putnam.

"Will you sit down? Take some cider?"

"Not at this time, thank you, Reverend. But a celebratory jug may be in order very soon now."

"When will Goodwife Cory be visiting?"

"Tomorrow."

Parris looked toward the almost dead fire. "I apologize for the lack of comfort in my humble abode. I have only one servant now to do everything."

"It was fortunate your girls did not accuse John Indian along with his wife."

"It was fortunate he did not torture them."

"Quite."

Parris picked up the poker.

"Needs more logs," Putnam observed.

"He should be back soon."

"Where are the girls?"

"In the field."

"The training field?"

"Aye."

The field next to the parsonage was used for exercises by the village militia.

"You should not let them go there. That is a likely spot for Satan and his witches to hold meetings."

Parris, without disturbing the embers, reinserted the poker in its black cast-iron holder next to the water bucket.

"Next to the parsonage?" His underlip jutted.

"Where better? The most devout Christians are the devil's best prizes. You just said so yourself in your sermon."

"Our enemies could use this . . ."

"Not if they are seen there themselves. In the field. With the devil."

The noise of the front door being yanked open sent the two men hurrying into the hallway even as Betty disappeared at speed up the stairs.

"Betty!" Parris called, staring after her. She slammed the bedroom door. The front door still stood open and Abigail came through it, scowling, her cap half off her head.

"What ails Betty?"

The older girl's shoulders twitched.

"Come in the living room," Parris ordered.

She did so, Putnam following.

"Did Betty see someone?" Parris asked.

She turned away.

"Abigail!" Parris moved to seize her by the shoulders but Putnam stepped between them.

"Perhaps she saw Martha Cory?" Putnam gave her his widest, most ingratiating smile. "You are a clever girl, Abby, you would know, even if she didn't tell you."

Abigail's scowl softened. She said softly, "No, she never saw Martha Cory."

"Then what happened to make her fly in like that? I bet you know, you are as sharp as any of them, even my Ann."

"Tituba."

"She saw Tituba?"

"No. She wants to visit her in prison. She wants to give her flowers."

"*What?* Has she forgotten she's a *witch*?" Parris shouted.

"She thinks that's the fault of the devil, not her."

"You know that isn't true, don't you, child? She chose to be a witch! She could have said no!"

"Yes, Uncle. Betty's stupid."

"Abigail!" Parris exclaimed angrily but Putnam quickly interrupted, "She's a baby, she doesn't understand things like you do. I expect *you* have seen Martha Cory's specter."

Abigail was about to say one thing but then, staring into Thomas Putnam's eyes, said another.

"Just now. In the training field."

Putnam turned to Parris. "I told you that's where they hold witch meetings."

Abigail experienced the joy of her uncle and Ann Putnam's father both smiling their widest smiles at her at once.

Morning daylight and damp spring air came through the window as the fire blazed brightly. Mistress Putnam held her sewing and pretty, smiling Mercy Lewis worked at her spinning wheel. Only Ann was unoccupied. Her father had told her he had asked the woman to come between ten o'clock and noon. He had also said something else, concerning Mercy, after which Ann had taken the girl outside to the copse. When they came back Mercy's smile was wider than usual.

White-haired Uncle John Putnam was already here, sitting by the fire with an air of complacency, his hands on his knees. Ann waited for the knock. But there was no knock. Martha Cory opened the door and walked in, her posture defiant, face angry. Thomas Putnam, who had been waiting outside, followed her in.

Martha had known Ann all her life though, since she was still only a child, had scarcely ever talked to her.

"I have been asked to come and see you."

Ann started screaming. Her hands flew to her throat and the scream turned to choking; her eyes rolled up in her head; her feet twisted so strangely she staggered, tripped, and would have fallen but that Mercy Lewis caught her. Her hands twisted as though palsied and her hips and knees turned in different directions. She called, "Stop it! Martha! Stop it!" By this time her mother too was screaming. Ann hissed, "There's a yellow bird sucking there, between your fingers!"

Martha Cory held up her hand and, with a mocking expression, rubbed where she was pointing to show this could not be so but Ann ignored her and ran across the room, colliding with a stool, shouting, "I see a spit on the fire with a man on it! Goody Cory, you're turning the spit!"

Martha laughed, turned, and marched toward the door.

"The girl's mad. Get her a physician." Mercy Lewis snatched up a stick and struck at some invisible object on the hearth.

"Martha hit her with a rod!" Ann wailed.

The corporeal Martha turned back to face her. "Just you wait!"

"Get that evil witch out of here!" said John Putnam, standing up.

Thomas pushed Martha toward the door and Mercy shouted, "I won't! I won't!" at the invisible object.

"What does she want of you?" John Putnam asked.

Mercy's hands went to her neck and she ran toward the fire. Thomas and John seized her and sat her down on a chair while Martha stood in the doorway. Martha left. The chair moved toward the fire as though pulled by invisible hands, as everyone said afterward. No one mentioned that Ann happened to be directly behind it. Mistress Putnam ran out to fetch neighbors. The news of what was happening spread through the village in no time.

Venerable, respected John Putnam corroborated everything Thomas and his wife and daughter said. That afternoon he and Nathaniel Ingersoll rode to Salem to make a formal complaint against Martha Cory to the magistrates.

The night sky was starless. A chink of candlelight showed at a window behind which Thomas Putnam sat at his desk covered with papers, doing the job he hated most. Balancing the books was both boring and depressing since every calculation reminded him that he should have been rich but was poor. According to tradition and justice, as eldest son he should have inherited the family estate but it had gone to the youngest, his half brother Joseph. Their father had eight children by his first wife and this one by his second, whom he had doted on despite the boy's ungrateful, selfish nature. Joseph got the homestead and Thomas just a modest house and farm. His anger at this outrage had grown greater as the gulf in fortunes between himself and his half brother widened. Joseph had married an heiress, and not just any heiress, but the daughter of Israel Porter, the leader of the faction that had opposed his attempts, which had at last been successful despite them, to found a Salem Village church. That faction was growing ever more powerful since Israel's prosperity had risen while his own had declined, as Porter bought mills and made lucrative links with merchants in the town while Putnam stayed a mere farmer. Thomas imagined Israel's face turning blue and his eyes bulging as his hands tightened round the man's neck.

Israel and Joseph were as close as any father and son-in-law could be, always walking together through Salem Village or riding together along the road to Salem Town. Thomas now imagined them swinging together from parallel nooses. But alas. Not possible. Men were almost never convicted of witchcraft. Of course they might be if their wives or other relatives were. . . . He pictured Elizabeth Putnam, Joseph's beautiful wife, Israel's daughter. Yet the family was so powerful and revered. . . . And of course Joseph and his wife were also Thomas's relatives. . . .

But Israel and Joseph had allies considerably less daunting than they were, unrelated to the Putnams. Two of them Thomas hated nearly as much as his half brother and Israel themselves. They were nobodies who'd maneuvered their way into the possession of the largest estate for miles around. Thomas's jaw hurt with clenching as he considered Goodman and Goodwife Nurse's incredible good fortune in getting a mortgage on three hundred acres of land. One day they would be more prosperous than Thomas himself. Yet Francis Nurse had started life as nothing more than a traymaker and, worse, Rebecca Nurse was from a family in Topsfield that claimed to own lands the Putnams well knew were rightfully theirs. That woman, mother of eight and grandmother of heaven knew how many, was famous for her piety. She would have greatly enhanced the new Salem Village church if she had deigned to leave the Salem one. That she did not, Thomas believed, was on purpose to spite him. Thomas had thought of her before anyone else, even Martha Cory and John Proctor, after Betty and the others saw Tituba's specter walk through the wall. That is, before anyone else except for one man, far away, in the devilish region full of Baptists and Quakers.

Martha Cory still caused concern. She had not yet been examined, or even arrested, though John Hathorne had assured him she would be. She was no slave, beggar, or misfit but a respectable, intelligent woman and, what was more, a member of the church. She might convince Hathorne, by her dignity, reasoned arguments, and appearance of piety, that she was innocent.

Independent witnesses were required, carrying weight and authority. John Hale, often in the village from Beverly, believed everything he saw. Another minister, not as credulous but more venal, would fit the bill perfectly. Such a man might be more than a witness, he might be an advocate. A certain tall, shabby figure, so fair of hair and complexion he looked almost albino, smiling with self-importance and eagerness to please, had for some days been in Thomas's mind. Deodat Lawson might be a weakling and fool but could deliver a good sermon, and could be counted on to do whatever he believed in his own interest, however morally dubious. Thomas pushed aside his accounts and seized a blank sheet of paper.

But thoughts of one Salem Village ex-minister led back to thoughts of another. Thomas envisioned the short, swarthy figure with the muscly, lithe torso under the clerical coat, gazed at longingly by the females in the meetinghouse as he puffed out his fine chest, shouted, whispered, and smirked. One woman who had gazed with particular admiration had been a beautiful, well-connected creature, the widow of John Hathorne's brother, whom Thomas had himself, when the pastor arrived in the village, been wooing for over a year. When Burroughs's first wife died, the widow lost all interest in Putnam. Soon afterward she discovered an unsuspected need for individual religious instruction; within months Burroughs had married her.

Later, Thomas had wedded Ann Carr. She'd had expectations from her father but they had never been realized.

Putnam threw down his pen and stood up. He would write the letter in the morning when his mind was at its clearest. He had somehow to convince Deodat to come quickly before Martha was examined.

And if Deodat was to serve his full usefulness, Rebecca Nurse should also be accused, and if possible arrested, before he got to the village.

Careful thought; careful planning.

In the morning, even before writing his letter, Thomas spoke to his daughter. In the afternoon, witnessed by her mother, Mercy, and, once again, venerable John Putnam, Ann saw Rebecca Nurse, sitting in her dead grandmother's vacant chair by the fire, her hand to her side where it hurt her, staring at Ann as though intending to kill her.

Chapter Twelve
Boston; Salem Village
March 1692

THE INVITATION CAME EARLY IN THE MORNING, FETCHING THE Reverend Deodat Lawson from a disturbed slumber induced by drinking too much cider the previous night. The letter the disheveled servant put in his hands was both bullying and wheedling, saying, after a flowery introductory paragraph, that John Hale of Beverly was now in the village, seeing for himself the extraordinary events of which Thomas had already informed him and which were growing more unusual each day. The people being named were no longer just outcasts but respectable women. His uncle John Putnam and Nathaniel Ingersoll had made a formal complaint to the magistrates about Martha Cory, wife of Giles Cory, a church member, and she was to be examined on Monday. The saintly Rebecca Nurse had been mentioned. More people had joined the band of accusers, including some older, married women. What was more, the accusers had whispered that the deaths of Lawson's own daughter and wife, which had occurred when he lived in Salem Village, had been brought about by witchcraft.

Deodat had been the village pastor before Samuel Parris but never ordained, despite Putnam's best efforts, due to the Porters' and others' opposition. When his wife and daughter had died of an unidentified illness he had left for what he had hoped was a better post in Boston. It had proved disappointing and his career was still floundering. As he read Putnam's letter, exciting new possibilities opened before him. His own wife and daughter's dying of diabolical malice would add to his standing. Though the Reverend John Hale counted himself the supreme expert on witchcraft, he'd had no relatives die of it.

Deodat had his horse saddled immediately after breakfast.

No sooner had the pastor installed himself in his firelit room in Ingersoll's tavern than there came a tap on the door.

"Who is it?"

"Is that Reverend Lawson?" came a breathless female voice.

"It is. Who may that be?"

There was a pause.

"Who is it?" Lawson repeated.

"Mary Walcott, sir," came the same voice.

Deodat's heartbeat accelerated.

"Captain Walcott's daughter?"

"Aye, sir."

Deodat remembered Mary from four years ago, when she was thirteen, already endowed with a womanly figure. Her mother had died when she was small and her father had remarried Thomas Putnam's sister Deliverance, a name alluding to the Puritans' safe arrival from the old country. No personal match between character and name had been intended; none existed. The second Mistress Walcott had never willingly delivered anyone from anything. She had certainly had no desire whatsoever to deliver her stepdaughter from her motherless state. But her marriage contract had obliged her to take on the plump, clumsy creature with irritatingly big, imploring eyes, always whining about being hungry, cold, or in pain. To her extreme annoyance, she had discovered the girl had taken to inflicting more of the last of these sufferings on herself by cutting her arms. She had walloped her to give her even more to cry about, Deodat remembered. As the village pastor, making frequent visits to parishioners' houses, he was privy to most things. He recalled again Mary's big pale blue eyes with their needy, guileless expression.

"I come to greet you from my father and stepmother and the Reverend Parris," the girl said in a singsong chant in the same breathless voice. Lifting the candle, Lawson opened the door. He was astonished to find the big blue eyes almost on a level with his. He was even more astonished, glancing down, to view unusually large breasts, particularly enticing in the warm colors and flickering shadows of candlelight. He stepped aside. Mary smiled coyly, making matters worse.

"C-come in," His unexpected stammering made him blush, which happened all too easily, given his skin's extreme fairness. Mary entered the room, the coy smile still on her face, the expression of her eyes much as he remembered though not quite as guileless.

"My father and stepmother send you their greetings." The eyes gazed into his. "So does my uncle, Mr. Putnam. So does Reverend Parris. The pastor says would you be so kind as to visit him at the parsonage when you're ready."

"Why, thank you, Mary, I'd be glad to."

Deodat's four years of near-celibacy since his wife died had taken its toll. He was strongly tempted to reach for one of those breasts. Mary screamed. Good God, had she guessed?

"What ails thee?" he cried.

"My wrist!"

He thought she said, "My breast!"

She lifted her arm. He flinched. However, she did not slap his face but pointed at her wrist, shouting, "Look!" He raised the candle. There were tooth marks deep in the flesh, either side of the wrist bone.

"Good Lord! How . . . ?"

"A witch bit me!"

"What! When?"

"Just now!"

"Here?"

"Aye!"

"Did you see her?" Deodat stared round.

"Yes! No! Just a shadow. . . . She's gone now." She gazed at him with those not quite guileless eyes. He looked round again, seeing nothing in the candlelight but the bed and a chair with his shabby holdall dropped on it. Gently he lifted Mary's hand and inspected the marks closely, then, in the most pastoral possible manner, put his arms round her, patting her back and murmuring soothingly that he and the other reverend gentlemen in the village would seek out the witches and hang them.

"Oh, thank you, Mr. Lawson!"

With an immense effort of will he let go of her and stepped back, to see her gazing at him with apparent adoration. With another immense effort he turned away, telling her to find Hannah Ingersoll and ask her to put balm on the wound.

Once she was gone, he soothed his own affliction.

The three of them, Lawson, Hannah Ingersoll, and Mary, arrived at Samuel Parris's together. The Salem Village pastor concentrated all his attention on his predecessor, shaking his hand for what seemed to Lawson a full minute. They had never met before though Lawson had seen Parris here and there in Boston and heard a great deal about him. Various acquaintances had mentioned his failures as a businessman, then his turning to the ministry, first as an amateur, then a professional, in due course finding fame as a fiery preacher. Lawson had heard this last claim with particular interest since he prided himself on his own skills at lighting fires in souls with his oratory. He was curious as to what the Salem Village flock thought of Parris's efforts compared with his own. In Boston, Parris had wormed his way into the acquaintance-ship of several top ministers, Lawson knew, but he failed to be charmed by the gushing manner behind which he sensed coldness. However, he was aware that the two of them would now be working together and responded to Parris's overtures with an almost equally energetic show of feigned friendliness.

"There, you see, are my poor afflicted children." Parris pointed to two young girls sitting dejectedly on stools near the fire, the larger one looking sullen, the smaller one dejected. "The little one is Betty, my daughter, the other my niece, Abigail Williams."

"A witch bit Mary's wrist, Mr. Parris!" exclaimed Hannah. Mary raised her bandaged arm but the pastor scarcely glanced at it.

"As you see, you find us in deep trouble," he said to his visitor.

"I saw the witch bite Mary's wrist for myself," Lawson told him.

"You *saw* the witch?" Parris seemed startled.

"I mean I was there when Mary was bitten. The witch was invisible."

"Oh yes, of course."

Abigail rose from her stool. She was an ungainly girl, Deodat observed, with legs too long for her body and hunched shoulders. Suddenly running to the fire, she was chased by Hannah Ingersoll, who Deodat realized must have been expecting this. Hannah tripped against the bucket of water in front of the hearth and fell on her face. When she lifted her head there was blood near the hairline. Abigail stopped and stared, in what seemed genuine horror, as Hannah struggled to her feet, blood trickling into her eyes. When Hannah wiped her face and moved toward her, Abigail ran again but faster and collided with the table. Mistress Ingersoll seized her but the girl wriggled away and, flapping her arms, ran about frenziedly, shouting, "Whish! Whish!" as though trying to fly. It seemed to Deodat she was now beside herself, however in control at the start. Parris shouted to her in a tone of desperation, "Who do you see?" Abigail stopped, lowered her arms and looked at him as though suddenly remembering.

"Goodwife Nurse," she said.

"Where?"

Abigail pointed, it seemed at random.

"They have been seeing Rebecca Nurse for days," Parris told Lawson.

"Good heavens! She is the saintliest woman in the village! She must be seventy by now!"

"Do you not see her?" Abigail pointed toward roughly the same spot. "There she stands!" Suddenly she held her arms up in front of her face as though defending herself from attack. "No, no! I won't! I won't!"

"Won't what?" Lawson asked curiously.

"I won't sign your book! I am sure it is not God's book! 'Tis the devil's book! Begone!" Abigail started running again, once more chased by Hannah Ingersoll, whose face was now covered in blood. Turning, Abigail saw this, screamed, ran to the fire, seized a glowing stick, made as though to throw it at Hannah but changed her mind, and sent it the length of the room. Parris moved to restrain her, shouting, "Stop that!" but she ran even closer to the flames, seizing and throwing more firebrands, one of which just missed Lawson's head. Then she ran right round behind the flames to the back of the chimney and Parris retreated. Her skirt caught fire and she ran out again and collapsed as Hannah grabbed her and dragged her to safety. Parris threw the bucket of water over her and Deodat stamped out the flames.

Chapter Thirteen
Salem Village
March 1692

THE PEWS WERE PACKED FULL, EXCEPT FOR ONE AT THE FRONT, AS were the benches behind them and the galleries above. There were people standing in the aisles. Deodat felt he was the Almighty looking down on souls gazing up at him on judgment day. The sensation was not displeasing.

He knew the one empty pew belonged to the Porter family but their absence scarcely marred his pleasure and excitement as he stood ready to start the service. This occasion felt like returning home in triumph. When he had departed five years before, after the Porters and their allies refused to ordain him, he had felt slighted and rejected even though he knew their opposition was to an ordained minister in principle, not to him as a candidate. Now he felt welcomed back with all the appreciation, perhaps even love, he could wish for.

Mary Walcott gazed at him with particular eagerness. Her wrist was free of its bandage. She smiled. With reluctance he shifted his gaze to Abigail, sullen but composed, and Hannah Ingersoll, staring up, a small scar over one eye. Little Betty Parris was next to her, eyes lowered. In the pew behind them was a puny creature to whom Lawson had just been introduced, Elizabeth Hubbard, and the thin-faced doctor whom Lawson knew had been the first person to say the girls were bewitched. On the other side of the aisle, at the front, was Thomas Putnam's eldest daughter, and next to her a pretty, fair-haired girl of seventeen, whom Lawson had just been introduced to as the Putnams' maid Mercy Lewis. Her parents had been murdered by Indians. Among the women on the benches were various middle-aged and even elderly women whom the witches were also now attacking, according to Parris.

Mixed with his pleasure and excitement Lawson felt nervousness. In this congregation were not only the tortured but one of those said to be torturing them, sixty-year-old Martha Cory, who sat on the front bench behind the pews, back straight, defiant. The warrant for her arrest had been issued the evening before but, since this was the Sabbath, had not yet been delivered. A constable would give it to her early the next morning; she would be examined later that day. Her husband, Giles Cory, across the aisle, had himself accused her of witchcraft, as William Good had accused Sarah Good, now in prison. Deodat, when hearing about this, had wondered if these two men wanted to see their wives hang or were just venting their aggression, after many years of scolding, without thought for the consequences. It occurred to him now, as he looked at Giles Cory's stupid face, that he might truly think his wife was a witch. He lowered his head to say a prayer.

"May the blessed Lord . . ."

A shriek pierced the pale spring light filling the meetinghouse. Ann Putnam was on her feet. People were trying to calm her and, to Lawson's surprise, succeeded. She sat down again. Not knowing what else to do, he lowered his head again and continued the prayer, trying to say it as quickly as possible without too obviously rushing. Thankfully the congregation stayed quiet and he raised his head to see composed faces. He sat down and Nathaniel Ingersoll rose, followed by the congregation, with much rustling. The innkeeper produced a little pitch pipe from his pocket with a flourish, sounded a note, and then, in his mellifluous baritone, sang to the customary simple melody the first line of the twenty-third psalm. The congregation sang it after him, tunelessly. He took them through the whole psalm, beating time in the air, clearly enjoying himself even if nobody else was. When the congregation sat down again Abigail Williams, who had not joined in the singing and wore a glowering expression, shouted at Lawson in a crazed, mocking tone, "Stand up and name your text!" Outraged voices shushed her. Their tone was quite different from when they'd calmed Ann Putnam. This time they had been taken by surprise and were angry. Abigail slid down in her seat, covering her face. Again, not knowing what else to do, Lawson stood up and started reading the text of his sermon from the open Bible before him.

"For my thoughts are not your thoughts." He managed with difficulty to keep his voice from shaking. "Neither are your ways my ways, saith the Lord. For as the heavens are higher than the earth, so are my ways higher than your ways, and my thoughts than your thoughts." The words gradually calmed him and, it seemed, his audience.

"For as the rain cometh down, and the snow from heaven, and returneth not thither, but watereth the earth, and maketh it bring forth and bud, that it may give seed to the sower, and bread to the eater, so shall be that goeth forth out of my mouth: it shall not return unto me void, but it shall accomplish that which I please, and it shall prosper in the thing whereto I sent it."

Lawson had found this, down the years, an extremely useful all-purpose text. Almost anything could be made relevant to the notion that when God expresses his higher thoughts to his people, he achieves a beneficial result.

"It's a long text!" Abigail's voice was as crazed and mocking as before. Lawson grasped the pulpit desk with both hands, eyes still lowered. But the ensuing commotion went beyond shushing and he looked up to see several people on their feet. Deliverance Putnam was leaning over the partition and shaking Abigail as though trying to jerk her head off. Parris strode toward his niece from a chair below the pulpit. There was quickly repressed laughter from the galleries. Lawson himself struggled not to laugh. After more commotion, and a few final shakes from Deliverance, Abigail slid down in her seat again, Parris walked back to his chair, and everyone sat.

Lawson extracted the several pages of his sermon from under the open Bible and placed them over the page he'd just read from. It seemed bizarre to ignore Abigail's antics but he felt it would make the situation seem even more bizarre to acknowledge them. He started reading. This sermon was a humdrum affair and he did not try to enliven it, as he would usually have done, by gestures or voice effects. The situation was volatile enough as it was. But after he had read for five minutes without interruption he began to gain confidence and started glancing up between sentences, meeting faces now showing less fear and more interest and, in some cases, even enjoyment. However, at a moment when his eyes were back down on the paper, Ann Putnam screamed, "Look where Goodwife Cory sits on the beam!"

The girl was on her feet, pointing at a rafter. Martha Cory rose, staring at Ann with outrage. Mercy Lewis shouted, "She's suckling her yellow bird between her fingers!" Ann, shielding her head with her arms, screeched, "She's coming down!" All the girls performed the same actions and shouted the same words, cringing as Martha Cory's specter apparently swooped on them. An elderly woman in neat boots leaped up and ran the length of the aisle, cap strings flying. Ann's mother fell to the floor in a faint. Only Betty Parris stayed in her seat, Hannah Ingersoll's arm around her shoulders, the girl's face buried in her bosom.

Quiet was in due course restored, Mistress Putnam revived, and Martha Cory pushed back down on the bench by her neighbors. Lawson resumed his sermon and continued without interruption until the last sentence. After a final prayer, as the congregation rustled its way out of the building, Samuel Parris met him at the foot of the pulpit.

"I am most distressed this should happen in my meetinghouse! I apologize!"

"My dear Reverend Parris, I've now seen for myself the havoc the devil is wrecking here."

"You saw the children could not help themselves."

"I feel sorry for them."

"Abigail meant no impertinence."

"Of course not!"

"Would you be so good as to accompany me to the tavern? I would invite you to the parsonage but I have little there to offer you."

Deodat had been looking forward to his tankard of cider for some time and, trilling "Delighted," set off at speed down the aisle. Samuel Parris hurried after him, saying, "I fear there are some who do not feel as sorry for them as you do. Some even doubt their torments are caused by the devil."

"Can that be possible?"

"Martha Cory claims she is no witch and the children are deluded and I am afraid there are those who believe her. Vile remarks have even been made about the parents and guardians, including myself."

"Abominable!"

They reached the door. Parris said, "Israel Porter, the most important man in the village, stayed away from the examinations and now stays away from meeting. You saw for yourself his pew was empty. Not even his wife came. The Peabody farmer John Proctor says the children should be hanged!"

"I remember him well."

"Owns an inn *and* a farm."

"Was he present? I didn't see him."

"He never comes, though his wife does. But not today. The children have started seeing *her* specter."

"*Have* they? The devil works strangely." Deodat gestured politely for Parris to precede him through the door but Parris stood his ground, saying, "Thomas Putnam and I have been wondering if we could ask you the favor of writing a special sermon for Lecture Day on Thursday."

"I would be honored!" Deodat felt a surge of thrilled gratification.

"Given your learning and piety, if anyone can show us the way in these difficult times, you can, my dear sir."

"I shall do so to the best of my ability!"

"The doubters must be enlightened as quickly as possible, for the sake of their own immortal souls."

"I shall endeavor mightily to enlighten them!"

"Some of our villagers believe church members cannot be corrupted by Satan."

"I only wish that were so!"

Parris bowed, gestured Lawson out, and followed him. In the faint warmth of the midday early spring sunshine, he glanced round at the little dark brown houses and up to the watchtower, the rails round its open platform silhouetted against the blue and white sky.

"Who could have imagined God would allow Satan to choose our little village to launch his attack on New England?"

"Who indeed?"

Deodat felt utterly drained as he lay in bed in the tavern that night. The day had been long and earlier in the evening he'd taken several jugs of strong cider. He'd dozed off with his clothes on and woken up later with a headache, drunk some water, undressed, and retired to bed again.

The next morning he was torn between making a start on this sermon of sermons and attending the examination of Martha Cory. It did not take long to decide on the latter since he felt avid curiosity and, besides, he was considering writing an account of these events, to be published as quickly as possible while the excitement was still at its height.

At the meetinghouse Thomas Putnam invited him to sit in his pew.

The girls and older women who had joined in the hysteria during Lawson's service all went into fits as soon as Martha entered. Their number had been added to by a woman so ancient she was hardly able to stand yet somehow managed to throw herself to and fro with the rest. All the females screamed, sometimes individually, sometimes in unison, that Martha Cory was attacking them and that they saw the yellow bird flying round the room and sitting on the rafters. When Martha stamped her foot, they stamped theirs. When she turned her head, they turned theirs. One woman threw her muff at the victim, then her shoe, hitting her head. The female who had run down the aisle at yesterday's meeting did so again, waving her arms. The even more ancient crone sprawled on the floor, legs apart, skirt high, gnarled calves in full view. As all this was going on, Martha tried to answer Hathorne's questions, saying she was innocent and had never had anything to do with witchcraft in her life. Once or twice she laughed with contempt. When Hathorne chided her, she denied having laughed, not knowing she had. The congregation furiously shouted she was lying. She claimed the girls were mad, to which Hathorne replied that no one believed this but her.

When he said this, Thomas Putnam, sitting next to Deodat, breathed an audible sigh of relief. He and everyone else knew the examination was to all intents and purposes over.

Half an hour later Martha was committed to jail.

Deodat labored at his sermon till late evening, sending down for a meal but restricting himself to only one jug of cider. Given the occasion and topic, this sermon, he hoped, would be published, perhaps even before his narrative of the witchcraft. It might reach the eyes of the highest in the land, maybe Increase Mather himself. By the end of the day he had still not quite finished it but felt confident of doing so by Thursday.

Chapter Fourteen

Salem Town
March 1692

JOHN HATHORNE'S BULK LOOKED AS SOLID AND IMMOBILE AS THE chair he was sitting on. He looked up from reading a closely written document.

"Can this be?"

"All this and more."

"Witnesses?"

"The Reverend Lawson."

"Most people think her a saint."

"My wife fought for hours with her specter as she tried to make her sign the devil's book, as I've written. Rebecca Nurse first visited my daughter days ago and has tortured Mr. Parris's niece almost to death. Reverend Lawson saw that too."

"A great many people would find this hard to believe." Hathorne pushed the document to one side. Thomas shook his tightly curled head.

"Not Mistress Holton, for one. Goody Nurse bewitched her husband to death several years ago."

"I remember something of that. But I believe most people thought Goody Holton may have made a mistake. There had been a dispute about hogs, I recall."

"They broke through the fence from the Holtons' land to the Nurses'."

"Then Goodman Holton died."

"I think we know why."

Hathorne remained motionless for a few moments, then began slowly moving his huge arms in what proved a largely successful attempt to reach for a pile of papers on one end of the desk and pull it toward him. A few sheets escaped but he reached again and captured these too, placing them on top of the others. Slowly he went through the pile till he found what he wanted.

"I have a communication here from Israel Porter."

Thomas gave an involuntary jerk.

"This was the first I had heard of the accusations against Nurse." He pushed the paper across the desk to Putnam.

Thomas's skull felt tight as he made out the signatures at the bottom of the page—Israel Porter, Elizabeth Porter, Joseph Putnam, Daniel Andrew, and Peter Cloyce—and then went back to the beginning to read, "We whose names are underwritten, being desired to go to Goodman Nurse's house to speak with his wife, to tell her that several of the afflicted persons mentioned her, we found her in a weak and low condition, telling us she had been sick almost a week."

Thomas's chest felt as tight as his skull.

"We asked how it was otherwise with her and she said she blessed God, she felt more of his presence in this sickness than sometimes she had but not so much as she desired."

Gradually his dread was turning to rage, relieving the tightness. How *dare* they try to outmaneuver him like this?

"And then of her own accord she began to speak of the affliction that was amongst them and in particular of Mr. Parris's family, and how she was grieved for them, for people said it was awful to behold, and she pitied them with all her heart, and prayed for them."

That slimy, scheming Israel Porter.

"But she said there were persons spoke of that were as innocent as she was. We told her we heard that she was spoken of also. Well, she said, if it be so the will of the Lord be done. She sat still, amazed, and then she said, well, as to this thing, I am innocent as the child unborn."

Thomas looked up to find Hathorne watching him.

"These are powerful voices in Rebecca Nurse's favor," the magistrate said.

"Not as powerful as the truth."

After a pause, Hathorne asked, "Your wife and daughter are completely without doubt that Rebecca is a witch?"

"They are as without doubt as I am that I'm sitting here."

"If she comes to be examined they may be stilled by her appearance of innocence, and by knowing she is thought of in the village as a saint."

"How can they be stilled, when her specter is tormenting them? It will torment them as surely when she is being examined as when they are sitting at home."

Hathorne looked down at his papers and up again. "If Rebecca Nurse is jailed as a witch, the skeptics in the village will be silenced."

"Not just in the village. Throughout Essex County."

Hathorne said thoughtfully, "Throughout Massachusetts."

Putnam's surprise showed only for an instant. He asked evenly, "There are skeptics in Boston?"

"There are skeptics all through New England!" Hathorne for once sounded almost animated. "They threaten God's realm!"

"The devil finds easy prey in such people."

"Aye. When men doubt the existence of witches they are soon made witches themselves."

"Yet firm believers are the devil's greatest prizes." Putnam paused. "The best prize of all is a minister." He showed the gap in his teeth. Hathorne gazed back at him without speaking. Putnam continued, "Where there's a skeptic who is also a minister, the devil is sure to come knocking."

"A skeptical minister?" Hathorne half-mused, half-prompted.

"A minister with no wish to be ordained, even when the opportunity is handed him on a plate. A minister who preaches to Anglicans and Baptists. A minister living cheek by jowl with the heathens. A minister who scorns good Puritan church members."

"A minister puffed up with pride and self-love," Hathorne murmured.

"Even now Satan may be recruiting such a minister to lead his army of witches."

"I shall draw up the arrest warrant," said Hathorne.

There was a momentary pause.

"For Rebecca," he added.

"Ah, yes, for Rebecca."

After another pause, Hathorne said, "Your daughter's visions clearly attest to the old woman's guilt. I suspect she will be seeing others before long."

The next morning Goodwife Nurse was brought from her sickbed to the meetinghouse. Deodat watched from the end of a bench near the back, convenient for a quick unobtrusive exit. Rebecca could barely stand and had to support herself by clutching the partition at the front of the Putnam pew, used as the dock today while Thomas and his wife sat with the Ingersolls. The Porter pew was full to capacity. Its inhabitants, mostly men, sat silently all through Hathorne's questioning, the girls' screaming, and the crowd's shouting, until Hathorne asked Rebecca Nurse why she shed no tears when she saw how the girls suffered and knew she was the cause. She replied faintly, "You do not know my heart." A tall man with a lined face and clenched jaw moved in his seat. The curly-haired younger man next to him shouted, "She speaks true!" Hathorne looked at him and the older man put a restraining hand on his shoulder.

"You would do well to confess and give glory to God," Hathorne said loudly to Rebecca over the cacophony made by the accusing girls and the crowd.

"I am as innocent as the child unborn."

The curly-haired young man stood up but was pulled down again by the older one.

After an hour, when Deodat saw that Rebecca's allies could not alter the course of events and the old woman was destined to join Tituba, Sarah Good, Sarah Osborne, and Martha Cory in prison, he slid from his seat to get back to work on his sermon. But before he reached the door it opened to show a tiny, ragged child with wondering blue eyes, followed by a constable and, behind him, a gaunt man dressed in rags. Deodat sat down again. The group passed and the constable pushed the child into the Putnam pew with Rebecca, shutting the little gate after her.

"Look at Dorcas Good!" Hathorne ordered the girls, who had been doing so already. But now they could no longer see her since the child was shorter than the pew. Ann glanced at Hathorne for guidance as to whether to go into fits. His answer was simply to wait. A few moments later she began writhing and shrieking, followed by the rest.

"Dorcas Good, do you see what you do to them?" Hathorne asked. It was clear to the congregation she could not see anything except the pew wall and Rebecca Nurse's skirt. The curly-haired young man in the Porter pew gave a loud, contemptuous laugh.

"Stand her on the seat!" Hathorne shouted. The constable reached both arms into the pew and lifted her up. Dorcas's head appeared, in its tiny white cap.

"Not so roughly!" cried her father.

"Who made you a witch?" Hathorne bellowed. "Tell us no lies!"

Dorcas looked all around her in terror; the girls kept shrieking.

"What familiar spirits do you use?" Hathorne bellowed louder. At that moment Ann Putnam, shouting, "She bit me!" ran up and thrust her wrist in his face.

"These are little tooth marks!" Hathorne shouted.

"My daughter's no witch!" wailed the ragged man. He tried to open the pew gate but the constable pulled him away. Dorcas stared at him and wailed, "Papa!" in her tiny child's voice. Mary Walcott ran to Hathorne and showed him *her* wrist.

"That girl just bit herself!" shouted the curly-haired man. "I saw her!"

All the girls were now running up to Hathorne, displaying their wrists.

"My daughter's innocent!"

"Remove William Good!" Hathorne shouted.

The constable pulled him roughly from next to the pew and down the aisle.

"They used just their front teeth to make the marks look small," shouted the curly-haired man.

"Dorcas Good will be taken hence to the prison keeper's house to await further questioning," said Hathorne loudly but barely audibly above the cacophony.

Deodat made his exit.

Later, after an hour's work on his sermon, while sipping a second mug of cider and eating a meat pie in Ingersoll's main room, Deodat saw Dorcas come in through the door, a slice of cake in her hand. There must have been some delay in taking her to the prison keeper's. She gave him a sweet smile. A constable hurried in after her, took her by the arm, and hauled her out.

"Can this be right?" Lawson said aloud before he could stop himself. Nathaniel Ingersoll, clearing a table nearby, looked at him sideways and said slowly in his beautiful baritone, "A witch is a witch however tiny."

"But even if she is a witch, can she *know* she is?"

Ingersoll kept looking at him and Deodat said hastily, "Yes, of course she can."

Later, as he was going to the meetinghouse, he saw the same constable hoisting the child onto a horse in front of Rebecca. The old woman put her arms round her but the look on her face showed she was absorbed in her own agony.

Chapter Fifteen
Salem Village
March 1692

"AND THE LORD SAID UNTO SATAN, THE LORD REBUKE THEE, O SATAN, even the Lord that hath chosen Jerusalem, rebuke thee. Is not this a brand plucked out of the fire?"

The silence unbroken, the faces before him enraptured, Deodat, having declaimed his text thrillingly, adopted an almost conversational tone to start reading the sermon.

"It seemed good to the great and glorious God, the infinite and eternal Elohim, in the beginning to create the heavens and the earth."

His tone built to the rhetorical as he described in ornate language God's creation of the angels, beautiful and beloved in his sight, their rebellion against him and his angry, sorrowful banishment of them to the lake of eternal perdition. After a pause during which he felt he held the whole congregation with his gaze, Deodat lowered his voice and started again slowly, warning of Satan's bottomless malice and envy and untiring assaults on men's bodies and souls as part of his battle against God. His delivery became more emphatic and louder as he told in alarming, eloquent detail of Satan's methods and means of attack, his ruse of turning people into witches to work secretly for him to take over God's world, and his teaching them how in turn to seduce others by offering them earthly delights. He explained that the people Satan most desires to make witches are church members. The more devoted to God they are, the greater his pleasure in inducing them to sign their names in his book.

At last Lawson came to the "direful operations of Satan in the midst of us" for which everyone had been waiting. His delivery built to its greatest crescendo as he urged "unregenerate sinners" in the meetinghouse to stay no longer under the dominion of the Prince of the Air.

"Surely no sinner in this congregation who is sensible of his bondage to Satan, that cruel tyrant, can be willing to continue quietly in subjection to him one day or one hour longer!"

Mary Walcott gazed at him with adoration, little Betty Parris stared around fearfully, clutching Hannah Ingersoll's arm, and Abigail, next to her, twitched her shoulders. The congregation, packing the pews, benches, and galleries to capacity, looked at one another. Thomas Putnam showed the gap between his teeth. Lawson adopted a quieter but even more menacing tone to emphasize the particular dreadfulness of full church members serving the devil, but he soon reached another loud climax when he said that for church members to eat the bread and wine of Satan makes us cry out, "Be astonished O ye heavens at this, and be horribly afraid, and be ye very desolate!" After ten minutes in a slightly lower key he reached his next climax, crying, "I am this day commanded to cry an alarm unto you to arm, arm, arm, against Satan!"

Thomas Putnam's tooth-gapped grin was by now at its widest and John Hathorne's heavy eyes shone. Lowering his voice, Lawson said, "And may we be faithful unto death, in our spiritual warfare, so shall we assuredly receive the crown of life."

The next part of his sermon was directed specifically at the magistrates, exhorting them to endeavor by all ways and means to discover "his instruments of these horrid afflictions."

"We entreat you, bear not the sword in vain," he intoned. John Hathorne and Bartholomew Gedney looked gratified and Hathorne's huge head lowered and rose again in a slow, discreet nod. Deodat ended by circling back to his beginning, pleading that Jesus would "quell, suppress, and utterly vanquish this adversary of ours, with irresistible power and authority." More quietly than at the start, he again declaimed the sermon's text.

He looked up, to rapt faces. His sermon was a triumph.

That night the screams from Betty and Abigail's bedroom brought Samuel Parris running in his nightshirt. A chink of first light through the shutters showed two shadowy figures next to Betty's bed, one standing, one crouching. The standing one shouted, "Save me, Father! Save me!"

Parris ran toward her, colliding with Abigail's bed on the way. The crouched older girl was whimpering.

"He's here!" Betty screamed.

"Who?"

"Satan!"

"Where?"

She pointed to a corner and Parris swung round to see a dark shape. As his heart jumped, the shape moved.

"Begone!" he screamed.

"Father in heaven defend us!" cried Betty.

Parris felt no doubt that he was seeing the devil though nothing was visible but a shadowy man's form. He stepped to the window and threw open the shutters. When he looked round, the form was gone.

"Vanished! Afraid of daylight! Get into bed."

Betty quickly did so.

"Did you see him clear?" he asked. "What did he look like?"

Betty shook her head, clutching the blankets, unable to answer. Abigail was still crouched and whimpering.

"*You* get into bed too."

She did so, pulling the covers over her head. Parris looked down at his daughter.

"You are leaving here tomorrow."

"Tomorrow?"

"Thomas Putnam has made the arrangements. Reverend Lawson is taking you. He has agreed to go through Salem to Boston."

"Oh, Pa, must I go?"

"It is decided."

Abigail's head emerged. "Am I going too?"

"No. Go to sleep, both of you."

"Do not leave me!" Betty cried. "Do not leave me! Satan might come again!"

"Very well, I shall stay here till you sleep."

He did not have to stay long. Betty was soon breathing deeply. But, hidden under the blankets, Abigail still lay awake, seeing nothing now but remembering those blazing red eyes in the corner. She had seen him first, Betty only after she told her he was there. If he came again after tonight, she'd be with him alone. But she did not want to go with Betty. She would not scream again. She would say nothing to anyone.

Chapter Sixteen

Maine
April 1692

As winter turned to spring Burroughs took to sleeping on a rope bed in his study. The warmer weather made this not only possible but necessary since everyone, including Mary, now discarded their outer clothing on going to bed. However, he often grew tired of the cramped space and low, sloping ceilings under the eaves, and escaped whenever he could.

One bright morning after an hour's work on a sermon, he persuaded himself he needed to check the repairs to the palisade and walked down the two flights of narrow stairs, through the main room, and out of the building. The blue sky, early pale green leaves, new grass, and succulent yellow buttercups lifted his spirits. Now that the weather was easier for traveling, he expected the reinforcements to arrive any day. Many of the inhabitants shared this hope and even those who did not were less unhappy than they had been. There had been no sign of Indians for some time, there were crops in the ground, and the daily diet often included rabbit and game brought back by armed hunting parties. Some people had moved back into the less well fortified dwellings and the garrison houses were less cramped. Burroughs assumed even Mary was more reconciled to staying than before. He had no way of knowing this for certain since they only ever talked when they had to, about care of the children and other practical matters.

The sounds of spring—birdsong and the rustling of leaves and buzzing of insects—were drowned out by a whinnying from the barn. Burroughs ran there to see the tall wooden doors unbolted and ajar. He pulled one of them wide open; he could not see Waramaug. He hurried to the stall gate and looked over. No Waramaug, only straw. It was the mare in the next stall who had whinnied. She did so again, moving forward, craning her neck toward Burroughs over her gate. All the horses, who now came to the front of their stalls, seemed unsettled, shifting and tossing their heads. Burroughs's immediate fear was that an Indian had climbed over the palisade in the night and stolen Waramaug. The natives were past masters at slow, stealthy movement; the man on watch might have failed to see him. But how could the Indian have got out again with a horse, without opening the gate? Could the guard on duty not have seen *that*? Burroughs patted the mare, saying gently he would find Waramaug, then left the barn, shut and bolted the doors, and ran to the watchtower. The man on duty was facing away, toward the forest; Burroughs shouted up. The watchman turned and called in astonishment, "Mister Burroughs! What are you doing here? I didn't see you come back!"

"Come back? Where from? I have not been away!"

"I saw you leave!"

"How could you? I'm here!"

"I saw you clear as day!"

"When?"

"Half an hour ago!"

"That wasn't me!"

"You were riding your horse! Wearing your minister's jacket! Your long hair was hanging down your back!"

Could an Indian have got in and stolen one of his jackets? But no one could climb the palisade without a ladder and Indians did not have ladders. If they had erected some structure to reach the top the watchman could scarcely have missed it. And in any case it was too high to jump down from without breaking a leg if not a neck.

"Who is missing?" Burroughs shouted as he walked through the main room where the women were washing clothes in wooden tubs while the men mended tools or repaired boots or cleaned guns.

Everyone looked at one another.

"Someone rode out on my horse!"

They started saying names but then remembered this one was on the watch and that one was sick in bed and another was working in the vegetable patch.

"Mary isn't here," Rebecca said suddenly. "I don't know where . . ."

"How long has she been gone?"

"Let me see, must be about half an hour."

Burroughs ran up the stairs to the family bedroom where his clothes were stored in a chest. He threw open the lid and saw at once that a jacket and breeches were missing. Running down again, he shouted to Captain White, passing him on the stairs, "I'm taking your mare."

She must have found the wait for reinforcements unbearable. This was absurd. This was agony.

The hoofprints on one of the paths leading from the town showed she had gone toward York, no doubt her destination Boston. The mare was as eager as he was to move quickly and soon they were galloping as though in a race whose prize was life eternal. He should catch up with her soon. She had not ridden a horse since she was rescued and was now riding one she had only sat on once before, so she could not possibly cover the ground as quickly as he could. He had often borrowed Peter's mare when Waramaug needed rest.

How could Mary torture him so? When he caught her he would whip her! For stupidity and disobedience and breaking her promise, though she had not actually promised.

The trees were starting to bud and he could only hope she had not decided to take Waramaug off the path to hide till any search parties passed. She would know he'd discover what she'd done and come after her or send others after her. If not for her sake, then for Waramaug's. But there were still hoofprints in the slightly damp earth and he kept hoping to see his horse's dark flanks past the next bend or over the next rise, and experiencing anguish at not doing so, and urging the mare on still faster.

Then he saw her. He gave a shout of agony. She was lying by the side of the path, twisted round, knees raised, body broken. He pulled the mare to a halt, jumped off, ran forward, and dropped to his knees.

"Oh, praise be to God!"

He was looking at two large, intertwined branches, torn off a tree in a storm. One end was the raised legs, the rest the crushed body. Head bowed, he thanked God again, then leaped back on the mare, urging her quickly to a gallop. His stomach was still churning; he was covered in sweat.

Why hadn't she told him? Because she thought he would stop her, and he would have. But if he could not have stopped her, he'd have gone with her. But she didn't know that. Why hadn't he talked to her? Told her if she truly could not bear it here he would take her to Boston?

Because he was wrongheaded, stubborn, and a tyrant, as both his wives had told him.

The hoofprints continued, clearer in some places than others, giving reassurance that she'd at least been safe this far. They were leading him close to what was left of York.

The gate and palisade were the charred ruins he remembered, no longer blocking anyone's entry. The hoofprints were leading him among blackened remnants of dwellings, some recognizable, some not. Wildflowers and weeds were already obscuring the little wooden crosses placed on the low mound where most of the dead had been buried.

Peter's mare whinnied and he saw Waramaug a hundred yards away hitched to a doorpost still standing though door and walls were gone. Burroughs almost shouted Mary's name but realized this could alert Indians, if the mare's noise hadn't done so already. She was still whinnying; he rode her quickly to the post and leaped off, tying her next to Waramaug. They at once started nuzzling. Looking round, he recognized a half-burned house; it was the one from which Mary had run and on the far side was Mary's father's grave. He quickly walked round the ruin and saw a kneeling figure that for an instant seemed himself. Head bowed, long dark hair hanging down his minister's jacket, the figure faced a wooden cross. He approached and Mary looked round, scrambling to her feet.

"My father's here, isn't he? This *is* his grave?"

Burroughs seized her in his arms and hugged her to him so tightly he felt her heart beating.

"Thank God!" he shouted. "Thank God!"

She tried to pull back but he squeezed her against his chest even more closely. "I thought you'd gone to Boston!"

"Boston?" Her voice was muffled.

"Never leave like that again!"

"I can't breathe!"

He let go of her a little and their eyes met. He crushed his mouth against hers and their kiss seemed a foretaste of heaven. Afterward he demanded, "Why didn't you tell me?"

"Tell you what?"

"You wanted to come here."

"You would have said no!"

"I wouldn't!"

"You would have been angry!"

"I wouldn't! I love you!"

"I thought you despised me!"

"I thought you despised *me*!"

"No! How could I?"

"Marry me!"

"*Marry* you?"

"Is that so unthinkable?"

"Yes!"

Burroughs drew back. "Because I'm so old?"

"I meant yes I'll marry you!"

He pulled her to him again and this time their kiss seemed heaven itself.

Chapter Seventeen

Salem Village
April 1692

"I FEAR THIS WITCHERY GOES FURTHER THAN ANY OF US THOUGHT."
Putnam held up his mug for John Indian to pour in more cider. "It's
not just silly old women now. There's a man, a leader."

John Indian continued round the room, refilling the mugs of men
and girls gathered in the parsonage, with more for the men.

"No male witch has ever been hanged in New England," observed
Parris, adding, after taking a sip, "Proctor has influence."

Putnam took a long gulp. "The complaint will be against Elizabeth Proctor, not John. But John is sure to go to the meetinghouse with
his wife. He will show his true colors then. Forget him. I did not mean
him. There is a more important enemy."

"What enemy?" Parris's underlip jutted.

"A minister turned bad."

Parris abruptly stood up. "He is a long way away."

"In God's eyes, no distance."

Nathaniel Ingersoll's face looked wise but his eyes puzzled.
"Who?"

"He was in your tavern often enough, wooing his new bride. Ten
years ago now."

"Ah. They say he preaches to Quakers out in Maine," observed
the innkeeper in mellifluous tones. Hannah had mentioned this at
breakfast.

"They say worse than that."

"What do they say?" asked Ann Putnam.

"Know'st whom we speak of?"

"I think I do, Father. He preached in the village when I was a baby."

"Then you know what they say."

"He murdered two wives."

Parris strode to the fire.

"There is *some* man who is a leader of witches in New England," Putnam said quickly.

Parris turned back.

"I'll wager he has recruited more followers than any of us knows yet."

"Many of them church members!" piped Ann Putnam.

"Some taken years ago, out in Maine, but now in our midst."

Parris walked to his chair.

"I will wager they gather to take their devilish sacrament here in our village," Putnam added.

"In our village?" Abigail, who had been slumped on her stool, jerked upright. "Where?"

"Some field with enough space for ten or twenty or thirty or even forty witches."

"The training field?"

"Maybe."

"How would we know him, Mr. Putnam?" Mary Walcott asked, big blue eyes wide. "This leader of witches? What would he look like?"

"He'd be little and dark."

In the night Satan came again. He did not speak but stared with his blazing red eyes, in the room that without Betty seemed emptier than the emptiest clothes chest, the emptiest cider barrel.

The next morning Abigail gazed out on the field where she and her cousin had so often played, picking flowers in the spring and, in the fall, scooping up armfuls of leaves of scarlet, orange, and russet. A misery filled her that was greater even than the sadness that at one time had propelled her to taunt Betty and scowl and be silent with her uncle and pretend Tituba had induced her cousin's fits. Greater even than when she'd copied Betty's shaking and twitching. Then she'd had control of her thoughts; now they controlled her. Then she'd felt part of the world she lived in; now she seemed behind an invisible wall, all alone. Then one moment had followed another in a continuous stream; now instants of time seemed separate, as though she were reborn every moment, restarting a tedious, unending journey.

The twisted branches moved a little in the lightest of breezes. The shadows beneath them moved too. Gradually each began taking shape and coming into the pasture. Soon the field was crammed full of them. From behind the wide, pitted trunk of the dead oak appeared a woman with high cheekbones and a ruddy complexion, placing a chalice next to some glittering candlesticks on the tree stump as smooth as a table. Another shape, who in bodily form had marched out of the meetinghouse, slamming the door, stood with a basket of bread in her arms. The shapes began forming a line. Whoever was administering this mockery of Christ's body and blood was in shadow but his form seemed that of a man, small and dark. Tituba's specter suddenly swung to face Abigail.

"This is your blood!" Her voice was loud and clear. "We'll drain every drop, we've drunk of it today twice already, we'll drink of it again."

Abigail meant to tell no one but it poured out of her when Mr. Putnam came again to visit. She was given cider and cake and warm smiles and told if she truthfully answered the magistrates' questions, with a few additions suggested by her listeners, there'd be rewards both on earth and in heaven.

Chapter Eighteen

Salem Town
April 1692

THE TOWN MEETINGHOUSE WAS IDENTICAL IN STRUCTURE TO THE one in Salem Village but almost twice as large and with windows of glass. The massive oak roof stood higher than the buildings around, dominating the corner of Main Street and Town House Street, even though these two handsome roads were lined with fine houses surrounded by lawns. The splendid setting inspired awe in everyone, whether accusers or spectators, who had taken the three-hour journey by foot, one on horseback, from the sprawling rural settlement. Together with townsfolk, they filled the building to capacity.

John Hathorne took a minor role here. He was seated, with Bartholomew Gedney, at the far end of a table along which were ranged several of the most important men in New England, including Samuel Sewall, the eminent merchant, member of the Council and judge, a man whose deep piety did not prevent him from enjoying the pleasures of life to the utmost, as evinced by his several chins and large stomach. Beside him was the most distinguished Council member of all, William Stoughton. This man was deputy governor and a close friend of the supremely powerful minister, Increase Mather, at present in England though due to return shortly with the new charter he had been negotiating with the king. Stoughton was an even closer friend of Mather's almost equally powerful son, Cotton Mather. The governor of the colony, Simon Bradstreet, was absent due to age and infirmity and lack of enthusiasm. It had been Stoughton's decision, after consultation with Cotton, to give this strange, unprecedented witch scare colonial importance, by staging this examination in town.

John Hathorne was all too aware of being deposed from preeminence. He felt, rightly, his dominance was diminished by Stoughton's air of supreme legal authority. Though, like the rest of the magistrates in Massachusetts Bay, the deputy governor was without training in the law, he had had years of experience as a magistrate and judge. Even on the physical level, Hathorne felt lessened. His bulk appeared less impressive next to Stoughton's neat form.

Stoughton's character was one with his looks. He prided himself on his thoroughness, never leaving the smallest detail to chance. He had large, clever eyes and a thin-lipped, tightly closed mouth.

At the other end of the table from Hathorne and Gedney sat Samuel Parris and John Hale, Parris dark-complexioned with full lips and plentiful hair, Hale pale-skinned and fine-featured. The first had been appointed scribe in place of the less than satisfactory, indeed, barely literate, Ezekiel Cheever, and already held his pen in his hand. The second sat back in his chair with a stillness masking excitement. Yet a third minister, Nicholas Noyes, sat on the table's end. Stoughton leaned forward to ask him to start the proceedings with a prayer. The wide-girthed reverend rose and bowed his large head. He prayed for five minutes and said, "Amen." Then he looked around with an air of self-satisfaction and heavily sat down again. Stoughton, spitting each consonant, called, "Elizabeth Proctor!"

Everyone turned as out of the shadows at the end of the meet-inghouse came a woman who could scarcely have looked less like a witch. There was whispering as she passed the folk from Salem Village and the poorer ones of the town, in their simple trousers and shirts and plain dresses, and the smarter Salem Town people in brightly col-ored clothes, with ribbons, braids, and feathered hats. Elizabeth was middle-aged but slender, dressed in simple village fashion, her face lined but still pretty, its expression composed, her fair hair peeping out from under her cap above her forehead. The marshal walking behind her with raised staff opened the little pew door and pushed her through. Flustered for a moment, she quickly composed herself and stood facing the table at which the magistrates and ministers were sitting, along with the accusers Ann Putnam, Elizabeth Hubbard, and Abigail Williams on one side and Mary Walcott and John Indian on the other, together with the middle-aged woman, called Bathsheba Pope, who had thrown her shoe at Martha Cory. Being a slave did not negate John Indian's preeminence as a male; Stoughton turned his eyes to him first.

"John, who hurt you?"

"Goody Proctor."

Tituba would have been proud of him, speaking with conviction, a humble but confident look on his high-cheekboned face. He felt certain she sympathized with his determination not to join her in prison. He had visited just once, to see the dungeons rather than her, as she well knew, and straight afterward turned accuser.

"What did she do to you?" Hathorne asked.

"She brought the book to me. She choked me."

"Do you know Goody Proctor?"

"Yes, here she is." He pointed.

"When did I hurt thee?" Elizabeth demanded.

"Many times!"

"Oh! You are a liar!"

"What else did she do to you?" Stoughton asked him.

"She bit me till the blood came."

"You lie!"

Stoughton turned next to the girl beside John, plump Mary Walcott, and they went through the same questions and answers. At the end, Mary's eyes rolled and the rest of the girls glanced at her and each other as though wondering whether to join in. However, Ann Putnam made a slight head movement and they stayed as they were. Mary, finding herself alone in her eye rolling, stopped it. Stoughton asked her, "Does Goody Proctor come alone?"

"Yes but sometimes with Goody Nurse and Goody Cory, and many I don't know."

Ignoring the middle-aged woman next to Mary, Stoughton swung his head to the nearest girl on the other side, his air changing from astringency to keen interest.

"Did you see a company of witches at Mr. Parris's house eat and drink?"

"Yes, sir, that was their sacrament," Abigail said.

"How many?"

"About forty." Abigail glanced at Thomas Putnam in a front pew and added, "And Tituba and Elizabeth Proctor were their deacons."

"What was the sacrament?"

"Tituba said it was our blood, and they had had it twice that day."

"Give me water," cried Elizabeth. A tall man at the back, wearing a cloak with its hood up, tried to rise but was pulled down by those round him.

"Tituba said it was our blood, and they had it twice that day!" Abigail repeated.

Elizabeth collapsed, her head banging the partition as she slid to the floor.

"Tituba said it was our blood, and they had it twice that day!" Ann echoed, pointing to the pew where Elizabeth could no longer be seen. "Mistress Proctor's gone to the prison, to fetch Tituba and Goody Nurse!"

"Stand up!" shouted Stoughton. Elizabeth hauled herself to her feet, using the wall of the pew.

"Elizabeth Proctor, recite the Lord's Prayer!" Stoughton demanded.

"Our father, which art in heaven. . . ."

"Speak louder!"

"Hollowed be thy name. . . ."

"Hollowed!" Stoughton repeated the mistake with incredulous fury.

"A tongue slip!"

"That was no tongue slip, that was a depraving of the words. That was a curse, not a prayer!"

There was a bellow from the back of the court. Everyone swung round to see the tall hooded man standing up, struggling to get free of those holding him. Ann Putnam gave a scream; the others did so too, including Abigail, still swaying. Raising his voice above their noise, Stoughton shouted, "Does this woman hurt you? Speak true!"

"She hurts me! She hurts me!" Ann shouted. The others echoed her.

"What do you say, Goody Proctor?"

"I take God in heaven to be my witness, that I know nothing of it!"

The hooded man broke free and strode up the aisle. Stoughton stood up.

"Goodman Proctor is at Mrs. Pope's feet!" Ann told them.

The stout middle-aged woman fell on her bottom as if her feet had been yanked out from under her.

"What do you say to that?" Stoughton shouted to John Proctor.

"I did not go near her!"

"Your specter knocked her down!"

"My specter? What specter? There's no such thing as a specter!" Proctor bellowed.

"Are you saying the ministers lie?"

"If they do not lie, the devil deceives them!"

Abigail pointed at Elizabeth.

"She hurts me! She hurts me!"

"Dear child, I do not hurt you, it is not so," said Elizabeth. "Remember, there is a higher judgment, dear child, than this, that we must all answer to one day."

Abigail staggered as though hit. Ann pointed upward. "Look you, there is Goody Proctor on the beam!"

Abigail screamed as if in pain. John Proctor strode toward her.

"Abigail, who hurts you?" shouted Stoughton, leaning over the table.

"Goodman Proctor!"

Proctor stepped forward to stand over her. The girl quickly ran round him and, to everyone's amazement, jumped up on the table. Proctor came forward and she leaned toward him and spat on his hood.

"He stabs me! He stabs me here!" shouted Ann Putnam, clutching her side. Parris leaped round the table, grasped his niece, and yanked her to the ground.

"Goodman Proctor, you see what you do to them!" shouted Stoughton, standing up. "Confess!"

"'Tis *you* should confess!" Proctor roared.

"Marshal, take them to jail."

Chapter Nineteen
Salem Village
April 1692

THERE WAS A SMALL BACK ROOM AT INGERSOLL'S TAVERN THAT ORDI-
nary visitors never saw. It had one window and a steeply sloping ceiling,
making it unsuitable for almost any purpose. If a narrow bed had been
squeezed in there the sleeper would have stunned himself when getting
up in the morning. Three teenaged girls and two younger ones now sat
close together on the floor, each with a mug of watered-down cider.
The door was ajar to allow in heat and light from the next room, at
present unoccupied but ready with a fire in case of unexpected arrivals.
A dimly glowing lantern hung on a nail on the wall.

"What you smilin' at, Mercy?" asked Ann Putnam sharply.

"She's always smilin'." Little Elizabeth Hubbard hugged her bony
knees under voluminous skirts.

"Smilin' at breakfast, dinner, and supper," Mary Walcott said,
wriggling.

"Better a smilin' servant than a frownin' one," said Mercy, still
smiling.

"Why d'you call yourself a servant?" asked Ann.

"'Cos I *am* a servant." The smile on the pretty face tightened.

"That's not very grateful to my parents who feed and clothe you
like one of their own children."

"I'm still a servant."

"I'll give you an order then."

The girls went very still.

"Stop smilin'!"

Mercy did so and the pretty face became almost ugly. Then Ann
Putnam smiled herself.

"Older sister, more like, 'stead of servant." She put her skinny arms round her for a moment, then turned away, picked up her cider, and took a sip. Mercy smiled and looked pretty again and the other girls shifted and giggled and sipped their drink, except Abigail, who glowered at Ann, shoulders twitching. Mercy drew herself up, legs crossed under her skirts, back straight. "I was smilin' for a reason. I was wonderin' somethin'."

"What were you wonderin'?" Ann peered into Mercy's eyes, dark in the dim light.

"Do them witches do it in prison?"

"Do what?" asked Ann.

"*It*. Do Goodman and Goody Proctor . . . ?"

"Oh, *that*."

"What?" asked Elizabeth Hubbard, her arms still round her knees.

"Don't pretend you don't know!" Mercy snapped.

"I *don't* know!"

"I do!" said Mary Walcott, waving her half-empty cider mug. The flesh under her chin bulged where it was pressed by her cap string.

"I should think so!" said Mercy. "Who knows, you might be married soon, you're old enough." She added, "Come to that, I might be married soon too."

"Is anyone offerin'?" Ann sneered.

"Might be!"

"You're lyin'!"

"I'm old enough to marry soon too," said Elizabeth.

"No one'll marry you if you don't get any bigger," Mercy said. "D'you really not know . . . ?"

"Like this!" Abigail fell on her back, Ann and Mercy either side of her, jerking her pelvis.

"Stop it!" shouted Mary, then shrieked with laughter.

"Sinner," Ann hissed. Elizabeth laughed; Mercy giggled.

Mercy asked Abigail, "Have you seen your uncle and aunt . . . ?"

"So what if she has," snapped Ann Putnam.

Abigail lay still, staring at the ceiling.

Ann said, "It's nothing much to see."

"It is if there's no blankets on the bed and they've got their clothes off," said Mercy.

"Mercy!" Ann snapped. "When did you . . ."

"You've never . . ." Mary breathed.

"I'm not sayin' I have or I haven't."

"What? *Done* it?" gasped Mary.

"No, *seen* it! How could I have *done* it? I'd be whipped, thrown out of doors, die of cold, and go to hell."

"Sarah Osborne did it when *she* wasn't married," Ann said.

"And Martha Cory," said Mary.

"They're not doin' it now, there's no men in those dungeons, except for John Proctor, and his wife's in there with him. That's what I was wonderin', if them two do it and the other witches pretend they can't see but they're watchin'."

"But how could they, chained to the wall?" Ann's eyes glinted.

"What? See?"

"No, do it!"

"I wish I could see." Elizabeth had curled on her side.

"See them doin' it?" Mercy asked.

"No, see 'em chained to the wall!"

"Does the warder take them chains off sometimes?" Abigail wondered, sitting up.

"Course not. They might attack us again." Ann said.

"I hope they never take Goody Proctor's chains off, not till she dies." Abigail's shoulders twitched. "She talked like I was a baby, sayin', *dear child*, I'm not her *dear child*, I'm no one's *dear child* . . ."

"She's *havin'* a baby," said Ann Putnam.

"How d'you know?" Abigail asked.

"Father told me."

"When's it comin'?"

Ann shrugged.

"Will they let her out when it does?"

"No," Ann said. "The baby'll be a witch too. Anyway, who cares about them Proctors? Mister Proctor's just an ordinary witch like those silly old women."

"Silly old Tituba, silly old Sarah Good, silly old Sarah Osborne," chanted Elizabeth.

"I hope them chains cut them Proctors' legs till they bleed." Abigail's face had gone dark red.

"If it weren't for us they wouldn't *be* in chains," Ann said. "They wouldn't be in prison. You'd better keep control of yourself next time or they'll send you away like crybaby Betty."

Abigail turned to lie facedown on the floor.

Silly old Martha Cory," Mary said.

"Silly old Rebecca Nurse," chanted Mercy. "Silly old Bridget Bishop. Silly old Mary Warren."

"Silly old Giles Cory," said Mary.

"Giles Cory's not a silly old woman," objected Elizabeth.

"He's a silly old man," replied Mary.

"But the leader of the witches isn't silly." Ann glanced round the company.

"George Burroughs," said Mercy.

"Sshhh, don't say his name, he might fly in through the window!"

"He's out in Maine."

"Not his specter."

"Why? Have you seen it?"

"Yes."

"When?"

"Yesterday."

"How did you know it was him?"

"He told me his name."

"Was he little and dark?" asked Mercy. "But very strong?"

"Aye."

"I know 'cos I lived with him." Again, Mercy was smiling. "When I was little, in Maine. After my parents were killed by the Indians." She still smiled. "He was married to his second wife then." Her voice dropped. "She was the second he married and the second he killed. She was on a ship going back to her family because he was so cruel and he sent out his spirit and killed her."

"Did he try to make you a witch?" Mary Walcott gazed at her with her enormous blue eyes.

"Yes but I refused. There was others that didn't."

"Lydia Hobbs," said Ann with venom.

"He frightened me." Mercy shuddered, though still smiling. "But I shouted no, no, I won't sign your book!"

"I hope I never see him," Elizabeth whispered.

"You will!" cried Ann. "He's their leader! He'll torture you!"

"Sometimes I wish we could stop." Elizabeth curled up tighter.

"Stop?" Ann stared at her.

"You know."

"You can't stop!"

"Sometimes I wish . . ."

"So do I, sometimes," said Mary.

"We can never stop!"

"They'd say we'd bin shammin'." Mercy smiled.

"We've got spectral sight," Ann said fiercely.

"But there's nothin' there," said Elizabeth. "We think there is when we're seein' it but . . ."

Ann pinched her. Elizabeth yelped, then wailed, "You're lucky, you've got a mother and father."

"Don't moan, none of us except Ann has a mother and father," Mary chided.

Elizabeth sat up, short as a child.

"You've got a father."

"Not a mother though."

"A stepmother."

"A stepmother's no good. She's worse than *no* mother."

"You're not a *servant*," said Elizabeth.

"But *you're* a servant to your own uncle and aunt, not to strangers, like me." Mercy was not smiling now.

"We're not strangers," Ann said to her.

"I didn't mean you were strangers, I meant you're not relatives. You're not . . ." Mercy went from looking unhappy to looking ugly to bursting into tears.

"Shush!" snapped Ann.

"No one cares!"

"Course they do!"

"If I died, no one would miss me! I saw my father lying separate from his head, I saw my mother with a knife through her neck!"

As Mercy sobbed, Abigail sat up, shaking.

"Covered in blood!" she gasped. "Covered in blood!"

"Who?"

"My mother! She was comin' towards me to kiss me . . . There's them Indians, as killed her!" She pointed at the door. "There's Tituba!"

"Stop it!" snapped Ann.

"It's them as murdered my parents!" Mercy shouted.

Abigail scrambled to her feet. "There they are." She kept point-ing, taking a few quick steps backward.

"Stop it, there's nobody there!" shouted Ann. "Both of you, be quiet! I told you, you'd better get control of yourself, Abigail, or they'll send you away just like Betty."

Abigail collapsed on the floor again, arms over her head.

"Time to go home, girls! I'll be back in five minutes!"

Nathaniel Ingersoll's face had appeared round the door; it disap-peared as suddenly. Ann said urgently, "Listen, all of you, listen care-fully, at the next examination there'll be Lydia Hobbs. She's told everyone she's a witch but not who made her one. Mr. Hathorne wants his name."

"Will they arrest him just because of what *she* says?" asked Mary "She's daft. She claims when she was out in Maine she used to go roam-ing the woods by herself to meet Satan. Now she says he sits on her bedpost."

"There'll be other evidence too. But hers should nail him, no mat-ter how daft she is."

John Putnam, Jonathan Walcott, and Nathaniel Ingersoll came together at Thomas Putnam's house and sat with him in his study, talk-ing of village affairs. A scream from the living room sent them running through the door. Ann Putnam stood, staring toward the center of the room, her cap on the floor, her hands clutching the tightly curled hair falling round her face.

"Are ministers witches too? What is your name? I will complain of you, however much you're a minister!" Walking backward, in a ter-rible whisper, she said, "I will *not* write in your book though you tear me to pieces! Oh, it is a dreadful thing that a minister should come to per-suade me to give my soul to the devil!" She backed against the wall, knocking over a chair, and then slid to the floor. She sat for a while, looking as though listening to something, then her head dropped to her chest and she reclined as though lifeless. The men righted the chair, carried her to it, and sat her there. She stayed slumped for a moment, then whispered that the minister was George Burroughs and he'd told her he'd had two wives and bewitched them to death, killed the wife and child of the previous vicar, and bewitched a great many soldiers. He demanded that she, Ann, write her name in his book or he would torture her. He said to her that he was a leader of witches and would make more and more of them till they'd conquered New England for Satan.

Chapter Twenty

Salem Town
April 1692

SPRING MELTED THE LAST OF THE SNOW, LINGERING IN SHADED corners and along the edges of tree-covered paths, and put blossoms on the trees and flowers in the earth. The journey from the village to the town had become easier than when Thomas Putnam had gone on the first of these errands at the beginning of March. He now mounted his horse and set off down the road leading through pleasant farmland and woods, skirting the estuary with its widening water and limitless skies, passing a hill on the right and turning onto the street lined with fine houses that led to the center of town and the home of John Hathorne. In his saddlebag, stowed under bread and cheese wrapped in a cloth, lay two pieces of paper, one inscribed with a long list of names, the other headed "Salem Village" and the date, twenty-first of April, 1692.

Putnam had expected to leave the list and the letter with a servant. But the man who opened the door said Hathorne was at home and would see him. Seated behind his wide mahogany desk, the magistrate extended his hand without rising.

"I thought you might come today, Thomas."

They shook hands.

"Your honor has heard tidings?"

"I know your daughter's torments continue."

"They grieve a father's heart."

"Pray be seated. None of the other girls' sufferings have lessened either, I hear."

"They grow worse."

"'Tis a harsh judgment God has sent down for our sins. We must endeavor mightily to find and destroy every witch in New England."

"Most important, we must find and destroy the wizard who leads them." Putnam felt his boldness in venturing such a decisive opinion. Yet he sensed how far he could go. His instinct proved sound. Hathorne replied, "That is so." He reached forward. "I see you have papers to give me."

Thomas handed one over. Hathorne read several names he'd expected, of Putnam's long-standing village enemies, and one he hadn't.

"Mary English? Her husband's the richest man in Salem!"

Putnam did not inform Hathorne that he had induced Ann and the others to name Mary English precisely *because* she was the wife of the richest man in Salem. There was no class of person he loathed more than the merchants of Salem, living in splendor in huge houses, making the Putnam clan look provincial and powerless. As indeed they were, alas. But his thoughts quickly moved to the man he hated even more than any rich merchant. He said, "This conspiracy goes further than anyone could have guessed."

Hathorne looked up at him, face expressionless.

"There is another name after Mary English."

Hathorne looked again.

"Lydia Hobbs? That daft daughter of the idiot mother? Who came here from Maine?"

"She was made a witch there. She has said so herself. By whom I dare not say, though I can guess."

"She has not named him?" After a pause, Hathorne added, "Or her?"

"Not yet." The two men gazed at each other, then Putnam said, "I have another paper here I would crave your honor to read." He pushed the rolled parchment across the desk. "It's a letter I wrote, thinking it unlikely you'd have time to receive me."

Hathorne rolled open the paper on the mahogany surface and held it down at both ends with bulging fingers.

"It warns of horrible tidings," Putnam said.

Hathorne read, "Much honored. After most humble and hearty thanks presented to your Honors for the great care and pains you have already taken for us, for which we are never able to make you recompense . . ."

The lengthy preamble, bombastic and fawning, went on for

almost a page but Hathorne kept reading, guessing what might be coming. He had other Salem Village informants besides Thomas Putnam. At last the missive reached the heart of the matter but, instead of coming clear, continued to tantalize.

"We thought it our duty to inform your Honors of events as yet unknown to you, high and dreadful, of a wheel within a wheel, at which our ears do tingle."

It ended there, without describing the events. Hathorne smiled. Clearly the next name Putnam was assiduously preparing to put to him was one he was still afraid he would balk at, despite insinuations already made and accepted. For all his cunning, Putnam could not comprehend that Hathorne would need no persuasion at all, once the ground was made ready, to send an arrest warrant to Maine. He had not yet guessed the magistrate hated the Reverend George Burroughs quite as much as he did.

Chapter Twenty-One

Salem Village
April 1692

HATHORNE RAISED HIS JOWLY CHIN TO ADDRESS THE UNKEMPT YOUNG woman in the pew that served as a dock. He was glad to be in the Salem Village meetinghouse again, conducting the examinations himself, not watching Stoughton take his place. The young woman was the last of the day and Hathorne hoped for success with her. The previous three, Bridget Bishop, Giles Cory, and Mary Warren, had all refused to confess, but Hathorne felt no loss of energy. It was as though his great bulk could support him for days, like a camel's hump or whale's blubber. Besides, he had hope, not only that he would get a confession, but that he would elicit that name. He did not have the authority to issue a warrant for the arrest of a resident of Maine. Only the Council in Boston had that. So he would need the best evidence to persuade them, which was always a confession, naming names.

The girls stood quietly to one side of the table, having emerged just moments before from the displays induced by the previous prisoner. Hathorne often marveled at their powers of recovery, choosing to believe their fits were genuine despite the overwhelming evidence to the contrary. He, like Stoughton and others, had chosen credulity over skepticism regarding every phenomenon forwarding this witch hunt.

"Lydia Hobbs, have you consorted with the devil?"

The girl, her matted hair falling from her cap, was clearly pleased by her place at the center of attention. Hathorne waited. Lydia said loudly and dramatically, throwing her hands in the air, she would speak the truth. Hathorne waited again. Looking all round the room and narrowing her eyes she said, quietly but just as dramatically, she had seen "sights."

"What sights?"

Dogs, cats, rats, and birds of various colors, she claimed with relish. What other sights?

After a long pause that made it clear she had no intention of being rushed, she said, "Men," and the meetinghouse went expectantly quiet. Asked what men, she said, again after a long pause, "A little dark man." Hathorne leaned forward to ask if the little dark man was known to her by name. She said he was "like an Indian" and she'd known him "in Maine." Again, Hathorne asked if he was known to her by name. After keeping everyone in suspense for a full half minute, she said no. Hathorne stayed impassive and went back to asking questions about animals, when she had seen them and how often. This went on till the congregation started shuffling, muttering, and yawning. Lydia looked around with annoyance. Hathorne leaned forward and asked again if she knew the name of the man she had seen. She cocked her head and peered at him sideways as though seriously considering whether to deliver the prize.

"She's hurting me!" yelled Abigail, twitching her shoulders. Lydia stared round at her.

"Kill the witch! Kill the witch!" shouted Abigail, now clutching herself, bending forward. Lydia stuck her fingers in her ears. John Hathorne, for once losing control, loudly and angrily again asked the name of the man. Lydia, her fingers still in her ears, shouted, "I can't hear! The specters are making me deaf! I can't hear!"

John Hathorne glared at Abigail and ordered the marshal to take Lydia away.

As the girls left the meetinghouse Parris grasped his niece's arm and pulled her up the path past the training field to the parsonage. He said nothing; his underlip was jutting. He threw open the door and pushed Abigail inside.

"What's the matter?" she whimpered.

"We never want you at an examination again."

"I didn't mean to! It won't happen anymore! I'll only do what the others do! I'll guard myself better!"

"Too late."

"Are you sending me where Betty is?"

"I would if they'd have you." He strode away.

"Uncle . . ."

He kept walking. Abigail took a step toward him, then stopped, watching his stiff back ascend the stairs. Then she went into the living room, where she stood for a while, then wandered round aimlessly, gazing at the chairs and stools without seeing them. Going back in the passageway, she opened the door to Mrs. Parris's bedroom and stared at the sleeping form under the bedclothes, the head on the pillow lying sideways with its closed, thickly veined eyelids. Shutting the door, she walked slowly upstairs and past the minister's study to the chamber where she and Betty used to lie in beds next to each other. She sat on her bed and stared at the empty one, its rough sheet still a tangle from when Betty had left it. Then she climbed under her own covers. As her eyes started to close her mother came forward to take her in her arms but blood spurted from her neck as the ax fell. Leaping out of bed, Abigail ran to the door. But she did not open it. There was nowhere to go. She turned to the wall and banged her head on it repeatedly, then climbed into bed again and eventually fell asleep.

Chapter Twenty-Two
Salem Village
April 1692

THE SKY WAS CLEAR BUT FOR A FEW PUFFS OF WHITE CLOUD, THE air balmy. Samuel Sibley saw Abigail hurrying with odd, stiff, shuffling steps along the roadside. She gazed round at him, and, startled by the look in her eyes, he pulled his horses to a halt and asked her what ailed her.

"A little black minister!"

"Where?"

She still stared at him with those weird eyes.

"He lived at Casco Bay. He told me he'd killed two wives and made witches."

"George Burroughs! Is he here now?"

"Aye."

Sibley clambered down from the cart, took a three-pronged iron fork from the back, and held it ready to throw. "Where is he?"

Abigail pointed. He threw the fork. She whispered, "You hit him!"

"Wounded?"

"No. His coat tore."

"Where's he now?"

Abigail stared round.

"Gone?"

She nodded.

"Are you better now?"

"Aye." But the look in her eye still chilled his soul. He gazed at the ungainly figure, the prominent rear end tightly encased by her long skirt, shuffling back and forth to no apparent purpose, glancing at Samuel without seeming to see him.

"Go you to Ingersoll's?" he asked.

Abigail looked as though he had reminded her of something she'd forgotten. Again she nodded.

They went on side by side, Sibley leading his horse with the cart rattling behind. He had never felt such strangeness emanating from anyone. Abigail still walked with those stiff little steps, sometimes glancing round. What was she seeing?

"Does George Burroughs come to you often?" he asked. Abigail seemed not to hear. When Sibley repeated the question she ran on, then waited till he caught up with her.

At Ingersoll's, she went inside while he tethered his horse. After a moment's hesitation, he kept hold of the pitchfork in case he needed a weapon and went into the inn, proceeded to the great room, and ordered ale and meat. There was no one else there but for the servant, who left to fetch the victuals. The room was still empty when Abigail came in and cried, pointing to the window. "There he stands!"

"Where?"

Abigail's arm fell. "He's gone now but there's a cat there."

Sibley threw the pitchfork where she pointed.

"You killed it!"

"Where's it lying?"

"Nowhere. Sarah Good carried it away!"

As Sibley looked into Abigail's narrow eyes it was as though the person who ought to be looking back out at him was absent. He had never felt this even when caring for Elizabeth in her fits. She had suffered agonies but had still seemed herself. It appeared something had stolen Abigail's soul. Sibley left to find Hannah Ingersoll.

Abigail gazed out of the window, past the yard where chickens strutted and squawked, to the parsonage field, visible through a gap in the trees. Shadows emerged one by one, gathering at the tree trunk. Abigail turned and walked from the room and the tavern, up the road, toward the parsonage.

She was unaware of the blue sky and scented breeze. The world she walked in was without color or odor. She entered the parsonage and climbed the stairs to Samuel Parris's study, where he sat at his desk. As he looked up at her, his underlip jutted. She gazed without speaking. He stared back for a while, then looked down again at his papers. She turned and went back down the stairs.

She knew what she needed and where it was. She found a length that suited her purpose and carried it to the field. The specters were gone now. She walked across the rough grass to the far end, where stood the dead oak, leaning as though about to collapse but never quite doing so. Climbing onto a low branch, reaching up to a higher one, Abigail tied the loop.

Her mother was coming toward her to take her in her arms as she had before the ax fell.

At midday, puzzling over how to phrase an idea in his sermon, Parris looked out of his study window for the first time that morning, to see a strange dark shape hanging in the oak at the end of the field. Not until he walked out under the hot sun and was halfway down could he see what it was.

Soon everyone in the village had heard that in the training field, where the witches' Sabbaths were held, George Burroughs had tortured Abigail so badly she'd taken her life.

Not much later everyone in town heard it too.

John Hathorne set off for Boston to see the deputy governor.

PART
TWO

Chapter Twenty-Three

Maine
May 1692

THE BRANCHES MOVED IN THE FAINT BREEZE, JUST VISIBLE IN THE first light of dawn. The shadows beneath them moved too. George Burroughs hoisted his gun. Nothing. His eyes had played tricks. He lowered the weapon. He had stood on this spot, on the watchtower inside the palisade of tall wooden spikes, countless mornings as the light changed the sky. In the garrison buildings and smaller houses behind them, the rest of Wells was still sleeping. Little remained of the dwellings that had once stood outside. It was almost a year ago, as he watched on this platform facing those trees in the same early light, that the shadows had turned into substance. They had appeared from under the branches, skin gleaming, knives glinting. Within a few silent seconds they were everywhere. Even as Burroughs was blowing the trumpet to sound the alarm screams filled the air; within moments the near naked forms ran into the houses; by the time George and the other men ran out past the palisade the buildings were burning and the Indians running away. A score of men, women, and children had been killed, fields of corn destroyed, and most of the houses burned to the ground.

The Indians had attacked again later that day, and again the next morning, and again every day for three days. All the settlers squeezed themselves into the garrison buildings, as they had again, nine months later, after the massacre at York. At last the Indians were decisively fought off and did not return, thanks largely to Burroughs's courage and leadership.

After the attacks, Burroughs had sent a letter by ship to the Council in Boston, pleading for help. He heard nothing. The Indians stayed nearby. It was impossible for the settlers to work in the fields or look after their few remaining animals. More soldiers and provisions were desperately needed. Two months later, in July, Burroughs had written again, pleading even more urgently, saying that since "the enemy is beating upon us, we can think of no other but we are fair for ruin."

Still he heard nothing. He wondered if the shipmasters had failed to deliver the letters. In September he had written yet again, saying, "We are brought very low. . . . The corn is not enough to keep us one half year. We humbly request your honors to continue soldiers among us and appoint a commander over them" and send "corn and clothing and a hogshead of salt, all ours being spent."

The letter was taken by two of the soldiers best known to and most trusted by Burroughs. They rode their horses from the town under cover of darkness to make their perilous way along paths beside the coast and through the forest to Dover, then Salem, then Boston. The journey was nigh on two hundred miles and would likely take more than a week. Burroughs hoped for the reinforcements to arrive a week after that. None came. The soldiers never returned.

Five months later, in February, came the attack on York that devastated that town and sent scores of survivors to stream into the already crowded Wells garrison. Burroughs had penned his most eloquent letter to the Council so far, the one he had shown Mary, begging for enough soldiers not only to defend the town but go out after the enemy, to discourage them from attacking again, if not to destroy them. This time he sent two copies, one by ship, one by soldiers.

It was now May. Still no reinforcements had arrived. The three months had passed, that the townsfolk had agreed to wait before leaving. Conditions were easier than a few weeks before; no Indians had been seen since that time. Many of the settlers who had wanted to leave were reconciled to staying for a little while longer. Others were readying themselves to hold Burroughs to his promise.

The sky was growing lighter, the shapes of the trees more defined, the shadows more clearly visible as nothing but shadows.

Burroughs found himself remembering his first days in Maine, as a young man, as at home in this frontier landscape as if he had been born here. With a sense of freedom and excitement he had never known in the staid town of Roxbury, or at tightly controlled Harvard, he had roamed the forests, fished in fast-running streams, shot rabbits and wildfowl, and often made his bed for the night under the sky. He met and befriended non-Puritans, including Indians, whose hunting and tracking skills and easygoing natures astonished and charmed him. One young Abenaki man became a close comrade. They fished and hunted together and sat by campfires under the stars telling stories of encounters with coyotes and bears, trials of strength and, as they grew closer, things that had scared them as boys and, as they grew closer still, things that still scared them now. They talked of the hostility between natives and whites but neither felt any disloyalty to their kind. As well as he could, Burroughs explained his religion, and listened in turn to tales of spirits dwelling in the forest and wind, and of the holy men who communed with them and restored health to troubled bodies and souls. His instructor once took him to a place his tribe counted sacred, a clearing by a stream where his ancestors lay. Burroughs never doubted the truth of the religion he'd been brought up in but respected that of his friend. He pondered the paradox of this but did not try to resolve it, trusting in God's deeper wisdom.

This friendship counted for more than his marriage. He had wed his young wife in Roxbury before knowing her except as a pretty, pleasant woman, and brought her to Maine with their daughter, Rebecca, born nine months to the day after the wedding. He and Hannah's happiness did not last long. They quickly found themselves at loggerheads about almost everything, including living in a frontier outpost. Soon he was keeping out of her way. Though acknowledging her virtues as a mother, he judged her deficient in all other areas, even appearance. With hard work and motherhood her pretty features were hardening and her smooth skin becoming lined. He was appalled that she could not keep quiet among neighbors and friends about things that ought to concern just the two of them, including her angry belief that she had been tricked into living in this dismal, dangerous place by Burroughs's pretense that it was paradise. No amount of explaining that he had never meant to mislead her either lessened her fury or stilled her wagging tongue. He could not admit to himself she had a degree of right on her side. The gulf between them grew from wide to unbridgeable.

With the coming of King Philip's War, his Indian friend's tribe attacked the settlement Burroughs lived in, forcing the inhabitants to flee to Massachusetts. Back in Maine five years later, he heard his friend had been killed. He made new Indian comrades but none ever meant as much to him.

Since then there had been two more children, and the move to Salem Village, where his wife died after a short illness, brought on by burns from flames catching her dress while she was cooking. Burroughs could not mourn her though he had greatly pitied her suffering. He was pursued by beautiful, rich Sarah Ruck, the widow of a wealthy officer and former sister-in-law of the magistrate John Hathorne. Within months he had married her. They had gone back to Maine, had three more children, and then, as she was traveling by ship to visit her family in Salem, she too fell ill and died.

Now, by divine generosity, he was married to Mary.

They had ridden from her father's grave in York to the nearest town with a minister, over the border in New Hampshire, and asked him to marry them two weeks later, the earliest date possible under Massachusetts law. Having pinned the required notice on the meeting-house door, they stayed at the inn—in separate rooms—and rode back to Wells the next day. The townsfolk's reception overwhelmed them. Everyone had feared they were dead and here they were, not only alive but betrothed. The New Hampshire wedding took place with a large party of soldiers and settlers in attendance, including Burroughs's older children, but the celebration in the inn afterward was brief since they had to return to Wells before nightfall.

Burroughs now bowed his head.

"Our father, which art in heaven, hallowed be thy name . . ."

He finished the prayer, said the "Amen," and looked to see if the new watchman was on his way. The man emerged from the garrison house, pulling on his jacket. Burroughs lifted his gun, climbed down the ladder, exchanged greetings, and, when his replacement disappeared upward, took a deep breath of pine-scented air, hoisted up his fowling piece with one hand, held it with its six-foot-long barrel horizontal in front of him for thirty seconds, which he counted out loud, and then lowered it. This feat was generally considered astonishing; word of it had spread through New England; people who had never even seen it spoke of it with awe. The truth was simply that Burroughs had exceptionally strong shoulders and arms that he had developed further by this regular weight lifting.

But he had done nothing to discourage the colony-wide amazed admiration of his strength. Quite the reverse, once even playing a trick on some soldiers by appearing to lift the fowling piece with not just one hand but one finger. His Indian friend, hidden behind the tree Burroughs stood next to, had been holding the butt. On another occasion he had lifted a six-foot-high barrel of molasses from a boat and set it on shore, with his Indian friend underneath, pushing upward. His reputation had continued to grow since the stories kept spreading and he never refuted them. That reputation was as important to him now as when he was a boy, traveling to Massachusetts with his mother, beating anyone his age, and many older, in fistfights. He had been small then and was still short as a man, but much stronger than many men taller and larger. Though he had delighted in gaining the highest academic honors when graduating from Harvard, he'd derived even more pleasure from winning every test of physical prowess.

Bringing the gun to his chest, he walked to the garrison house, where he leaned it against the dark wooden wall beside the door. Thirty or more people were settling themselves along the maplewood table that ran the length of the room. His wriggling smallest son was held down on his stool by his twelve-year-old daughter, the boy's half-sister, leaning across from her own seat, hands on his shoulders. The boy saw Burroughs, squirmed out of the girl's hold, and ran to his father who lifted him, carried him back, sat him down, and told him to behave himself. Mary, helping set out breakfast—newly baked bread, strawberry jam, maple syrup, and cider—looked as luminous in the warm light of morning as she had by candlelight last night in their little room under the eaves. He and she exchanged glances of remembrance. He made his way to his place at the head of the table.

"No eggs?" he asked.

"Coming, now you're here, Mr. Burroughs." She went to the fire and returned with a steaming earthenware bowl. "One spoonful each." She ladled a helping of the yellow and white mixture onto his plate.

"Why no more?"

"Rachel died last night. Only ten laying hens left."

"Can't we put the cock to work to make more?"

Mary leaned her hip lightly against Burroughs's shoulder. "The hens say he's hopeless."

"All crow and no show."

"Unlike a certain person not far from where I'm standing."

He put his arm round her, letting go again as she moved on round the table. His physical love for this woman was more intense than any he had ever experienced. She seemed to him the most seductive creature he had known in his life, every part of her slender but sweetly curved form the right shape and size for his taste. And she enticed him not only with her body but her eyes, her voice, and her very presence that seemed frank yet hiding unreachable depths.

"There's more to her than other women," he had said to Peter White, when his friend, after congratulating him on his good fortune, reminded Burroughs he had sworn he would never marry again.

"I agree with you. If I could find another one like her I would wed her at once."

When everyone was served, Burroughs asked for silence and said grace. After "Amen," he took a chunk of bread and started to eat, chewing as slowly as he could to make the food last. There was never quite enough. The man next to him brought up the subject of repairs to the palisades and soon all the men around were discussing this. Most of the women ate standing, though the oldest and boldest—*not* Mary and Rebecca, who were on breakfast duty this morning—found places at the end of the table. There were rosters for the cooking and serving of meals as for all the work of the garrison.

When Burroughs finished and rose, his youngest son ran from his stool and hung on to his leg while his second youngest blocked his way, his round face pink, shouting, "Father! Come see the garrison I made! There's a minister in it! I made him out of a peg! Come see!"

"Not now, I have a sermon to write." Burroughs noticed the boy's pained look and patted his head, saying, "Tell your peg minister to write a sermon too."

"He can't write yet!"

"Ask Rebecca to help him."

"I can't write a sermon!" His daughter, still carrying a cider jug, showed her neat, slightly protruding teeth in a smile. To Burroughs the roundish face, with its small nose and look of sensible good nature, was one of the two dearest on earth, as dear as his new wife's. He and Rebecca had been through danger and tragedy together, fleeing south from Maine when she was a baby, enduring her mother's painful death, sharing the responsibility for the younger children, and then surviving the Indian attack a year ago. He had become everything to her, and she to him, after her mother died, and though his remarriage lessened their closeness a little, it did not fundamentally alter it. When his second wife died it became again as strong as it ever was. Despite his happiness with Mary, Rebecca still held the same place in his heart. He told her, and meant it, that she had always supported him as much as he did her. He now said, playfully, "You have helped me write *my* sermons."

"Helped you? I've listened to you grumble about them!"

"You mean I have listened to *you* grumble about them!"

"Just the tedious parts."

"What's tedious?'" asked the pink-faced brother, while the youngest still hung on Burroughs's leg.

"Father's sermons."

"Tedious?" queried Mary. "Boring, perhaps, never tedious!"

"What's the difference?" Burroughs asked.

Mary mused, then said, "Boring makes you yawn, tedious sends you to sleep."

"She just thought of that!" shouted the small boy.

"Well I am almost flattered she thinks they are no worse than boring, even if her definition's her own." Burroughs tried to free his leg, pulling gently at his youngest son's shoulders. "Let go, my boy, I've got to write one now."

Rebecca prized him off and lifted him up, giving him a kiss.

"Get away while you can."

To reach the study under the eaves that now doubled as his and Mary's bedchamber, Burroughs had to pass through a storeroom. This was easier than it had been since the corn was low and the apples all gone. Though he missed the variation in diet, he was relieved to be rid of the stench of overripe fruit. Under the sloping ceiling, a desk, chair, stool, and small bookshelf took up most of the space. The rope bed hung on the wall like a fishing net. Taken down and fitted on little legs stored in a corner, after the other furniture had been pushed against the wall, and when two bodies were cuddled together, this simplest of beds was as comfortable as the costliest of four posters. Burroughs now sat down, pulled his sermon papers toward him, and bent his head, lifting his long dark hair behind his shoulders with both hands. He quickly reread the text on which he was basing his sermon: "Sojourn in this land, and I will be with thee, and will bless thee; for unto thee, and unto thy seed, I will give all these countries . . ."

Leaning back, lifting up the papers with both hands, he put his feet on the desk and read the text again, this time aloud. Then he read it a third time, projecting his voice to the rafters, the cadences giving expression to his mood of euphoria, the words seeming to tell of his own new possessions, in the countries of the heart.

There came a knock on the door. Burroughs lowered his feet and the paper, his jaw tightening. His most obvious fault, about which he prayed to God frequently, was his temper. Deeper faults were invisible to him. Letting out his breath, he forced cheerfulness and friendliness into his tone. "Come in, whoever you are."

"Last time I looked in a mirror I was Captain Peter White."

Burroughs's anger dissolved. Peter was his most liked and admired companion. They had been at school together in Roxbury, though Peter was three years younger than Burroughs. The choice for Captain White between Harvard and the army had been made for him by his father's losing his fortune in King Philip's War, the same conflict as had forced Burroughs to flee from Maine fifteen years earlier.

"Your glass doesn't lie, you are Peter White," said Burroughs. "Handsomest fellow in the colony."

This was close to the truth, even if Indians as well as whites were included. Burroughs sometimes envied his friend's looks, though more often, and more strongly, his height. If he were as tall as Peter he'd truly be a giant among men. But his appearance even as it was seemed to cause women to admire and feel drawn to him as much as to any man. It had Mary, which was all that mattered now.

"Let me guess. Grave illness? Childbirth? Indian attack?" Burroughs said this lightly, hoping it would prove merely the jest he meant it as.

"None of those, thank God." His friend pulled up the stool and sat down, leaning the gun he carried with him against Burroughs's desk. "I wondered if I could persuade you to come on the patrol with us this morning."

Burroughs looked down at his papers, then out of the window, barred but without glass, shutters open, showing a dappled blue and white sky. There were few things he enjoyed as much as working on a sermon but one of them was going out on a fine day with Peter for company. He calculated how many working hours were left before ten o'clock on the morning of the Sabbath.

"I had meant to finish this this morning, or at least this afternoon."

Peter looked at the papers on the desk.

"Much still to do?"

"So far I only have the text and one or two notes."

"What is the text?"

"Genesis twenty-six."

"Sojourn in this land . . ."

"The same."

"Very apposite."

"Despite all their hardships his people must be grateful for the new country He's given them."

"I do not want to pull you away but the patrol is safer when you are leading it."

Burroughs again looked out the window. "There is little danger of an ambush. No sign of anything suspicious on my watch."

Peter said, "Now that it is spring, I feel uneasy. With the leaves out 'tis so much harder to see if there are Indians hiding in the trees."

As Peter knew it would, this talk of spring and the leaves made going out irresistible.

"Very well."

"Good!"

"As I say, I believe there's little danger. All the same I wish the reinforcements would come."

Peter started lifting his gun but put it back down.

"You still think they *will* come? Now? After three months?"

"Boston promised."

Peter laughed.

"We stand between them and the Indians!"

"But not between them and their political foes. Perhaps we *are* their political foes."

"How *can* we be? We're all New Englanders."

"We are as tolerant of different faiths here as the exiles in Rhode Island. They would be better off without us."

"As our rulers they are responsible for our safety, whatever their view of us."

"They aren't our rulers now. Till Increase Mather gets back from England with the new charter, we do not know who rules us."

"Well, till we *do* know, they have a duty to protect us."

"A duty but no motive. They would prefer to protect only Puritans."

"There are Puritans here!"

"Outnumbered by Anglicans, Baptists, and Quakers."

"I'm a Puritan! They ought to protect *me*."

"Are you? You never take communion. Your new wife is an Anglican. Except for Rebecca, none of your children are baptized."

"How could I have got them to a minister past Indians and wolves?"

"Hannah and Elizabeth were born in Salem Village, an hour's ride from a minister."

"Do you reproach me?"

"*I* do not reproach you! It would not matter if I did! 'Tis whether the rulers in Boston reproach you that matters."

"*Might* it matter?"

"I do not know. They are fighting for their political lives. There is much stronger opposition than there used to be. If they are to hold on to power, this colony must stay a Puritan stronghold."

"Is that all they care about? Power? The devout Increase Mather? The pious *Cotton* Mather? The good-natured Samuel Sewall?"

"Not *all* they care about perhaps. But what they care about most."

"Not Sam Sewall. I know him well. He has been my friend since Harvard."

"Friendship means nothing when power is at stake."

The two men had had this conversation, or several very like it, before. They smiled in acknowledgment of this and rose to their feet. Peter said, "The men are waiting at the gate."

No sign of human activity. No newly cut wood, or stripped bark, or smoldering embers, or trampled undergrowth. The coastal path was untrodden since the rainfall last night. Out in the bay the waters lay still. There were no dots on the horizon that might turn into canoes.

"Safe for today," Burroughs said, as they walked back along the path between the woods and unplanted fields.

Peter said, "All the same, I'll check that the lookout's at his post."

Burroughs stopped, staring into the grass, then lifted his gun. A great boom and a cloud of white smoke filled the air. Burroughs lowered his weapon, took two steps, and lifted a little rabbit by its ears. The men grinned and shook their arms.

"Just a baby one," Burroughs said. "Strayed too far from its family. Still, it will flavor our vegetables."

"You'll get an extra kiss from Mary," Peter said.

"We must get back. She will be wondering what that shot was."

And, indeed, she was waiting at the gate. Silently, she clasped Burroughs in her arms. He handed the rabbit to Peter so as not to bloody her dress. When she moved away, she said to Captain White, "Give him me, I'll skin him and put him straight in the stew."

Rebecca was the next in Burroughs's embrace. Then, more noisily, the rest of the children.

Two hours later the inhabitants were swallowing tiny, pungent portions of meat with their customary potatoes, carrots, and rutabagas. Peter was absent, having taken his platter to the watchtower. When he came back, sooner than expected, he walked quickly toward Burroughs, who, seeing his expression, at once rose to his feet.

"The reinforcements have come!"

No greater noise had ever been heard in that room. Over thirty people screamed, whooped, jumped, and wept. Even a baby clapped her hands.

"Wait! Wait!" shouted Peter. "What I saw was only the field marshal with six soldiers. More may be coming but we will not know till we speak to him."

"Then let's speak to him."

Outside, Burroughs crossed the grass, followed by the rest of the people from the garrison house, and soon the other garrison houses. He swung open the gate and walked forward rapidly. The marshal and his soldiers came as quickly toward him. John Partridge, field marshal for New Hampshire and the closest army officer to Wells, was a large man in tall boots and long jacket over breeches, sporting a surprisingly clean neckerchief and tall hat. Carrying a staff taller than he was, he personified powerful, beneficent authority.

"Welcome!" Burroughs shouted.

"George Burroughs?"

"Aye."

"I arrest you in the name of the Crown."

Mary screamed. The marshal switched his staff to his left hand and, with his right, took a paper from his pocket. Two soldiers seized Burroughs by the arms.

"What's happening?" shouted Peter, running forward. Soldiers seized him too.

"George!" screamed Mary. Soldiers held her back.

"For God's sake, what's going on?" Peter asked.

"I'm instructed by the authority of this document to arrest George Burroughs in the name of the Crown!"

"What for? What's he done? It's a mistake!" people shouted.

The marshal read aloud in a voice that carried clearly in the still afternoon air, "You John Partridge are required in their Majesties' names to apprehend the body of Mr. George Burroughs, at present preacher at Wells in the province of Maine, and convey him with all speed to Salem before the magistrates there to be examined, he being suspected for a confederacy with the devil."

"Confederacy with the devil!" Peter repeated in amazement, then laughed. There was a cacophony of shouts of shock and disbelief. Burroughs jerked his right arm out of the grip of the soldier who held it, seized the paper from the marshal and silently read it.

"Talk to Samuel Sewall before you take me anywhere!" he shouted, eyes still on the paper. The soldier seized his arm again but he did not let go or raise his eyes until he reached the last sentence, over the signature of the sheriff, which said, "I having received particular order of the Governor and Council of their Majesties' Colony of Massachusetts."

Sewall was a member of the Council. Could he know of this? Could he have approved it?

Partridge grabbed the paper. "There's a ship waiting."

Burroughs half turned but the soldiers pushed him forward. He could have knocked them down but knew this would achieve nothing. Six armed men would prove too many even for him. His fellows, rightly, would not fight. Whatever the subtleties, Massachusetts still governed Maine. He glimpsed Mary's distraught face and outstretched arms as she screamed his name with a frenzied desperation he would never forget. The soldiers marched him away, possessed of nothing but the clothes he wore.

Chapter Twenty-Four

Salem Town
May 1692

THE FEAR AND HATRED IN EVERYONE'S EYES WAS AS BAD AS THE LOSS of his freedom. He was used to love and admiration, even awe. He now felt himself almost the worthless creature they were saying he was.

There had been no room in Salem jail so they had locked him up at the top of Beadle's tavern. The room was similar to his study in Wells but that did not make it more likable. On the contrary, he loathed at first sight the dusty rafters, truckle bed, rough bench, three-legged stool, and small window, foretelling the feelings long imprisonment must bring.

He had hoped to be examined the day he arrived. He wasn't. Nor the next day, nor the one after that. Each morning the room grew warm and then sweltering, cooling down only when night fell. A tiny window gave fresh air but looked out on a dark wooden wall no more than a yard away. Yet Burroughs knew he was lucky to be here instead of in a dungeon. He could at least pace the room; he was given edible meals three times a day. All the same, the frustration of waiting made it hard for him to resist smashing down the door, running from the inn, and making for the harbor. But he knew he would be recaptured and almost certainly taken to prison. They would find room for him somehow.

Now and then he had company in the form of curious tipplers from downstairs who had persuaded or bribed Beadle or a servant to unlock his door. Most stayed only a few moments, barely daring to step in the room or speak a few words. But on the third day a fat-cheeked, loose-mouthed, watery-eyed fellow, smelling strongly of ale, appeared without warning, walked right up to him, and stared. Burroughs rose from his stool. He could easily have overpowered the diminutive ser-

vant by the door but knew his shouts would bring more servants, followed by soldiers.

"Who might you be?" Burroughs asked his visitor.

"Name's Keyser." The fellow took off his cap, still staring, then
lurched.

"I remember you from Salem Village!"

"Live in Shalem now."

"Take the stool. Talk to me."

"Can't!"

"Why not?"

"You're a minishter!"

"Is that a reason not to talk to me?"

"You're learned." The man lurched again.

"All the more reason to talk to me."

The smell of ale came in waves. The man muttered something
Burroughs did not catch.

"What did you say?"

"You're a follower of the devil!" The watery eyes were wide with
fright at his own daring. Burroughs was tempted to punch him. But he
managed to speak calmly. "Do you truly believe that? Do you truly
believe I have sold myself to Satan? Why would I as a paster lose my
immortal soul for promises of mere power and wealth?"

The fellow backed away. "Shatan's telling you to say that!"

"I have never seen or spoken to Satan in my life!"

But Keyser backed all the way out and the diminutive servant went
after him, locking the door.

Other visitors, together with the innkeeper and his servants, gave
Burroughs an idea of the extent of this witch scare. Balancing the
drunken exaggerations of the tavern guests against the caution of the
innkeeper and others whose incomes depended on Salem's good name
and prosperity, he calculated there were about thirty in jail. Not in one
jail but three: Salem, Boston, and Ipswich. He was astonished to learn
that some of those held were respectable women: Martha Cory, Elizabeth Proctor, and the highly esteemed Rebecca Nurse. He had known
all three and admired them when he lived in Salem Village. With even
greater wonderment he learned that four accused people had *confessed*
to being witches. One was apparently a slave called Tituba, another a

wild, attention-seeking girl called Lydia Hobbs, whom he had known slightly years ago in Maine before his stay in Salem Village, the third that girl's cretinous mother. The fourth, he heard to his horror, was a child of four. He presumed all these females, young and old, *must* be witches or else why would they say so? He knew nothing of Tituba but it seemed possible that Lydia and her mother had stuck pins in dolls and mumbled spells. Perhaps the little girl also had done so. But had any of them seen the devil? Could that be possible?

Burroughs felt even greater surprise when he heard that some of the accusers were girls he'd known as children. One, Mercy Lewis, had lived in his household after her parents were slaughtered by Indians. He and his wife Sarah had been good to her, in due course sending her to Salem, where they thought she would be safer than in Maine. She had never grown close to them but had seemed grateful for their care.

Burroughs had no idea what to think about the girls' accusations except that in his case at least they had made a mistake. But if they had made one mistake they might have made others, and surely had, in the cases of Martha, Elizabeth, and Rebecca. Yet why had the ministers and magistrates not guessed they were deluded? The girls had made the allegations but the magistrates ordered the arrests. Whatever John Hathorne's faults, and Burroughs knew from their several meetings he was proud, coldhearted, and self-satisfied, he did not seem a fool. Burroughs hoped to question, as well as be questioned, when he was finally examined. Hathorne was bound to be one of his interrogators, as Salem's chief magistrate, and Burroughs's relationship with him by marriage would surely oblige him to listen and give answers. Hathorne had disapproved of the marriage, viewing Burroughs's social standing as inferior to the Hathornes', but could not deny it had happened, and provided him with four nephews and nieces.

Burroughs wondered if God could have chosen to punish Salem Village for its vicious enmities and backbiting. Could he have chosen to strike down Burroughs himself for his anger and pride? Perhaps for his laxity as a Puritan?

Burroughs had persuaded the innkeeper to lend him a Bible and that, with his certainty of proving his innocence, made the next few days and nights bearable.

On the sixth day, after breakfast as he sat looking out of the tiny window at the wall whose dark wooden slats were as familiar to him as the bed, bench, and stool, a constable marched in, took his arm, and started pulling him to the door. Burroughs shook him off.

"I will come with you without compulsion!"

"Walk ahead of me then. Out the door, turn left."

"Where are you taking me?"

"To your examination."

"Without warning?"

"Prisoners don't get warnings."

Burroughs followed the constable's barked directions along a passage, down a flight of stairs, along another passage, and through a low door, to find himself in a small room facing four men seated at a table. Two of them he had expected to see, two he hadn't. The marshal pushed him down on a stool. One of the two who surprised him, and indeed greatly surprised him, was Samuel Sewall, whom he had last seen across another table, in Boston, chins wagging with laughter as Burroughs told his tale of lifting the barrel of molasses to shore with the help of an invisible friend. He had told no one else about this trick except for his two wives. Was Sewall at this examination to speak for him, he wondered? Though he'd approved that arrest warrant? Burroughs nodded and smiled but Sewall nodded back so slightly that the three chins scarcely wobbled. Burroughs told himself he must be sticking to protocol. On his right was John Hathorne, huge and motionless, showing no expression. On the other side was the second man Burroughs was surprised by. He also showed no feeling, though in his large, clever eyes was a hint of curiosity. Burroughs wondered why the deputy governor should have come all the way from Boston to question him, unless he happened to be in Salem already, but even so. . . . The fourth man at the table was Hathorne's fellow magistrate Bartholomew Gedney, nondescript, wearing a supercilious expression.

"You understand why you are here?" Stoughton carefully enunciated every consonant.

"I know I have been accused of confederacy with the devil. I am innocent of the charge. There has been some terrible mistake."

Stoughton's eyes lost their curiosity. The thin lips closed even more tightly. Burroughs felt disappointment, having hoped to make a connection and alter the atmosphere. The disappointment deepened when Stoughton said, "This is not the time to protest your innocence but the time to answer our questions." He looked down at a paper on his desk, then up again. "When did you last take communion?"

Startled, Burroughs exclaimed, "It is so long ago, I cannot tell!"

Stoughton kept looking at him. "You are a full member of a church, are you not?"

"Aye, I was received into Roxbury church as a boy."

"Yet two years ago when you were in Boston on the Sabbath, and went to meeting, you did not take communion."

Burroughs turned his eyes to Sewall. They had gone to that meeting together. Samuel knew why he had not stayed for communion. The chins trembled a little but his old friend did not meet Burroughs's eye.

"Mr. Sewall was there . . ."

"I am not examining Mr. Sewall! Did you take communion?"

"I did not take communion."

Burroughs had not felt at ease in that meetinghouse in Boston, the service so formal and stiff compared to the ones he'd become used to in Maine. Sewall had made no objection to his not staying for the sacrament and had met Burroughs later to dine, drink, and laugh. Burroughs felt a growing sense of unreality in this room with these people he had known as a fellow student or relative by marriage, or, in the case of Gedney, a minor magistrate who'd kowtowed to him.

"Samuel!" he said. "You must remember!"

"Silence!" Stoughton shouted. "When you are asked to speak, you will address *me*! When you are not asked to speak, you will stay silent. I heard you were at Charlestown one Sabbath, when communion was given, and again you did not take it. Is that true?"

"That is true."

The reason had been the same, hardly a reason he could give to this man who was revealing himself as the most unforgiving of Puritans. Though all the magistrates stayed expressionless, he sensed condemnation in the room. Yet he could scarcely believe his own insight. These men were intelligent and learned. Their reason and good sense must tell them he was neither a foe to the Puritan faith nor a wizard.

Stoughton seemed to be waiting.

"You must know I was not able to go to communion for many years in Maine. There are no ordained ministers there. I had grown used to not going. I agree I should have taken advantage of my opportunities to do so in Boston and Charlestown."

Stoughton's expression did not change. He said, "We have heard your house in Maine was haunted."

"*Haunted?* Nay!"

"There were toads seen in the yard."

"Toads? There may have been toads." Burroughs was about to add that the toads were there naturally, not as demons in disguise or witch's familiars, but before he could do so John Hathorne leaned forward and accused him of making his second wife swear she would not write to her father unless he—Burroughs—gave her his permission to do so. Burroughs, astonished, denied this. He knew that Hathorne, and everyone else who had known them, knew that he and his second wife had often disagreed, as also had he and his first wife. Yet this accusation, of trying to come between Sarah and her family, came as an utter surprise. Other allegations might have some substance, but not this. He was about to say so when Stoughton spat out, "Is it true that none of your children but the eldest are baptized?"

"Aye. They . . ."

Stoughton rose. "We will go to the next room."

The constable pulled him up from his stool.

They went through the door Burroughs had come in by, the magistrates first and then Burroughs, followed by the constable. Taking a few steps to the next door, they entered a larger room where, to Burroughs's bewilderment, huddled a crowd of women ranging in age from about eleven to sixty and, to one side of them, a smaller group of men, mostly in uniform. As the magistrates entered all were silent, but as soon as Burroughs appeared the females started screaming and clasping different parts of their bodies. Stoughton shouted to Burroughs to turn round to face the magistrates, who were settling themselves at a table. Burroughs did so and the females went silent. The deputy governor, now seated, looked past him to call,

"Ann Putnam, know you this man?" A high, whining voice wailed, "His two wives appeared to me in their winding-sheets and told me he killed them!"

Burroughs spun round. At once all the girls again began screaming and clasping themselves. Which of them was Ann Putnam? It might have been any of them apart from Mercy Lewis, whom he now recognized. She looked much as she had three years before, with that pretty, heart-shaped face, except that she was taller and more fully developed. It was so strange to see her screaming and twisting for no apparent reason when in her terrible grief she had been silent.

"Ann Putnam, did George Burroughs bring you the book and make you write in it?" asked Stoughton.

"Aye! Aye!" called the whining voice, from a girl with small, close-set eyes. So this was Ann Putnam, hardly more than a baby when George had last seen her.

"Mary Walcott, did George Burroughs bring you the book and make you write in it?"

"Aye! Aye! George Burdette, he brought me the book . . ." The speaker, or rather shouter, was a plump girl of about seventeen with big blue eyes.

"Elizabeth Hubbard, did George Burroughs bring you the book and make you write in it?"

"Aye! Aye!" cried a small, scrawny-necked creature.

Stoughton now turned to Mercy Lewis.

"Mercy Lewis, did George Burroughs . . ."

"Aye! Aye!"

Mercy's pretty face and figure made her twisting and turning seem almost a dance, but this made it no less chilling—if anything, more so. Burroughs tried with his stare to make Mercy look at him but she seemed oblivious to everything but her own frenzied movements.

"Susannah Sheldon, did George Burroughs bring you the book and make you write in it?"

"Aye! Aye!" called a young woman Burroughs thought he also remembered from Maine.

"Bathsheba Pope, did George Burroughs . . ."

Pope's gyrations caused her to trip over her foot. She shouted "Aye! Aye!" from the ground, while rolling bulbous eyes.

So it went on. Every female said "aye," but many who tried to say his name stumbled over or misspoke it. A wrinkled old woman called him John Bundy, then Jim Burry, and, on a third try, Jos Buckey.

"What think you of these things?" Stoughton asked Burroughs.

"I understand nothing of any of it!"

Stoughton gave a tight smile.

Burroughs said, "You may observe, when they try to name me, they cannot!"

"What of that?"

"They do not know who I am!"

"They know you are confederate with the devil!"

"They mistake me for another!"

The writhings then became even more frenzied, the shriekings even louder. They reminded Burroughs of the movements and sounds made by the wounded and dying after an Indian attack. But these were more terrible because their cause was invisible. At last Stoughton ordered the girls taken away. Most of them calmed as they exited, though not the old, wrinkled woman, who had to be carried out by two constables.

When they had gone, Stoughton turned to the men, most of whom Burroughs recognized as soldiers he had once known in Maine. To his surprise he spotted among them the fat-cheeked fellow who had visited him a few days before, smelling of ale. A moment later he recognized old John Putnam, Thomas Putnam's uncle, who had turned against him during his years as pastor in Salem Village. John still had the same air of complacency, though his hair and face were both whiter. Stoughton fixed his large eyes on Burroughs's former visitor.

"Elizar Keyser, pray read us your testimony."

With an air of importance, Keyser stepped forward, the ale smell almost as strong as in the inn. Clearing his throat, he unrolled a foolscap-sized parchment and started reading.

"On Thursday last, being the fifth day of May, I wash at Thomas Beadle's tavern in Salem, and a man of my acquaintance who wash there at the same time and in the same room asked me whether I would not go up and see Mr. Burroughs and dish . . . discourse with him. I told him I wash not willing to meddle and that my opinion wash, that he wash the chief of all the persons accused for witchcraft and the ring-leader of them all."

Keyser looked up but, meeting unimpressed stares from the magistrates, quickly looked down again. Burroughs expected Stoughton to tell him to stand down since he was surely too drunk to be a reliable witness. But Stoughton merely nodded to Keyser to continue.

"The shame afternoon, I having again occasion to be at the said Beadle's house, I went to the chamber where Mr. George Burroughs kept and observed that said Burroughs did steadfastly fix his eyes upon me."

Burroughs remembered well Keyser's fixing his eyes upon *him*.

"The shame evening being in my own house, in a room without any light, I did see very strange things appear in the chimney. I suppose a dozen of them, which seemed to me to be something like jelly that used to be in the water."

"Jelly that used to be in the water?" Burroughs marveled silently at the concept. Keyser must have gone on drinking after he'd got home.

"It quavered with a strange motion, and then quickly dishappeared. Soon after that I did see a light up in the chimney about the bigness of my hand. I called the maid, and she looking up into the chimney saw the same, so I did consider it was some diabolical apparition."

Keyser looked up again at the magistrates. The maid might also have been drinking, Burroughs reflected.

"Captain Simon Willard, pray read us your testimony," called Stoughton.

Clearly disappointed at having to leave the limelight so abruptly, without congratulations or praise, Keyser stepped away. The soldier who took his place had a sharp chin and diffident air Burroughs remembered, though the man must now be fifteen years older. He had been a decent enough fellow, Burroughs recalled. Without looking at the minister, he read a rambling account of hearing that George Burroughs could lift a very heavy gun with one hand and that he, Burroughs, had himself agreed he could do that. Burroughs shook his head in amazement. What was the purpose of this? He recalled confirming the gun-lifting story to a party of soldiers; perhaps this witness had been one of them. At that time he had never admitted his trickery to anyone but his wives. He looked at Samuel Sewall, still the only other human being to know of it, apart from the

Indian who had helped. Sewall would not meet his eye. The soldier turned over the paper and read an equally rambling account of Burroughs's lifting a barrel of molasses from a canoe and setting it on shore.

Suddenly the minister realized that the accusation being leveled against him was of devil-given strength. But surely Sewall must remember his telling him these stories. Burroughs opened his mouth but Stoughton shouted the name of the next witness. As the soldier stepped forward Burroughs tried again to speak but the constable hissed at him to keep his mouth shut.

In dreary succession all the soldiers repeated the same tales of the gun and the barrel. None claimed to have seen these feats but merely to have heard other people tell of them. When the last soldier finished, Burroughs tried again to speak but again Stoughton called a name.

It was John Putnam. As the white-haired old man stepped forward Burroughs recalled his having him arrested for debt at the end of his time in Salem Village, though Burroughs was ready and willing to pay what he owed. John Putnam now swore he had seen Burroughs lift his gun with one finger.

"That's a lie!" Burroughs roared, goaded beyond caution. John Putnam was not repeating rumor or fantasy but committing perjury.

"Silence!" shouted Stoughton. His large eyes fixed Burroughs with a furious stare as he said, "The prisoner will speak only to answer my questions. Otherwise he will be taken away and the proceedings continued in his absence." Turning to John Putnam, he asked more quietly, "Captain Putnam, have you anything more to say?"

"I have, your honor." John smiled smugly.

"Pray say it."

"When George Burroughs and his first wife lived for nine months in my house in the village, while the parsonage was being repaired, I observed he was very cruel to his wife."

"Did he ask you to witness something?" Stoughton prompted.

"He asked me to witness a covenant to be signed by that wife, to swear never to speak about his secrets."

"Did you agree to that?"

"No, I did not. I told him he and his wife had already made a covenant before God."

"Marshal, take out the prisoner."

"Your honor, I beg to be allowed to defend myself!" Burroughs shouted, astonished.

"Mr. Burroughs, this is an examination to determine if there is sufficient evidence to commit you to prison and bring you to trial. As chief magistrate I have no doubt whatsoever that the evidence we have heard today is more than sufficient. Constable, remove the Reverend Burroughs from this room and escort him to jail."

Chapter Twenty-Five
Maine
May 1692

TWO LEATHER HOLDALLS HAD JUST ROOM IN THEM FOR A SHIRT, changes of underlinen, and stockings for two men and one woman, brushes, soap, cloths, a sewing kit, Peter's medical bag, and a Bible.

The accused man's wife and best friend, their bags slung over their shoulders, set off at dawn on the hour's walk to join a vessel berthed yesterday with space for them. It had taken two weeks of daily trips to the harbor to find this.

Fear of Indians as always kept the pair silent. But as they emerged from the trees the lightening sky, salty tang, and wide expanse of quiet water filled them with new hope. If George had not already been freed, they would establish his innocence and free him.

A rowing boat was waiting to take them to the small sailing vessel anchored in the bay. The captain himself helped them on board and showed Mary to a hammock in a cubby hole with a curtain to pull across for privacy. A spare hammock was slung up for Peter in the galley.

The captain, who was bringing a group of fur traders and their wares to Massachusetts, had told Peter yesterday that he had heard the accusers were a band of wild girls and young women. News of the Salem witch scare had already reached Canada. But he knew little else and was dumbfounded to hear the respected George Burroughs had been seized. It was due to his sympathy for his wife that he had found room for her and Peter on his ship.

Thankfully, though the sea was fairly calm, there was enough wind for the vessel to set sail. Mary and Peter stood on deck as it moved slowly out of the harbor and, after an hour or so, out of sight of the shore. This was the first time Mary had left Maine but the excitement she'd have felt in any other circumstances was swamped by her hopes and fears for George.

Over a rough breakfast in the galley the fur traders told their fellow passengers all they had heard about the witch hunt: that the trouble had started in Salem Village but was now spreading to outlying areas, and that many respectable and even rich people were being accused. There had been amazed talk of it during the time they'd been in Halifax before boarding ship. To Peter and Mary's questions about causes and legal process they had no answers or guesses, except for one old man who said sourly that he suspected people were settling old scores.

The strangeness of this witch hunt, unlike anything that had happened before in the colony, though there'd been plenty of convictions and hangings of individual witches, was becoming ever more unfathomable.

Later in the day, the wind strengthened and the ship moved faster and less smoothly. But, despite its pitching and her worries, that night Mary fell asleep easily. This ship seemed like a cocoon. Her father had been a fur trader, before marrying and settling as a homesteader, and she had warmed to her open-minded, good-hearted shipmates. They treated her not just with respect but consideration and kindness.

The three-day voyage, for all its discomfort and constraints, proved strangely restful. It gave freedom from responsibility, unbinding Mary's spirit though her body was confined.

Peter was thankful to see her looking stronger and healthier than at any time since her husband's arrest. He felt easier in his mind now that they were at last on their way.

Chapter Twenty-Six

Salem Town
May 1692

BURROUGHS GAZED INTO HIS WIFE'S EYES, AS DEFINED AS IF MARY were before him in the flesh, their brown flecked with green, shaded by dark lashes. He slid down until just his shoulders were propped against the wall, seeing the lines and shadows of worry and exhaustion, which did not lessen the eyes' beauty but enhanced it, adding an adorable pathos, all the more poignant for the eyes' shining intelligence. Burroughs lifted his hand, imagining he touched the soft olive skin of Mary's cheek and the dark, wiry hair tumbling to her shoulders. As her eyes gazed back into his, he felt her giving herself to him moment by moment as though her commitment was renewed with each breath. He imagined laying his hand against her slim neck and running it over her collarbone to the hollow under her shoulder. As strong as the desire he felt for her was his love of her love for him. He pulled her toward him, sliding down further till they lay together on the ground. He felt her put her arms round his neck and grasp him to her tightly. Running his hand down her side to her waist and up over the curve of her hip, he pulled her still closer until her body and his seemed to merge.

When Burroughs opened his eyes and looked up at the tiny barred slit at the top of the wall where it joined with the ceiling, pale gray showed it was day. Apart from that oblong of sky and the rotting timber walls and the stench, damp, and silence, his world consisted of thought. He struggled to his feet, the shackles biting his ankles, causing him to clamp tight his jaws in angry defiance. He lifted his arms above his head and held them at their full extent for several seconds, then stretched them out to the sides, then brought them down behind him, pulling back his shoulders, clasping his hands together. Next, parting his hands, he took six small steps forward. Then turned and took six small steps back. This was as far as the chain padlocked to the hoop would allow. He performed the sequence ten times, then sat down again, leaning back against the wall. Bowing his head, he said softly, "Our father, which art in heaven, hallowed be thy name . . ." After the "Amen," he stayed, head still bowed, but soon again began to pray.

"Almighty God, for all my wickedness, in thy infinite mercy, forgive me. I know not what sins I have committed, unrepented of, that have caused thy displeasure against me. I beg thee to give me wisdom to understand what I have done, to repent and find favor in thine eyes. Let my ordeal end swiftly, I beg you, or, if that cannot be, give me the strength of body and mind to endure it." He paused. "Pray keep my wife Mary and my daughter Rebecca and all my other children safe and in health, and, if such be thy will, bring us once more together, if not in this life then joyfully by the grace of thy blessed son Jesus Christ, in the next. Blessed be thy name. Amen."

He brought his hands to his face. He could hear his wife screaming his name and see her terrified eyes as the soldiers marched him away and he remembered, long ago, his daughter Rebecca clinging to him, sobbing, when her mother lay dead. He remembered an older Rebecca hiding herself in a closet when he ran out of the house in Wells with his gun as the Indians attacked. So many dangers and misfortunes and now, at the end of them all, this inexplicable horror, worse than anything he could ever have imagined.

"Oh God, my gracious God, what have I done to offend thee?"

Did God judge, as Stoughton and the rest of the magistrates seemed to have judged, that he'd been untrue to his Puritan faith? He had not always obeyed every Puritan edict. In the wilderness some seemed trivial. Yet he had never thought himself anything but a faithful member of the church his mother had helped him join as a boy.

"Pray God, give me guidance, in this misfortune and in all things."

The pain of the shackles on his legs forced him to stand, stretch, and shift again. He refused to acknowledge the scamperings and scratchings of the rats, as he refused to acknowledge the sliminess of the walls and the foul stench of filth and the hunger. Lifting his head, he intoned more loudly than before, giving the words as much expression as if he were addressing his congregation in the meetinghouse, "*The Lord is my light and my salvation; whom shall I fear? The Lord is the strength of my life; of whom shall I be afraid? When the wicked, even mine enemies and my foes, came upon me to eat up my flesh, they stumbled and fell.*"

He had learned this psalm, the twenty-seventh, by heart during his days in the tavern in Salem. Doing so had helped pass the time; having done so, he found now with no Bible to read, helped him keep his wits. He continued loudly to recite until, nearing the end, his voice dropped and he intoned more softly, "*Teach me thy way, O Lord, and lead me in a plain path, because of mine enemies. Deliver me not over unto the will of mine enemies: for false witnesses are risen up against me, and such as breathe out cruelty.*"

He pictured the girls in their fits, among them Mercy, her pretty face distorted. *Cruelty?* Was that cruelty? Surely not meant as such. What could she, or any of them, have against him, that they should wish to be cruel? He had taken the orphaned fifteen-year-old into his home, clothed and fed her. She would come to his study, with the air of a soul who had lost everything, which was sadly indeed what she was, and stand without speaking next to his desk. He would tell her she should have faith, that her parents were saints in heaven, and that one day they would all be together. He would ask her to join him in saying the Lord's Prayer and when she stayed mute he'd recite it alone. At last she'd taken to whispering the "Amen," leaving straight afterward to go back to her tasks. Most of her time was spent preparing food, washing dishes, dressing and feeding the smallest of the children, concentrating wholly on what she was doing, never talking or smiling.

In due course this had started to change. One day she'd joined Burroughs in saying the Lord's Prayer and soon after that she'd started talking to him and his wife about everyday things, and gradually by stages she'd turned into an ordinary girl again. Except that she'd developed a strange way of always smiling.

Eventually Burroughs sent her to a family in Salem, a safer place than the outpost in Maine. He'd heard she'd gone from there to the Putnams, with whom he'd earlier had so much trouble. He wondered if Putnam treated her well. He suspected he must, or the village would talk.

"*I had fainted,*" he intoned softly, "*unless I had believed to see the goodness of the Lord in the land of the living.*" He had felt close to fainting, in the examination room, as the girls screamed and writhed.

Was Samuel Sewall's not speaking for him, and not coming to visit him, true cruelty? But his friend must have his reasons. Perhaps he knew he could wield more influence on Burroughs's behalf if he did not appear to be partial, his judgment clouded by affection.

"*Wait on the Lord: be of good courage, and he shall strengthen thine heart: wait, I say, on the Lord.*"

The gray oblong turned to blue. The creaking of the door presaged a smell that might once have made Burroughs's stomach turn but now clamped it with hunger. The keeper took his time shutting and locking the door, then hobbled the few feet across the cell and lowered himself to place the bowl of gruel, spoon, and mug he was carrying on the ground next to Burroughs. He took a small piece of bread from his pocket and held it so Burroughs had to half rise and stretch to get hold of it. Burroughs ate it in seconds, then slurped the gruel, then drank the none too clean water. When he finished the keeper, standing over him, said, "You're a man of learnin'."

Burroughs waited for whatever this was leading to. He knew the keeper well; he loved to tease. The minister had come to loathe the characteristic uneven sound of his footsteps, caused by a club foot, and his sarcastic smile and the mean glint in his one working eye. The other orb was swollen and glazed, resembling a peeled quail's egg. A hint of sightless blue pupil disappeared under the eyelid. Burroughs suspected he forbore to wear an eye patch out of contempt for the prisoners.

"You'll likely know what's goin' on."

Burroughs only knew the keeper had news but no intention of sharing it without fawning and coaxing. He leaned back against the wall and said carefully, "My learning's of little use to me now. I'd be most grateful for anything you can tell me. I've no other means of getting information."

"Very true. Not one visitor have you had since you've been here." The widening sarcastic smile produced an intricate network of lines on the weather-damaged face. The keeper could not always have worked underground. Burroughs suspected he'd been recruited as a jailer only when the dungeons started overflowing with witches. He went on, still smiling. "Most of them have visitors. Even that foul witch Sarah Good has a husband who comes sometimes. Mind you, it's my opinion he comes to see her daughter, not her."

"Alas, my wife's too far away to come visiting."

"I forgot, you *have* had a visitor. And a very important one. I expect you asked *him* one or two questions."

He was referring to John Hathorne, who had come to see Burroughs a couple of days ago, to try to extract a confession. He had failed.

"He didn't answer them," Burroughs said. "Please, if you have news from outside, do me the great favor of telling it." Burroughs tried to sound eager yet humble. He must have succeeded well enough since the keeper said, "Well, I will. The new governor's come."

"The new governor?" Burroughs was taken completely by surprise. Whatever news he was expecting, it wasn't this.

"Come with the Reverend Increase Mather all the way from England."

"Who . . . ?" Burroughs checked himself and asked, in a humbler tone, "Do you by any chance know who he is?" The keeper said proudly, "Course I know! Sir William Phips, made a knight by raising sunken treasure and giving every piece to the king. Well, he said he gave every piece to the king."

"An unlikely new governor!"

"Who are you to know who's unlikely?"

"Are you *sure* 'tis William Phips?"

"Course I'm sure! *Sir* William, if you don't mind!"

"He was poor as an Indian till he raised that sunken treasure."

"How d'you know?"

"I remember him in Maine. Years ago. He was born there; he was nobody."

"If he's nobody, why's he a friend of Reverend Mather?"

"That's what puzzles me."

"See, the devil doesn't tell you everything!"

"The devil doesn't tell me anything! I rely on you alone, good keeper, and no one else in this world or the other, for my knowledge. Has Sir William Phips brought the new charter?"

Again with pride in his voice, the keeper said, "He has."

"Then my trial should be soon."

The jailer stacked the mug and spoon in the bowl very slowly, which meant he had more news.

"Are there other new appointments?"

The keeper's air as he limped to the door told him that, whether there were or whether there weren't, it was not that he wanted to speak of. But Burroughs asked anyway, since he wanted to know, "Is William Stoughton still deputy governor?"

"He is." Looking round and seeing Burroughs's face, he said, "Enemy of yours? Must be, since he's an enemy of the devil."

"I am as much of an enemy of the devil as he is."

"Strange enemy, doing his work for him."

"I have never done his work for him."

"That's not what Mr. Hathorne thinks."

"He'll change his views at my trial."

The keeper thrust a key from the ring on his belt into the keyhole but did not turn it. Burroughs asked him whether there'd been any more arrests.

"*Many* more."

This still wasn't it.

"Any comings and goings in the dungeons?"

The keeper turned slightly and Burroughs knew he'd got there.

"Did you not hear anything?"

The thick timber walls made the dungeons virtually soundproof, as the keeper well knew. Burroughs managed to hold on to his temper.

"No. Nothing."

"Ah, yes, there've been comings and goings, important comings and goings." The keeper turned fully from the door.

"New prisoners?"

"Nay, we're full to bursting."

"Visitors?"

"And what visitors!"

"John Hathorne? Bartholomew Gedney?"

The keeper half turned back. Burroughs had been meant to make one or two wrong guesses first.

"I wonder who they saw," the minister said quickly. "Sarah Good?

Sarah Osborne?" He chose unlikely candidates to give the keeper ample chance to show scorn.

"Sarah Good! Sarah Osborne! Call yourself learned?"

"As I've said, my learning seems of little use to me now."

"What would he be doing with *them*?"

"I couldn't say."

The keeper looked suspicious and Burroughs realized he might have overplayed the dumbness. The keeper well knew why Hathorne had visited Burroughs.

"I suppose John Proctor is more likely. Hathorne must be hoping for his confession more than anyone's, apart from mine."

"Nay! Not John Proctor!" The keeper's sightless eye bulged slightly. "And *Mister* Hathorne, if you please. You may be learned but you're in jail for witchcraft, don't forget. You may be a hero in Maine but here you're less than a greenfly on horseshit."

"I'm in no danger of forgetting, believe me. *Elizabeth* Proctor?"

"Nay!"

"Martha Cory?"

"Far off!"

Burroughs injected more humility into his tone. "Pray tell me."

"Lydia Hobbs!"

"Lydia Hobbs? But she's confessed already!"

"Not enough!"

"Not enough! She's said she's a witch. What more can she say?"

"She can say who *made* her a witch."

"And did she?"

"Aye!"

From the density of lines on the keeper's ugly face Burroughs knew who she'd named.

"How did you hear this?"

"I listened at the door. If you don't think I should have, you won't desire to know more."

"Lydia Hobbs said I made her a witch?" Burroughs's surprise was already fading.

"Near enough."

"Near enough?"

"As good as."

"What *did* she say?"

"Mr. Hathorne asked if you brought poppets of your wives to stick pins in and at first she said no. But after half an hour she changed her mind and said yes."

"Is that all she said?"

"That's enough to hang you."

"The new governor's here! I'll soon face my judges in court!"

Satisfied with the quick breathing he'd induced from his charge, the keeper unlocked the door.

Chapter Twenty-Seven

Salem Town
May 1692

PETER AND MARY DECIDED NOT TO GO TO THE PRISON UNTIL MORNING. They assumed this was where George was, though they could not help but hope he'd been examined and let go. They'd never be admitted to the jail after dark, except perhaps by means of a large bribe, which they couldn't afford. Having asked advice of the ship's captain, they made their way in the near blackness, asking directions when they could, to Salem's only inn.

Peter gave his own name to the innkeeper but Mary said hers was Cheever. She felt it best no one knew of her relationship to Burroughs until they saw how the land lay. It was common knowledge throughout New England that relatives of accused witches were always under suspicion. She and Peter told Samuel Beadle they were cousins, traveling from Maine on family business. The innkeeper looked quizzical but did not challenge them.

After a meal in the main chamber, where due to the lateness of the hour they sat alone, a servant took them upstairs and along a corridor, where he saw Peter into his room. He stopped at the next door. Swinging his candle into his left hand, in readiness for opening the door with his right, he remarked softly that until a week or so ago, for six days, the leader of witches had lain directly above where Mary would be sleeping. He raised his eyes to the ceiling. Mary clasped her mouth.

"Don' let the thought disturb your slumbers! 'E's in prison now, in chains, so 'is specter can't come 'ere."

Mary took a deep breath. "In *Salem* prison?" she asked.

"'Ave no fear! 'E wouldn' wan' to come back 'ere anyway! Spent long enough in that room to last 'im a lifetime!"

"Has he been examined yet?"

"'Ere, downstairs, in the very room where you bin eatin'! Well the magistrates talked to 'im in the room next to it but 'e was moved in the main room for them girls to prove 'e was witchin' 'em."

"Them girls?"

"They was shouting and screaming fit to split yer eardrums if yer'd bin on the ocean 'alfway to England."

A knock on a wall and angry shout of "Quiet there!" sent the small servant scurrying off, after pushing the key into Mary's hand, muttering, "'Appy dreams!"

For a few moments Mary stood unmoving. Should she knock on Peter's door to tell him at once what she'd heard? The impropriety of the action, since he might already have undressed, was weighted by the unavoidable physical closeness in which he and she had lived for three days. However, her dilemma ended when Peter opened his door and came out, still in all his clothes. She stepped forward to meet him halfway between the two rooms and said softly, "Did you hear?"

Peter put his finger to his lips, beckoned her to come in his room, and, when she did, shut the door behind them. Pointing at the wall of the chamber on the other side from hers, he whispered, almost inaudibly, "Talk very quietly. There's someone in there." His words were proved true by a loud snore through the wall.

"He's been examined!"

"He's in prison?"

"Aye." Mary stared at him, hardly comprehending that the hope they had lived all this time, of George's being freed as soon as he was questioned, was lost. And the strange role of those accusers, who screamed when he was in the room, filled her with new dread.

"We mustn't give the *remotest* cause for suspicion. We will have breakfast in the normal way with the other guests."

"I'm afraid."

"We'll free him. But it's imperative we stay calm."

"I know that. Don't fear, I will."

"Good night, Mary. Try to sleep."

As she lay in her feather bed of a softness and comfort she'd never known existed, the slumber that had come so quickly in a hard, narrow hammock in a pitching ship stayed distant. When it crept up at last, it brought nightmares.

But on waking, the sense of horror was replaced by resolution. She threw open the shutters, put on her clothes, washed her face, walked down the corridor, and knocked on Peter's door. He opened it at once, dressed and ready.

The breakfast table was laid with pewter spoons, mugs, and bowls glinting down the length of the gleaming reddish-brown board. Mary had been surprised the night before by the metal platters and knives; she'd never before eaten off anything but wood. She was even more surprised now to see the pewter set out at breakfast; she'd assumed it was only for best, later in the day. Seating herself midway down the table, joined by Peter, she hoped they would be well placed when others arrived to start conversations with as many people as possible, to learn all they could.

The small servant entered with corn bread, milk, and cider, saying with narrowed eyes to Mary that he hoped she'd slept well. She merely nodded. He left to return with more food, followed by a pair of fellow guests, who seated themselves as far away as possible at the table end. A man and woman with uniformly pinched features, they looked as though they had no wish to talk to anyone, including each other. As Peter and Mary helped themselves to food, the other seats began to fill. Soon they were in conversation with a leather goods maker and a mariner, telling them the story about themselves as they'd told the innkeeper, and at the same time rapidly gaining information. Mary felt a surge of hope on hearing that Burroughs's old friend Samuel Sewall was one of the judges. The leather goods maker said the first trial was less than a week away and the mariner mentioned that pretrial hearings were still taking place. At this the pinched-faced woman, glancing round with vicious eyes, spoke for the first time to declare that devils were being discovered all over Essex County. Her husband added, staring straight ahead of him, that he feared for the future of the province. The manufacturer, cutting up food on his plate, said a day of prayer and fasting had been ordered three days hence to appease the God who was smiting New England for its sinfulness. Mary asked for details of the day, explaining that they had never had one in Maine.

"What!" barked the pinched-faced man. "Why not? Ain't they God-fearing Puritans there?"

"I've heard a lot of them ain't," said his wife, with a look of undisguised venom at Mary. "Some of them are *Quakers*."

"I'm not a Quaker," Mary said quickly. The mariner explained that from dawn to dusk, except for attending two three-hour services in the meetinghouse, everyone would be expected to stay in their homes, eat nothing, and pray. He himself would of course be on board ship by then but would fast and pray in his cabin.

The manufacturer remarked that he had heard the clerk of the court was Stephen Sewall, Samuel's brother. By this time many of the guests were preparing to leave and the pinched-faced couple had risen from the table. Mary asked, as lightly as she could, if anyone knew anything about a man meant to be one of the witches called George Burroughs.

"A minister," said the mariner. "I heard he was kept in this very inn before going to prison. There was something else about him but I can't recall what it was."

The pinched-faced woman, still by the table, was looking back at Mary and the pinched-faced man, through gritted teeth, pronounced, "He's the leader of the witches. The devil's right-hand man."

Mary stood up and started stacking plates ready for clearing, a moment later managing to say, "No wonder I had heard of him."

Some guests had left and many more were on their way to the door. The pinched-faced couple nodded good-bye and walked off stiffly. Peter and Mary surreptitiously slipped an item or two of uneaten food into their pockets and bade farewell to the table companions who remained, wishing the mariner, who was sailing that day, a safe voyage.

Outside in the street the sky was clear, the air fresh, the morning not yet too hot.

"Leader of the witches," Mary repeated, with horror.

"Not necessarily reliable information. About what is generally believed, of course."

"Why would he say it, if it's not what everyone is saying?"

"There cannot be many male accused witches. He may say it about all of them."

"Seems unlikely."

"Aye. Wishful thinking, perhaps."

"Who *are* that couple?" Mary wondered. "What are they doing here? They do not look like they could afford to stay at the inn just for the pleasure of following the trials."

"I would guess he is a farmer. But they could scarcely afford to neglect their farm either."

"I wouldn't dare question them."

"The less we talk to them, the better."

"Which way?" Mary wondered. They both stared around. "Down here."

As they walked the street struck her, now that she saw it by daylight, as grander than anything she had ever imagined, with its large houses, most with more than one chimney, some with gables, and, most amazingly, all with glass in the windows. Peter knew no more than she did where the prison was and when they were out of sight of the inn she asked directions from an ancient, bleary-eyed man she hoped would neither see nor remember them well enough to describe them if questioned. The man pointed with a shaking finger and mumbled a few words. Soon they found themselves in Main Street, lined with equally large houses together with a few shops including a baker and grocer. At the first they bought a large loaf of bread, at the second some early apples. Still following the man's brief directions, they turned into an alley. This, in stark contrast to the road, contained a few dismal dwellings on one side, a large, scrubby field on the other, and, at the end, a rambling, dark timbered building with small, barred windows that proclaimed what it was as loudly as if it had had a sign on the door.

The time they spent at that portal, requesting to see the Reverend George Burroughs and waiting while Peter's bag was searched and a guard was sent for to take them to the dungeons, was longer than the time it had taken them to walk there.

Chapter Twenty-Eight

Salem Town
May 1692

WHEN THE KEEPER WAS GONE AND THE DOOR LOCKED THERE WAS silence. No sounds from outside—no birdsong such as he and Mary had delighted in when they woke in their attic on those blissful mornings in Wells. Oh God, why couldn't he keep control of his memories? They came like assaults, sharpening his anguish. He tried to fill the silence with visions of what his happiness would be in a month or less from now, after he had been acquitted, back in Maine with Mary and Rebecca and the rest of his children in the glorious summer sunshine with the trees in full leaf. But to think of all this was soon to feel more pain and feel the silence stifle him.

The only sound that regularly penetrated the walls of his dungeon was the clanging of a door. That sound came now; the guard must be taking food to the shackled wretch in the next occupied cell. Burroughs had no idea who this was. He had been brought here in darkness and given no notion of the layout of the dungeons or who was in which, though the keeper had later let slip that his cell was at the end of the row and the wall to the right, as Burroughs faced the door from inside, was an outer one. All he knew was that the warren of dungeons must cover a large area, given the number of prisoners it held. But he guessed that despite this the cell next to his must be empty. He'd often banged and called but got no response. He sometimes heard the keeper open the door and moments later shut it, clearly without having entered the room. He could learn nothing more from the man himself about this. The keeper enjoyed telling him how angry Sarah Good was and how pale Elizabeth Proctor, and how large her belly, and how John Proctor pestered him with questions almost as much as Burroughs himself, and how Sarah Good's four-year-old daughter, made a witch by her mother, had gone silent and staring as she lay shackled to the wall in her specially constructed small leg irons. But he refused to tell him who was where along the corridor.

Once Burroughs had heard nothing at all for a whole day, between the keeper's two visits, morning and evening, and he started losing all sense of time. To fight off the notion that he'd died and gone to hell, he made himself recall how he got here, remembering the short walk from Beadle's, with a constable each side of him, and going through the door of the prison, stumbling down steep stairs and along a passage, and finally being thrown in this cell, with the keeper slamming the door on him.

He knew that on the floor above the prisoners could look out through the windows, mingle, talk, and plot. Those were ordinary criminals—thieves, drunkards, and adulterers—not followers of Satan.

It was now time for the next task in his daily routine: practicing his defense for his trial. He had several times begged the keeper for pen and paper but been refused since he had no money to pay for them. So he kept his arguments marshaled in his head. He knew what he wanted to say to refute the ramblings of Keyser, the wild allegations of the soldiers and John Putnam's accusations. Keyser was drunk, the soldiers reporting mere rumors, and Putnam plain lying. He had never bewitched anyone, his strength was his own, he'd never held a gun with one finger without help, and his wives had died of ordinary illnesses. It was true he'd asked his first wife to sign a covenant, but that was to stop her talking to strangers about personal matters, for her sake as much as his. Now and then he felt he'd achieved soaring eloquence and longed to be standing at that moment in court.

He was less clear what to say about the charge of "confederacy with the devil" to harm Ann Putnam, Mercy Lewis, and the rest. Given their shocking demonstrations at his hearing, it might not be enough merely to deny it. He might have to *prove* it was wrong. He had read in a book that the devil could not give someone the power to inflict harm at a distance by magical means, but he could not recall title or author. Peter White would know. Yet surely they couldn't hang him just because of those fits, without other evidence. . . . Again, Peter would know.

He sometimes wondered if Peter would follow him to Salem but did not dare hope. It did not occur to him that Mary might attempt such a journey, with all its dangers and hardships. Besides, she had no money to pay for her passage, or the expenses of staying in Salem.

Now he had a new accusation to refute. He would argue that Lydia Hobbs had always been wild and strange and, what was more, was now in a dungeon, hoping for release or at least to be removed to easier conditions upstairs.

Still sitting on the ground, leaning against the wall, the longing to be free of the shackles almost overwhelmed him. Lying wounded in battle had never amounted to torture like this. Physical pain was as nothing compared to this helplessness. He sat forward; his chest tightened; his vision blurred; he gasped, struggling to breathe. For a moment it was as though a demon truly possessed him.

"Aaron," he cried. "Abednego. Abel." He took a quick breath. "Abigail. Abner. Abraham." Another breath. "Absalom. Achan. Achish." He went all through the As, then the Bs. Gradually he calmed, leaning back against the wall. "Cain. Caleb. Carmi." He realized he'd missed one. "Canaan!" he shouted. "Cursed by Canaan!" He remembered Noah had uttered the words but did not pause to recall why. "Casluhim, Chelal, Chemosh, Chenani."

He had compiled this list of Old Testament characters from memory of his Bible reading, to recite when his wits were deserting him. He finished the Cs and started on the Ds.

"Daniel!" Were there any he had missed? He did not try to remember in case he lost his hold again. Instead he started telling the story of the boys seized from the children of Israel to serve the Babylonian king, reciting the very words of the Bible. He reached, "The king spake to the master of the eunuchs, that he should bring certain of the children of Israel."

But before he could go on there came a scream of terror such as he had never heard in his life. It was stifled, then came again, then once more was stifled. He struggled to his feet. The voice that had screamed shrieked, "I can't . . . I can't . . . " The keeper rasped, "Shut it!"

Burroughs's door flew open and a girl about the same age as his daughter, her cap hanging off her head, fell into his cell. The door was pulled shut. Burroughs ran forward but was agonizingly stopped by the shackles.

"She's dead!" the girl screamed.

"Who's dead?"

"Eyes staring!"

"Who?"

"Sarah Osborne. He was locking me in with her!"

"Tell me everything quickly. He'll come back soon. Who are you?"

"Margaret Jacobs."

"Arrested for witchcraft?"

"I can't believe it! Me! So fearful of God! They arrested my grandfather too."

"Have you been examined?"

"He was locking me in with her!"

"Be calm." He knelt down. She moved forward and grasped his arm.

"Mister Hathorne tried to make me confess but I wouldn't, though he told me they'd put me in a dungeon, and Grandfather said they might as well call him a buzzard as a wizard, and they took him away, I don't know where, he's eighty years old." She burst into tears.

Burroughs guessed the jailer had gone to find help to remove Sarah Osborne's body. He knew now why he'd never heard anything from the far side of the left wall. The woman must have been, if not dead until now, in an unwaking sleep.

The girl clutched her head in her hands and found her cap was hanging off. She pulled it up, pushing her hair under it. Burroughs saw she was a little younger than Rebecca, with large gray, intelligent eyes in a square face. She gulped back her tears.

"Is your grandfather Mister George Jacobs?"

"Yes. Do you know him?"

"I knew him years ago when I was pastor in the village. He's a man of courage and sense. Be assured he will survive this or, if not, he will die at peace with his God."

"Are you Reverend George Burroughs?"

"I am."

"They wanted me to say you were our minister at witch meetings. But how could I belie myself?"

"Brave girl!"

"But to put me in a cell with a dead body!"

"They are taking her away. That is why he's put you here. But he will be back for you soon. Let's agree to a code."

"What kind of code?"

"One knock as a greeting, two to say we have news."

"The wall's thick."

"You could use your shoe."

"But if we have news, how can we tell it?"

"Through the keeper. Coax and flatter him. If necessary bribe him. Have you money?"

"Yes, Grandfather gave me some." She began unbuttoning the high neck of her dress and pulled at a string hanging inside. "D'you need some? Let me . . ." She pulled out her purse.

"No, no, put it away, you'll need it yourself. The jailer will bring you extra food for about sixpence, I would guess, and paper and pen for a little more and deliver a note to any prisoner you want to get word to for a shilling or so. But never offer him more than a penny or tuppence at first. Bargain with him."

"You need extra food too! You're so thin! Let me . . ."

"By no means!"

When it was clear that Burroughs would not take her money, she tucked the purse in her dress again.

"You're a good girl, your grandfather must be proud of you."

"No! I'm a coward! I'm afraid!"

"*I'm* afraid. Everyone here is afraid. Remember I am just a few feet away. Knock whenever you want and I shall knock back and you will know you're not alone."

"Will you pray for me when I'm in there?"

"Knock three times and we will both say the Lord's Prayer, knowing the other's saying it too."

"Oh, Mr. Burroughs, that will comfort me so!"

"Try to keep your mind busy. Tell yourself Bible stories. Recite psalms. That's what I do."

"I will. That will help me, I know. Oh, how long will we be here?"

"I hope our trials will be soon. You should be warned, they will visit you again to try to make you confess."

"You mean Mr. Hathorne? He'll come to the prison?"

"And perhaps Mr. Gedney."

"Mr. Hathorne said if I confessed I could stay upstairs in the open prison and live. He said if I didn't confess I'd be thrown in the dungeon and stay there till I was hanged."

"He said *that*? He did not say that to me. He knew I would know he was lying."

"What *did* he say?"

"That I ought to confess for the sake of my soul. But that is just why I cannot confess, for the sake of my soul."

The door opened and the keeper limped in. He reached down but Margaret scrambled up and out of the door before he could touch her.

Bangs on the wall came at regular intervals through the night. They were barely audible but Burroughs always heard them and replied. Usually there was one knock but once there were three and then, after signaling back, he bowed his head and recited the Lord's Prayer as loudly as he could.

At last, when the night was almost over, he fell deeply asleep and did not wake until the keeper came with his food. The oblong high in the wall was bright blue.

"Have you seen Margaret this morning?" Burroughs asked at once.

"Margaret? Oh, Margaret. I suppose you think she's in the next cell?"

"Why, yes."

"Why, no. Mr. Hathorne came at first light to talk to her. Soon after, they took her upstairs."

Burroughs had made a series of scratches with his thumbnail on the damp timber wall, in the corner under the window, to which he added one each evening, when the keeper left. There was a satisfaction, as faint as the scratches themselves, in marking the endurance of another twenty-four hours and coming closer by that length of time to his trial. Yesterday, for the first time since he'd been here, owing to his preoccupation with everything Margaret had told him, and wondering about her state of mind as she lay beyond the other wall, he had forgotten to denote that day's passing. Now, when the keeper had left, but without even the usual faint satisfaction, he made yesterday's mark.

Soon after he did so, as he was trying to find the strength of mind and body to begin his day's routine, he heard in the passage outside his door a woman's droning voice interspersed with the keeper's barking tones. He could not catch any words. A few moments later he heard the clang of the door to the cell Margaret had been taken from. He waited for the door to clang again, then after a few moments, shouted and banged on the wall. No response. Perhaps the new prisoner was deaf.

Calling on all his resolution, telling himself if he kept strong he could yet prove his innocence despite all the voices against him, he got to his feet and lifted his arms high to begin his series of exercises. But he had no sooner finished them and knelt to pray when his door opened. It was hours until his second meal was due. Hope and dread, of good or bad news, made his heart race. But the keeper just stood in the doorway and looked at him, that expression of contempt on his face that Burroughs had come to know well. No doubt only belief in his own superiority made the man's vile existence endurable. He clearly had no reason to be here now but to wait for Burroughs to beg for information about the new arrival. With a sigh, Burroughs obliged.

"Pray tell me, who is the new prisoner?"

"A foul witch!"

"Old? Deaf?"

"Old enough to have buried two husbands and married a third. Like you with your wives. *She* killed hers by witchcraft an' all."

Burroughs did not respond.

"Deaf except to the devil," the man added, the entire network of lines coming into view on his face.

"From Salem Village, is she?"

"Oh no, they're not coming from there anymore; they're finding them in Salem Town now. Bridget's been a witch for twenty year, she was accused years ago but the jury found her innocent. That won't happen this time, there'll be too many speakin' against her."

"Bridget? Bridget Oliver?"

"Bridget Bishop she is now. You know her? Was it you made her a witch?"

"I never even met her."

"She gave young William Stacy, who drudged for her, three pennies and when he'd gone a few yards down the road he looked in his pocket where he'd put it and it had vanished like snow!"

"Perhaps his pocket had a hole in it."

"Are you saying Bridget Bishop's *not* a witch?" the keeper asked nastily.

"All I'm saying is these stories don't *prove* she's a witch."

"Are you saying William Stacy's lying?"

"I'm saying he may have made a mistake."

"One night he felt something cold pressing on his teeth so hard it woke him and he saw Bridget Bishop sitting on the end of his bed. He can't have made a mistake about *that*."

"I heard all this and more when I came to Salem Village. I am surprised she wasn't accused earlier."

"I told you, she was."

"I meant in this witch scare now."

"She was examined near a month ago but they sent her to the jail in Ipswich, we were too crowded."

"Why have they brought her here now?"

"Get some money, Mister Burroughs, and I'll answer more questions." The keeper hobbled from the room, still smiling his widest, nastiest smile.

Not long after, the man opened the door again. For an instant Burroughs thought he had died and gone to heaven. Stumbling to his feet, he opened his arms and his wife ran into them. They hugged and kissed until they both gasped for breath. Peter White stood behind her. The keeper shouted, "Ten minutes," banging the door.

"My love," Mary gasped. "You're, oh God, you're skin and bone." She stepped back, to view him. "You're a skeleton."

"I'm alive!"

Her eyes were on his ankles. "Those irons. My God!"

"How did you get here?"

"Cargo ship." Mary knelt at Burroughs's feet, tentatively touching the shackles. "Can you move?" She looked up at her husband's face.

"Six small steps."

She stood up and threw her arms round him again. Peter waited until they loosened their grip on each other a little, then asked, "How are you, dear friend?"

Without letting go of Mary, Burroughs stretched out an arm to embrace his comrade too. He could not keep back tears.

"Forgive me my weakness."

"Forgive *us*, for not getting here sooner!" Mary leaned her head on his shoulder.

"'Tis a miracle you are here now!"

"In time to help you, we pray God."

Peter said, "We arrived last night. Stayed at Beadle's."

"That's where they kept me!"

"We know."

"The food's good. I thought so even then."

"What do you get here?"

"A bowl of gruel and a crust, twice a day."

"We've brought you food!" Mary moved away and dug into Peter's bag, which he had dropped on the ground.

"You come like angels, better than angels, God forgive me."

Peter stepped away and Burroughs staggered slightly. Mary helped him down onto the floor, then sat next to him and put the loaf and other food they'd bought on his lap. Only when he had eaten it all did he take Mary in his arms. Peter had turned to study the lock and hinges of the door as though trying to work out a method of releasing Burroughs from his cell. By squeezing and stroking her, Burroughs reassured himself his wife was truly a flesh-and-blood woman, not a vision. Her back and shoulders seemed bonier but the curves of her body as seductive as ever. He checked himself from caressing her further but instead, pulling back his head, gazed into her face again. Her eyes were more beautiful than he had remembered but her olive-skinned cheeks thinner and paler. He kissed each of them, then her mouth.

"Still as beautiful," Burroughs said softly. "I must look so different."

"No. You're just the same. Thinner, that's all. We'll be back with more food as soon as possible. Oh, George, is this where you sleep, on this earth floor?"

He nodded.

"We'll bring you blankets."

Peter turned back to them. "Tell us all that's happened. The keeper will be here soon."

"My good friend!" George exclaimed, marveling anew at his and Mary's being here. Peter squatted next to him, suddenly making him acutely aware of his emaciated body.

"We heard you've been examined and charged."

"Aye."

"Who examined you?" Mary asked.

"Stoughton, Sewall, Hathorne, and Gedney."

"*Stoughton!* The deputy governor!" She and Peter had heard of this appointment from the fellow guests at the inn.

"They suspect I'm a ringleader."

"Does *Sewall* think that?"

"I do not know. He did not say one word for me. My hope is that he's biding his time."

"Has he come to see you?"

Burroughs shook his head.

"Who first complained of you?" Peter asked.

"I suppose the girls."

"They would not go to the magistrates on their own."

"They were there, at the examination. You should have seen them."

"Screaming, we heard," Mary said.

"You cannot imagine it!"

"How can this be?" Mary marveled. "What is causing it?"

"The witches, they say. In other words, at my examination, me."

"*How?* You weren't touching them!"

"My spirit came out of my body to torture them, it seems."

"How can anyone believe this?"

"If you saw those girls you would know. 'Tis not natural, what they do. I myself started wondering if I could be causing it."

Burroughs told them about Elizar Keyser and the soldiers and John Putnam. His legs, which he had kept bent, were hurting badly and, wincing, he lowered them. The change gave momentary relief but the shackles weighed even more heavily and soon he pulled them up again.

"May I look at those ankles?" Peter asked.

"If you wish."

Burroughs tried to hide his pain and shame as Peter lifted the trouser leg overlapping the hoop of the shackles. But his smile turned to a grimace as Peter, peering closely, gently wiped the wounds with a cloth from his bag. Mary watched, trying not to flinch. She said, "Next time we'll bring water."

"And bark oil." Peter carefully laid back the trouser leg.

Mary stared around at the dripping walls and low ceiling, its damp timbers studded with small holes. "We're getting you out of here."

"Not a good billet, dear friend," Peter said.

"I must confess, time moves slowly."

Peter put his hand on his shoulder. A moment later he said, "We heard the prisons are overflowing now. They will *have* to start the trials soon. But with the new charter they will need to set up new courts."

"I know nothing of the new charter except that Increase Mather has just brought it from England."

"It wasn't what he had hoped for. It confirms Boston's rule over Maine but gives us religious freedom."

"We had that anyway!"

"Not just in Maine, in Massachusetts," Mary explained.

"Is that possible?"

"Now nobody can be forced against their will to worship as a Puritan."

Peter said, "It gives the vote to every man with property, not just church members."

A door clanged.

"The keeper's coming. Tell me quickly, how are my children? How's Rebecca?"

"Much better for knowing we have come here."

"I have a letter from her." Mary took a twice-folded paper from her pocket and gave it to George, whose hands shook so much it was hard for him to open it. In the dim light he could just read the handwriting, neater and smaller than when he used to enclose her hand to guide it.

"Honored father, I rejoice that as you peruse this my stepmother and Captain White are with you, to give you comfort and aid. I pray for you every hour. My heart is so full I hardly dare write more. Revered father, my greatest hope is that we meet again soon on this earth, but if that be not God's will, then joyfully one day in heaven. I remain your everloving daughter, Rebecca."

He read it again, devouring each word as though it was food. The tall "H" and long tail of the "R," and the restrained tone brought his daughter into the cell by his side. His eyes filled with tears.

"She's a jewel," Peter said quietly.

"*Her* tears were flowing, when she gave it me," Mary said. "She wanted to come with us but I said she had to look after the children. We did not want to expose her to danger."

"Does she understand why I am here?"

"She does but knows 'tis a terrible mistake," said Peter.

"And the other children?"

"They all know everything apart from the littlest, who just knows you have gone to Salem, that's got bigger houses than Wells."

They all laughed, but stopped abruptly, the sound strange in their ears in that place of desolation. Burroughs carefully refolded the paper and put it in his pocket.

"You came by ship, you say?"

"Took a while to find one," Peter said, "or we would have got here earlier."

Burroughs glanced from him to Mary. There was no man and no woman on earth he trusted more, yet, for them to be alone together on a journey, helping and supporting each other . . .

Peter stood up and Mary squeezed George's arm, looking into his eyes. "It felt like an eternity, away from you."

With a gut wrench, Burroughs knew he had nothing to fear. Mary smiled. After a breath, he asked, "How did you pay?"

"The captain gave us free passage. He just charged us for our food."

Peter said, "He knew why we were coming."

"We've got money, however," Mary said. "Everyone in the garrison who had any gave us some."

"Bless them!"

She produced some coins. "These were given to us specifically to give to you."

"No! You need them!"

"We have more. The people of Wells meant these for you." She slipped the coins in Burroughs's pocket.

"I hope I live to repay them."

"Amen," Peter said.

"You will!"

"We will get you out of here even before the trials if we can," Peter promised. "Till then one of us will come every day."

"If ever we do not it's because we're detained working to free you."

The door creaked.

"Another five minutes, I beg you!" Mary called, rising.

"Time's up." The jailer came in, blind eye bulging. Burroughs rose too and Mary hugged him before moving to the door.

"We will come back with more food as soon as we can."

"Not today you won't," barked the jailer.

"Just to bring him some more bread?" Mary pleaded.

"Not today."

"Tomorrow then?"

"He may not be here tomorrow."

"What do you mean?" Peter asked.

"The trials are starting!"

"Tomorrow?"

"Nah, not tomorrow."

"Then why won't he be here?"

"He'll be here."

"He's teasing you," Burroughs said.

"When *are* the trials starting?" Peter asked.

"Soon."

"We heard, in a week."

"Why d'you ask then?"

"For confirmation from a reliable source. Who's first on the stand?"

"That'll cost you a sixpence."

"Give us three guesses," Burroughs requested.

"Three won't be enough!"

"Sarah Good?"

"Nah!"

"Elizabeth Proctor?"

"Nah!"

Burroughs pointed at the wall. "Her through there?"

"You saw me looking!"

"Maybe!"

"A witch if ever there was one."

"*Just* her, or others?"

"Just her, to start with. No more now! Come on! Out!"

Chapter Twenty-Nine
Salem Town
May 1692

MARY PULLED THE THIN BLANKET OVER HER SHOULDERS AND CLOSED her eyes. After leaving the prison she had broken down, shaking and sobbing, overwhelmed by the distress she had kept at bay for George's sake. Peter, almost equally shaken, had stood silently beside her, fighting back tears. At last they both composed themselves enough to hurry back to Beadle's, where Mary felt she must have time alone and went up to her room. There she found herself shaking again, with tears pouring down her face, and got into bed to try to rest and grow calm.

But she could not blot out the vision of her husband in the dungeon, with hollow cheeks and ragged beard. His teeth had seemed bigger and sharper than they used to, with more of the gums showing, and the dark brown gaze of his eyes, the whites bloodshot, was no longer full of manliness but uncertainty. She had lied when she said he looked the same, yet she had felt she had not, because the emaciated face was a mask and the eyes, despite their loss of strength, were as full of love for her as ever. She drifted into sleep but images of George reappeared, within walls streaming blood. A noose dangled from the ceiling; the timber it hung from crashed to the ground.

"Are you there, Mary?" It was Peter's voice, through the door.

"Coming!"

She must stay strong for George's sake. Once outside she said, "We have to decide what to do next."

When they were seated in the main chamber, alone though the long table was already laid for midday dinner, Peter said softly, in case anyone could hear from the hallway or even the next room, they should wait for Bridget Bishop's trial before making further moves.

"But that's a week of doing nothing."

"Anything we try to do in our present ignorance may harm George, not help him. Seeing how the trial's conducted will give us a much better idea of how to continue."

"I should go see Samuel Sewall."

"He's in Boston."

"That's not far."

"It would take four hours to walk there, four back. You can see him here in Salem after the trial."

"If I can reach him."

"He's bound to stay with his brother Stephen for the night. You realize you will be putting yourself in great danger, pleading for George as his wife, already for that reason alone under suspicion of witchcraft."

"An old friend *cannot* believe George is a witch, or that I am."

"Perhaps *I* should talk to Sewall."

"No. I should. As closest kin to him."

"At least wait till after the trial."

Reluctantly, Mary agreed. Since it seemed there was truly nothing else she could do, she would spend all her time with George. She would be with him in the cramped, dark, filthy cell all day every day and even during the nights, if the keeper would let her. Because of the need to conserve money, she and Peter were both determined they should continue to gain entrance without payment.

"I will go and see George tomorrow morning by myself. The keeper might be more likely to let me in without a bribe, and perhaps let me stay longer. Besides . . ."

"I shall walk you there."

They were silent a moment.

"What shall we do now?" Mary wondered. "It is maddening, to be here in Salem and yet helpless."

"Let us take a walk through the town."

As soon as they set out, as though God were telling Massachusetts the planned day of fasting and prayer were not enough to placate him, the skies darkened. However, impatient to get a better sense of this strange place, where almost no one questioned the claims that in Maine seemed incredible, they did not turn back. Soon afterward a few thin breaks in the clouds suggested the threatening rain might pass over.

After exploring lanes they had not been down before between the tavern and Main Street, they turned in the opposite direction from the prison, heading for the sea. Soon roaming at random, they viewed wide streets and tall houses and stretches of water that never quite revealed open ocean despite the salty tang in the air. But the sky again turned black, the views became hazier, and the contours of the distant hills more obscure. The masts and sails of ships that had come in and out of view as they walked now merged with the clouds.

They started making their way back along streets they had not walked before and thought would get them to Beadle's as quickly as possible. But halfway down a quiet road lined with modest houses they found themselves at the little gate to a cemetery. Mary persuaded Peter they should go in. Glancing at some of the headstones, she saw this was where Salemites had been lain to rest since first arriving from England sixty years before. The place seemed a refuge, filled as it was with men and women who had known their own agonies but not those that were turning their town into an unimagined hell.

"Let's stay here a little while," said Mary. "If it rains we can shelter under there." She pointed to a solitary broad oak near the gate.

The field of wooden crosses and granite headstones was separated by a low stone wall from the river whose opposite shore could barely be distinguished from water and sky. Peter walked to it, sat down, and gazed out across the estuary. Mary moved to a chest-high family tomb standing near the tree.

A diamond-shaped panel high on one side was inscribed with the word "Gedney." The magistrate of that name would be in here one day, Mary thought, as she walked round the tomb slowly. She would be seeing the magistrate of this name soon, at the trial. Was he a bad man, or a fool, or neither of these, but merely mistaken? Or *not* mistaken, except about George? Were there really witches in Salem? She and Peter had discussed this as they walked, as they had on their journey and with George, coming to no definite conclusions. All they knew for sure was that Burroughs was innocent and there must be some bizarre, unimaginable explanation as to why he'd been accused.

She left the tomb and walked toward the wall to join Peter. As she did so her attention was caught by a small headstone in the midst of simple wooden crosses. Kneeling down, she read the name "Mary Cory," the words "wife of Giles Cory" and a death date ten years before. She knew Giles Cory was in prison for witchcraft. If they hanged him, would they bury him here, with this wife? Mary remembered that his present wife, Martha, was also in prison. If they hanged *her*, would they bury her here too?

If they hanged George . . .

But they could not; she would free him. The sky darkened further: the smell of the air changed; a moment later, lightning and thunder struck at the same moment. She and Peter started running for the gate. As they passed through a drop plopped on Mary's forehead; as they ran up the street they were deluged. Mary leaped into the doorway of a house and hammered on the door. A moment later a fat-cheeked girl was gazing at them with her mouth open.

"Please, may we take shelter till the rain's passed?"

"Father!" the girl screamed, as if being attacked.

"Please, let us in!"

"Father!" The girl's voice rose as high as if the attack had turned murderous. Mary smelled ale, then saw a replica of the girl's head, thirty years older and male, over her shoulder.

"Who is it?"

"A man and lady saying can they come in." The girl sounded calmer now that her father was there.

"Don't mind Susannah," the man said. "She's not used to opening the door. Our maid left us. Come in."

Father and daughter scrambled out of the way of the rain-sodden visitors.

"It's the fireplace you'll be wanting," the man said. "Susannah, fetch some ale."

"Where is it?"

"In the pantry."

The girl hurried off, arms swinging.

"This way." The man led them into a room where a fire smacked and hissed. Their clothes at once gave off great clouds of steam. "It's not usually lit in the daytime but the maid took all the bread with her and Sue's having to bake more."

Susannah, returning empty-handed, shrieked with laughter.

"What's the matter, girl?" asked her father.

"They're like steam kettles!"

"Where's the ale?"

"Couldn't find it."

"Lord above." The man hurtled out of the room. The girl stood, smiling plumply, eyes shifting.

"He's got a bottle in his chamber," she said. "But I knew I shouldn't fetch *that*."

"Quite right," Peter said.

"Why did your maid leave?" Mary asked.

"She saw things."

"Saw things?"

"Shapes."

"Shapes?" Mary imagined oblongs and squares.

"You mean specters?" asked Peter.

"I see them too!"

"Do you?"

"Well, I did one time."

The man came back with a jug in one hand and some mugs in the other. "The creature left them in the lean-to."

"See, not in the pantry, not in the pantry!"

"Hold your tongue. You can pour."

As she did so her eyes kept shifting as though having trouble following the directions from her brain.

"Her mother died five years ago," the man said, as though by way of explanation. The girl handed Mary a mug so full it spilled over.

"Oooh, beg pardon! Quick, drink some!"

Mary did so, getting froth up her nose. Susannah carried another mug to Peter, who smiled at her. She blushed.

"Don't forget your old father!" the man cried.

"No, no, my old father!"

Soon he had a mug too.

"It is most kind of you to let us dry off by your fire," said Peter.

"I'm sorry it's lit."

"*Sorry?* We'd hardly get dry if it wasn't!"

"But you can't see it as it was. I assume that's what you came for."

"As it was?"

"When I saw the light in the chimney after George Burroughs witched me."

Mary lowered her mug. Susannah refilled it, causing it to spill again, this time on Mary's dress. The girl seized a cloth from a rail by the fire and rubbed, turning a large patch of brown fabric black.

"You are Elizar Keyser," Peter said.

"Why, yes, didn't you know?"

"No, we did not," said Peter. "Forgive us. You thought we'd come to look at your fireplace?"

"Why, yes! All sorts come to look at it!"

Mary was trying vainly to stop Susannah from rubbing. Peter gently took the cloth from her, then relieved Mary of her mug and put it on a table.

"What do you show them, precisely?" he asked Elizar.

"Why, where the light was." The man pointed. "Back there, above where the flames go. About the size of my hand. Quivered and shook till it disappeared up the chimney."

"What made you think Mister Burroughs caused it?"

"The way he stared. I knew he was witching me and then I saw the light and the other strange things." His eyes were open wide. "Things like jelly . . ."

"That used to be in the water," Peter finished for him.

"You were there! At the examination!"

"No, but we have heard about your evidence."

Elizar raised his fat chin. "Everyone's heard about it."

"Mr. Keyser, don't you think you might be mistaken?" Mary asked.

"*Mistaken? Mistaken?* I saw his look! I saw the jelly! My maid saw it too!"

"But he had not witched *her*!"

Elizar looked startled. This thought had clearly never occurred to him.

"Perhaps both you and she were mistaken. It is easy to imagine things."

"*Imagine* things! I don't *imagine* things!"

"Anyone can imagine things."

"I imagine things!" shouted Susannah.

"You don't know what it means," her father barked.

"Yes I do!"

"What?"

Her eyes swiveled.

"It means seeing things that aren't there," Peter told her.

"How can you see things that aren't there?" asked the girl.

"That is what imagining is."

"Then I don't!"

"Susannah's a good girl. She's never caused me any trouble," said Elizar.

"Unlike those girls in Salem Village," Peter said, as Susannah beamed till her cheeks bulged like two bookends, keeping the fierce smile within bounds.

"The girls in Salem Village? I didn't mean them! *They're* not causing trouble. It's the witches as are causing the trouble! Them women and George Burroughs!"

Mary kept quiet, knowing the danger she could put them in if she started to speak on this subject.

"Urrrhhh, those witches!" Susannah twisted her body, for a moment looking like one of the girls in her fits. Peter quickly finished his beer and said the rain seemed to have eased.

"No need to go yet! Susannah, refill his jug!"

"No, we really must go. Come, Mary." He put his hand on her arm.

"Thank you for the ale." Mary headed for the door. Peter thanked Keyser too and smiled kindly at his daughter, again making her turn red.

Outside Mary walked at top speed; Peter ran to catch up with her. The air was luminous after the rain, the sky light, the leaves of hedges and trees sparkling.

"This is what George is up against," Mary exclaimed.

"Drunken fools listened to."

"But truth will out."

"We'll make sure of it."

They walked on, deep in thought.

"Did he really see something?" Mary asked.

"No question. After six or seven mugs of ale."

"What was that jelly that used to be in the water?"

"Whatever it was, he saw it after knocking back three or four more."

"Would it look different from jelly that *had not* been in the water? Why would anyone put jelly in water?"

"Every family has its secrets."

"A Keyser custom."

"Brought from England."

They were smiling but the moment of lightheartedness was fleeting. Mary said, "At least that famous fireplace got us dry. Let us keep walking. Since the rain has stopped there's no need to go back yet."

"It must be dinnertime."

"Are you hungry?"

"Not very, thanks to Samuel Beadle's generous breakfast. Let's keep on along the shore. That way we'll have no trouble finding our way back again."

They passed a big house fronted by rosebushes. They had seen big houses in other parts of Salem but none as large as here.

"Who do these belong to?" Mary asked.

"Merchants. Ministers."

"I never saw anything like them."

"Nor I. They are finer than the finest in Boston."

"Look at that one."

They stopped. In a large open area on the top of an incline, overlooking the water, was a wooden structure whose two magnificent gables, at right angles to each other, four tall chimneys, and rows of fine windows proclaimed an assured, almost casual, preeminence.

"Whose is *that*?"

"It's not just bigger," Peter observed. "It's different. Simpler but more magnificent. Such large windows."

A serving woman with a pail emerged from the front door and Mary ran up the grassy incline.

"May I ask whose house this is?"

The startled girl said, "Why, it belongs to Mister Philip English!"

"Who is he?"

"Don't you know?" Suddenly the girl looked alarmed. "Are you one of them accusers?"

"Goodness no! We are just visitors admiring this house!"

"Mister English ain't here." The girl turned and hurried in.

"He is a merchant who heard there was a warrant out for his arrest," Peter said when she rejoined him. "Someone mentioned him in Beadle's. They said he'd fled."

"Ah, I remember that now. Why would anyone think a *merchant* was a witch?"

"If we knew that, we would probably know everything we need to about this witch hunt."

Mary turned to take a last look at the house before they walked on. "I thought Puritans lived simply."

"Only if they cannot afford to do otherwise."

"Do you still consider yourself a Puritan?"

"I still belong to the Roxbury church. But I must admit there is a great deal about the religion that puzzles me. It always has, but the doubts are more insistent now."

"What puzzles you most?"

"I suppose the doctrine that God decided at the beginning of time who will go to heaven and who to hell."

"So someone who has been good all his life could go to hell?"

"Yes, though I do not think many Puritans really believe that."

"How could they? It makes no sense."

"The Anglican faith is certainly easier to understand."

"Kinder too. Look what these saintly Puritans are doing to each other."

"I cannot argue with that."

They were silent a few moments. Then Peter said, "You are thinking about George."

"I am always thinking about George. At that moment I was thinking how strange it is that if he had been a minister in Salem he might be sitting in one of these mansions instead of that dungeon."

"He could never have been a minister in Salem."

"He was one in Salem Village."

"And hated it."

"I have never really understood why. We had so little time to talk about anything before he was arrested . . . I know they wanted to ordain him but he would not . . ." She stopped. "Is that connected with his arrest, do you think? Are the people there still angry? Are they pretending to believe he's a witch so as . . . ?" She could not finish the sentence

Peter stopped too. "I have been wondering."

"But those girls . . . Why should *they* care."

"They might just be pawns."

"Who of?"

"I cannot see the whole picture yet."

"Their fathers?"

"Maybe. They might be pawns too."

"Of the magistrates?"

"Possibly."

"What good would it do any of them, if George . . . ?"

"Ssshh." Peter glanced round but there was no one near. "What I am most afraid of is that the Boston rulers want him out of the way."

"Why would they? George has not the smallest interest in politics."

"He is a force for change just by being who he is. He is a living demonstration that there are different ways of being a good Puritan. He's famous and admired all through Massachusetts."

Mary almost whispered, "Can we save him?"

"We must."

Chapter Thirty

Salem Town
May 1692

AT THE BOTTOM OF THE STEPS THAT LED TO THE DUNGEONS, MARY'S resolve almost left her. She looked back up and was tempted to retreat. However, she quickly turned, raised her hand, and banged hard on the door. A keeper—not the one she'd met yesterday but a well-muscled man with two functioning, though watery, eyes—opened the door and at once stepped back for her to enter. He seemed to know who she was even before she told him her name and led her straight to Burroughs's cell. To her great relief he did not ask for money.

The day was brighter and the dungeon a little lighter than yesterday. Burroughs hugged and kissed her, then took the bread and cheese she'd brought and quickly devoured it. When he hugged her again the caresses quickly became intimate. Mary pulled away and, opening the little bag hanging round her waist, told George she had Peter's bark oil for his ankles and scissors for his nails and beard.

"Am I disgusting to you?"

"No! Of course not! I love you more than ever. This dungeon . . . I need a little time . . ."

"I have so longed for you!"

"I've longed for *you!*"

There was a bang on the door and the one-eyed keeper hobbled in, his face a network of lines.

"What d'you want?" George forgot, for once, not to speak as he felt.

"To make sure this lady is safe."

"I am her husband!"

"Wives aren't always safe with their husbands. You killed your first two, Mr. Burroughs."

"That's a lie!" Mary shouted.

"So *he* says. I think I'd better stay with you to make sure nothing happens."

"That's absurd! He loves me!"

The keeper kept grinning nastily and Mary realized her naïveté. She changed her tone. "Please be kind enough to leave me alone with my husband. It is no more than fair and natural."

The keeper leaned against the wall.

"I will give you a penny if you promise not to come back till tonight," Burroughs said.

"Tuppence."

An agreement was reached on a penny ha'penny for two hours. The jailer made short work of Burroughs's saying he had no way of knowing when their time was up.

"You'll know when I bang on the door."

Once the keeper was gone Burroughs told Mary again how much he had longed for her and her love for him overwhelmed her. Despite the horrors surrounding them, man and wife were as able as in the little room under the eaves to lose in ecstasy all sense of their separate bodies and souls.

They had put their clothes to rights, and were sitting in each other's arms against the wall, when the door creaked open and the keeper's leering face appeared.

"You said you'd knock!" George shouted.

"Forgot. Another penny and I'll go away again."

Mary got to her feet, saying she would come back after her midday dinner, perhaps with Peter, definitely with more food. The keeper made no objection. Mary guessed he would wait to try to extort more money until she returned, and hoped to outwit him with coaxing and promises.

At the meal in Beadle's most of the same guests were present as at the two breakfasts they'd had there, and there were new faces too. During more talk of the witch scare a recent arrival mentioned Burroughs, marveling that he had been brought for trial all the way from Maine.

"*They're* from Maine," said the pinched-faced woman, nodding toward Mary and Peter. They glanced at each other. They had discussed whether and when they should reveal their true identities since this couple and some other guests were becoming increasingly suspicious. They had been unable to give details of their family business in Salem and knew no Cheevers or Whites in the town. Someone had mentioned there were Cheevers in Salem Village and was surprised when Mary had to admit she did not know them. The pair feared dangerous anger if they were caught out in lies.

Peter now, after apologizing for having previously misled such good and trusting people, told them the truth.

The reaction was surprisingly subdued. One man asked how Burroughs was faring in prison and said there had probably been a mistake. Many people seemed embarrassed or bewildered. However, the sour couple got up and left the table.

Talking more freely once they were gone, some people said they did not know what to think, wondering why Burroughs was imprisoned if there were not strong evidence against him, others suggesting the accusing girls might have confused him with another man. One guest ventured that the devil might have appeared to them in Burroughs's form. Mary did not try to argue George's case, for now wanting information, not converts, and to avoid causing hostility that might lead to an accusation of witchcraft against *her*.

Someone remarked that the couple who had just left clearly thought Burroughs guilty.

"'Tis no matter what they think," said the leather goods maker they had talked to their first morning. "They are going back to Andover today."

"Why were they here?" Mary asked.

"Courting a rich relative who's dying. Hoping he'd remember them in his will. He left the land of the living the day before yesterday."

"Did they get anything?"

"Not a farthing."

Mary could not but smile.

"Did *they* tell you this?"

"No, I heard it from a friend of the relative I sold a couple of saddles to. He said their miserable faces by his bed day and night probably speeded his end."

That afternoon the keeper let them into Burroughs's cell without demanding payment and Mary realized he was expert at gauging when extortion would succeed and when it wouldn't. She resolved that by playing the game carefully she would gain almost as much time as she wanted with her husband at a price she could afford.

Burroughs talked of his certainty of Mary's persuading Sewall to persuade Governor Phips to free him without trial. Peter tried to temper this optimism but Burroughs's warm memories of his friend weighed more than that friend's silence at his hearing and failure to visit him in jail.

Neither Peter nor Mary talked of the danger of her being accused as a witch if she made herself known to anyone directly involved in the trials. George's faith in his friend was too great for him to think of this.

The next day was the one appointed for fasting and prayer. George had observed sardonically that for him every day was one of fasting and prayer. Or had been, until Mary came to Salem, he added, hugging her tightly.

Mary and Peter stayed in the tavern except to go to the services in the meetinghouse. To do anything else would have aroused too much suspicion. George understood and approved, in these circumstances, their not visiting him for twenty-four hours.

By the time of the first trial, after another six days, Burroughs and Mary felt as close again as though they'd never been apart.

Chapter Thirty-One

Salem Town
June 1692

BRIDGET, STOUT AND BEWILDERED, WAS THE FIXED POINT AMID chaos. She stared about her in the dock mounted on the platform at the end of the room. Constables were sorting witnesses from spectators, directing the first to the front rows of benches, the second to those further back; the room was growing noisier and more crowded by the moment. It was on the second floor of the Town House, in the middle of Town Street, on an island of well-trodden grass, with horses and pedestrians passing or loitering on either side. The ground floor was normally used as a school and forty or so boys, given the day off, were among those now finding seats. Their pushing, wrestling, and bursts of stifled laughter added to the mayhem. As the temperature rose, people fanned themselves with their kerchiefs or summonses or hands. Men and women sat together, unlike in the meetinghouse. Some were uncorking bottles of beer and unwrapping meat pies, having left home in Salem Village or further off at first light. Below the platform stood a table and bench gradually filling with neatly dressed men, all respectable farmers and tradesmen, looking self-important, apprehensive, or dazed. The air seemed almost to shimmer with mounting excitement. The examinations had been thrilling enough but now a woman with a long-standing reputation for witchcraft was on trial for her life.

Mary and Peter squeezed onto a bench near the back, Mary apologizing to the rabbit-toothed woman she had obliged to move up. As he sat down Peter was forced to pull his knees up so far, they almost reached his chin. Mary was surprised to see that the accused witch did not have the agitated, scrawny look she had expected but was portly and passive. On the shortest of necks was an unusually large head crammed into a cap far too small for it. With heavy jowls, a slightly open mouth, and heavy-lidded pale blue eyes, one drooping lower than the other, she appeared to understand little of what was going on.

Two men mounted the platform. Peter told Mary the thinner one was William Stoughton and the fatter Samuel Sewall. Four other men, one of great height and massive bulk, followed them up as three more came through the door.

"*More* judges?" queried Mary.

"These last must be ministers," said Peter.

The rabbit-toothed woman sitting next to Mary turned and stared. "You don't know those gentlemen?"

They were now also mounting the platform.

"I'm afraid not," Mary said.

In a tone of incredulity, the woman explained they were Samuel Parris of Salem Village, Nicholas Noyes of Salem, and John Hale of Beverly. The judges arranged themselves at a table next to the dock, the ministers at a smaller one next to that.

"Which is which?" Mary asked.

"The darkest one's Reverend Parris."

He was staring round, underlip jutting.

"It was in his house it started. The stouter one's Reverend Noyes and the one he's talking to is Reverend John Hale."

This last man, white-haired and handsome, was glancing around with a kindly, courteous air.

"Who are the other judges besides Stoughton and Sewall?" Mary asked Peter. He did not know. Mary asked the woman.

"Where have you been living?"

"In Maine."

"Even in Maine you must have heard of John Hathorne!"

"Well, we may have heard of him but we do not know what he looks like. Which one is he?"

"The big one. That wig must have cost him a fortune. The others are Mr. Gedney, Mr. Richards, and Mr. Saltonstall. All eminent justices. But Mr. Hathorne . . ." She shook her head with an admiration amounting to awe. "He examined all them witches, up in Salem Village." She lowered her voice. "See that rich gentleman . . ." She nodded her head sideways. Mary peeped round her to see at the end of the bench a

well-built man of medium height in a white neckerchief and velvet
jacket and breeches, with a look of intense concentration on his dark-
complexioned face. She whispered, "That is Nathaniel Cary. Mr.
Hathorne examined his wife!"

"He looks like a merchant."

"He *is* a merchant! From Charlestown! But all his riches didn't
stop his wife being seized as a witch. At her examination Mr. Hathorne
treated her no different from a farmer's wife or beggar."

"Where is she now?"

"Why, in prison, of course." The woman grinned with pleasure
and Mary turned away.

A moment later, when a tall man shifted along the bench in front,
blocking her view, she stood up. The jurymen were all seated, squeezed
together at their table below the platform; the space between them and
the front benches was being kept clear by the constables. Judge
Stoughton rose and Mary sat down again.

"We will begin our proceedings with a prayer," the judge enunciated as if the court were full of foreigners who could scarcely speak
English. "Mr. Parris, would you be so good?"

Parris stood and bowed his head. Everyone else on the platform,
apart from Bridget who seemed not to hear, bowed theirs too, Sewall's
three chins squashing his collar. Parris, in mellifluous tones, apologized
for New England's sins, asked for forgiveness, and begged for God's
help and guidance to the court in its endeavor to rid the province of
evil. After the "Amen," he sat down. Stoughton said, "Clerk of the
court, have Bridget Bishop take the oath."

A twitching creature with thin hair mounted the platform and approached the dock with a Bible. Peter whispered that this was Stephen
Sewall, Samuel's brother. Mary marveled at the lack of similarity.
Stephen was as spare as Samuel was ample. He had not one chin, let
alone three. He placed the Bible on the ledge in front of Bridget.

"Place your l-left hand on the book and h-hold up your r-right."

There were some titters, quickly hushed. Bridget Bishop apparently had not heard. Stephen Sewall repeated the order more loudly,
though with as much stuttering, and she suddenly banged her left palm
down on the book as though swatting a fly. There were shocked, disap-
proving noises.

"Right hand!" someone called. "Put it up!"

Stephen pushed her hand in the air, then told her to repeat after him that she swore by Almighty God that the evidence she would give was the truth, the whole truth, and nothing but the truth. She stared at him. But when he declaimed, "I s-swear by Almighty G-God," she heard, or remembered, and repeated the words in a loud, droning voice. When the procedure was completed, William Stoughton asked her how she pled. The alleged devil's accomplice cupped her ear. The judge repeated the question more loudly.

"I can hear!" cried Bridget Bishop, affronted.

"Then answer!"

"What was the question?"

There were titters, shouts, and guffaws. Stoughton repeated with even greater clarity and force, "Do you, Bridget Bishop, plead guilty or not guilty?"

"Not . . ." croaked Bishop, then cleared her throat and shouted, "Guilty!"

"Did you say guilty?" inquired Stoughton maliciously.

"*Not* guilty!" she shouted angrily. The judge called, "Dr. Barton!"

A man with unnaturally black hair mounted the platform and was also sworn in. Stoughton said, "I believe you have this morning performed an examination of the body of this prisoner?"

"I have, your honor, together with nine midwives." He pointed down and Mary stood up to see on the front bench a row of wide backs, bulging necks, and tightly tied caps. She sat down, wondering, if George came to trial, whether this collection of females would examine *his* body. They would find no marks except for a small knife scar made by an Indian in the attack in Maine long ago. But he would *not* come to trial. It had become clear even in these first minutes that justice was unlikely to be served here. She resolved anew that she would convince Samuel Sewall of George's innocence before he was put in the dock.

"And you also performed an examination on the bodies of five other prisoners?" inquired Stoughton.

Bridget was again cupping her ear.

"Just so, your honor," said the doctor.

"And this process was to ascertain if there existed any teats on the prisoner's body for the feeding of imps, toads, or other familiars?"

"Yes."

"Pray tell the court what you found."

"By diligent search we discovered a preternatural excrescence of flesh between the pudendum and anus."

There were gasps.

"In which prisoners did you find this excrescence of flesh?"

"Bridget Bishop, Rebecca Nurse, and Elizabeth Proctor."

"Are such excrescences usual in women?"

"No. They were unlike anything we found in the other women we searched."

"You may stand down."

Amid the muttering and whispering Bridget shouted, "What did he say?" No one enlightened her. The judges consulted, Sewall's chins vigorously wobbling. But a sudden commotion at the back of the courtroom made everyone turn. Up the aisle strode a marshal with a staff followed by ten or twelve women and girls. Looking purposeful, they walked to the space under the platform, then, staring up at the prisoner, suddenly, all together, began a performance the likes of which Mary had not been able to imagine despite George's descriptions. He had not conveyed how unnatural, even impossible, their actions and postures looked as they turned their necks almost to face backward or pushed their tongues out and down to their chins or corkscrewed their bodies.

"Is Bridget meant to be causing this?" Mary whispered.

"I believe so."

The prisoner gazed at the girls with an amazement that swiftly changed to contempt. Judge Stoughton spoke to the marshal, who spoke to a constable, who hauled her from the dock and down the steps. Her underskirt was hanging lower than her dress and her cap was too small for her head, giving her the look of being too stupid or slovenly to clothe herself properly. She struggled but the marshal kept his grip and pushed her up to one of the girls, at that moment standing still but with her arms and wrists twisted as though palsied. He pressed Bishop's hand against her shoulder. The accuser at once untwisted her upper limbs and walked away.

"What on earth happened there?" Mary asked.

"The touch test. The idea is that the power of the witch, causing the girl to have fits, flows back into the witch with that touch, so the girl becomes well again."

Bridget was taken to the next girl. The result was the same. At last all the girls stood normally and Bridget was hauled back up to the dock. The judges leaned toward each other to talk.

Mary stood up again to take a good look at this collection of females. They varied widely in age and appearance, ranging from children to teenagers to middle-aged women to an ancient crone sprawled on the floor, skirts above her knees. There were just two pretty girls in the group, one of whom, Mary guessed from her age, must be Mercy Lewis. The other pretty one was plump, with enormous blue eyes. Next to Mercy was a child of about twelve with a prominent nose. She suddenly started writhing again and the others followed suit. Stoughton sharply ordered Bridget to turn her eyes away from them. When she failed to do so, the judge shouted more loudly. She jerked her head to look at the wall and the girls at once stilled. Someone tugged at Mary's dress from behind and she sat again. She whispered to Peter, "How could they explain that could happen, without their doing the touch test all over again?"

"I have no idea what Stoughton's explanation would be," Peter replied. "There is a great deal about all this that baffles me."

"Most baffling is how those girls do those things."

"Ann Putnam!" called Stoughton. "Does the prisoner afflict you?"

The large-nosed girl cried, "She oftentimes bites me and urges me to write my name in her book."

Bridget Bishop, her gaze going again to the girls, clasped her hands. Ann Putnam clasped hers and fell to the floor with a scream.

"Bridget Bishop!" Stoughton shouted. "Look away! Everyone can see that when you look at them you torture them!"

She jerked her head away but immediately forgot she was supposed not to look at the accusers and did so, causing more screams. Stoughton shouted the same question to each girl as to Ann, and each shouted the same answer. While this was going on, it came to Mary that the underlying reason Bridget was here was that her stupidity, obstinacy, and deafness got on everyone's nerves.

"She's no more a witch than I am," Mary whispered.

"Ssshhh!"

"The girls are mad or pretending."

"*Sssshhh!*"

The loathing for the prisoner in the courtroom was palpable. Peter put his mouth to Mary's ear to say softly, "If Stoughton gave the word, these people would tear Bridget to pieces. If they heard what you are saying, they'd tear *you* to pieces."

The girls calmed down enough to speak and, one by one, recounted tales of the prisoner's specter taking them to the river and threatening to drown them or meeting with other witches in a field and taking the sacrament from the devil. Suddenly the girl Stoughton had addressed as Ann Putnam cried out that the ghosts of the people Bridget Bishop had murdered were appearing in the courtroom. Bridget, for once catching the words, violently shook her head; the afflicted shook theirs.

"Hang her!" cried someone.

"Cursed witch!"

"Devil!"

Stoughton did nothing to silence this. Bridget shook her fist. All the girls shook theirs. Bridget stamped her foot. They stamped theirs. The crowd roared.

"Turn the prisoner away from them!" shouted Stoughton. The marshal did so; the girls fell silent.

"The afflicted may go now," said the judge.

They were led from the room, some smiling, the old woman waving.

The next part of the trial consisted of a series of male witnesses telling rambling tales of Bridget's having harmed them by witchcraft by giving them money that disappeared from their pockets or half-smothering them in their beds or killing their cows.

"Why are they bringing all *this* in?" Mary whispered. "She is not charged with any of this, just torturing the girls."

"They want a conviction. They will use anything. Don't expect logic."

The last witnesses were a father and son, standing on the platform together, who said they'd been employed by Bridget to help take down the cellar wall where she had lived, and found several poppets made of rags with headless pins stuck in them.

"How do you explain this?" Stoughton shouted at Bridget.

"Explain what?" She cupped her ear.

"These poppets."

"What poppets?"

"You deny them?"

"Deny what?"

"These poppets."

"What poppets?"

"Bridget Bishop, do you know what poppets are?"

"Of course!" Bridget sounded aggrieved at this suggestion of ignorance.

"Then please explain why you had poppets."

"I never saw no poppets."

"These men testify they saw poppets in the cellar wall of your house."

"I don't know what they saw."

"They say they saw poppets."

"What poppets?"

The crowd roared with rage mixed with laughter. Mary whispered, "Doesn't he know walls of poor houses are often stuffed with rags? They might easily look like poppets to men who thought a witch lived there."

"You ought to be her counsel."

"She ought to *have* counsel."

"Defendants are not allowed counsel in capital cases."

"But it is in capital cases they need them the most!"

When the father and son descended the platform Mary assumed the trial was over bar the verdict and sentencing. But Stoughton called Dr. Barton again and ordered him and his nine midwives to perform another physical examination on the body of the prisoner. He explained that the court would remain sitting until he came back with the results. A marshal explained this to Bridget and, despite her struggles, managed with the help of a constable to drag her down the steps and the aisle. The doctor and midwives followed them out.

During the long, hot wait, Stoughton stared ahead while the other judges talked to one another and the spectators whispered, muttered, yawned, groaned, and finished their pies. Peter stretched his long legs sideways into the aisle and Mary's thoughts turned, as always, to George.

"I wonder if I can catch Samuel Sewall as he's leaving the courtroom."

"Better to go to his brother's house later."

"He might go straight back to Boston."

"No. It would be night before he got there."

"Perhaps I should try to catch John Hale. He looks as though he might listen to reason. He must have some influence."

"Not much, as a local minister, but he'd be easier to approach. You could talk to him and then go to Stephen Sewall's house."

At last the doctor, midwives, and Bridget returned. The doctor announced that the preternatural excrescence on Bridget's body could no longer be found and gave as his expert opinion that it must have been sucked dry by an imp.

Stoughton turned to the jury.

"Gentlemen of the jury, the time has come for you to consider your verdict. As you are no doubt aware, the indictments of this prisoner state that by her wicked arts, witchcraft, and sorceries within the township of Salem, Mercy Lewis, Elizabeth Hubbard, and Ann Putnam have been hurt, tortured, afflicted, pined, consumed, wasted, and tormented. Now, gentlemen of the jury, you may have observed that the bodies of these and the other afflicted persons are not in fact pined, consumed, and wasted. What you are to consider is whether the said afflicted suffer in a way that might naturally lead to their bodies becoming pined, consumed, and wasted. This is pining and consuming in the sense of the law."

Stoughton went on to summarize the rest of the evidence in a way that left no doubt he believed it proved Bridget was a witch.

The jury left the room. They soon brought back a guilty verdict. Stoughton delivered the death sentence.

Outside the courthouse the air was almost as sultry as within. Mary and Peter positioned themselves on a slope leading up to a fine house, across the grass and road. They had a good view of the crowd still emerging. People were heading off on foot toward the center of Salem and Boston Road, which led north to Salem Village and other towns. There was a long wait before the important people started to appear, the first being Dr. Barton followed by his midwives, the next Nicholas Noyes. Then the accusers came out in a bunch and behind them Samuel Parris, talking to someone half-hidden. Parris moved and Mary saw his companion was John Hale. She walked quickly down the hill; Peter followed, saying, "Wait till he's alone."

She stopped. They watched as Parris and Hale talked some more, then Parris moved off behind the Town House and Hale headed for a large dwelling beyond it. Mary set off again after him; Peter stayed behind. She caught up with Hale some yards from the house.

"Reverend John Hale?"

The pastor turned and stopped. "Good day."

"May I speak to you privately?"

"To what good fortune do I owe this request from such a beautiful lady?"

"Alas, not good fortune. My husband has been arrested for witchcraft. After watching this trial, I am gravely concerned about his chances of justice."

"If we are to speak of this, it should indeed be in private. Do you live in Salem?"

"I am lodging here."

"At Beadle's?"

"Aye."

He explained that he had some business to attend to, and must travel back to Beverly later that evening, but could spare her half an hour, an hour from now. Thomas Beadle would let them use a private room without charge. Mary should arrange this, giving his name, and he would meet her there.

"May I ask *your* name?"

"Mary."

"Your last name?"

"I'll tell you at Beadle's." She smiled. Hale looked troubled and Mary was afraid he would renege on his agreement. But instead he too smiled, with great charm, and said, "Then I shall remain in suspense for an hour." He bowed and walked off to the mansion he had been heading for.

The change in the innkeeper's demeanor toward Mary, when she asked for a private sitting room for the minister John Hale, was so extreme it was comical, even in the midst of worry and dread. He had treated her and Peter with marked coldness since he realized they were not only poor but the wife and friend of a man in jail on charges of witchcraft. His look changed whenever he saw them, its affability curdling like cream in the sun. They wondered whether he was seeking a pretext to ask them to leave. However, now he was all deferential friendliness. Leading Mary to the most comfortable sitting room in the inn, he pulled a chair to the window overlooking a yard full of roses. He offered her cider, for free. She declined.

When John Hale walked in she was seated, having tidied her hair as best she could without a looking glass and resettled her cap. He bowed, telling her not to get up. They exchanged greetings and he lowered himself onto a chair facing hers, a few feet away.

"Will you take a glass of wine?"

"No, thank you, Mister Hale."

He was in his early sixties but still handsome, with small yet distinguished features in a face whose symmetrical lines only added to its charm. His complexion, though pale, looked healthy and his hair, though white, covered his head.

"Let us come straight to the matter in hand since our time together is so limited. You say your husband has been arrested for witchcraft?"

"Aye!"

"Do you believe him to be innocent?"

"I know him to be innocent."

"Has he been examined?"

"Aye, and jailed."

"On what evidence?"

"The accusing girls'."

"Was anything else brought against him?"

"Bizarre claims that he is unnaturally strong."

"But this is George Burroughs!"

"Aye!"

"You should have told me!"

"I was afraid you would not see me."

"He is a leader of witches."

"That's not true!"

"How can you know?"

"He's my *husband*!"

He rubbed his chin with a knuckle. "How long have you been married?"

"Two weeks."

He smiled. "How long were you engaged?"

"Two weeks. Are you suggesting he might be a witch without his wife knowing it?"

"My dear, I am simply attempting to establish the facts."

"The facts are that he is a good, brave, conscientious minister who has battled the Indians to everyone's admiration and amazement as well as writing wonderful sermons and never sparing himself in tending to his flock. They would do anything for him. It is incomprehensible anyone should think he is in league with the devil."

"I was at his examination myself."

"Then you heard all those lies. That is what they were. My husband's very strong but I have never seen him do anything more than what is humanly possible. None of those men ever even said they had *seen* him lift a gun or a barrel of molasses with one finger. They had just heard others talk of it."

"John Putnam said he saw him."

"He was lying. He bears him a grudge. Mr. Hale, believe me, my husband is as innocent as you are."

"Mrs. Burroughs, how do you account for all the things the girls accuse him of, the tortures, the asking them to sign the devil's book, the promise of riches when Satan conquers this land?"

"Perhaps the devil comes to them disguised as my husband."

"The devil cannot disguise himself as an innocent man."

"How can you know that?"

Hale looked surprised, but then smiled, again with great charm.

"It is generally agreed among persons famous for piety and learning."

"Whatever those persons may think, he must have disguised himself as my husband unless the girls are mistaken about seeing him. Or worse than mistaken. One of them, Mercy Lewis, lived with his family in Maine when her parents were killed. Perhaps *she* holds a grudge."

"That is to say she may be lying! That would make her a murderer."

"Because my husband could hang on her evidence?"

"Quite so."

"She may not see the consequences so clearly. She may be acting on impulse. She is young."

The reverend leaned forward, again smiling charmingly.

"Would you like to meet her? Perhaps she can enlighten you. Or perhaps *you* can enlighten *her*."

"Meet her? Can you arrange it?"

"By all means."

"Yes, I *would* like to meet her."

"Can you travel to Salem Village tomorrow? It is a long way, nigh ten miles."

"I would walk much further than that to free George."

"Then I will arrange for Mercy and yourself to meet privately at Ingersoll's tavern at, say, twelve o'clock."

"Thank you, Mr. Hale. I am sorry not to have convinced you my husband is innocent, but that makes your attempt to help me all the kinder."

"You will see your husband before you go, I assume?"

"I will go to see him now."

"He can tell you the way to the village."

George gazed at Mary with eager hope.

"Remind Mercy of how I talked to her and prayed with her when she lived in our house. She need only tell the court she is mistaken and the case will be dropped."

"But the other girls . . ."

"They will follow her lead."

"There are those girls who have confessed they are witches and you made them so."

"If the accusing girls say they are mistaken, the confessors will recant."

When Mary got back to Beadle's from the prison, she found Peter talking to the merchant who had been pointed out to her in the courtroom. He wore the same velvet jacket and breeches as then but a new, or newly washed and pressed, white neckerchief. He also wore the same look of intense concentration, changing to a vulnerable, startled expression as Peter greeted Mary. Both men rose. Peter introduced her to Nathaniel Cary and asked how she'd fared with John Hale. Before she could answer Cary pulled up a chair for her and called for more cider.

"Or would you prefer wine?" he asked.

"No, cider, thank you."

"And some cakes," Cary added to the servant.

"You must let us pay our share," Peter said.

"On no account. Your means are limited, I know. I am a rich man, though alas my wealth seems of little use to me now. It has not helped my poor wife."

He looked so distressed that Mary put her hand on his arm, saying, "I am sure you are doing all you can."

Nathaniel nodded. The cider came and, after a few sips, Mary gave a brief account of her meeting with Hale.

"I will go with you to Salem Village," Peter said.

"Now I must tell you *my* story," Cary said. "You'll soon understand why I wish to do so at once."

"There need be no reason," Mary said. "We want to hear it."

"I would have waited," said Cary. "But, as it happens, 'tis good I tell it now." He sighed. "Two weeks ago I heard that my wife had been named as a witch. I decided we should investigate the matter so we rode to Salem Village from Charlestown to find an examination about to take place. Everything we saw in the meetinghouse was just the same as what we witnessed today, except in some ways worse. When the prisoners touched the accusers, supposedly to cure them of their fits, Mr. Hathorne pronounced the girls cured before anyone could see any change!"

Mary stared at him. "What, before they went quiet?"

"Just so."

"But that is outright deception!"

"Sshhh!" Nathaniel glanced around but the only other guests were out of earshot.

"Go on," Mary urged.

"As we sat there, no one paid any heed to us, except once and that was when one of the girls came and asked my wife her name. During a pause in the proceedings, I talked to John Hale."

"John Hale!" Mary was taken completely by surprise. Peter nodded, as though he had guessed.

"I knew him a little. Mr. Hale said he would arrange for my wife and me to meet privately with the girl who had accused her, Abigail Williams."

Mary gasped.

"He told us we could meet her at Samuel Parris's house alone. But when the examination was finished, he informed us we could not meet there after all but must go to the tavern. We waited there. At last Abigail Williams came in, not by herself but with all the girls. They started tumbling about, crying, 'Cary!' Then a marshal came in with a warrant in his hand from the justices for my wife. They were sitting in the next room, waiting for her."

"Unbelievable," Mary said.

"Hale tricked you," Peter added.

"If I had not experienced it myself, I would never have believed it. I had thought him a decent, honorable man. I believe he *was*, till corrupted by this witch hunt."

"I see why you had to tell us this story at once," Mary said.

"You must not go to Salem Village tomorrow."

"Why would he do this? Why would he want your wife arrested as a witch? And why me?"

"I cannot understand it except to assume that he's carried away by his enthusiasm for rooting out witches. He believes those girls completely, it seems. As does Stoughton and the other judges, it appears. But why Abigail Williams accused my wife, I cannot imagine. She did not know her; she had never even met her."

"I have not even been suspected yet as far as I know," Mary said.

"Perhaps Hale thinks if your husband is a witch, *you* must be one. Luckily he seems not to think the same way about me. Of course, men do not fall under suspicion so easily."

"If it were not for you, I would soon have been heading for jail."

"I had my concerns about Hale when I found out whose house he was visiting," said Peter.

"Whose?" Mary asked.

"John Hathorne's."

Nathaniel gazed away from them. "When I saw how they treated my wife at her examination I thought nothing could be worse, but then I saw how they treated her in jail."

"What happened at the examination?" Peter asked.

"They made her stand with her arms stretched out at the sides till she was in agony. I asked to be allowed to hold them up for her but they refused. She asked me . . ." He stopped and shook his head, then cleared his throat. "She asked me to wipe the tears from her eyes, and the sweat from her face, which I did, but then she asked if she might lean on me, saying she was going to faint, and Hathorne said since she had strength enough to torment the girls, she must have strength enough to stand."

"Such cruelty," breathed Mary.

"I protested but Hathorne said if I could not be silent he would send me from the room. Then an Indian slave was brought in who fell and tumbled about like a hog. When asked who tormented him, he answered that my wife did. Hathorne ordered her to touch him, with her head turned away, and the constable guided her hand but the slave seized it and pulled her down on the floor and rolled her around in a most barbarous manner."

"How could you endure it?" cried Peter.

"I could not, and shouted to them to stop, and said God would have vengeance! But they seized me and held me, and Hathorne read out the order to send her to prison."

"Did they let you go with her?" Mary asked.

"Yes, but we did not go that evening. I got a room for us at Ingersoll's, at great cost even though it was a tiny one with no beds in it. Ingersoll is doing well out of this."

"As are a lot of people, one way and another," Peter said.

"Did she go to jail next morning?"

"Aye, to Boston. But then I managed to move her to Cambridge, thinking she might be better treated there, as well as being closer to home. But the jailer put chains on her and she went into convulsions till

I thought she would die, I really thought she would die, and I begged that the chains be taken off, but in vain. She is still in them." He turned away from them, quickly wiping his eyes. "I came here to see if there was hope of her acquittal. But, as we saw, there is none."

"I am planning to talk to Samuel Sewall," Mary said. "He is George's old friend from Harvard. I will convince him George is innocent, and your wife is innocent too."

"As I suspected, he is staying with his brother, Stephen," said Peter. "I made inquiries earlier. He will be there at least till dinnertime tomorrow."

"I know the house," said Cary.

Mary leaped up. "Take me now."

"It is too late at night," Peter said.

"We will go tomorrow straight after breakfast," Nathaniel promised.

But the morning next Mary went first to the prison to tell her husband what Cary had said about Hale. Burroughs was incredulous, then outraged. But Mary had a more encouraging piece of news, which was that one of the judges at Bridget Bishop's trial, Nathaniel Saltonstall, had resigned from the bench. Mary told George of her plan to go from here to see Sewall. He reminded her of all the good times he had had with his friend and the warmth Samuel had invariably shown him, until now. For which no doubt there were reasons he did not yet understand.

They prayed, then sat holding each other, drawing strength from their love. But both were aware every moment that the woman due to be hanged within a week lay in the next cell.

Chapter Thirty-Two

Salem Town
June 1692

MARY BANGED AT THE DARK WOODEN DOOR UNDER A LARGE PORCH. The sky had darkened as she had walked from the prison to Beadle's, where she had collected Peter and Nathaniel Cary, who now waited at a distance to see her admitted. She stepped back to survey the front of the house and a raindrop plopped on her forehead. Wiping it away, she moved under the porch again. She had been repeatedly mending and brushing her clothes since arriving in Salem and, despite the drenching at Keyser's, they still looked respectable. But if they continued to be deluged and dried she would end up seeming a beggar. She banged again, harder. There was a creaking and rattling, the door opened, and a flustered, bushy-eyebrowed young woman with floury hands stared out at her.

"What do you want?" The girl's tone and air were rushed not impertinent.

"I wish to speak to Mr. Sewall, if I may."

"Mr. Stephen Sewall?"

"No, Mr. Samuel Sewall."

"Aye, most visitors are for him." The girl wiped her hands on the large apron tied round her waist. "What's your name?"

Mary told her. She assumed that in this case the chances of being granted an interview would be greater if her identity were known.

"Come in."

Mary followed her through the door.

"Wait there."

The servant ran across the hall and up a mahogany staircase with curved banisters. Mary stared round in amazement. The silver platters ranged along high shelves and the vases full of flowers and rugs woven from red and blue thread created an effect of immaculate opulence she would have assumed could only exist in a palace in England. She had been surprised by the chairs, carved settles, occasional cushions, and polished wooden floors in Beadle's tavern but the furnishings here surpassed those as much as they surpassed the furnishings of her father's house in York. Yet she felt uncowed by the splendor she saw; she walked round the staircase and peered down a corridor. A girl of about eight or nine was disappearing through a door.

"G-good morning. I believe you wish to see my b-brother?"

She swung round. Stephen Sewall's chinless face with sharp features and red, spotty skin looked alarmed.

"Yes, very much, Mr. Sewall. Thank you for receiving me."

"Your name is M-Mary B-Burroughs?"

"Yes. I am the wife of the Reverend George Burroughs, your brother's old friend from Harvard."

Stephen seemed at a loss as to what was appropriate behavior toward a woman whose husband was a friend of his brother yet suspected of witchcraft. His eyes showed bewilderment and he scratched the back of his head. Like his brother, he wore no wig, but to greater disadvantage since his hair was much scantier. Mary guessed he had wanted to confirm her identity and discover why she was here, and what her state of mind was, before disturbing his eminent sibling. Presumably the maid had orders to inform him first of all visitors.

"Did you know my husband too?" she asked.

"Oh, n-no, no, I was at H-Harvard five years after Samuel." He paused. "I was only there a few months. I left to be a m-merchant's apprentice." He said this as though he was afraid of appearing to pretend to be something he wasn't.

"The apprenticeship certainly led to success." Mary glanced round the hallway with an admiring smile.

"Th-thank you!"

"And you have a young family! I saw your little daughter a moment ago."

"My d-daughter! Heavens! W-where?"

"At the end of that corridor."

"W-what was she doing there?" He hurried to the staircase to peer down the passage. "She's not there now! W-was anyone with her?"

"No, she seemed to be by herself."

"I must g-go and find her!"

"But Mr. Sewall, why should she *not* be by herself? At least, when there are others in the house?"

"A child of two?"

"This girl was about eight!"

"That is not my daughter!"

"She did not look like a maidservant."

"That is Betty Parris!"

"Betty Parris?"

"The daughter of the Reverend Samuel Parris. The first g-girl to be afflicted by the witches, along with her cousin Abigail W-Williams, who is dead now."

"Why is she here?"

Her f-father sent her to us, to be out of the way of the trouble. Samuel P-Parris and I are d-distant relations."

"Are you? I did not know. Is Betty still afflicted?"

"No, praise be to God. John Hale came to talk to her and she has been better ever since."

"John Hale?"

"The minister in Beverly."

"I have met him."

"Have you?"

Mary quickly calculated how to use this fact to best advantage and said, "He graciously offered to arrange for me to meet one of my husband's accusers, Mercy Lewis."

"Did he?"

"It was his kindness toward me that emboldened me to visit your brother."

This worked just as she had hoped.

"I see. If you will be good enough to wait here, I will ask my brother if he has leisure to see you."

"Thank you!"

He vanished up the stairs.

Despite the speed of Stephen's departure the wait was long. Mary gazed round the opulent hallway and decided that once she got George out of jail, she would try to persuade him to start a new life back in

England. She had no wish to go back to the dangers and hardships of Maine but could hardly imagine settling in Massachusetts after what had happened. Could he work in England as a Puritan minister, she wondered? Things had changed for the better for Puritans there since the first immigrants left, she knew, but she was not sure how they stood nowadays.

At last Stephen returned.

"H-he'll see you. Come up."

Mary suddenly felt nervous. Stephen ushered her ahead of him up the stairs, along a corridor and through a door. The judge was sitting behind a small desk, reading a document. He looked up, then stood. His fleshy cheeks were framed by long, thinning hair, white at the top but darkening to gray where it billowed out at the ends like waves approaching the beach.

"How do you do? Please sit down." The eyes deep in the puffy face were cautious. They shifted away from her as Stephen Sewall, flurried and panting, pulled up a chair. The great man's patience was clearly stretched nearly to breaking point by this bumbling brother. Once Mary sat, the judge did too. Stephen excused himself, with much stammering, and left.

"Thank you so much for receiving me."

"What can I do for you, Mrs. Burroughs?" The judge sat stiffly, looking at her with an expression suggesting he was keeping all his kindness and humanity under careful control.

"Nothing for myself, Mr. Sewall. I have come to ask you to do something for my husband, whom I know you were friends with at Harvard."

"Alas, I have no power to alleviate his conditions." The judge looked away.

"I do not ask you to alleviate his conditions."

The wary eyes met hers but at once again shifted. "Then for what *are* you asking me?"

"To free him. He is innocent."

"Free him? How can I free him?" The judge seemed suddenly almost as flurried as his brother. "He is in prison by the magistrate's order!"

"But he's innocent!"

"If he's innocent, he has nothing to fear!"

"I wish I could believe that."

"He is to be tried by a bench of five eminent judges and a jury of Puritan church members."

"Judges make mistakes. So do juries. Let me convince you of his innocence. Then I know you'll want to help him."

"He must be tried according to the law!" Sewall picked up the document on his desk and put it down again. Mary fixed her eyes on his face but he would not look at her.

"Mr. Sewall, I know I am but a woman without legal knowledge, but precisely because I'm a woman I have a better understanding of other women than a man could. I know how confused and mistaken young girls and even older women can be. I fervently believe that the judges should beware of giving the girls' evidence so much credence. The devil may have deluded them or they may be out of their wits."

Sewall turned sideways in his chair, crossing his legs, then uncrossing them.

"I attended Bridget Bishop's trial," Mary added.

"Then you saw for yourself how dreadfully the afflicted persons are tortured! Such fits could not be produced by epilepsy nor any other natural cause and they would be impossible for the children to create of their own will and volition."

"I am not certain of that."

"I know of no one else who is uncertain."

Mary wondered whether to mention the judge who had resigned from the court but decided that this might be unwise.

"If their fits are caused by the devil, the devil may delude them about what they think they are seeing."

"The court does not think so."

"The court may be wrong."

"The court of Oyer and Terminer was set up by the governor of Massachusetts and is presided over by the deputy governor, the province's greatest legal authority."

"The court may still be wrong. Mr. Sewall, I ask with the greatest humility that you and your fellow judges consider very carefully if the girls' evidence is reliable. Perhaps you could suggest to Mister Stoughton that he examine each girl one by one to ask about the exact nature of their visions and to inquire of their motives. Or you could undertake to examine them yourself and tell him your findings."

"Mrs. Burroughs, I honor you for your attempts to help your husband but the law as presently constituted in our province of Massachusetts must take its proper course." Sewall stood up. Mary did so too.

"I know that one of the judges, Mister Saltonstall, has resigned from the court." Mary felt now she had nothing to lose.

"I cannot speak for Mr. Saltonstall." Sewall's chins trembled.

"Mr. Sewall, do you really believe your old Harvard friend could be guilty of witchcraft?"

"The devil may ensnare anyone, Mrs. Burroughs. I cannot presume to make a judgment about a man's guilt or innocence except on the basis of the evidence brought before me at his trial. I must say good day to you." He walked to the door.

"Mr. Sewall, you *know* George. You know he is devout, truly devout; you know whatever his faults he is a *good* man, always caring for others more than himself. He rode to York to rescue the people there from the Indians, purely out of goodness. You've known him for years, you *know* he cannot be a witch."

"If you do not leave now I'll have you removed."

"Allow me one more minute."

He opened the door, then stepped back to the desk and picked up a handbell. Mary walked out of the room and down the stairs. As she reached the hall she heard the judge shut his door and found herself alone. Her heart was beating fast, her mind in turmoil; she could not decide whether to go and find Stephen Sewall or simply wait here. How could this be over so quickly? For an instant she wondered whether to go up again but knew at once she should not. Walking round the hall, she looked down the corridor where she'd seen Betty Parris. On impulse, she darted down to the door she had seen Betty go through and opened it. She found herself looking at a well-furnished, colorful room, apparently empty. But when she stepped in and gazed round she saw two alarmed eyes staring up at her from a small, pale face.

"Don't be scared!" She walked toward the girl, seated in a chair next to a large, empty hearth, an open Bible on her lap. "I mean you no harm!"

The girl kept staring, eyes still as frightened.

"Truly, there is nothing to be scared of. I was hoping to speak to you for five minutes. My name is Mary Burroughs. May I sit down?"

"Are you real?"

"Real?"

"Not a vision?"

"Oh! No! Not a vision! Quite real. As real as that poker."

"Truly?"

"Here, feel me." Mary came close and held out her arm. Betty touched it, then smiled.

"Flesh and blood," Mary said. "May I sit down?"

"Aye." The girl, less flustered now, smiled and waved toward a chair on the other side of the hearth. The room was not as opulent as the hall but highly attractive, with pretty patterned wallpaper and two windows showing rosebushes and neat shrubs. Betty seemed to have use of it as her own, judging by the sewing box, knitting, and books on a table beside her and some rag dolls sitting in a row against a wall. Her sweet face exuded innocence. Could it really have been this little creature who had set the ball rolling that had propelled George to jail?

"Are you still seeing specters?" Mary asked, warmly and gently.

"Oh no, not since my fits, but I'd never seen you before, so I was afraid they might be coming again."

"Those fits must have been horrible."

"Oh yes! Worse than the worst nightmare!"

"Lord be praised they're over."

"Are you a friend of Mrs. Sewall?"

"No, I have been visiting Mr. Sewall, Mr. *Samuel* Sewall. Were you reading your Bible? Can you read? Few girls can."

"Yes, my father taught me the alphabet and then I learned the words by myself."

"The same thing happened to me, though my father helped me with the long words and the ones with odd spellings."

"Mr. Hale does that for me."

"Does he?" Mary couldn't hide her surprise. "How kind of him!"

"He's the kindest man I've ever met. He told me that when the devil came I should read the Bible out loud till he was frightened away."

"The devil came to you?"

"Lots of times."

"You saw him like you are seeing me?"

"Except the room seemed to go dark." Betty's voice softened almost to a whisper.

"What did he look like?"

"Short. A high black hat. Flaming eyes." The girl shuddered. Mary felt she should stop asking questions but could not.

"Did he talk to you?"

"Yes."

"What did he say?"

"'Be ruled by me! Be ruled by me!'" The child's voice had deepened. She looked away, seeming to forget Mary's presence. Mrs. Burroughs felt a chill. Could this have happened? Was the devil truly here in Salem? Had George himself been seduced by him? And been lying, even to her? No, no, this is madness. Good and clever people know it's all a delusion—Peter, Nathaniel Cary, and even some of the townsfolk in the tavern. They are just too frightened to speak out. Betty *believes* she saw the devil but she's as deluded as so many others.

"Did Satan say anything else?" Mary asked gently.

"'I'll give you whatever you ask and take you to a city of gold.'" Betty spoke now in her own voice.

"What did you answer?"

"No!" The girl almost screamed, looking straight at Mary. "No! No!" She took a deep breath, growing more composed. "When I came here from the village I thought he would not come to me again but he did, but still I said no. I told Mrs. Sewall and she said he was a liar and if he came again I should tell him so and bid him go away. Next time he came, I did tell him so, and he left, but he came again, and then Mr. Hale told me to read the Bible aloud to him."

"And did that make him stay away?"

"No, I could not do it, the words stuck in my throat."

"Then how were you cured?"

"Mr. Hale asked me about how the fits started and I told him we'd been very wicked and used the egg and glass to tell our fortunes and he said God would forgive me and we prayed and I said again and again I was sorry, and Mr. Hale said the devil would never come again, and he hasn't!"

After a long moment, Mary said gently, "Abigail wasn't so lucky."

Betty frowned and Mary wondered if she knew what had happened to her cousin. Betty stayed silent. Mary said, "The other girls are still suffering. Ann Putnam and the rest."

"They have fits at the trials," Betty answered.

"You mean, not at other times?"

"I don't know. Abigail told me Father was sending me away because I still had real fits instead of making myself have pretend ones when they needed them."

"She said *that*?"

"Aye."

"Did anyone else say that?"

"No. Father said they were sending me away to try to make me better."

"Did you tell him what Abigail said?"

"Oh, no." She was clearly surprised by the suggestion.

"Did you want to be sent away?"

"No! I wanted to stay with the others! I was afraid to go to a strange house by myself. But Mrs. Sewall's been kind to me."

"Did you tell her what Abigail said?"

"No. She said what Father did about coming here to get better."

"Would you like to be back with the others?"

"I wouldn't want to have fits again."

"But would you like to see the trials?"

"I don't know." Betty gazed out of the window. "Those people, the witches, they'll be hanged . . ."

"If they are found guilty, yes, they will be hanged. Do *you* think they are guilty? Do you think they are witches?"

She realized Betty was not listening. The girl said, "They say Bridget Bishop will be hanged very soon."

"Yes, very soon."

"I know she's evil . . . but still, to be hanged . . . " In a small voice, Betty went on, "They say Abigail was hanged." She gave a quick, small shudder, and Mary glimpsed something of what her fits would have looked like.

"I am very sorry."

In the same small voice, Betty asked, "Will Tituba be hanged?"

"I do not know."

A look of agony crossed Betty's face. She burst into sobs. Mary knelt and grasped her in her arms. The door opened and Stephen Sewall came in.

"What on earth's g-going on here?"

"I beg pardon." Mary rose. "Betty and I were talking of the trials. She got upset. I need to see Judge Sewall straightaway."

"I'll f-fetch my wife. You had no b-business coming in this room. You must g-go now."

"Forgive me, Mr. Sewall. I felt so sorry for Betty, I wanted to talk to her. I meant no harm. I need to speak to your brother most urgently."

"You c-cannot!"

Mary walked from the room, mounted the stairs, went along the corridor and straight into the study without knocking. The judge was standing, his billowed hair catching the light from the window, chewing something, brushing crumbs off his hands.

"I have to talk to you at once!"

"This is an outrage!"

"I have just spoken to Betty Parris who told me the girls are pretending. Abigail said to her she was being sent away because she could not simulate fits when needed like the rest of them."

Sewall's eyes flicked from side to side.

"I swear she spoke true!"

"She's mistaken. You have no business here. Leave at once."

"But, Mr. Sewall, you *must* talk to her!"

He walked to the desk to pick up the bell. Mary said quietly but with passion, "If those girls are pretending, it means an innocent woman will die and other innocent people will die, including my husband."

Sewall shook the bell.

"Come and talk to Betty with me, *please*."

"Leave now or be dragged."

There was a knock on the door. Stephen Sewall came in, his previous look of alarm heightened to terror.

"I want Mrs. Burroughs removed. With the doors locked behind her."

"C-come with me."

"My husband's life is at stake! Your *friend's* life's at stake!"

"He is not my friend."

"What happened? What did he do to you? Why don't you care about him?"

"I will not speak another word to you, Mrs. Burroughs."

Mary stepped up to him and touched his arm. "Think of what Betty said!"

He shook her off, chins vibrating; his brother opened the door and called loudly for a manservant. Mary ran past him and down the stairs.

BURROUGHS WAITED IN NEAR DARKNESS FOR HOURS. THE LITTLE oblong of window was gray; there was not even light enough to read the Bible Mary had given him. He could do nothing but try to imagine what she was saying to Sewall and he to her. But every moment that passed gave him more hope. At last there came the creaking of the door but when Mary came in he saw at once on her face she had bad news. Peter, behind her, looked as grave. When she told George what had happened, however, it seemed better than he'd feared.

"You could not make him listen! It was not your fault. If I could only talk to him myself."

Peter turned away. Mary stared into George's eyes, not knowing whether to argue with him or leave him with hope.

"We have to decide who she will see next," Peter said.

"I must act fast," Mary said. "I do not know how long I have till I'm arrested. Since Sewall condemns *you*, he must surely suspect *me*."

"He does not condemn me! I cannot believe it. I shall write a letter to him. Peter can take it."

"I have little hope a letter will achieve what Mary could not. If Sewall cared about the truth, her new information would have *made* him listen."

"To think, those girls are pretending . . ." Burroughs marveled.

"William Phips might care," Peter said. "The English would depose him if they knew the trials were a sham. But he is away, leading the fight against the Indians."

"Stoughton would not care," Mary said. "I would wager my life he already knows they are pretending."

"The Mathers might care. I heard that Cotton wrote to the judges advising them to beware of spectral evidence."

"Could Cotton Mather get George freed?"

"Without doubt. Phips does what he and Increase tell him to. If they spoke against the trials, he would stop them."

"How can I reach him? Cotton? "

"Perhaps at Bridget Bishop's hanging." Peter paced back and forth. "But you are in great danger now, Mary. I think I should take you back to Wells. Then *I* shall talk to Cotton Mather."

"I'm not going."

"Sewall might have gone straight to Hathorne. He may have put out an arrest warrant already."

"Sam would not do that!" Burroughs shouted.

"Even if *he* would not, others might. He will talk to people about Mary's pleading for your freedom, or Stephen Sewall will, and *someone* will go to Hathorne."

"They could arrest me in Wells, like they did George."

"It would need a special order from the Council. In your case, they might not go to so much trouble."

Burroughs, convinced by Peter's arguments, took Mary by each arm and looked in her eyes. "You must go."

"No."

"You must not risk your life for me."

"You cannot help George if you are in jail," Peter said.

"I cannot help him if I am in Wells. I am staying."

Chapter Thirty-Four

Salem Town
June 1692

THE WOMAN CONSUMED THE APPLE WITH SAVAGERY; THE SOUND WAS stomach-turning. If Mary could have escaped from her she would have, but they were pressed so close it was impossible to move. She'd had no idea such a large crowd would gather so early. They had meant to visit George before following the procession to the gallows, but it seemed the throng had amassed before dawn. They had not even been able to get close to the door of the dungeons, let alone through it.

Mary had heard an older man say to a younger, his eyes wide, "William Stacy woke up one night to see her on his bed."

"What happened?" asked the younger man.

"She hopped round the room. Then went out."

"Is that all? He should have pulled her under the covers!" The young man, grinning, had pushed back his hair.

"'Tis no jest! She could have sent him to hell!"

"She's an idiot."

"No! She's an agent of the devil!"

Mary had reported to Peter what she'd heard.

"I wonder how many in this crowd really believe she's a witch."

Mary had glanced around. "Most of them, I suppose. People have been saying it for twenty years."

They had been pushed forward by the crowd but soon afterward had come to a stop. With the advantage of his height, Peter was able to see the door to the dungeons. Mary could see and hear only the people around her. She tried not to listen to the apple-eating noises and not to dwell on what she'd soon be witnessing. But a particularly loud apple crunch sounded in her ears like a neck snap.

Mary knew that if Bridget jumped she would break her neck and die instantly. However, it was more likely she would be pushed from the ladder and her death would be agonizingly slow. Mary thought of George thinking about this, perhaps at this moment. More likely, he would be trying to put it from his mind, reading his bible or praying. She could not visit him now unless she stayed Behind after the cart had moved off and missed the chance to speak to Cotton Mather.

The woman finished her apple except for the core, which she popped endwise in her mouth, stalk and all. She saw Mary observe this and quickly chewed and swallowed.

"I don't believe in waste."

"Waste not want not," Mary politely agreed.

The woman craned her neck. She was two or three inches taller than Mary, thin and scrawny. "They'll be fetching her any minute," she said. "They brought the cart half an hour since."

To Mary's dismay, from somewhere in the folds of her skirt, the woman produced another apple.

"Want it?" she asked, holding it out.

Mary was tempted, so the woman would not eat it herself, but her stomach turned and she declined. To her relief, the woman put it away again. Feeling guilty for such ungenerous feelings, she asked, "Do you know Bridget Bishop?"

"I've lived near her eight year, since she married her present husband, the sawyer."

Her manner was noncommittal. It was impossible to tell what she thought of her neighbor's alleged crimes. The thin, worn face suggested a life of hard work, anxious counting of coins, and avoidance of trouble. The lank hair under her cap showed wisps of gray.

"A sad thing, to see her go to the gallows," Mary ventured.

The woman looked at her warily. "'Suffer not a witch to live.'" But she did not sound convinced.

"How can we be sure she *is* a witch?"

"Sshhh," Peter hissed.

Mary gave him a nod of reassurance. The woman noticed it and peered round Mary to look at him.

"This is Mr. Peter White, I am Mrs. Mary Burroughs."

"Goodwife Alice Perkins," said the woman. Luckily "Burroughs" rang no bells with her.

"You say you have known her eight year?"

"Eight year last Easter. Since she married Goodman Bishop. He had been living there by himself. She moved in just after Easter week."

Mary, to keep the conversation going, said, "I bet the house needed a spring cleaning."

"She didn't give it one!"

"No?"

"Not so you'd notice. She hung out a few blankets and hit them with a stick but forgot to take them in again and they got drenched. Always did everything wrong. Porridge where her brains should be."

"We were at her trial."

"Were you? She's deaf. And touchy. You shout; she takes offense."

"She did that then. Were you there?"

"Aye." She seemed about to say more and then did not.

"So strange, those girls."

She did not reply.

"You live near her, you say?"

"Two houses away, along Back Street."

"Did she ever witch *you*?"

The woman shot Mary another wary look. "I couldn't say. My pig died but it had been ailing for a week."

Peter called, "They are bringing her out!"

Alice Perkins went on tiptoe and said, "Her underskirt's showing."

"They are getting her on the cart. There's Parris. And John Hale."

"Is Cotton Mather with them?" Mary asked.

"Not as far as I can see."

"*He* won't come," said Alice. "Not to see a sawyer's wife die." She glanced at them, looking alarmed, as though what she had said about one of the mightiest ministers in the province might seem blasphemous.

"You are right," Mary agreed. "He's too important. He would not have time. You could not blame him."

"She cannot climb up!" Peter told them. "Her leg is stiff, by the look of it. Now the constable's pushing her. Cannot he *see* she can't bend her leg?"

"Witch!" a man shouted in a deep, complacent voice.

"Witch! Witch!" came from several other people.

"Wi-i-i-tch," screamed an old woman, in a frenzy. A short man next to Mary with toothless gums yelled something incomprehensible, his mind presumably filled with visions of Bridget since he was too short to see her.

"There's Mary Walcott. And Ann Putnam," said Peter.

"Those girls are here? To see *this*?"

Before Peter could answer, the crowd roared.

"What's happening?"

"The constable is trying to lift her and she's hitting him."

"Her cap's off! She's nearly bald! I never knew that!" Alice shouted. Again the crowd roared.

"She's in the cart. Now the constable is trying to make her sit up. He's thumping her! She'll have bruises tomorrow, poor soul." Peter realized what he had said and went silent. Mary imagined purple stains on a corpse. Was this possible? With the soul gone the body is a shell. But is there life in flesh without spirit, allowing bruises to rise after death? What is it, that animates? Mary suddenly realized she was asking herself questions she had never thought of before.

"Ann Putnam's in the cart," Peter called. "Now her father's pulling her out again. Bridget Bishop is sitting up at last. Oh, now the constable is making her *stand* up."

They were shoved from behind by the crowd.

"The cart's moving," Peter said.

For a while there was mayhem as people pushed forward and constables held them back. But at last the cart was truly on its way and everyone was surging up Prison Lane toward Main Street. Mary could see only the people around her and a sliver of sky. After a few minutes the throng veered to the right and ten or so minutes after that veered again, into Boston Street. Another five or ten minutes later they turned onto a path that led uphill.

Once they started climbing the throng became quieter, the pace slower. After a while they reached level ground, coming to a stop. Peter pushed Mary forward till she glimpsed the scaffold, silhouetted against the perfect blue sky, like the frame of a partly constructed building but with a rope hanging at its center. A moment later Mary saw the top of a ladder, leaning against the beam next to the rope.

"She'll roast to a turn, where she's going! With all that fat on her!" someone shouted.

The jokes and insults started coming thick and fast; Mary put her hands over her ears but still heard them.

"She'll beat her old man black and blue when they meet again!"

"She won't be too deaf to hear the sinners screaming!"

"'This MUST NOT happen to George,'" sounded in Mary's head as though someone else was saying it.

"She's going up now," Peter said.

"Hats off!" a man yelled.

"At least they're showing respect," Mary said.

"No, it's so they can see better," Peter told her. "The executioner's making her turn round and face the crowd."

A man in front of Mary shifted sideways and she saw Bridget's head, the cap crammed back on.

"Someone's tying her arms behind her back. The executioner's on the ladder, two steps down from her."

The crowd hushed. Mary saw the executioner now, as he climbed above Bridget. He was dressed in constable's clothes, indistinguishable from those of a prosperous farmer except for the helmet and belt. Reaching for the noose, he pulled it sideways and down over Bridget's head. Then he climbed back down, out of sight.

"Confess!" someone shouted.

"Confess! Confess!" cried others.

"Sshhh, she's speaking!"

The crowd went quiet. But there was no sound from the woman on the scaffold.

"I think maybe her lips moved without saying anything," said Peter.

"Goody Bishop!" called the resonant voice of Samuel Parris. "We beseech you to confess to witchcraft and sorcery. If you do not confess, this is your last moment on earth before you stand before your God. If you confess, you will live for as long as he in his wisdom shall grant you."

"Her eyes are open," Alice said. "But she doesn't seem to hear."

"Foul witch!" screamed a little girl's voice. "You'll soon be burning!"

"Who's that?" asked Mary.

"Ann Putnam," said Peter.

"Foul witch! See how Satan's betrayed you! You'll soon be with him forever!" the girl called.

"Goody Bishop!" Parris spoke again, louder than before. "Have you nothing to say? This is your last chance!"

"Not guilty!" Bridget shouted.

"Say the prayer, Parris," someone said.

"Who's that?" Mary asked.

"John Hathorne."

"Is Cotton Mather here yet?"

"I cannot see him."

Parris recited the Lord's Prayer, loudly and quickly.

"Do your work, hangman." The voice again was Hathorne's. The executioner, now once more in Mary's sight, struggled to get a hood over Bridget's head. Then he tightened the noose. A moment later he shoved her from the ladder like a dog from a chair. She dropped, hung limp for a moment, convulsed, then went limp again. Then she struggled as though trying to walk, treading air. After a long while she went still. Mary turned away.

"Is it over?" she asked, when the crowd grew noisy again.

"I think so."

Still Mary did not look.

"A doctor is climbing the ladder," said Peter. A moment later he told her, "He's nodding to the hangman."

People started to move. Mary turned and saw Bridget's body swing slightly as the doctor climbed down. The crowd went still again when the hangman took off the hood. It gasped as one at the bulging eyes and twisted features.

"I want to leave. I want to see George."

Peter took her arm and hurried her away, Alice following. Most people were moving now but some were staying to watch as the dead woman was cut down. The three made their way as quickly as they could down the hill.

At the bottom the crowd began to thin; some people turned north up Boston Road, some walked toward Salem, some started turning down side streets. Close to Beadle's tavern Alice said, "I'll say good-bye here. I live that way." She pointed to a narrow road to the right, in the direction of the river. A flock of gulls swooped low in the perfect blue sky, screeching as they passed. Mary took and pressed Alice's hand. "Let us hope for better times soon."

"Amen."

"Good luck to you," Peter said.

Alice hurried off. A voice called their names. They turned to see Nathaniel Cary hurrying toward them. Soon afterward they were in Beadle's tavern together, deep in conversation, making a plan for the next morning.

Chapter Thirty-Five

Boston
June 1692

WHEN MARY HAD TAKEN HER FATHER'S HORSE AND GONE GALLOPING along the Indian paths through the woods around York she had sat astride, her skirts hitched above her knees. If any Indian had spied her, he had decided to leave this crazy white woman alone. Some of her happiest moments had been spent thus, riding by herself, exhilarated beyond thought, care, and fear. But now she was at odds with her steed, who was as dissatisfied as she was. Bella was a beautiful mare, pure black in most lights but dark chestnut when the sun caught her flanks, and well behaved, but she had flattened her ears and swished her tail when Mary sat on her with both her legs to one side. Nathaniel Cary had spared no expense but had not had time to find a horse used to a woman riding sidesaddle. Once seated, Mary had talked gently to Bella to calm her. But both rider and steed missed the pressing together of human and horse flesh.

"We're passing Gallows Hill." This was almost the first time Peter had spoken this morning. Mary wondered if she had displeased him but then remembered he often went quiet, withdrawing into himself, when full of anxiety. It had happened as they came close to Salem after journeying from Maine. She had tried to coax him to speak but he had started to seem almost angry and she'd stopped.

Looking to the left, she saw the hill she had not been able to see when they came this way yesterday, surrounded as she had been by the crowd.

"It's so steep. How did the cart get up?"

"The path we took is further along. The ascent is gentler there." He sounded more himself again. Looking up the hill, Mary thought of

Bridget in the crevice between rocks, covered with a thin layer of earth. They had heard in the evening that this was how she had been buried. Mary wondered where her soul was. What a shock Parris and the rest of them would get if they met her in heaven. That is, if they went to heaven. Bridget surely would. What had she ever done wrong, apart from hanging blankets out to air and forgetting them, and wearing caps too small for her and underskirts too long?

Soon they had passed both path and hill; marshland stretched to the sea. On the other side of them lay fields of barley and wheat and occasional houses. In another half hour the road dwindled to a track and entered the woods. Soon it narrowed and they were obliged to ride single file.

"Stop for a minute," Mary called. "Do not look round. I am sick of riding sidesaddle."

She balanced in her one stirrup, hitched up her skirts, and swung her left leg over the horse's back in front of the saddle. Since there was no stirrup for her left foot, she pulled her other one out to ride with her legs gripping the mare's flanks. Bella whinnied with approval.

"Let's go!" she shouted. "We can gallop now!"

During the next hour's ride she almost forgot where they were headed. Nothing existed but the pine-scented air, the thin strip of sky between faraway top branches and the pounding horses' hoofbeats. The bands of fear round her heart loosened. For the first time since George was arrested, except for the moments when they were lost in each other's arms, she felt ease.

All too soon the woods reverted to farmland. As they stopped, and Mary transformed herself back to respectable womanhood, the bands squeezed her heart again. The track was wider now and they rode side by side, passing small houses, then a larger house with a yard sporting cabbages and chickens. A woman appeared in the doorway and stared. A few minutes later the countryside shrank to stretches of grass, roadside trees, and occasional herb gardens or vegetable plots between buildings. They rounded a bend and there, set back from the road, was a house three stories high with two tall poplars on either side of a magnificent doorway. It was separated from neighboring dwellings by a large expanse of grass.

"Let's ride to those trees there," Peter said.

A hundred yards down the hill, just before the next house, stood a small group of pines. The riders halted, dismounted, and tied their horses to one of the trees, its roots half in the dirt of the road, half in the grass. Here they could not be accused of encroaching on anyone's private property.

"I'm afraid," said Mary.

"All you can do is tell him what you know."

"Everything may depend on this."

"He will choose to listen or not. That depends on *him*."

"But I have to be persuasive."

"Your innocence and honesty should be persuasive enough. Just tell him what Betty said, word for word."

They stood facing each other, Mary trying to conquer her anxiety by gazing into his calm face.

"Wish me luck." She quickly turned and walked up the slope across the grass. As she disappeared behind a poplar, Peter sat down under a tree, leaning back against the trunk. He felt sure Cotton would receive her but had no idea how he would respond to what she had to tell him. Peter had met him only once, in Boston's North meetinghouse.

"He's vain," he had thought, as he had watched him mounting the pulpit in his elegant vestments and splendid wig. The sermon had confirmed this assessment, filled as it was with overly ornate language and thinly veiled boasts. Afterward, among admiring church members, Mather had seemed distracted and distant though showing elaborate courtesy to anyone bold enough to speak to him. After that meeting Peter had read a book he had written about bewitched children. He had found in the prose the same self-importance as he had seen at the meeting. And also found a childish relish for magic and miracles. He hoped now the man was honorable enough, despite this predilection, to accept that the girls might be frauds. His advice to the court about spectral evidence gave some hope of this.

A well-dressed man walking down the road glanced curiously at the traveler sitting on the ground next to tethered horses. He nodded to him but, to Peter's relief, did not speak.

So lost in thought did he become that Mary's reappearance took him completely by surprise. He scrambled to his feet, causing mane tossings, tail swishings, and hoof stamps.

"He's deranged!"

"What?"

"He ought to be locked up. He tried to make me lie down so he could put his hands on my chest to soothe me."

Peter raised his fists.

"Naturally I refused. I made him listen to me. I told him everything Betty said."

"Did he believe you?"

"He seemed to at first but later he talked as though he still thought the girls were truly bewitched."

"Will he talk to Phips?"

"I do not know but Phips has already asked him to write a letter to the court on spectral evidence and he claimed he would advise them to be wary."

"He wrote a letter like that before."

"I said that. I said he ought to advise them to discount spectral evidence completely. Then he talked as though he might but later he seemed to contradict himself. He is as slippery as an eel."

"What on earth are his real motives?"

"Heaven knows! I wonder if he knows? He's a lunatic! He told me he'd seen a vision of an angel. Then he started telling me to lie down again. I had to get away."

"I should have come with you."

"He would not have seen us."

"At least this letter gives a little hope."

"All the ministers in Boston will read the final draft and approve it, he said."

"That gives *more* hope! Not *all* of them can be taken in by those girls."

"Nathaniel Saltonstall was not."

"Was not Mather *shocked* by what Betty told you?"

"He did not seem to be. But perhaps, underneath . . . But you cannot tell *what* he's thinking, I wonder if *he* can."

Chapter Thirty-Six

Salem Town
June 1692

Nathaniel Cary was in an agony of impatience, having spent the day in the tavern while Peter and Mary traveled to Boston. He could have gone with them and continued home to Charlestown but felt he could use his time better here, keeping his ears open for news. But the wait had been hard. When he was not talking to people who might provide information, he could do nothing but think of his wife. He and she had never been parted, during their forty years of marriage, and when in trouble had always been able to help and console each other. Her health had never been good; he was used to hiring the best doctors, ordering delicate food, and nursing her himself. Now she might die and he was helpless.

The summer equinox was near and dusk came late now. In the early evening light Nathaniel paced the tavern's main room from the wooden post and tall settle at one end, past the large table and fireplace, to the small tables and chairs near the door. The few people sitting there, with mugs of ale or plates of food, no longer troubled to look at him.

At last, as he paced in the direction of the door, Peter and Mary came through it.

After brief greetings, since none of them wished to say anything of substance in front of other guests, they all set off for the stables so Nathaniel could pay for the horses. On the way, Mary told him what had happened and he surprised her by saying he had already heard about the letter of advice. But he had not known it would be sent for approval to all the ministers rather than being Cotton's sole handiwork and was much rejoiced to hear it.

"I know the way they are thinking. They will never approve it unless it condemns spectral evidence."

"Stoughton will be *forced* to ban the girls from the courtroom if it does," Peter said.

"That could end it all," Mary said.

"Yes, all the other evidence will be seen for the nonsense it is."

"And my wife will be saved! I hardly dare believe it."

They stopped talking as they entered the stables. As Nathaniel paid the stable owner Mary patted her mare's neck in a loving good-bye.

"Now for Beadle's," said Cary. "As we eat we will decide what we do next."

"I must go to George!"

"Eat first; you must be starving; then take George food. We should discuss our plans before you see him."

Over their meal Nathaniel told them he had heard that Rebecca Nurse would be the next to be tried, though no one knew why the court had chosen her before anyone else. Peter suspected they wanted her trial over and done with because the opposition to it was mounting. Several petitions for her release had been sent to the court. Cary found it hard to believe the magistrates were so cynical, then remembered how they had treated his wife, and realized anew that any baseness was possible. But he pointed out that *someone* was anxious enough the court should administer justice to ask for that letter from the ministers. Could it really have been Phips, as Cotton had claimed? He was a man of action not reflection, to put it kindly. Perhaps it had been Stoughton himself, at last having doubts. But Peter reminded him of the judge's behavior at Bridget Bishop's trial and said he was certain it was Phips who had asked for the letter. He had reason to be nervous of the English Crown's view of the trials.

Cary told them he had heard arrests were spreading to ever more outlying areas and the examinations by Hathorne and others had kept pace. There were now a hundred and fifty in prison.

"How can we see this letter of advice?" Peter asked.

"I may be able to get a copy."

"Do you know any of the ministers?"

"Not well enough, but a friend of mine does." Cary rose. "Let us collect the food for George and be on our way. I intend to reach Cambridge tomorrow by midday to spend some time with my wife. After that I shall cross the river to Boston to see Brattle."

"Brattle?"

"Thomas Brattle. The friend I just spoke of."

"I've heard of him!" exclaimed Peter. "Extraordinary man, everyone says."

"A philosopher and fellow of the Royal Society as well as very successful as a merchant. He has opposed these trials from the start but is keeping quiet till the right time to speak."

Mary said, "That surely must be now."

Chapter Thirty-Seven

Salem Town
June 1692

"A VISITOR FOR YOU!"

George struggled to his feet. This would be Mary, back from Boston. But the keeper was grinning with pleasure and George was suddenly afraid it was Peter come to tell him that she had been stopped on the road and arrested. However, the person who came through the door was someone he did not recognize at first, then saw with shock and pity was Margaret Jacobs, looking older by years than the month ago when he had last seen her. She at once knelt at Burroughs's feet.

"Forgive me!"

The keeper gave a harsh laugh, going out and banging the door on them. Burroughs squatted down, facing her.

"For what?"

"My false confession against you!"

"They were too much for you!"

"I couldn't eat or sleep or bear myself! I thought the devil would carry me away! I've retracted it!"

"Retracted it? Brave girl! Good girl!"

"I'd rather die with a clear conscience than live with that guilt!"

"Stand up!" He helped her to her feet.

"They're putting me in there again." She pointed at the wall. "But I cannot visit you anymore. I've given the jailer my last penny."

"We can talk in our code! We'll say the Lord's Prayer together, whenever it will help you. You are not alone. I am close by."

Chapter Thirty-Eight

Salem Town
June 1692

TWO DAYS AFTER CARY LEFT FOR BOSTON HE WAS BACK AGAIN AND, minutes after his arrival, Mary sat in Beadle's main room with a paper in her hands, Nathaniel on an opposite chair, Peter standing behind her. She read quickly, hopes rising.

"Look! It says the magistrates should be wary of spectral evidence in case it results in their believing things 'on the Devil's authority!'"

Nathaniel beamed.

"You realize that means he thinks the girls might get their information from the devil."

"Indeed I do."

She read on silently for a while, then aloud again. "He says, 'A demon may, by God's permission, appear even for ill purposes in the shape of an innocent, yea, a virtuous, man.'" She turned her head to look up at Peter, reading over her shoulder. "That is the opposite of what John Hale said. They *cannot* use spectral evidence after this."

"Hard to see how."

She looked down again.

"Look—it rules out the touch test!"

"At least says it's unreliable."

"And the Lord's Prayer test."

"Yet all these criticisms seem to imply the trials should go on," Peter cautioned.

"But what other evidence is there? In George's case, that he is strong and a drunken fool saw lights in the fireplace and John Putnam claims he was cruel to his wife."

"I agree it seems unlikely a man could be hanged on such gossip."

240240 FRANCES HILL

"It says the judges should try to avoid the courtroom's being noisy. And, oh my goodness, that 'exceeding tenderness' should be used toward the accused! That *would* make a change. And especially toward those with an unblemished reputation! George's reputation is unblemished, whatever anyone says." Mary looked up again, eyes glowing. Peter could not help but laugh and when she realized that what she had voiced was self-contradictory, she joined in. Then she jumped up.

"I must go to him."

"A moment." Nathaniel also rose. "I have waited to tell you some bad news till after you heard the good."

Mary's heart contracted. "There's a warrant out for my arrest?"

"No, not that. Quite different. Wells has been attacked."

"*What*?"

"By the French and Indians who are allies now. Boston heard this morning."

"George's children!" Mary almost screamed. "Are they . . . ?"

"I do not know."

Peter took a few strides back and forth. "Bad as York?"

"I believe so, or nearly."

"Oh, my dear God," Mary said. "Come to the prison. Tell us everything on the way. I have to tell George."

"Please forgive me but I must go straight back to Cambridge to my wife. In any case there is no more I can tell you. I have no details."

Mary handed him the letter and kissed him quickly on the cheek, saying, "God protect you, my dear friend."

Running up the steep stairs to her bedroom, she closed the door, tidied her hair, and collected the bread and meat wrapped in a cloth she had saved from midday dinner, then fell on her knees, overcome by hope for George's life but fear for his children's. She prayed fervently, asking God for strength. As she was rising, there came a knock on the door and when she lifted the latch and pulled it open Peter stood before her, stooping slightly under the low ceiling. She saw in his face more bad news.

"Tell me at once."

"The girls will still give evidence."

Mary's insides dissolved.

"It seems Phips has ignored the ministers' advice."

"How do you know?"

"A man downstairs just talked to someone at the Town House. Let's go. It is better George hears this from us than the guard."

"Does Mister Cary know?"

"He does. I caught him at the stables to tell him. He has gone now. After hearing this he wants to see Brattle as soon as possible, even before his wife."

"Where is the man you talked to?"

"In the main room."

But the only person still there was a servant wiping one of a row of earthenware jugs. However, as they were turning to go, Mary to her astonishment saw Nathanial Cary appear from behind the tall-backed settle at the end of the room. She nudged Peter, pointed, and they walked in that direction. Nathaniel, in his riding coat and spurs, was talking either to himself or someone hidden by the settle.

"I thought you had gone!" Peter exclaimed.

"Oh, Peter! As I was riding down the road I met this gentleman riding towards me." He waved toward the back of the settle. "He came here from Boston as soon as he got the bad news. Come on out, sir, 'tis only the good people I told you about." He explained, "Mr. Brattle does not want to be noticed and questioned."

The man who emerged was short and ugly with bulbous eyes under huge eyebrows from which wiry hairs stuck out at all angles. He scrutinized their faces, then bowed.

"Mr. Brattle prefers no one knows he is here," Cary said. "Except the two of you. Mr. Brattle, may I introduce Mrs. George Burroughs and Mr. Peter White."

"So pleased." The little man bowed again, then said very softly in an unusually quick voice with gasps for breath between phrases, "I am extremely sorry my reason for doing so is bad news."

"That Phips ignored the ministers' advice?" Peter asked as softly. "I have just heard that myself."

"He did not ignore it!"

"What? Will the girls be banned from giving evidence after all?"

"Alas, no . . ." The elf-like face puckered with disgust.

"Explain to them what happened," Cary exclaimed.

"You read the letter?" Brattle asked.

"Aye."

"That letter was never shown to Phips."

"What? Why?"

Brattle gave a forceful sigh as though needing to vent anger before he could speak again. He glanced down the room; the servant was still wiping jugs. Cary said, "Let us go to my bedchamber. Would you be willing to, Mrs. Burroughs?"

"Of course."

As they started walking, Mary asked Brattle urgently, "Do you know about the attack on Wells? Are there survivors?"

"I was about to tell you, Mrs. Burroughs. There were, and your husband's children are among them."

"Oh, thanks be to God!"

"I am glad to have *that* good news for you, at least."

Cary's bedroom, the best in the tavern, was furnished with a table and chairs as well as a splendid four-poster bed. When they were all seated, he said, "Mr. Brattle, please explain to them."

Brattle's response came at high speed with many gasps and sighs between phrases.

"Copies of Mather's letter, the one you read, were delivered to the ministers who read and approved it. I acquired one from my friend, which I copied and gave to Nathaniel and he showed to you. But later the same friend gave me a subsequent letter just the same as this but with a paragraph added. This letter had never been approved by any minister. It had never been *sent* to any minister, not even Increase Mather. My friend acquired a copy from Cotton Mather's house by means I shall not elucidate. That letter's added paragraph had been penned by Cotton Mather *after* the first letter had been given approval. It was this new version he sent to the governor and deputy governor. I have the copy here." Producing a paper, he handed it to Mary. "It is the last paragraph that has been added. Please read it aloud to us."

Mary opened the paper,

"'Nevertheless, we cannot but humbly recommend unto the Government the speedy and vigorous prosecution of such as have rendered themselves obnoxious, according to the direction given in the laws of God, and the wholesome statutes of the English nation, for the detection of witchcrafts.'" She looked up at Brattle. "What does he mean by this?"

"What he means is to overturn everything gone before. He says one thing and then suggests the opposite. He states that the forms of evidence used to convict should be dropped, and then implies that the forms of evidence used to convict should be kept." Brattle gave another forceful sigh. "There can be no speedy and vigorous prosecution of witches without spectral evidence, as Cotton Mather well knows. He explicitly advises against using it, then implicitly advises *for* using it. It is the implicit advice Phips and Stoughton will follow. The trials will go on as before."

Chapter Thirty-Nine

Salem Town
June 1692

THE UNCERTAINTY WAS ALMOST INSUPPORTABLE. OFTEN BURROUGHS found himself thinking he would rather know for certain he was going to die if he knew when he was going to die. He would chide himself for the sinfulness of desiring his own death, but the thought would soon return.

Night differed little from day except that it was without hope of the creaking of the door heralding Mary's entrance. The frequent thuds on the wall in darkness and silence were a blessing in the assurance they gave him of the existence close by of another human being, a curse in telling him that she was enduring sleeplessness and fear just as he was. He always faithfully struck back and, if she banged three times, recited the Lord's Prayer as loudly as he could. He hoped she could just hear his voice through the wall though he could not hear hers.

Thoughts of Margaret's suffering widened to embrace an awareness of all the others in this prison, and of all human beings, living and dying in misery and pain. For his unknowable ends God had made men and women capable of causing terrible harm to one another, of not only, in the words of the psalm, breathing out cruelty, but of acting out cruelty. Those who thought themselves most righteous, it seemed, often inflicted most suffering. The world seemed upended; everything he had known was called into question. But he still trusted in his God. Without faith in his justice and wisdom, he would have despaired.

It was in deepest night that Burroughs heard the clang of the door to the next cell. His first thought was that Margaret had again agreed to confess and was being taken upstairs. But on reflection he could not believe this. She had told him she was a thousand times happier with a clear conscience in the dungeon than with a tortured one in the prison above. He had believed her. Then Burroughs heard faint voices, their number, let alone words, impossible to make out. He shouted, "Who's there?"

He heard the clang again. After waiting a few moments, he banged twice on the wall. There came two knocks in return. This meant, whatever had happened, Margaret was alive in her cell and alone, or just with another prisoner, not a magistrate or guard. He could find out no more till the keeper's morning visit.

The little window had turned pale blue before the man appeared.

"Is there someone with Margaret?"

The guard held a piece of paper scrunched against the bowl of gruel.

"Is that for me?"

"D'you think *I'm* going to eat it?"

"I meant the paper."

"Oh, the paper!"

"Give it to me."

"What's the hurry? You aren't going anywhere, Reverend Burroughs."

As so often, Burroughs was tempted to knock him to the ground. As always, he resisted. The keeper went through a charade of trying to give him his gruel and the paper at the same time and dropping the second in the first. Burroughs snatched it from the liquid, wet and brown but still legible, though scrawled in great haste.

"My mother is with me, very sick. My grandfather is to be moved here. I promised the jailer money if he lets you visit us. Margaret."

"Wait!" Burroughs called.

The keeper had reached the door. He turned, blind eye bulging. Burroughs said, "Please, allow me this. You will be paid soon." His tone was of a man with reason to be proud showing humility. It failed.

"Those shackles never come off. You know that. Your wife's begged me often enough. Next door's promised me money when the grandfather gets here but how do I know if he's got any? The sheriff's probably seized everything he owns."

Burroughs leaned back against the rough wall and gazed into the keeper's one working eye. Remembering Mary's meeting with Brattle, and making an effort to speak calmly, he said, "The day may come soon when everything changes. Powerful people know I am innocent. Some have opposed these trials from the start. Now they are starting to act. When I go free I may be in a position to help you get better employment."

The man's expression became thoughtful. A few minutes later, for the first time in over a month, George lifted a leg unburdened by iron. He had forgotten what walking free felt like. He went out of his cell and into the next one, the keeper close behind him. When he stood with other human beings as a man instead of a leashed animal he had tears in his eyes.

But self-regard was dispelled when he made out in the dim morning light the bone-thin woman lying on the ground. He knelt down next to her. She gripped his hand and gazed at him, trustingly and longingly, as though he could deliver her from all this. He well remembered her coming to services long ago when he preached in the village. Then she was bonny and youthful; now she was old.

"Good Reverend Burroughs!" Despite its faintness, her voice was fervent.

Margaret, shackled nearby, said quietly, "My mother was taken today. Not arrested, just taken."

"The officer came to our house."

Burroughs leaned closer to catch the old woman's words.

"I was alone with the children. My husband had gone. He'd heard he was accused."

"Father fled," Margaret said, in a small voice of shame.

"The officer told me to go with him to Salem. He said if I did I could come home again soon." Her eyes stayed on Burroughs's face. "I asked, what about my children? As we walked down the road they ran after us, crying. He said again, you can come home to them soon. But when we got to Ingersoll's there were those girls and one of them shouted, 'She's Jacobs, the old witch.' I fainted. When I came to I couldn't walk. They carried me here." Her grip on Burroughs's hand tightened. "What will happen to my children?"

"The neighbors will care for them," said Margaret, stretching her arms out toward her. Mrs. Jacobs turned.

"If only you were with them!"

"Never fear, they will keep your children safe," Burroughs said. "You will be united with them again, once this is over."

She turned back to him. "What are we doing here? What have we done?"

"I wish I could answer."

A week later Burroughs *did* have an answer, or part of an answer, though not one that would have consoled Mrs. Jacobs. Peter and Mary had gained a great deal of information about the people now named to be tried along with or soon after Rebecca, from a family fleeing Salem Village. Once they realized Mary and Peter were deeply suspicious of the witch hunt, and Mary was married to George Burroughs, they were willing and eager to tell everything they knew.

Most of those to be tried, and many other prisoners too, were associated in some way with the successful, admired Salem Village patriarch, Israel Porter, the enemy of Thomas Putnam, father of the most vocal accuser. Thomas and his close friends and relations had lodged most of the formal complaints.

Mary realized, from their description of him, that she had seen Putnam at Bridget Bishop's hanging, near the scaffold while the crowd was dispersing. She'd disliked the look of him, with his gap-toothed, malevolent smile.

Mary and Peter would have liked to go to Salem Village to try to find out more but did not dare, fearful that Mary might be arrested. This was an ever-present danger in Salem Town but would be much greater there. They well remembered what had happened when Elizabeth Cary had visited.

They had never seen Israel Porter as far as they knew. Their new acquaintances told them that these days he kept to himself, rarely leaving his homestead, let alone the village.

Several prisoners had something else in common besides their association with Israel: they came from the outlying region of Topsfield and were wives or daughters of men who owned land there. As though watching fog lift from those same lands, Mary and Peter came to understand that this ownership had been disputed for three generations by none other than members of the family of Putnam. Many of the prisoners had another common bond, as their informants knew all too well: they were skeptical of the witch hunt.

"But none of this was true of Bridget Bishop," Mary had said later to Peter.

"She has been known as a witch for twenty years. They could scarcely omit her. And since everyone believes she's a witch, the jury was bound to find her guilty, making it easier to get other convictions of more respectable people."

Mary reported this conversation to George.

"Bridget Bishop was lucky to get off the first time she was tried, all those years ago," he observed.

A little later, after telling him more of her new information, Mary asked, "Why would Thomas Putnam hate you?"

"I did not know he did, but I know he was angry because I didn't want to be ordained."

"Why didn't you want to be ordained? We have never talked about it."

George leaned back against the wall, his black hair hanging to his waist. He had been afraid the prison authorities would cut it, or even shave his head, but they had shown no such inclination. He had come to realize they had had no motive in setting up as prison keepers except to make money. Serving justice, even inflicting punishment, were incidental to this end. His dark brown eyes, no longer hollow and strange but showing the old courage and strength, gazed past Mary as he gave the question careful thought.

"I realized quite soon that the village was a viper's nest. If I had been ordained I would be working with the Putnams and their allies as one of them, against the Porters and their friends. I wanted no part of it."

"Were you a friend of Israel Porter's?"

"Not a close one. But I liked him."

"It seems Thomas Putnam never forgave you."

"I never knew I mattered that much to him. He found another minister to ordain soon enough."

"That lawsuit of John Putnam's against you. What was it?"

"He had lent me money for my first wife's funeral to be repaid from my salary. But the church committee stopped paying that because of the disputes about ordination, so I left to go back to Maine, arranging to return to the village on a particular day to settle all my debts. When I duly came back, and arrived at the meeting, Putnam had me arrested. I was held in jail overnight but when the magistrate heard the case he dismissed it."

"You mean you were arrested by John Putnam for a debt you were just about to settle?"

"Aye. I was not too concerned; I knew I'd be let off."

"Why on earth did he do it?"

"He seemed to have taken leave of his senses."

"But *why*?"

"Sheer dislike of me, I suppose."

"But *why* did he dislike you so much?"

"No good reason."

"There must have been *some* reason, even if it wasn't a good one."

"My first wife and I had to live in his house for nine months while the parsonage was rebuilt. There were strains between us." Burroughs wriggled his back against the wall to ease its aching.

"What strains?"

"None of it matters!"

"It matters a great deal. Understanding this might help your defense."

Burroughs brought his knees up and put his arms round them.

"My wife Hannah kept tittle-tattling to *his* wife. She was a foolish, selfish woman, my wife that is, though his was too. They thought they were so pious, the pair of them, but she is dead now, I should not talk about her like that."

"You should! For your defense. What did she tittle-tattle about?"

"Never mind."

"I need to know."

"I do not want to tell you. We have never quarreled before, Mary."

"We are not quarreling now. Surely, whatever she talked about, you can tell *me*?"

"It's you in particular I don't want to tell."

"Why?"

"You might stop loving me!"

"That's impossible."

"You can't know that!"

"I can."

"Promise me?"

"I promise. What was it?"

Burroughs took his arms from his knees and pushed his legs down.

"This reputation for great strength I have . . ."

"Yes?"

"It's based on tricks."

"Tricks?"

He explained. Mary erupted with laughter, the sound for the briefest of instants transforming the cell's dank air into sunlight. George reached for her hand. "Aren't you shocked?"

"Oh, George, why should I be shocked? It was just silliness!"

"My first wife thought it abominable! So did John Putnam's wife! So do I, looking back."

"But what has it got to do with John Putnam's disliking you?"

"He and his wife always took my wife's part in our quarrels. I asked them to witness a covenant signed by her, saying she would not talk about my secrets, but they would not."

"Was not it too late for that covenant anyway? Had not she already told them?"

"I did not want her telling anyone else!"

"If she had, you would not be facing these accusations now."

"That is not so! John Putnam knew of my tricks, yet he still bore witness against me."

"That is true. But this is all so petty! Could he really want you to hang just because you tried to make him witness a covenant?" She paused. "Were he and Thomas Putnam very close?"

"Very close."

"Perhaps Thomas egged him on. I heard he courted your second wife."

"She never seriously considered him."

"Whether she seriously considered him or not, he might have been stung by her preferring you. He must surely have envied you for catching her, famous as she was for her beauty and wealth. He may have envied you in any case for being a better man than he is."

"Am I?"

"In every way."

"I doubt he thinks *anyone's* better!"

"He may not think it but deep down he must know it. Thomas Putnam is a nasty, envious, cowardly conniver. In his heart, he must know he is."

"You have never even met him!"

"I have seen him."

"I do not know if he's that bad."

"He is worse. He made all these complaints against everyone, including *you*."

Mary was about to go on and then stopped. She and Peter had learned about the association Putnam had formed with John Hathorne and about Hathorne's ties to Cotton Mather and William Stoughton. Fragments of information from different people were coming together to form a complete picture. But she did not want to share this with George until she was certain.

There seemed no more she could do until after the next trials. Their outcome would make clearer what their next moves should be. Thomas Brattle, they knew, was determined to approach William Phips as soon as he came back to Boston.

The day before the trials started, news arrived of Nathaniel Cary. He had not been seen or heard of since Thomas Brattle brought them Cotton Mather's second letter and she now discovered he had helped his wife escape from prison and flee to the colony of New York where they were received by the governor in Albany. Cary could only have done this by bribing the jailer, his money proving useful at last. She and Peter rejoiced for him but felt the desolation of having no equivalent means to secure George's escape, and of losing such a powerful, good-hearted ally.

It transpired that Rebecca's trial was not after all to be the first but the last of the five to be held over several days, since she was ailing. Mary made herself attend the first four, including those of scraggy, swivel-eyed Sarah Good and passive, brave Elizabeth Howe. Despite, or because of, Cotton Mather's advice, everything followed the same pattern as at Bridget Bishop's ordeal. Watching those women subjected to Stoughton's relentless, poisonous questions, and the touch tests and Lord's Prayer tests and the screams and contortions of the accusers and the jeers of the crowd, Mary found it hard not to run from the courtroom. There seemed more accusers every day, women of all sorts and even some men, including an Indian. At each trial the doctor with unnaturally black hair descanted on protuberances, pudendums, and anuses while miserable-looking witnesses gave rambling accounts of obscure injuries inflicted long ago.

All four women were convicted.

Mary foresaw Rebecca, seventy and still in ill health, going through this, and felt she could not bear it. By the morning of the trial, her reluctance to attend was like a weight in her bones.

"Stay here," Peter said. "When the jury brings in the verdict I will come and tell you."

"Come the very minute . . ."

"The very minute."

Mary sat alone in the main room after everyone left for the trial. She had her Bible on her lap but could not have made out the words if she'd tried. If Rebecca were convicted surely George would be too. But Rebecca could not be convicted; she was pious and good and clearly innocent; yet the girls might terrify the jury into finding her guilty. And if Rebecca were convicted surely George would be too . . . But Rebecca could not be convicted . . .

Occasionally her anxiety subsided, as though body and soul could not bear its intensity any longer and the loop of thought was broken. She remembered George walking beside her inside the palisade, saying, "I've never loved anyone like this," and when she said he must have loved his other wives he replied, "Not like this," and smiled the most wonderful smile, one she would never forget. She saw his dark-skinned, hard-muscled naked body approaching her as she lay in their bed and felt his arms round her. Her heart thumped; her face flushed; she rose to her feet.

"Oh, God, please save him!"

The words filled the empty room. She remained standing. Should she go to the courthouse after all? But she might not even get in. Then Peter burst through the door.

"She's acquitted!"

"Oh, thanks be to God!"

They ran out into the street and were at the Town House in two minutes. A crowd of women were in ecstasies, waving their arms, writhing and howling. Mary noticed the crone who had made a spectacle of herself at Bridget Bishop's trial, and suddenly realized she wasn't in spasms of joy but a fit. And so were all the women. She caught the shouted words, "Get off me, Rebecca!" and, from another female, "She's killing me!"

The shouts merged in a cacophony. Mary felt physically sickened by those twisted, spiteful faces, their black-toothed mouths gaping. She and Peter pushed their way past them and into the Town House, up the stairs and into the courtroom. There the crowd was so dense they could not move forward. The accusers at the front were just as vociferous as the women outside. Rebecca Nurse, still in the dock, looked bewildered and close to collapse.

"When did this start?" Peter asked someone nearby.

"Just after the verdict."

Stoughton banged the palm of his hand on the table. The crowd hushed but the accusers still kept shrieking.

"Members of the jury! You have reached your verdict as is your sworn duty. It is *my* sworn duty to accept it. But it is also my duty to inform you of anything material in the consideration of your verdict that may have escaped your attention."

The accusers now hushed too.

"You may not have caught the words Goodwife Nurse uttered when Lydia Hobbs entered as a witness, which were, 'What, do you bring *her* here? She is one of us.' I will repeat that. 'What, do you bring *her* here? She is one of us.' May I remind you that Lydia Hobbs has confessed to being a witch. I put it to you that Goodwife Nurse can only have meant one thing by her remark, which is that Lydia Hobbs is 'one of us witches,' and thus Rebecca Nurse is another."

"Merciful heavens," breathed Peter. Mary gripped his arm. Looking straight ahead of her, Rebecca's expression gave no clue to her thoughts. The whole courtroom was now silent, waiting for the response from the foreman. He cleared his throat, then spoke softly, inaudible at the back of the room. Stoughton conferred with the other judges, then said, "I give you my leave." There was an eruption of shouts. Word traveled back that the foreman had asked if the jury could withdraw.

"This is beyond everything," Peter said.

"We should tell him he can't do this."

"And get arrested?"

The heat and pressure of the crowd was almost overwhelming and Mary leaned against him.

"Do you want to leave?" he asked.

"I can keep standing if I lean on you."

He put his arm round her. Neither cared at this moment what others might think, or what they themselves might think later. Soon the jury returned.

"Foreman of the jury, tell us your decision."

Again the foreman's words were inaudible at the rear. But word came back that he had asked if he could question the prisoner. Stoughton said, "You may."

The foreman mounted the steps and faced Rebecca Nurse. Her expression was still one of stupefaction. He said something in a respectful voice and word traveled to Peter and Mary that it was, "What did you mean when you said, 'She is one of us?'"

She did not look at him or answer. The crowd became restive. The foreman spoke again, this time to Stoughton. The judge said, "The court gives you leave." The foreman went down the steps and word came that the jury had gone out again.

When they returned the courtroom was deadly silent. The foreman spoke.

"What did he say?" people shouted. Stoughton said in his usual clipped tones, "The jury have found the prisoner guilty."

The courtroom erupted with a jubilant triumph beyond anything seen before. Mary fought her way down the stairs and outside, where the women were now in true paroxysms of joy. How could they already know? Perhaps someone had signaled from a window. When Peter caught up with her Mary gasped, "I can't go back in. I want to stay out in the air."

"Let us go to the graveyard. There will be no one there. At least no one we need to talk to."

The air was cooler there, with the light breeze from the water. As soon as they passed through the little gate Mary walked to Mary Cory's grave and lay on the grass next to it, closing her eyes, wishing herself under the ground with this woman who had known nothing of her husband's imprisonment, of his probable fate. . . . Perhaps she could drown herself in the river, loading her pockets with stones and jumping from the wall. . . . Better to die at once than watch George die on the scaffold. And yet, for him to have the noose placed round his neck without her in his sight . . . Besides, these trials were just beginning. . . . Things could surely still change. . . . She sat up, intending to join Peter, but he was sitting on the wall gazing into the water and she decided not to disturb him. She lay down again, curling into a ball.

The gray-green water slapped gently against the barrier guarding the settlers' bones; Peter could make out murky shapes that might be rocks or flotsam and jetsam washed here after days or weeks in the sea. They might be remnants of shipwrecks or unwanted items thrown from houses by the shore. In one of their walks around town he and Mary had seen a bed winched up to a rooftop and heaved with an almighty splash into the sea.

Peter found himself picturing such a bed in the house he and Mary might one day share. The house would be in Roxbury, next to the one he had grown up in, where his mother still lived. He pictured a fine son walking out of the door on his way to the very same school where he and George had first met. He would have given up soldiering and set up as a physician, to keep Mary in safety and comfort.

Shocked and appalled at these thoughts, which came against his will, Peter concentrated again on the objects in the sea; but their shimmering suggested Keyser's "jelly that used to be in the water," which brought his thoughts back to Mary. She had seemed so adorable in that rare lighthearted moment. He looked across at her, lying curled on the rough grass, the hair above her forehead just touching the base of the small headstone. She lay quite still and seemed asleep. He suspected it was because he was near that she had felt safe enough to drift into slumber. He could still feel her body, as it had been close to him under his arm, in the courthouse.

This must stop. He got off the wall. He would do everything he could to save his friend's life. George and Mary would grow old together. He would find another wife, or live alone.

He walked to where she was and gazed down for a while before saying, "Time to go."

She opened her eyes, then sat up, saying, "Strange dream." As she got to her feet, Peter checked the impulse to take her arm to help her, afraid of the physical contact after the thoughts he'd been having, in this evocative place.

"Let us go to him at once," she said.

"We need food."

"I don't want him to hear the news from the guard."

"I expect that has happened already. Let us eat first and then take food to him."

On the way back they walked with a space of a foot or more between them. Mary wondered if the new awkwardness on Peter's part was due to his not daring to tell her he despaired of George's chances. But after a few moments he said that Stoughton's having gone to such extraordinary lengths to secure a conviction gave hope.

"Why should it give hope?"

"Shows things are on a knife edge. Anything may happen."

Mary felt a surge of new confidence. "What would I do without you?"

"You have managed very well often enough by yourself! But I'm glad I'm sometimes able to help."

They spoke no more until they reached Beadle's. In the main room all the tables were filled and everyone had started eating but they pushed their way through the crowd, ordered two onion pies, one to share and one to take to George, and found stools in a corner.

"Look over there," Peter said suddenly, nodding toward the door. Mary leaned back on her stool to see past him. A close-knit group of men stood enclosed in an atmosphere of utmost seriousness that kept them separate from the rest of the room. In their midst was an old man, the only one of them seated.

"They're from Salem Village," Peter said. "I recognize some of them."

"That must be Francis Nurse, on the stool. What must he be feeling?"

"He looks done for."

"Who are the others?"

"That spindly man is Peter Cloyce, Rebecca's brother-in-law. We saw him at Bridget Bishop's trial. His wife is in prison too. I think the curly-haired man is Joseph Putnam."

"Thomas Putnam's half brother?"

"Aye. Another of them may be Israel Porter. I do not know which."

A servant approached the group and a man as tall as Peter, with a tightly coiled look and careful eyes, spoke to him.

"Maybe *he* is Israel," Mary suggested.

"Perhaps we should go and talk to them."

"They look as though they want to keep to themselves."

"I would like to know what they're planning."

"You think they're planning something?"

"I cannot believe they'll just accept this."

"Let us talk to them!"

"No, you are right, this isn't the time."

The servant brought the group mugs of cider. The isolation that enclosed them was broken for a moment but resettled. A little while later the onion pies arrived. Mary and Peter had just started eating, their platters on their laps, when they saw Francis Nurse being helped to his feet and the group of men moving to the door. Peter put his plate on the floor, got to his feet, and headed for the tall man Mary had thought might be Israel, reaching him just before he went out. The man's guarded look changed to one of intense interest as Peter whispered in his ear; he turned to face him and spoke a few words. The two shook hands, the man went out, and Peter made his way back to Mary.

"You were right," he said. "That was Israel."

"What were you saying?"

"I shall tell you as we walk to the prison."

By the time they reached him Burroughs had already heard everything about Rebecca's acquittal, then conviction, from Margaret Jacobs, who had heard it from her grandfather. Old George Jacobs had bribed the jailer to let him visit his grand-daughter, and then bribed him again to let her visit Burroughs. The middle-aged man and young girl were in the cell together when Mary and Peter were let in.

"Did Rebecca *really* say, 'She is one of us'?" Margaret asked. "Did you hear her?"

"Yes," Peter said. "She spoke softly but I caught the words. I was near the front at that time. I wondered what she meant. It certainly never occurred to me it was 'one of us witches.' That was ingenious of Stoughton."

After a few more minutes, he said he must go. He shouted for the keeper and, when he came, Margaret let him take her to her cell. Mary and George had a precious half hour alone together until the keeper returned and ordered Mary to pay money or leave.

"You had better go, my love," said George. "Come back in the morning."

"I will."

"As long as you are nearby, I have hope."

Peter left the cell but not the prison. When the keeper took Margaret into her dungeon he did not wait for him but kept walking down the passage. He guessed the keeper would not try to find him since he'd assume he was heading for the door to the street. Deprived now of the light of the lantern, he felt his way along the damp wall, his hands meeting rivulets of slime and patches of moss and, every few yards, the hinges and locks of dungeon doors. He turned right, then left, according to the directions he had memorized. The way seemed longer than he had expected and he started to fear he had gone wrong. But at last his hand met a corner and, turning, he saw a light and heard voices. A few steps later he made out a lantern and, a few steps after that, Peter Cloyce's spindly figure, holding it aloft. Gathered round was the group from the tavern, enveloped in the same air of gravity, made even more somber by this setting. Everyone seemed to be there but for Francis Nurse and Israel Porter.

Peter Cloyce stepped forward and introduced Captain White to several sons and sons-in-law of Rebecca together with curly-haired Joseph Putnam and a short, spare man called Daniel Andrew, married to Israel's sister. Cloyce told Peter that, before being brought to the prison, Rebecca had been taken to the meetinghouse in Salem where Nicholas Noyes had excommunicated her from the Puritan church. As he said this he could hardly hold back his tears. The group stayed silent after that until, a minute or two later, the door they were standing in front of swung open and, to Peter's surprise, a well-dressed young woman came out. She was followed by Francis Nurse and Israel: he realized she must be Israel's daughter. Behind Israel came a guard to whom Israel gave coins while Francis Nurse, with a shaking hand, held up a paper. Cloyce reached for it; Israel, turning, stopped him.

"Let us get out of here first."

The men and woman, with Peter at their rear, made their way by the light of Cloyce's lantern along the passages he had come by, then the length of another and finally up the steep stairs to the door to outside. In the cool evening air, under a sky still blue though the ground was now black, Israel took the paper from Francis and the lantern from Cloyce and read the words on it aloud. When he finished a breeze blew through the lantern's open panel, putting out the candle, but the men could still dimly see one another by the remnants of daylight.

"Rebecca dictated this," Israel said. "She has made her mark at the end. Governor Phips has just returned to Boston and tomorrow I will ride there to give it to him."

Chapter Forty

Salem Town
June 1692

"SHALL WE PROCEED TO OUR BUSINESS?" STOUGHTON ASKED. "LET US begin by asking God's blessing."

The men gathered in John Hathorne's study, which the deputy governor was using as his own while he stayed in Hathorne's house, closed their eyes and bowed their heads. Stoughton asked for their Eternal Father's continuing help in finding the right paths in their holy endeavors against Satan and his allies. After the "Amen" he glanced in turn at each of his colleagues, then folded his hands on his lap.

"Gentlemen, we find ourselves at a crossroads." He spoke as though addressing the courtroom. "The enemy of mankind is proving as wily now as at the time of the Creation. We face a more formidable foe than we guessed, though we should have guessed, since the scriptures tell us fully and clearly of his powers."

Hathorne's heavy face showed no expression but Samuel Sewall's chins trembled and Stephen Sewall's features clenched with fear.

"We need to arm ourselves with new weapons. There are witches to be tried more dangerous and more confederate with Satan than even the she-devil who yesterday so nearly escaped judgment."

Samuel Sewall raised his chins and Stephen Sewall's cheeks twitched but Hathorne stared straight ahead.

"W-what new w-weapons? What w-weapons, however new, c-can strike an invisible enemy?"

Stoughton shifted slightly at the length of time taken by the question. Samuel closed his eyes in shame of his brother; Hathorne did not stir.

"The best weapons we have now, thanks to God's goodness," Stoughton said, "are our brave witnesses to the wiles of the Evil One. But there are too many doubters. The terrible suffering Nurse inflicted in the courtroom failed to convince everyone there."

"Yet they were undeniable!" exclaimed Samuel Sewall.

"Those you call doubters," Hathorne said, "they may themselves be witches."

"The Nurse relatives may be," said Stoughton. "We know the two sisters are. They have duly been charged and will in due course face trial. Yet there are others who doubt the witchcraft but may not yet have been recruited by Satan. Some are in positions of power, not just in Salem Village but also here in Salem Town."

"W-who do you mean? Which positions of power?"

Again Stoughton stirred and Samuel closed his eyes. The younger Sewall reopened his mouth but Stoughton said quickly, "Members of the Salem Village committee."

"And the Salem Town committee." This was from Hathorne, still motionless.

"Men who can stir up opposition," said Stoughton.

"Israel P-Por . . ."

"Strong character," Hathorne said quietly.

"J-Joseph . . ."

"Married to his daughter."

"D-Dan . . ."

"To his sister."

"They could swing the whole village behind them." Stoughton closed his lips so tightly they vanished.

"Joseph Putnam has threatened to fight to the death anyone who comes to arrest him," Hathorne said.

"No doubt Israel Porter has too," Stoughton observed.

"As you say, we have no proof they are witches," Hathorne said. Stoughton stretched out an arm, lifted the jug placed on the desk, and poured cider into one of four mugs. As an afterthought, he glanced round, holding the jug up. Hathorne and Stephen Sewall shook their heads; Samuel Sewall nodded. Stoughton poured and handed him the mug. After they had both sipped, Stoughton put his mug down and said in his most venomous tone, "There is a woman presently in Salem, closely related to our most dangerous foe."

"W-who do you mean?"

"The wife of our chief enemy."

Stephen still looked blank. Samuel shifted uncomfortably.

"I wonder why she walks free," Stoughton said.

"She will not for much longer," Hathorne replied.

"But more threatening even than that woman, and the men we talked of, are the merchants, magistrates, and even some ministers who question the proceedings of our court. This insidious doubt and suspicion reaches to the very top of our province, demonstrating the fearful extent of Satan's power. We must find new means to combat it."

"W-What n-new means?"

"More confessions."

There was silence, then Hathorne said with a defensiveness close to anger, "We have Tituba and Hobbs."

"Obtaining those confessions was a tribute to your skill as a magistrate, Mr. Hathorne, but the rest of the witches have proved harder to persuade, as you from your own admirable efforts know better than anyone. We need not one or two but *scores* of confessors, who will tell not only of their devilish plans but of the meetings they have been to and the name of their leader."

"That leader is as deceptive as his master." Sewall looked at the floor, squashing his chins.

"He deceived *you*," observed Stoughton.

"I admit that for many years I thought him a God-fearing man."

"Despite his not having his children baptized."

"He had convinced me there were good reasons for that."

"There are never good reasons for breaking God's laws."

"How do we get those confessors?" Hathorne asked, folding his arms. Stoughton well knew the source of his defensiveness. Knew, but did not care. Hathorne's self-love was no concern of his.

"We must treat them less gently. For the good of New England."

Sewall looked up. "Less gently?"

"We must be willing to be harsh."

Sewall said, carefully, "Torture is proscribed by Massachusetts law."

"I do not speak of torture. I speak of less gentleness."

Sewall looked away. "As you know, the conditions in the dungeons are far from luxurious."

"The conditions in hell are a thousand times less so. Hell is where we will all find ourselves if we allow Satan to conquer our province."

"What mode of harshness do you contemplate?"

"At present the prisoners are allowed to sleep as and when they please. They themselves show no equivalent tenderness toward those they wrack with agonies all day and all night."

"As Mistress Putnam was wracked, on several men's testimony," Hathorne agreed, unfolding his arms.

"You would keep the prisoners awake all night?" Sewall did not look at Stoughton.

"I would suggest that for a period of time before interrogations the guards keep them standing."

"Some people can sleep standing," observed Hathorne.

"If need be, the guards can make a loud noise."

"Is that not torture?" asked Sewall.

"Torture! Pain from a physical injury is torture! Hurt that impairs bodily functions, or causes organs to fail, or threatens death, that is torture!"

After a pause, Sewall asked, "Would this be the extent of it? Robbing them of sleep?"

"Are you afraid to be determined in the fight against Satan?"

"I would wish to abide by the laws of our province."

"Extraordinary circumstances call for extraordinary measures. Our governor, Sir William, rather than old laws made in easier times, must decide the best methods for fighting the new enemy."

"Has Governor Phips asked for prisoners to be tortured?"

"I told you, I am not speaking of torture!" Stoughton's lips again disappeared.

Hathorne was leaning forward, listening with uncharacteristic keen interest. He sat back suddenly at the sound of a knock. Stoughton nodded at him and he barked, "Come in!"

A servant appeared, holding a paper, looking from Stoughton to Hathorne, who held out his hand. He read it and, with an almost imperceptible tightening of his features, passed it to the deputy governor. Stoughton perused it and let out a bellow that no one in that room would have known he had in him. Samuel took the paper as quickly as he could while avoiding seeming to seize it.

"This cannot be true," he said.

"W-w-w-w . . . ?"

"Phips has granted Nurse a pardon."

Chapter Forty-One

Salem Town
June 1692

THEY DID NOT HEAR THE NEWS UNTIL EVENING. WHILE THEY WERE seated with other guests in the fading light in the tavern, a man unknown to them came in and announced it to the room. After shouts of joy Peter asked, "Does her family know?"

"Aye, Israel Porter has returned from Boston by way of the village. He has taken some of them with him to the prison."

"Let us go too," Mary said.

"It's late."

"By now we could find our way there in pitch darkness."

In fact there was light enough still to see their way. A white moon hung low in the sky, its murky features forming an ambiguous smile. When they turned into the short street with little dwellings on one side and the empty expanse on the other, it was there before them, hanging next to the black building at the end like a dim beacon.

A small crowd had gathered near the door that led to the dungeons. As they drew closer, they heard angry voices and saw in its midst, glimmering in lantern rays, the white hair and eyebrows of Francis Nurse. Pushing through, they saw that Peter Cloyce was the lantern-bearer and Nurse's frail body was jerking like a puppet's as he shook his finger at the marshal. With him were Israel Porter and the men Peter had met the night before. The crowd seemed divided in sympathy between Nurse and the officer.

"Fetch her now! Fetch her now!" The old man's words were full of outrage yet pleading. His expression was ravaged, transformed from yesterday's passive despair. Israel stepped closer to the marshal. "The governor gave his order. She's free. You are breaking the law by not going down those steps now and releasing her."

"Don't you tell me the law!"

"I wouldn't have to if you knew it!"

"Shut your mouth!"

"Keep your temper!"

Francis was still wagging his finger. "Fetch her now!"

"Please explain to us," Goodman Cloyce, stepping forward, said evenly to the marshal, "why you *cannot* fetch her now? She is pardoned. I have not heard you deny that. Why not simply unlock the door and take us down there so we can fetch her out and take her home?"

"It's not for me to explain to you, I have no call to explain to you."

"You certainly *do* have a call to explain to us. The law says you should release her."

"I am the authority here! I could have you arrested!"

"Why would you want to have us arrested? We are here to collect our relative, freed by the governor. What offense is there in that?"

The marshal held his staff with both hands in front of him as if to anchor himself to the ground. Peter White moved forward.

"Have you orders from someone of higher authority to detain Goody Nurse despite the pardon?"

The man looked startled.

"Who gave you those orders?"

"I have no call to answer you!"

"Answer anyway."

The marshal lifted his staff and, carrying it high, strode away, shouting, "Leave now! Everyone leave! No more loitering! Get back to your houses!"

No one heard him. The crowd had turned to peer down the dark lane, their attention caught by hoofbeats. A horse and rider were coming into view. The marshal also turned, then walked toward them, followed by Israel, Peter, Mary, and others. The horse halted and the rider dismounted, a pale wig and fine linen collar glimmering in the light of Peter Cloyce's lantern, lifted high. People had begun murmuring a name. Beckoning a boy to take the reins, the rider produced a roll of paper from his pocket and handed it to the marshal, who made a small bow and tore off the seal.

"It tells you Rebecca Nurse's pardon is rescinded," proclaimed the clipped voice familiar to everyone there. "It orders you to keep her in irons. As you see, it is signed by the governor."

Francis Nurse collapsed like a puppet whose strings are cut. People crowded round him, some falling to their knees. William Stoughton looked at them with undisguised disdain.

"I advise you to get back to your homes."

Israel stepped forward. "May I ask the cause of this, Mister Stoughton?"

The chief judge stared at him. "I can hardly conceive it is the place of a Salem Village farmer to interrogate the deputy governor."

Israel's mouth tightened.

"You are Israel Porter, I believe?" Stoughton asked icily.

"Aye."

Everyone was listening, some looking, some not daring to.

"I advise you to take your friends home to their village."

Israel clenched his fists, breathing in sharply, but as he breathed out raised and folded his arms. "As you see, sir, Goody Nurse's venerable husband is lying here, collapsed under the news that his wife of sixty years is to be hanged, after hearing she had been spared. He deserves an explanation."

Stoughton lifted his sharp chin, appearing to wonder whether to continue to talk to this man or have him arrested. At last he said, his voice as clipped as before, "Ridding this land of Satan and his allies takes precedence over all other concerns."

The crowd stayed silent.

"That is all I have to say to you."

"That cannot be all," Israel said. "We desire, and have every right, to know why Governor Phips changed his mind."

"Have pity, sir," called a woman kneeling next to Francis.

"Have pity!" another echoed.

Stoughton half turned toward them.

"I beg of you!" pleaded a younger woman, her cap awry, hair straggling down her neck.

"Governor Phips made a mistake that he rectified. I think Mr. Porter knows what caused him to make that mistake. He owes no explanation to *him*. He owes no explanation to anyone." Stoughton looked at Francis, sitting up now, supported by Cloyce.

"Least of all to a man married to a witch."

"She'll be hanged! My wife will be hanged!"

Stoughton walked to his horse, the marshal and Israel and several other men following.

"There is something more I must say," Israel declared softly but forcefully. Stoughton stared round at him with astonishment, clasping his hands behind his back before anyone could notice they were trembling.

"What more can you possibly have to say?"

"Goodwife Nurse made plain after her conviction what she meant by the words 'one of us.' It was 'one of us prisoners.' As I think you know, that was written in the paper seen this morning by Governor Phips. She was too deaf to hear the juryman's question. In other words, the so-called evidence that made the jury change their verdict was worthless."

"All lies. I advise you never to mention this again. And I again urgently advise you to take your followers home." Stoughton snatched the reins from the boy, mounted his horse, glanced around disdainfully, and rode off.

Despite the marshal's frantic urging, the crowd did not disperse, instead growing larger. Word of the pardon was spreading, not as yet overtaken by the news of its reversal. Those arriving were expectant, even joyful. Everyone knew Rebecca; many had signed the petitions pleading her case; almost everyone had been shocked and dismayed by the jury's altered verdict. Mary watched each expression change in just the same way when people were told the bad news.

"How alike we all are," she thought. Then she remembered Stoughton. "No, he is different. . . . And Hathorne. . . . And Thomas Putnam. . . . They are different. . . . Are they the true agents of the devil, these righteous men without hearts?"

A woman's voice spoke her name and in the dim light she saw the worn face of Alice Perkins.

"You must get away from here," Alice whispered. "There's a warrant out for your arrest. You can't go back to Beadle's. Come with me."

"I must tell Peter."

But he was near enough to have heard.

"Where do you live?" he asked Alice.

"Back Street. Smallest house in the row."

"I shall come later."

The ever-darkening blue of the sky was close to black but there was just light enough to show outlines. Houses loomed on either side of them. There were no candles in windows; in the summer people went to bed with the sun. The silence was as complete as though the whole world had gone mute. Birds and insects had retired and night creatures not yet crept from their lairs. The two women's steps on the beaten earth made no sound.

Alice led the way off Essex Street down a side road. Mary kept checking all round her. She thought she saw a movement but there was nothing but darkness and she assumed she'd imagined it. A moment later a dim shape was almost upon her and she feared it was a spirit. But as it drew level the impression of stockiness and drabness was too workaday for that. Yet it might be a constable with a warrant! But the figure passed and she could tell it was just an ordinary poor man. He did not look at her or speak, as though they were all moving now through a world where the rules of neighborliness and courtesy no longer applied, where people did not even acknowledge one another. She felt relief, but only for an instant. It could not last in this landscape of fear.

The women hurried the last few yards to Alice's house and, once inside, bolted the door.

"You are safe now. No one will come looking here," Alice said.

"Thanks be to God. But 'tis not God I should thank but *you*, if that's not a wicked thing to say."

"No thanks necessary. The constables might search from house to house but not before morning. You must flee as soon as it's light."

"Where to?"

"Back to Maine, perhaps."

"They might come for me there, like they came for George. I hope Peter gets here soon."

"He'll know what to do."

"If I go, he will have to come with me. He'll be in danger too. And I cannot see how I could travel alone. I must tell George. No, I cannot. I'd be seized."

"I'll go and see him. I'll explain."

PART
THREE

Chapter Forty-Two

Salem Town
July 1692

BURROUGHS'S HIGH SUMMER WAS THE UNVARYING BLUE IN THE small window high in the wall. The overwhelming heat did not penetrate stone and earth and its occasional climax in thunder reached him only faintly. He felt a loneliness that was deeper than before Mary had arrived. He knew from Alice Perkins, who had paid him one short visit, that Mary had fled with Peter to New York colony, hoping the governor would receive her there, as he had the Carys. They had had no money to pay for passage on a ship and had set off overland on foot. He had stopped trying to imagine their journey, as his isolation deepened; he could hardly bear to think of her.

He went through his daily routines but with no sense of their forming any link with the world outside. Exercise was to keep stiffness at bay, not maintain vigor; his prayers now were inward activities, no longer a part of communal Puritan life. He recited his defense by rote without picturing the courtroom or those who would hear it.

He rarely spoke to the keeper. He never knocked on the wall except when Margaret did so. What was left of his money he used for extra rations out of simple, brutish hunger, not to keep up strength for the fight. His trial, set for the first week of August, seemed so remote as to be an abstract idea rather than something bound to happen.

Five women had been hanged now: Rebecca Nurse, Sarah Good, Susannah Martin, Elizabeth Howe, and Sarah Wildes. Burroughs heard this from the keeper, who told him with an astonishing tear in his one seeing eye that on the gallows Rebecca had made an eloquent farewell to her family and prayed in a most pious manner, ending with a perfect "Our Father." The tear vanished and the network of lines reappeared as the keeper went on to report that Sarah Good had cursed Reverend Nicholas Noyes, saying God would give him blood to drink.

"I wouldn't be 'im, not for all 'is money or big 'ouse."

Early one morning, as Burroughs sat praying, he heard, from a distance, a scream of agony. When the keeper came he asked what had happened. The man handed him his bowl without answering but also without his customary malevolent grin. Apparently even in his simple, cruel mind the ever-darkening landscape was causing unease. Burroughs asked again.

"Didn' hear nothin'."

Burroughs knew no coaxing would make him say more.

He could not accept the explanation lurking at the edge of his mind. This was still Massachusetts, the city on a hill, God's beacon to the world. His experience since his arrest had not yet told him that legal or moral rules no longer applied, that there'd been a total collapse of integrity.

The next morning, when the keeper appeared again, he said dully, "Message from George Jacobs."

"Where?"

"Here." He tapped his head.

"What is it?"

"John Proctor's sons have been tied neck and heels for eighteen hours. So have Martha Carrier's. Bent over backward."

"Was that the scream . . ."

"Wouldn't know." He handed Burroughs his bowl.

"Were they trying to escape?"

The jailer laughed with contempt.

"Why were they tied?"

"You're a man of learnin'! You tell *me*!" His scorn lacked its former relish. The explanation at the edge of Burroughs's mind forced itself forward.

"To make them confess?"

The keeper, by saying nothing, assented.

"Does Hathorne know?"

"He ordered it."

"Are you sure?"

"It was me as he ordered."

"You tied them?"

This time again the keeper said nothing.

"Does Stoughton know?"

"He knows."

"And Sewall?"

"Couldn't say. There's one more thing George Jacobs paid me to tell you."

"What?"

"One of them *has* confessed. One of them Carriers. He's a witch and you're a leader of witches, he says. All his brothers will break soon, all them Carriers. Not the Proctor boys though. They'll never break, however much the blood pours from their noses." He showed grudging admiration.

As the keeper was speaking Burroughs formed a desperate resolve and these last words fired him to act. He threw his bowl across the cell and, as the astonished keeper half turned, lunged at him, and brought his face to the ground.

"Give me the keys or I'll kill you." Burroughs took him by the hair and slammed down his head. He just caught the words, "Get off me. I'll do it."

He moved enough for the keeper to free his arms and untie the keys from his belt, then snatched them, and, shifting round to sit sideways on the guard, unlocked his shackles. Once free, he stood up and walked to the door.

"I am locking you in and if you lie to me I'll come back and kill you. How do I get out?"

"Turn right. The stairs are at the end."

"If you make a sound I'll return and you'll be dead."

Burroughs pushed the heavy door closed behind him and locked it. The passage was dark, the walls slimy. He felt his way to the end but found no step, just a wall, and thought the keeper had lied despite his threats. But, still feeling his way, he discovered a turning to the left. After several hundred yards came a small chink of light from above; Burroughs's foot bumped a step; he felt with the other foot for the next step and started to mount. Suddenly, with a creak, the door above him opened, its crack of light widening until two guards stood silhouetted against half-blinding sunshine. Burroughs leaped up, seized one, and threw him down the stairs; the other got him in an arm lock but he broke free and threw him down too. The first guard ran back up but Burroughs seized his shoulders and banged his head against the wall until he tumbled down onto the second man, just getting to his feet. Burroughs ran out, slammed the door, and leaped up the three outside steps to the street. Dazzled by the light, he slowed to a walk. People stared at the unshaven figure in filthy garments but no one tried to stop him.

Chapter Forty-Three

Massachusetts
July 1692

❧

MARY COULD SCARCELY REMEMBER LIVING ANY OTHER WAY, ENGROSSED every moment with urgent physical sensations—hunger, thirst, heat, pain, and exhaustion. And always afraid. They traveled through terrain ranging from dense forest to lightly wooded or open land, over gentle hills and low mountains, navigating by the sun, finding and following streams or old Indian paths that often dwindled to nothing or disappeared into impenetrable forest or tall bluffs. Wary of trails that looked as though Indians still walked them, they often found their way pathless. The Algonquin tribes of this region, unlike the Abenakis of Maine, were crop growers, building settlements of bark-covered huts with fields for beans, corn, and squash. Walking into a village was an ever-present danger.

The forest's huge oaks and white pines, many times taller than the houses in Salem, kept the ground clear of undergrowth but showed the sun only as a patch of red between branches. The travelers could move quickly but, on gaining higher ground or a clearing, sometimes realized they had mistaken their direction and cursed the loss of time. Peter's map of New England was of no use except in showing that their direct route was due west and that if they stayed on course they would avoid the few English settlements before Deerfield, on the far bank of the Connecticut River. It showed that when they reached it they would be halfway to Albany.

Their fear of the natives was acute. Many English settlements that had dotted this landscape had been destroyed in King Philip's War and the Algonquins hated and feared whites perhaps even more than the Abenakis of Maine did, well knowing they intended to resettle. "Praying" Indians, converted to Christianity by French Catholics and hostile to Puritans, sometimes captured English men and women and delivered them to French generals in Canada as hostages. This fate seemed to Mary hardly preferable to death, since it would remove her so far from George and any last hope of saving him.

If they'd had money and time they could have found a ship to take them to the mouth of the Hudson and up the Connecticut River to Albany. But they fled with nothing but the clothes on their backs, Peter's gun and knife, and a tinderbox, ax and cooking pot given to them by Alice.

Wolves and bears were ubiquitous and they glimpsed several of both, though none close. Thankfully in this high summer season all creatures were likely to be well fed and good-humored.

At least there was little fear they might have been followed. Even if the sheriff guessed their destination and overland route, and sent constables after them, it would be almost impossible to find and follow their trail. They could not completely rule out determined pursuit, however, given Mary's efforts to free the supposed leader of witches. They had encountered no human beings so far, though once on higher ground they had seen smoke in the distance from an Indian village or a party of fur trappers, resting by day to do their work by night. But they could hardly believe their luck would hold much longer. All things considered, they had little expectation of reaching Albany alive.

They would not starve, however, adept as they were at living off the land. Peter was as knowledgeable about plants and berries as an Indian and as skilled a huntsman as Burroughs. Mary was practiced at making fire using a tinderbox, dry sticks, and pinecones, and at gutting fish and skinning animals. They gathered blackberries and, on higher land, blueberries, as well as the mushrooms familiar to them from Maine and acorns still on the ground from last fall. They caught fish and crayfish with their hands and a spear fashioned from a log of white ash. They pulled freshwater mussels from underwater rocks, and lichen from stones for boiling into soup. Peter once shot and killed a rabbit that ran across their path. But he never dared do that again, such terror did they feel at the crack that resonated through the forest like doomsday. Indians could have heard it twenty miles off. Despite their knowledge and skill, it was hard to find and prepare enough food while covering ground quickly. Sometimes they walked fourteen hours in a day.

Mary's worst fear, apart from meeting Indians, was that George would be tried and executed before they reached Albany.

They slept on the ground at a distance of several yards from each other. Despite her hunger and anxiety, Mary always fell asleep instantly. The only time this was not so was when the sky darkened one evening and they smelled dampness in the air and rain started. As they became ever wetter they talked of building a shelter for the night by leaning logs against a tree trunk. But they wondered if the effort was worth the small degree of protection they'd gain. They came across a tree torn up by the roots, lying upward on a slope, its base high enough to provide shelter for both of them, curled up, one on either side of a low, thick central root. They decided to do without food that night and take shelter now. But Mary's sense of gratitude for the respite from rain was short-lived. Trying to get comfortable on the hard, damp earth, knees bent, arms tight to her sides, forced to shift as pieces of twig pressed through her clothes, hit by raindrops slipping through the roots overhead, hungrier than ever, she thought that surely nothing on earth could be any worse than this. But then she remembered George in his dungeon. This did not lessen her misery but made her better able to endure it. She fell asleep at last, for a little while, when the rain eased.

Every morning on waking, she and Peter said the Lord's Prayer together. All their other devotions were solitary. As she walked or foraged or cooked, Mary frequently begged God to give her strength and to spare George's life.

On the fifth morning they found they had walked into a clearing dotted with huts, fireplaces with racks over them, and a large central hearth surrounded by a circle of logs. Mary saw all this even as she was turning to flee. When they reached a safe distance Peter said, "Thanks to God's mercy there was nobody there."

"Where were they?"

"The whole village must have packed up and gone off to a river or even the ocean for the easy August fishing. We were lucky."

With renewed care, they set off again through the trees, the sun flickering through the faraway top branches. An hour or two later they walked through a section of forest composed of pines with spaces of identical size around each. This looked like a white man's plantation but the height of the trees showed it could not be. These pines had been here for far longer than white men. Nature, not humans, had apportioned the breathing spaces, large enough for each tree to grow tall though permitting no lower growth to survive. For fifteen or more feet up from the ground on each trunk there projected stunted, horizontal sticks—all that remained of live branches.

After a time this wood started to change. Oaks appeared; then a hemlock, swathed in busy, dark green leaves from the tip to the ground. They found themselves walking out into the fierce, unshaded sun of a clearing. But there were no signs of human habitation. The air had gone still, the forest sounds hushed. Alone in the center of a wide patch of rough grass stood a maple tree, its top perfectly arched, broad base luxuriant.

"Keep walking. Quickly." Taking Mary's arm, Peter strode past the maple toward an oak guarding the reentrance to the wood, its trunk more than twice the width of a door. They had almost reached it when from behind peeped a shaved head topped by a feather. As they turned, the native leaped out, bow and arrow aimed straight at them. Mary's first feeling was of devastating loss. Everything gone. In the next instant she experienced the full tragedy of unprepared death, without good-byes or retelling the story leading from earliest memory to now. But the native did not shoot but made barking sounds, adjusting his bow, apparently to take more careful aim. Peter held up his hands; the native jabbed the bow and arrow forward, nodding his head; Peter understood, took off his gun sling, and dropped it. The Indian ran forward and, transferring the bow and arrow to his left hand, dexterously picked up the sling and got it over his body. Neither Mary nor Peter moved an inch. Again lifting the bow and drawing the arrow, now at closer range, he inspected them. He was young, his almost naked brown body of the lithe thinness of very early manhood, the high-cheekboned face smooth as a plum. Mary met his eyes and in their cold curiosity saw a new threat. The Indians who had stormed York had committed every atrocity but that. Yet she had heard other tales. . . . Suddenly she remembered something George had shown her, that his friend Waramaug had shown *him*. She lifted her hand, palm outward, fingers outspread. To her amazement the Indian gave a laugh, showing perfect white teeth, and again switched both his bow and arrow to his left hand, to give the sign back to her. Then he turned and, the gun swinging from side to side on his chest, ran back past the oak into the forest.

"What was that?" Peter gasped.

"A peace sign."

"He may come back. After consulting with the elders. Let's run."

A good distance from the clearing they sat on mossy earth, leaning against a wide tree trunk, trying to talk but emitting more sighs and gasps than words. Peter gave up attempting to speak and put his arm round Mary.

"Feeling better now," she muttered after a moment. He took his arm away.

"You saved our lives."

"Can't be sure yet," she replied.

"We'll move on soon. Did you see the gashes on that maple tree?"

"No."

"They have been using it for syrup. That was a clearing they'd made. Maybe a meeting place."

"We should leave. Though I suppose if they want to find us they still can. George told me Indians can always find tracks even if there aren't any."

"I hope they won't think it worth their effort. Behind that oak the Indian must have thought we were deer and hoped for a good meal. But the only thing about us of any use was the gun."

"Not much of a loss. We never dare shoot it."

"I am glad to be rid of it."

"Walking will be easier." Suddenly Mary started laughing. "I'm surprised how glad I am to be alive!"

"Why should you be surprised?" Peter paused. "Yes, I understand. George . . ."

Mary scrambled up.

"Which way?" She searched in the trees for the sun and at last saw it, a giant burst egg yolk spread behind black branches. "That must be southwest."

"South, southwest." Peter pointed to a little to the right of the burst yolk. "That's due west." The trees in that direction gave them clear passage. Sounding diffident, as he adjusted his jacket, loose without the gun sling, he asked, "Are you quite recovered?"

"Quite recovered! We'll make good going now."

They did. And that night they had the good fortune to catch two fat trout. Mary, as always despite everything, when she lay down fell asleep instantly.

But Peter stayed awake. His love and desire for this woman had increased the more he'd come to know her and they were testing him now as much as all the deprivations of the journey. It was becoming harder than ever to behave toward her as another man's wife. The conflict between the desire to save his friend and the inadmissible wish that he'd fail lay just below the surface of thought, a constant weight on his spirits. In a part of his soul he wanted never to reach Albany.

Over the next days the need to stifle longing often made him cold. Mary understood. She too was fighting a battle. She loved George as much as she ever had but it was a sometimes almost overwhelming temptation to encourage this strong, handsome, good man to give in to his growing love for her and take her in his arms. After the first hours of buoyant relief on escaping the Indian, her shame at her own weakness and sinfulness was added to her fear of pursuit, of ambush by Indians, and of sheer physical collapse, making the journey still more arduous.

The travelers shared a moment of joy on seeing from a mountain top the thin blue serpent of the Connecticut River at the foot of distant gray hills. Beyond was a slender plume of smoke they guessed must come from Deerfield, a fortified town about the same size as Wells. A few miles past that was the border with the colony of New York, beyond which they were safe from pursuit and arrest, if not Indians, wolves, or hunger.

They knew there was no white man's habitation after Deerfield until Albany. As they rested, the river valley before them, Mary suggested they enter the town to ask for advice on the best route to the capital and to beg or buy provisions to help make sure they arrived there. They might make contact with someone who could ferry them over the river instead of having to build a raft from logs and vines as they'd planned. Peter said, "But the arrest warrant is as valid here as in Salem."

"They won't know about it."

"Hathorne could have sent a messenger."

This seemed to her unlikely but Peter looked obdurate and she said nothing more. They made their way down the mountain but toward evening began climbing again. Reaching a clearing, with no sign of recent habitation, they decided to stop, since the sun was too low now to be visible over the hill and the stream they had followed for a while was narrowing. Soon it would disappear altogether and they would be without water to drink. Only just enough daylight was left to give time to find food before sleeping. As they usually did, they rested for a few minutes before starting the search.

Mary sat, her chin on her knees, rubbing her blistered toes. Her boots lay toppled on their sides, the exposed soles white with wear. Peter leaned against a rock, his legs stretched out. He too had taken his shoes off. Mary noticed how long and bony his feet were, quite unlike George's, which were squarer and more muscular. Peter's seemed designed for daylong walks, George's for sprinting and jumping. Peter's were in surprisingly good condition, without bad bruises or blisters, and Mary wondered how George's would have been faring by now. Altogether Peter wasn't as physically strong as her husband—nobody was—but he possessed extraordinary stamina. And was utterly depend-able. She hoisted herself to her feet, pulling on her boots.

"Food and water!"

"I'll try to spear a fish while you forage."

An hour later they'd made a sparse meal of some small mush-rooms that had been growing on a log and a few blackberries and a cou-ple of crayfish Peter had caught in a pool a short way upriver. Dusk was falling in earnest. Mary wondered whether to leave discussing Deerfield until morning. But Peter always seemed especially remote in the morn-ings. Better have the talk now.

"Please do let's go to Deerfield."

"I said before, there's too much risk."

"In Wells the witch hunt seemed absurd. It'll be the same there."

"That was Maine. This is Massachusetts."

At the edge of the clearing stood the smooth stump of a tree chopped down by trappers. In the fading light Mary fancied it a polished dining table piled high with big brown loaves and dishes of succulent roast meat. An owl in the distance sounded a long cry. Per-haps he was hungry too . . .

"I am not sure I can keep on as far as Albany without more food than we've been getting."

"You've made it this far."

His brusque tone surprised her. Peter looked not only closed off but angry. This was so unusual, she suspected something was at work in him that was creating emotional turmoil and clouding his judgment. She usually trusted his decisions, knowing how carefully considered they were; now she believed on this occasion hers might be sounder.

"I am serious. I'm not being weak-willed. I often feel faint. Sometimes it is very, very hard to keep going."

He was silent.

"Is there some reason you're not giving, for preferring not to go to Deerfield?"

"Of course not. I told you, it is because of the danger."

"It's *small.*"

"But real."

"The danger of collapsing is *more* real."

"I don't agree." Peter hoisted himself up.

"The people in Deerfield will take pity on us. They're bound to."

"I know the pastor there. He is the most conventional Puritan you can imagine."

Mary felt a surge of hope, the opposite emotion to the one Peter had expected to evoke. How could someone he already knew refuse to assist him? But had he quarreled with the man? Was that the true reason he wanted to avoid Deerfield? Yet Peter never quarreled with anyone. Mary asked, "Where did you meet him?"

"At school."

"So you've known him twenty years!"

"But not seen him for fifteen."

"Were you friends? Did you like him? And he you?"

"He was some years below me." Peter was pacing now.

"I expect he admired you."

"If he did, that means nothing now that we're men."

"It might mean everything." Mary made a sudden connection. "He must have known George!"

"Yes."

"Did he admire *him*?"

"I do not know."

"An old school friend who looked up to you and George too would *surely* want to help you."

"Really? Remember Samuel Sewall? John Williams was an unimaginative boy. Even at school he was headed for the ministry. What is more, I seem to recall he married Cotton Mather's cousin."

Mary scrambled to her feet. "But in any case he will not know about the arrest warrant."

"If he does not, how can we explain our traveling like this?"

"We could say we left Massachusetts because of *possible* arrest."

"For that reason alone he might hold us by force and send word to Salem."

"Not if he's a friend."

"He is *not* a friend."

Mary felt convinced she was right, that not even the most rigid Puritan could refuse to help two travelers in such need, particularly if acquainted with one of them. She was equally convinced that not even the most rigid Puritan, living in this wilderness, could seriously believe there were huge numbers of witches in Salem, some of them pious church members. Or, even if they could, they surely could not believe, if they had ever known George, that he was one of them. And, even if she were wrong, without help she might not make Albany. What was it that blinded Peter to the true balance of risk? She watched him as he paced; he turned to look at her and something in his face before he quickly looked away again gave her an answer. He wanted to keep her to himself. Could that be? Could this journey, with the two of them alone together, be for him, despite all its hardships, an idyll?

She said quietly, "I am going even if you're not. I feel certain my chances of survival are better if I do."

To her surprise, he looked ashamed. She realized he had seen himself, for the moment of her insight, as she had. He said, with guilt in his voice, "Very well. We'll go to Deerfield."

When they first heard the river they thought it was rain. But then beyond the shade of the trees they saw sunlit leaves and knew the water was below, that the bright foliage was the tops of trees growing low on the steep bank. A few moments later they saw brown water and clambered down through tree trunks and shrubs to the edge. On the far side were only more trees, with no sign of Deerfield.

"Oh no," said Mary. "Which way? Should we try to cross?"

"Let's walk along the riverbank one way for an hour or so, then, if we don't see anything, try the other way."

"Let's try upriver first."

They climbed back up to walk along a narrow path that made easier going than the wet stones and sand by the water, though their view was blocked by trees and bushes. After about half an hour Peter shouted, "Look! Smoke! Above the trees!"

Then they saw a chimney. Scrambling down again to the water's edge, they could see the trees on the opposite bank further upriver had been felled and a palisade erected. Behind it was a watchtower. They waved and shouted and a small figure on the top of it waved back. Five minutes later a boat was rowing toward them.

Chapter Forty-Four

Deerfield
July 1692

PASTOR JOHN WILLIAMS'S SMALL DWELLING WAS SURPRISINGLY comfortable and attractive and Mary saw at once that his wife, who greeted them and asked them in, must be responsible for this. She looked comfortable and attractive herself, and concerned with the comfort and attractiveness of others. She gazed at Mary, as she led her to the best chair, with obvious admiration; Mary realized, to her surprise and mild pleasure, such beauty as she boasted must show through exhaustion, dirt, and unkemptness. After explaining that Reverend Williams was out, as she settled Mary among cushions, Mistress Williams sent the maid for sassafras tea, promising a good dinner the moment her husband came home. Peter gave Mary a nod and smile as he perched on a bench, acknowledging that so far her optimistic predictions were accurate.

"You have walked from *Salem*?" Mistress Williams marveled. "I could not have believed it was possible!"

The boatman, one of the small contingent of soldiers stationed in Deerfield, had told her at the door where they had come from as well as giving their names and the reason for their flight, repeating the modified version of the truth they had given him, that Mary was *suspected* of witchcraft. As they rowed across the river Peter had also explained he was an old acquaintance of Reverend Williams and a close friend of Mary's husband, who could not himself help Mary get away. Despite the boatman's obvious curiosity Peter had stayed silent on the reasons for this.

Mistress Williams had invited the soldier in with the travelers and he now reported Peter's old friendship with Reverend Williams, leaving alone the trickier matter of why Peter was Mary's traveling companion.

"To speak true, good lady," Mary said, smiling, "I think God must have been helping us more than we knew. That is the only way I can explain finding the strength to keep going. I cannot express how wonderful it is to be kindly received in such a comfortable, beautiful house." She shook her head, tears in her eyes. Their hostess looked from her to Peter, showing warmth and wariness in almost equal measure though the warmth clearly had her truest nature behind it. Mary saw no resemblance between her and her cousin Cotton Mather but for a certain air of bewilderment, the outward manifestation of a lack of easy, firm grasp of facts and possibilities. However, this characteristic in Cotton was combined with insecurity and vanity, whereas in his cousin it coexisted with anxious consideration for others.

"Your name is Captain Peter White?" their hostess asked her guest uncertainly, not to verify the fact, which the boatman had stated quite clearly, but to start the search for an understanding of Mary and Peter's relationship. Peter stood up, bowed, and sat down again, saying, "I am this lady's husband's closest friend. Do you know of George Burroughs? He was also at school with myself and your husband in Roxbury."

"Oh!" Mistress Williams's bewilderment now almost overwhelmed her. But after a few moments of deep frowning, she inquired, "How is it he's not with you?"

Mary, taking herself completely by surprise, burst into tears.

"Oh, my dear! No more questions! Here comes the sassafras tea!" Mistress Williams took a cup from the maid and brought it to her. "Sip that, my dear. We will not speak of this again till you have refreshed yourself and rested. Jane, fetch some cakes too! There are some on the side table, newly baked. And ale for the gentlemen."

"May I wash my hands and face first?" Mary asked.

"How thoughtless of me! Martha, take Mrs. Burroughs to my chamber and provide her with everything she needs to tidy herself."

After Mary returned, as they ate and drank, they talked of the hardships and dangers of their journey, to Mistress Williams's frequent exclamations of astonishment, horror, and sympathy. A little later the reverend came home. Of medium height, straight backed, with short brown hair and a solemn expression, he seemed exactly the decent, diligent, unimaginative character Peter had suggested. The boatman rose from his stool, brushing crumbs from his hands and introducing the visitors, who also rose. As the reverend gazed at them in astonishment, since few unexpected guests, let alone old school friends, ever came to this outpost, the soldier explained briefly, to accompanying head shakes from the reverend's wife, why they were here. The reverend stepped forward, shook Peter's hand, saying he had not changed at all from when he was a boy except for having grown taller, bowed to Mary, and bade everyone sit down again.

"I hope my wife is looking after you well?"

"Wonderfully!" Mary exclaimed.

"What a dreadful shock for you, Mistress Burroughs, to find your-self accused of witchcraft!"

"At least I am in excellent company. Some of the most reputable people in Massachusetts are accused."

"You must have little faith in the system of justice, to undertake such an arduous journey." The reverend sounded sincere, showing only a hint of reserve against the possibility Mary might not be the innocent she seemed.

"I am sorry to say I have no faith in it at all. Many people I know to be God-fearing, even saintly, have been charged and await trial. At least one has already been tried and found guilty! We were there; we saw shocking injustice done."

"A pious woman of seventy," added Peter.

"Some insanity seems to have seized them all," said the reverend. "We heard it started with a band of young girls acting strangely."

Mary knew, after a few more minutes' conversation, he was, as she had predicted, no longer the Boston Puritan he might once have been. What little news of the witch hunt had reached Deerfield had suggested to him unheard-of human madness rather than the work of the devil. For all his relationship by marriage to the Mathers, Pastor Williams was unimpressed by spectral sight or the overeager dispatches of arrest warrants by the magistrates or the securing of convictions by the judges.

Over a hearty dinner of pork, sweet potatoes, red cabbage, and a compote of dried fruits, as the arrivals told the Williamses more of the trials and described Bridget Bishop's hanging, the depths of John Williams's skepticism surprised even Mary. It soon seemed safe to reveal that his old school friend George Burroughs was one of those charged and in jail. Williams expressed shock and concern and Mistress

Williams seized Mary's hand, giving a cry of distress. Mary wondered if she should tell them of her meeting with Cotton and decided not to at this juncture.

By the time they finished their meal it had become clear that John Williams's views were at least partly the result of Boston's failure to send reinforcements to his town. As Peter had, in Wells, the reverend regarded a hierarchy that neglected the needs of its most vulnerable members as suspect. Its enthusiasm for the hanging of witches might well be no wiser than its lack of care for its frontier outposts. Mistress Williams fervently voiced agreement with her husband as he talked of this.

"Have you any influence with the authorities?" Mary asked him. "Could you possibly speak to anyone on behalf of my husband?"

"Alas! I am a pariah to them, with my constant requests for reinforcements! I could only hurt your husband's cause, not help it, by trying to speak for him."

"I wonder, do you have any influence with your cousin Cotton?" Mary asked Mistress Williams, who unexpectedly laughed loudly.

"I gather not," Mary said wryly.

"If I ever had any I lost it when we were seven and he wrote prayers for me to say, which I dropped behind the furniture. I was a God-fearing child but saw no cause to take religious instruction from a boy the same age as me, however pious and clever he thought himself. He reprimanded me repeatedly for my wickedness and told me I was sure to go to hell."

Mary felt the time had come to tell her about her visit to the pious, clever boy, no less deluded now, thirty years later. Mrs. Williams and her husband were in equal parts grimly amused, saddened, and disturbed.

"I fear a great wrong is being done in Salem," said the pastor.

"There can be no doubt of that," Peter agreed.

The next day their hosts provided Mary and Peter not only with clean clothes and ample provisions but also horses and the company of the soldier who had ferried them, who knew the terrain between Deerfield and Albany.

Chapter Forty-Five
New York Colony
July 1692

ON THE FIFTH MORNING OF THEIR RENEWED JOURNEY, AFTER MAKING excellent progress compared with their previous traveling, Mary woke feeling hotter than usual at such an early hour.

"Start of a hot spell, alas," Peter said.

They no longer had to catch or gather their food but simply unpack some from their saddlebags, but by the time they'd doused the fire and repacked their pots and utensils after breakfast, Mary was exhausted. As they rode through the trees the heat thickened until it seemed as if they were moving through some undiscovered element of a consistency between water and air. Mary began to feel nauseous and her limbs ached. She assumed this was due to the exertion of riding in this heat, but as the morning wore on she felt worse and after the midday meal it was hard to climb back on her horse. Now she guessed something was wrong with her besides the effects of the weather. She began to feel she was living through a nightmare except that her physical suffering kept reminding her she was awake. Suddenly she slid from her saddle, lay on the ground, and could not get up. She was conscious but her arms and legs would not move. Peter felt her forehead, took the saddle off her horse, and, with the soldier's help, lifted her so she lay on its back. Then he took the reins and led the creature while the soldier took the reins of the other two.

Later Mary had no memory of arriving at the governor's mansion or being carried by a servant to a well-appointed bedroom. The next few days were made up of emotionally fraught dreams interrupted by brief moments of waking. Her nightmares refused to dissolve even when she tossed and turned and called out and sat up. In one of them George was locked in his cell for eternity.

When anyone appeared she asked for news but they had none. At first she thought her attendants were spirits but soon came to realize they were servants, doctors, and the governor's female relatives, though she was unsure which was which. The only person she could identify with certainty was Peter.

"I would have died but for you."

"We might both have died if you had not made me go to Deerfield."

"I can hardly remember."

He sat down next to the bed and squeezed her hand so hard her wedding ring pressed her finger painfully.

"You are going to get better. At first the doctor was not sure."

"When will we hear about George?"

"Soon I hope."

Illness invoked clarity and honesty. "I love you, Peter. But I love George more. I would die to save him if I could."

For a few moments Peter could not speak. Then he said, a little hoarsely, "We will save him without dying."

She stared at him with continuing clear honesty. "If only we could be sure of that."

"We can be sure of one thing. We will do everything possible, and impossible."

"Thank you for your devotion to him. Perhaps I should not have talked of this but I needed to. I cannot help but know you love me."

"It is because I love you that I am resolved to do all I can to save him."

Chapter Forty-Six

Salem Town
July 1692

"I MUST APOLOGIZE AGAIN FOR DISTURBING YOU LAST NIGHT AFTER you'd retired!"

"N-no apology needed! You c-couldn't have had a better reason! Let me c-congratulate you again!" Stephen Sewall seized his brother's hand and shook it hard, smiling with a delight that broadened and softened his pinched features.

"I could not leave home till I had seen the baby suck!"

"Of course you c-could not!"

"It is such a relief to see that, after a difficult birth! A manservant will ride here if anything goes wrong, as I pray is unlikely now."

"Let us s-sit down. Our b-breakfast is waiting. We will drink a toast to m-mother and baby at dinner tonight."

"What a spread, brother!" Samuel put a hand on Stephen's shoulder as they moved to the table laden with a variety of food including a mountain of pancakes surrounded by berries and flanked by large jugs of maple syrup and cream. "This is in my honor, I know." He tugged his jacket up an inch or two and lowered himself into a chair.

"I know your special liking for pancakes. A new father needs sustenance."

"No one understands the joy of a new birth like one's own flesh and blood." Samuel glanced round the table laid for six. "Are your wife and family joining us?"

"They will come down later. I knew you wanted to start work as soon as possible."

"Thank you. I would have waited to ride here this morning if there had not been quite so much business for us to attend to today."

"Shall I ask the servant to help you to a little of everything?"

"Please!"

As the servant piled food on his platter, Samuel again glanced round the table.

"Does the littlest child eat with you now?"

"Oh, no, she still eats in the nursery."

"The table's laid for six."

"The extra place is for Betty."

Samuel went still. He had forgotten about Betty.

"She used to want to keep to herself but yesterday she agreed with my wife she would eat with us."

"Enough, sir?" the servant asked.

"Yes, thank you."

The servant moved away to fill Stephen's plate.

"How is she?" Samuel asked, his voice betraying no feeling.

"Well, thanks be to God. No more visions."

"The Lord be praised."

After Stephen had said grace they began to eat, saying no more on the subject of Betty, or anything else, and finishing before any of the rest of the family appeared. Stephen said a prayer, then he and Samuel left the room and mounted the stairs to his study. Samuel sat himself at the desk while his brother took a few steps to the window. Glancing down at the street, he leaned out, then quickly drew back.

"L-look!"

"What is it?"

"George B-Burroughs! C-coming to the door!"

Samuel knocked over his chair, running to see. "Any weapon?"

"N-No."

Samuel turned from the window and headed for the door. "Get away from there. Go out at back and fetch a constable. Two constables. I'll get him up here."

As the two men ran down the stairs there was a loud knock on the door. Stephen hurtled along the corridor to the back entrance while Samuel leaped down the last steps, ran across the hall, and grappled with the bolts. He opened the door just far enough to peep out.

"Let me in, Sam! I must talk to you!"

Burroughs's wild, malnourished appearance, seen close-up, astonished Sewall. But Stephen had been right about his carrying no weapon and there seemed nowhere in his breeches or shirt he could hide one. Samuel pulled the door fully open.

"Come in. Quickly. Before anyone else sees you." He shut and bolted the door as Burroughs stepped in, exclaiming, "Thank God you were here!"

"Follow me."

He quickly led Burroughs upstairs to his study, where he gestured him into a chair, lifted the one he'd knocked over, and placed and sat on it so they faced each other.

"It's good seeing you, Sam!"

"How did you break out?"

"Sheer force. I had to come here."

Impulsively, overcome by his appearance, which testified to intense suffering, Sewall reached toward him.

"My old friend!" Burroughs said fervently, seizing his hand.

"Let me get you food and drink."

"No. Do not move. I need to talk to you."

Sewall eased his hand out of Burroughs's. "You cannot stay here. Why did you escape? If you are innocent you have nothing to fear. This puts you in jeopardy. Why have you come?"

"They are torturing prisoners to make them condemn me. One boy has already confessed. By now maybe more."

Sewall hit his forehead with his fist.

"Did you know of this?"

"No, of course not!" Samuel's chins wobbled vigorously with the shaking of his head. "How, tortured?"

"Neck and heels."

"This is far beyond. . . . How long are they kept like that?"

"Twenty-four hours. Maybe more."

"How do you know?"

"The keeper told me."

Sewall jumped up and walked to the window.

"It must be stopped!" Burroughs shouted. "Now!"

Sewall turned, regaining control.

"Who ordered it?"

"Hathorne."

"Stoughton comes to Salem tonight. I will talk to him."

"Stoughton gave his consent! You must go to the prison now and stop it!"

Sewall looked at the desperate figure who had once been his friend and his lifelong instinct of self-preservation produced the words, "I have no authority to do that."

"The keeper would obey you! That is authority enough! I stand no chance of justice with these false confessors accusing me!"

Sewall walked back to his chair and sat down, dissembling concern, real enough moments before but now eclipsed by his habitual priority of security for his family and himself. Where were the constables? Why were they not here yet? He said, "Increase Mather is coming to the trial. He will see for himself if justice is served. If it is not, he will ask Governor Phips to order a retrial. You must go back to prison now."

"Not unless you come with me!"

Should he agree? Go with Burroughs before the constables got here? To prevent his possibly escaping them, and Salem? But once they reached the jail Burroughs would again demand Sewall countermand Hathorne's orders, perhaps refusing to enter till he did so.

"I shall speak to Mr. Stoughton tonight."

"But I told you Stoughton condones it!"

"How do you know?"

"The keeper told me."

"Why should you believe him?"

"He has no reason to lie!"

"With Increase Mather coming to the trial, you can be certain of justice."

"I wish I had your faith in him."

"He is the wisest man I know."

"You were his protégé; he always favored you."

"No godly man could doubt him."

"Do you think me ungodly? Do you think me *guilty*? Is that possible? You know I do not have supernatural strength. I told you myself about those tricks!"

Sewall stood up.

"Let me order you food and drink."

They heard footsteps coming to the door. Burroughs leaped up. The door opened and Stephen Sewall came in with two constables.

"What's this?" Burroughs shouted.

"You must go back to prison! For your own sake!"

"Not till I've convinced you of my innocence!"

The men seized Burroughs's arms; he threw them off.

"Fetch more constables!" Sewall shouted at Stephen, who stood as though paralyzed.

"Give me ten minutes more with you!" Burroughs pleaded.

"I cannot! This will go against you! Go back to prison!"

Burroughs seized one of the constables by the throat with both hands while thrusting his knee in his groin. "Come with me to the prison, Sam! Stop the torture!"

"I have no authority!"

Burroughs squeezed harder and the man began to gag. The other was still doubled over, his stomach having met the corner of the desk when Burroughs sent him sprawling.

"Let him go!" Samuel shouted.

"Only if you'll come with me!"

"I will!"

"You swear?"

"I swear!"

Burroughs released the man and headed for the door, the constables going after him, one still clutching his stomach, the other his groin.

"These men can walk with me, when they're able, but not try to touch me. Come, Sam."

"I shall follow you."

"No! Come with me!"

The constable Burroughs had kneed was behind him and now rallied with the energy of anger to strike his head hard with his stick. Burroughs fell, half got up, and collapsed again. The constable produced a rope that had been hanging coiled on his belt and, with his fellow's help, tied Burroughs's arms behind his back and began to drag him to the door.

"Sam, swear you'll follow me!"

"I swear!"

"Let me get up! I'll walk!"

The constables allowed Burroughs to rise to his feet, then took hold of his arms again.

"No need of that," Burroughs shouted. "Now that I have Sam's word, I give my own I won't try to escape."

"Unhand him," said Sewall.

"See you at the prison!"

The constables followed Burroughs through the door. After shutting it, Stephen Sewall asked his brother, "Are you going?"

"No. I had to lie to him. I have no authority to countermand John Hathorne's orders."

Chapter Forty-Seven

Albany
August 1692

MARY, OPENING HER EYES, SAW NATHANIEL CARY STANDING ABOVE her and sat bolt upright.

"Has George been tried?"

"Yes."

"Convicted?"

"I fear so."

She screamed, "Hanged?"

"No, no, not hanged."

"Oh, thanks be to God." She fell back on the pillows, her heart beating as wildly as when the Indian leaped out from the tree.

"There is still hope," said Cary.

"Date set?"

"No."

"I must go to him!"

"My dear, you are not well enough . . ." He laid a hand on her arm. "Thomas Brattle is here. He came from Salem with the news."

"Fetch him!"

"If the doctor thinks you are well enough . . ."

"I'm well enough."

"I shall speak to the governor's wife about it. Wait as patiently as you can."

An hour later, after having been brought tea by the maid, dressed in a clean nightrobe with a high, frilled collar, and propped on pillows that looked like mounds of pristine snow, Mary greeted Brattle eagerly, feeling a warmth resembling love for this gnomelike man bringing her news. He sat on one side of her while Peter and Nathaniel Cary arranged chairs for themselves on the other. The heat had diminished over the past several days; the scent of roses wafted through the room on a breeze from the window. Brattle scrutinized Mary, his bulbous all-seeing eyes full of concern, his eyebrows sticking out at every angle. He opened his mouth, sighed, seemed about to speak, and stopped.

"Tell me everything," Mary urged. "Nothing is worse than this suspense. Can you get him a reprieve?"

"I cannot promise. I shall try my very best."

"Where is Governor Phips?"

"Back in Boston. Just arrived. I leave at once to go to him."

"How I wish I could come with you."

"You could not even if you were well enough. You'd be arrested."

Mary fought back the sense of near despair at her helplessness. Peter took her hand, squeezed, and let go. Brattle said, "I swear I will do everything possible."

"Did you visit George in Salem?"

"No, I left at once after the trial. Time was of the essence."

"How was he on the stand?"

"Exemplary. He said, 'I am innocent,' loudly and clearly when they brought him in, and then again at the end when the jury gave its verdict. Otherwise he made no sound. He held himself tall and never lost his dignity."

"Oh, my good friend!" Peter exclaimed.

"My brave George!" cried Mary.

"The girls outdid themselves, I assume," Peter said with deep disgust. Brattle gave one of his quick, angry sighs.

"They showed the judges their arms where they claimed Burroughs had bitten them. I saw for myself one sink her own teeth in."

"Did you tell Stoughton?" Peter asked.

"Impossible in the chaos. And he would not have believed me. There was truly no point. Even more disgraceful was that the mad wretches claimed Burroughs's dead wives appeared in the courtroom."

Mary gasped.

"They said the ghosts were saying Burroughs killed them. But that was not the worst of it. There was a troop of so-called confessors claiming Burroughs was their leader. It was obvious they had been tortured. Some were young men who looked as if they had had the life almost beaten out of them and some were dull-witted old women so exhausted from being denied sleep they could scarcely stand upright."

"Oh, what iniquity!" Cary shouted. Mary pounded the bedcovers with her fists. Peter put his hand gently on her shoulder to calm her.

"Were others convicted?" he asked Cary.

"The Proctors, George Jacobs, and Martha Carrier. I heard just before I left that Elizabeth Proctor is pregnant so her life will be spared till after she gives birth."

"Was Increase Mather there?" Peter asked.

"Yes."

"What did *he* make of it?"

"He said to me afterward he himself would have convicted on the evidence brought. I asked why and he said the sheer volume of it. There was more than I have told you, claims of George's alleged devil-given strength and harshness to his wives and ancient sorceries. All of course worthless. I longed to reply to Increase Mather that there cannot be volume without substance but it would have achieved nothing except to make him even less willing to talk to me."

"Did you tell *him* about seeing the girl bite herself?" Peter asked.

"Like Stoughton, he would not have believed me and, again, I would have undermined my influence with him." Brattle stood up. "I must go."

"Was Samuel Sewall there?" Mary asked.

"He was one of the judges."

"A weaselly hypocrite if ever there was one. Oh, how I despise him. Did he speak?"

"Not a word."

"Have you *anything* to tell us, to give us hope?"

The large eyes shone. "The sheriff and his officers went to old George Jacobs's estate, after he was convicted, and took everything, even his wife's wedding ring."

"Why on earth should that give us hope?"

"Because the more outrageous this witch hunt becomes, the more people will question it. Already respectable Puritans are losing trust in their leaders and defying the laws they have always lived by. I learned Rebecca Nurse's sons sailed by night to Gallows Hill to rescue their mother's remains and rebury them in the family graveyard."

"Israel Porter got Goody Nurse a reprieve. You surely can do the same for my husband, and prevent Stoughton from rescinding it."

THERE WAS NOTHING BUT THIS. THE WORLD HAD PARADOXICALLY
shrunk and yet deepened. . . . On the ladder, moving and talking. . . .
Minutes later . . . moving but unaware he was doing so. Suffocation did
not scare him; it was pain to end all pain. But the transformation from
warm, breathing being to inanimate matter frightened him as nothing
ever had. He tried to tame the idea by thinking of sleep. But in slumber
the lungs breathed; the body stirred; the mind dreamed. In death his
body would be motionless and his mind no longer glimpse self-conjured
images but know the unknowable.

Pastel-colored expanses and dimly seen white-clothed figures
hung like a screen before the God it would be sinful to try to envision.

Yet even more sinful was to find little comfort in the prospect of
meeting his Maker in heaven, but instead long by some magic to be
released through the gateway of death to forests, the scents of roses and
pine and soft evening breezes.

He must pray, again and again, for help in his weakness, and for
forgiveness.

Less than forty-eight hours now. That longing for certainty he'd
had was part of life. He was dead now but for the dying, and longed for
uncertainty.

He had heard the news of date and time from supercilious
Bartholomew Gedney who had said, without enthusiasm, it was not too
late to confess and be spared. Burroughs knew Hathorne had sent Gedney because he had no wish to try to persuade him himself. He knew he
could not succeed and perhaps did not wish to. A confession from Burroughs would be a triumph but his death on the gallows a pleasure.

Burroughs had never even been tempted to confess. To agree that he was an ally of the devil would mean spending the rest of this life in shame and the whole of the next one in hell. The simple longing of flesh for continued existence could not vanquish his mind's judgment.

His thoughts traveled well-worn paths. Did Mary know he'd been convicted? Did she even know he'd been tried? Had she and Peter reached Albany? Had news of his conviction reached the governor? Even if Mary knew of his conviction, she could scarcely go back to Boston to seek a reprieve. She would be arrested at once. Might Peter go without her? If he did, and *were* to see the governor, what influence could he have, compared with the opposing voices of Stoughton and the Mathers?

George wondered if he could have done or said anything at his trial to alter the outcome. Remembering all those lies, he remembered grains of truth: the tricks amounting almost to sorceries; the suffering he'd caused his wives and sometimes others by his selfishness, anger, and intolerance. He thought of occasions when he'd been harsh, even cruel, and for the first time in his life recognized and named the hate and resentment that had paraded as righteousness. He begged God for forgiveness not only for his sins but for his hypocrisy.

He always ended his prayers with the "Our Father." He spoke aloud, slowly, pausing between phrases, hearing the words as he never had before. When he said, "forgive us our trespasses, as we forgive those who trespass against us," he understood forgiveness not as something begrudgingly granted but as a heart's gift. He remembered what he had said to Mary when she first came to Wells and better understood his own words. He had been thinking then of the love of a father for a daughter, of his own love for Rebecca, but it came to him now that all true forgiveness is forgetting.

As he pronounced "deliver us from evil," he knew that God's greatest blessing to mankind is that such deliverance depends on oneself.

That night, the next to last he would spend on this earth, he tried to sleep. But, though he could make his body lie quietly, his thoughts kept traveling the same paths and going off down new ones. He found himself remembering Rebecca as a child, and the births of all his children, with details long forgotten. He saw Mary again as he had first viewed her, when she fled from the flames and fell on her knees by her

FRANCES HILL

father, and he saw her face as she sat in front of him on his horse and turned round to smile.

He could not bear to imagine her future life here on earth but conjured a faint image of their reunion in the next, when their adoration would be as strong as any between living, breathing beings. He saw their faces and figures dimly but felt their all-encompassing love.

In the darkest part of the night there came three knocks on the wall. He banged three times in return, and recited loudly, "Our father, which art in heaven . . ."

He slept at last, waking when the scrap of sky was clear blue, and at once turned his mind to a subject he had so far avoided: what he should do and say on the cart to the gallows and then on the ladder. He must leave Mary, Peter, Rebecca, and all his children accounts of his death that would strengthen and console them for the rest of their lives. He must strive to make them prouder of his strength as he died than while he lived.

He intended to jump from the ladder before he was pushed, to break his neck and die quickly. But he knew his purpose might be thwarted and considered what he would hold in his mind if he suffered long last agonies. He tried to compose a prayer to express all he wanted to say to his God but, as he struggled for phrases, felt the endeavor was futile and arrogant and that he should simply repeat the "Our Father." When he met his Creator it would be with those perfect words on his lips.

It seemed to him a consolation that before he departed this life he would for a few final moments breathe the open air and see the sky and forest and fields and bid farewell to this beloved earth that had borne him and cradled him.

He had a visitor that evening. Margaret. For the first time she'd had no need to bribe the keeper, who had recovered from the injuries Burroughs had inflicted and, far from bearing him a grudge, seemed to view him with respect. Since the man had learned the date of his death this had increased almost to awe. He hardly dared speak to him. He did not do so now but left as quickly as possible, shutting the door with new quietness.

The gray eyes in the prematurely worn face stared imploringly into Burroughs.

"Please forgive me!"

"Why? For what?"

"For naming you when I confessed!"

"My dear girl!" He tried to go on but the words caught in his throat. He cleared it, to say in strong tones, "You have revoked your confession! There's nothing to forgive! I should ask *you* to forgive *me*."

"What have *I* to forgive *you* for?"

"For not having been able to help and comfort you more."

"You helped me as much as anyone in this whole world could!" She turned her head away. Neither spoke for a few moments. Then she said, "I've been to see my grandfather to ask *his* forgiveness." She brought her arms up over her face. Burroughs could just hear the words. "He dies tomorrow."

"He and I will travel on the cart to the gallows together. We will speak of you as the person who most helped us bear our imprisonment."

"I shall miss you so!"

"One day we will all be together in heaven."

"Yes! Yes!"

"For the first and last time, not separated by the wall, together in the flesh and not just the spirit, let us pray." He closed his eyes. Margaret did so too.

"Our father . . ."

They recited the prayer in perfect unison.

Chapter Forty-Nine

Salem Town
August 1692

THE LOW BUILDING SET ALONE AT THE END OF PRISON LANE, UNDER a sliver of moon and sprinkling of stars, drew toward it human forms, alone and in groups, until even before sunrise the unpaved street and empty field were full. Here and there in shifting lantern light gleamed the bright colored coat of a merchant or his wife's elegant cloak and feathered hat, a doctor's dark garb or tradesman's orange-brown leather jacket. There were no magistrates or ministers at first, but by the time red streaks appeared in the sky several had been ushered through the crowd by the constables and taken places near the door to the dungeons. When the sun's curved tip showed over the horizon the whole of Prison Lane and part of Essex Street were packed.

People started shouting for the leader of witches. There were cruel jokes and unsavory laughter yet with a staleness about them compared with when all this was new.

A single bird had begun to chirp like the pipe before the chanting of a psalm. This note was followed by a chorus far more musical than anything ever heard in a meetinghouse, striking a strange chord of hope in the death-promised dawn.

At last red streaks gave way to clear light. The merchants' wives' velvets and silks glowed among the tradesmen's leather and wool. The occasional black or brown face gave those next to them the pallor of corpses.

A chant was starting, with clear voices joining the rough ones.

"Bring 'em out. Bring 'em out. Bring 'em out."

Peter had been one of the first to arrive, walking from Beadle's in the darkness, stationing himself at the top of the steps leading to the dungeons. He remembered that after coming up from below George would be blinded by daylight and deafened by the noise of the crowd. But surely when his eyes had adjusted he would see his friend, taller than anyone else there.

"Please God, give him strength. Let him bear himself with dignity."

The door opened.

"Make way! Get back!"

A guard came up the steps; two more followed. A marshal moved forward to meet them from the back of the throng. At the steps he took control, loudly ordering the crowd back and telling the guards where to stand. Several constables joined him but, when a clattering of hooves was heard, he ordered them away again. People were pushing to get out of the way; the hoofbeats were growing louder. Peter jumped aside as two horses pulling a cart trotted past him. The driver was standing, balancing himself with legs slightly apart while using the reins with a self-conscious air of expertise. As soon as the cart rattled to a stop two of the constables started unfastening and lowering the railings at the back. The crowd edged forward again.

Suddenly an old man was on the steps, raising a walking stick as he shielded his eyes with his arm. He tried to support himself with his second stick but stumbled. A keeper caught his arm.

"Let me be! I can see well enough, half-blinded though I am by God's light after Satan's darkness!" Shaking off the guards, he reached the top step and moved toward the cart. But, for all his pride, he needed help climbing up. The floor was two feet from the ground. Once there, he refused further aid, getting a hand on the top rail with one stick under his arm while leaning on the other stick.

A commotion at the door heralded tall John Proctor standing at the steps, as blinded as Jacobs, pushing off a guard who was trying to pull him. Regaining his vision, he speedily set off for the cart, grasped the rail, and pulled himself up into it.

"Peter!"

Captain White swung back. George Burroughs was on the steps, shielding his eyes. Peter stepped toward him but a constable's arm was at once thrown across his chest. Behind Burroughs appeared the keeper with one working eye. Peter ducked under the constable's arm and ran forward, thrusting a paper into Burroughs's hand, no one seeing the action but the keeper, who chose to ignore it, shouting at Peter to get back even as the constable seized him and pulled him away. As the keeper propelled Burroughs to the cart the minister slipped the paper into his pocket; his face was haggard, its expression grim. But, to Peter's relief, he showed no fear. Shaking the keeper off, he reached the cart alone. There were mutterings from the crowd but no one dared shout since this prisoner was, even for those who believed him the devil, a figure of personal strength, with a minister's authority. Peter tried to follow him but the constable still held him back. The marshal shouted, "Stay where you are or I'll have you arrested."

Burroughs got into the cart and took his place at the rail. He looked across at Peter and waved an open-palmed hand slowly from side to side. Peter waved back with the same movement. Neither smiled. Not for the first time, but more intensely than before, Peter wished they could swap places. Burroughs should go back to Mary while he went to the gallows.

"I'll be following you!" he shouted.

"Shut your mouth!" the constable, holding him, barked.

A hideous screech made everyone turn. Martha Carrier was being dragged up the steps by two guards, her features distorted with terror. She struggled but could not slow the guards' progress. The crowd thundered insults, the more vociferous because they had not dared yell at Burroughs. There came shouts from all sides of the name Cotton Mather had given her, "Queen of Hell." Peter looked back at Burroughs, to see him finish reading the paper he had given him and put it back in his pocket. His expression had changed to one close to joy: he met Peter's eye, smiled, then raised both hands, joined and shook them. Peter followed his example. Massive John Proctor, next to Burroughs, raised his huge hands in the same gesture, then George Jacobs looked from one to the other and raised and shook his stick.

"Stop that, you prisoners!" shouted the marshal. They did not, and several men in the crowd raised and shook their hands too. A young man with floppy hair produced a hammer from his toolbox and shook that. Part of the crowd was roaring approval while another hissed and booed.

"Get her on the cart!" yelled the marshal.

This was no easy task. Carrier shrieked and cursed but at last lay slumped on the floor, her head against the bottom rail. George, Proctor, and Jacobs were now talking quietly together. Peter felt a bizarre sense of envy. These men were comrades in the most profound of all human experiences. The constables started pulling up and fixing the rails at the back of the cart and, as the one who had been holding Peter let go of him, he darted to Burroughs, who leaned over, seizing his hand.

"Brattle tried to get you a reprieve but Phips had left for Maine again and he could not even reach him." Peter spoke as quickly as he could, knowing he would be pulled away at any moment.

"Please thank him for trying and bless you for coming, my friend. And for what you brought me. It means everything." Burroughs put his hand on his pocket.

It was strange to hear his voice out here in the free air. The constable seized Peter's arm and pulled him away. Burroughs called after him, "Tell Mary, now that I have this, I go to my death wanting for nothing!"

"Off! Go!" the marshal shouted to the driver, who, still standing with his feet far apart, flicked the reins. The horses moved forward. The prisoners clung to the rail or each other except Martha Carrier, who still lay on the floor.

"Remember me, friend!" Burroughs shouted.

"I'm coming with you!"

The horses started trotting. Proctor and Burroughs supported Jacobs while the marshal ran on ahead and the constables surrounded and followed the cart and the now unrestrained crowd surged forward. Peter tried to push through but the constables blocked his way. As the procession made its noisy way out of Prison Lane and along Essex Street more people joined it from either side, soon walking two or three abreast, some shouting and jeering.

The horses slowed as they turned into Boston Street, where Gallows Hill rose up steeply on the left. At the corner when the cart turned to ascend, a group of people stood waiting; Peter saw curly-haired Thomas Putnam and his thin-faced wife and sharp-nosed daughter and other Salem Village accusers and relatives. They joined the procession behind the marshal, in front of the horses.

As the cart went slowly uphill the sun was also climbing and the air growing hot. Peter bumped into the man in front as everyone halted and word came back that the cart was stuck in a rut.

"The devil hinders it!" came a girl's high-pitched voice. Ann Putnam's, Peter recognized.

"The devil hinders it!" a woman repeated. Others took up the cry. At last the procession moved again, more slowly.

The dark beams of the scaffold with its row of dangling nooses framed a rectangle of blue sky. The cart stopped and so did the shouting. Peter, with the advantage of height, could see the male prisoners staring straight at the gallows. Martha Carrier, now on her feet, looked round distractedly.

"There's your doorway to hell!" yelled Ann Putnam. Peter glimpsed her father's tightly curled head near her. Martha Carrier mopped her face on her sleeve.

"You're hot now! You'll be hotter soon!" called Ann.

There were loud, nasty laughs but a few "tut tuts" and head shakings.

As Peter looked toward the gallows a man appeared from behind it on an elegant horse. Captain White felt a sense of aversion as he recognized Cotton Mather, sitting tall, staring round, nodding at people he knew, his wig as pristine and abundant as the one he'd been wearing long ago when Peter saw him preaching in the meetinghouse. With sudden determination, Captain White elbowed his way forward, prodding rib cages, treading on feet to get as close to the scaffold as he could. Now he saw not only Mather but other ministers and magistrates on foot. He also had a better view of the group from Salem Village, including Ann Putnam, who wore a look of naked viciousness.

Everyone went quiet when there appeared round the scaffold a large-chested man with glistening muscles, his torso bare but his haunches and thighs gripped in leather and his feet unshod, which gave him the look of a satyr. Despite his bulk he walked quickly to the ladder leaning against the scaffold and leaped nimbly up the rungs. He reached for a noose, inspected it, and made an adjustment. This was not the man who had hanged Bridget Bishop, who had been a mere local constable. This was a professional executioner brought especially from Boston. Two other men, similarly attired, joined him from behind the gallows.

A dreadful screech turned all eyes to the cart. Martha Carrier was being pulled from it, her cries a mixture of curses and pleas, some of the sounds scarcely human, her complexion ash gray.

Cotton Mather's complacent face under his shoulder-length wig glowed with excitement. His horse had the same air as its rider, its head high and alert. On a level with its neck appeared Samuel Parris's tall, buckled hat. The man beneath looked uneasy, his underlip jutting. Beside him handsome John Hale was smiling slightly and next to *him* John Hathorne stood expressionless while Bartholomew Gedney looked disdainful and William Stoughton, a few feet from the rest, surveyed the scene with tight mouth and large eyes. Half behind *him*, looking anxious, was Nicholas Noyes. Peter remembered with pleasure Sarah Good's curse on him.

There was no sign of Samuel Sewall.

The constables got Carrier, still screaming, to the foot of the ladder and Peter could not help but share the crowd's loudly voiced desire for her noise to be silenced, though by some other means than the one they wished to hasten. The executioner seized her from the constables and lifted her onto a rung. One of his assistants helped hold her there while the other tied her wrists behind her back.

The hangman's glistening torso, satyr's legs, and blank face seemed scarcely human. But when Peter glanced at Cotton Mather, then at Stoughton, he saw in the excited air of one and the large, cunning eyes of the other a more frightening inhumanity.

When the rope was round Carrier's neck Noyes tried to say a prayer but her screams rendered it inaudible. They ceased only when she dropped. The sound of her neck snapping came straight after the thud. The crowd had scarcely doffed its hats before it gasped at the changed color and distortion of her features. This executioner did not use a hood.

Was she in heaven, Peter wondered. He must not think of this. He must concentrate on his purpose.

George Jacobs was seized and dragged forward. He kept hold of one of his sticks but the other fell to the ground and, as he tried to reach it, the marshal knocked it away.

"Let me walk!" he roared. "Give me my cane!"

"He'll strike the hangman!" screamed Ann Putnam. "'Tis the devil's cane!"

Peter remembered that Ann, for all her evil, was only twelve years old. The full insanity of a child leading this circus of horror struck him with particular force. Her shouts continued and were echoed by the crowd but no one tried to silence them.

George Jacobs was bundled onto the ladder, now moved from its former position so it leaned against the frame three feet from where Martha Carrier was dangling, and Peter saw that the executioner had no intention of cutting down bodies until all the prisoners were hanged. If Cotton Mather or any of the other ministers or magistrates disapproved of this, they did not show it.

When George Jacobs was halfway up, the executioner turned him round to face the crowd. As his wrists were being tied, he shouted, "I am as innocent as the child unborn! I have lived eighty years and never wronged any man!" He stared around, the bloodshot eyes in his weathered face glistening. "I see many friends and neighbors here! I've lived with you all thirty-three years! You all of you know I've never wronged any man!"

There were murmurs of agreement but also shouts of abuse.

"Cain lived many years before killing Abel!" The powerful voice silenced the rest. Cotton Mather's horse shifted at such a sudden noise from its back.

"You lived long before the devil prevailed with you, Mister Jacobs. But he prevailed in the end! Confess now and save body and soul!"

"I will not save this old body to damn my everlasting soul! Executioner, put the noose round my neck!"

"He can't wait to feel the flames!"

"Can't wait to meet his master!"

Some in the crowd shouted their support of him but others echoed the insults. The executioner positioned the noose round Jacobs's neck and Nicholas Noyes stepped forward to pray. But Jacobs shouted before he could speak, "Forgive me my sins, O God, and let me behold thee in thy glory and praise thee forever!"

"Amen!" shouted many.

"O, wise and merciful father," Noyes began in a minister's singsong voice.

Jacobs shouted, "I come to thee, my God!"

"Amen! Amen!" many again shouted. Noyes looked up at Cotton

Mather, baffled as to whether or not to keep praying. Mather shook his head, then nodded at the executioner, who tightened the noose and pushed Jacobs off the ladder. The old man bounced, swung, and twisted. The hangman nimbly leaped down.

Jacobs's neck had not snapped; he suffocated slowly. Peter turned away. The crowd's noise continued though the insults had stopped. After ten minutes, the sounds ceased. Peter looked around: the body was still and George Burroughs was walking to the scaffold, a constable on either side though not touching him.

He needed no help in climbing the ladder and turning to face the largest congregation he had ever addressed. His body seemed to have regained all its former strength; his dark eyes glowed; his long black hair appeared a mantle of authority.

"Good people." He spoke with a veteran minister's assurance, his voice carrying strongly and clearly through the hushed crowd. "Good people, I stand before you today convicted of witchcraft. I, a minister of God for twenty years, have been accused, though not formally convicted, of striving to overthrow God's rule in New England. Good people, if this accusation were just, I assure you I would confess it at once and save my soul from an eternity in hell, denied that light of God's countenance that I have striven for all my life. I cannot confess because confession would be a blasphemous lie. As I stand here before you, about to meet the God to whom I must answer for all things, I declare my innocence, and pray that once the noose has done its work, I will behold him with his angels in heaven and dwell with him for ever."

Women were in tears. Men shook their heads. Ministers and magistrates glanced at each other. Cotton Mather's horse pawed the ground.

"I go to my death with one wish, that my blood and the blood of the others who die here today shall be the last to be shed as a result of these trials. If the innocence of all of us here, proved by our refusal to confess to uncommitted crimes as we face divine judgment, helps to bring these trials to an end, we will die not in vain, but for a good and holy cause. Reverend Mather, I beg you to pray with me."

"I cannot pray with an unconfessed ally of Satan!"

"I am none! No matter. Good people, you I know will listen to my prayers and with your own help speed them to heaven."

Cotton Mather was having trouble controlling his horse.

"Almighty God!" Burroughs slightly bowed his head yet his voice still carried through the crowd and down the hillside. It seemed to some it must be heard even in Salem.

"I beg thee, forgive my accusers, deluded by Satan, and forgive the judges and juries who found me guilty, and forgive the ministers for refusing to pray with me in my hour of need, and most of all, I beg thee, forgive me George Burroughs all my many sins. I pray for this blessed forgiveness through the precious blood of our beloved Redeemer. Amen."

There was a huge shout of "Amen!" Still with bowed head, Burroughs recited the Lord's Prayer, delivering it phrase by phrase with fervor and composure and completely without error. At the end the crowd was gasping in wonder that this convicted ally of Satan could do this. Ann Putnam shouted, "The devil dictated it to him!" No one echoed her.

Mather was still having trouble with his horse but managed to gesture to the executioner, who lowered the noose.

"No!" shouted someone.

"No! No! Spare him!" shouted others.

"Proceed!" Mather screamed, pulling so hard at the reins that his horse gave a high-pitched whinny of pain that seemed an echo of his master's.

The executioner tightened the noose and pushed Burroughs off the ladder. Burroughs could not jump; it happened too quickly. The crowd surged forward but the constables kept them from the scaffold: some shouted, "Cut him down!" but others, "Let him die!" It was clear to Peter there was no chance that the people opposed to Burroughs's death could overwhelm the forces of authority, even if they had courage enough really to try.

Quickly Peter moved out of the crowd in the opposite direction from the magistrates and ministers. Ignoring a constable's shout he ran round the back of the scaffold. From behind Burroughs's twisting body he reached up and grasped the wounded ankles and pulled as hard as he could. He heard the neck snap as a constable reached him; he let go, dodged the man, and ran back into the crowd. Few had seen what he'd done; those who had were yelling with approval or outrage. Other voices were shouting that Burroughs was innocent, a true minister of God, and that all the others were innocent, and that the hangings should stop. As it became clear throughout the crowd that Burroughs was dead, Cotton Mather shouted, "He was never ordained! He is not a true minister!" His horse reared but he managed to bring it back down and, standing in his stirrups, wig askew, screamed, "His words were lies! He's as cunning as his master! The devil is here with him!"

Women were sobbing.

"He's in heaven!" shouted one.

"He's with God!"

"The devil can disguise himself as an angel of light!" Mather roared.

The protests went on but Mather by force of his position gained dominance. At last he lowered himself to the saddle and was able to say calmly, without interruption, "John Proctor waits to be hanged. He is as guilty as George Burroughs and the rest who died here today. If he lives he will take Burroughs's place as the wizard leading Satan's army. Constables, fetch him!"

Peter pushed his way out of the crowd and down the hill as quickly as he could. There was nothing more he could do here. But there was much to do elsewhere, in the days and weeks to come, to realize his friend's dying wish that his blood and the others' would be the last to be sacrificed to fear, superstition, envy, and the lust for power of vain, shallow men.

Epilogue

THE SUN SHONE IN A BLUE, UNCLOUDED SKY ACROSS MEADOWS AND swampland on one side and houses and fields on the other. The heat of the high summer's day was not yet stifling and she walked without too much discomfort down the hill. Coming to a space between houses like a gap between teeth, she stopped and gazed over scrubby brown grass dotted with stones. What had happened to the building that once stood here? There was no sign of charring but if it had burned long ago the earth would have repaired itself and rain and snow washed the stones. Had enemies of the owners set fire to it? There had been enmity enough.

Walking onto the rough grass, she sat on one of the low stones, facing away from the road toward the fields. Hearing footsteps, she swung round.

"You did that quickly," she said.

"Luckily there were two spare stalls."

"What was here, in this space, do you think?"

"Whatever it was, it must have been abandoned years ago and the timbers taken for firewood."

"You don't think it was burned down?"

"Doesn't appear so." He walked to another of the stones and tried to dislodge it. "Doesn't budge. Part of the foundations. Of course the house may have been demolished."

"I wonder why, if they didn't want to build something else here?"

"We'll ask at the inn."

He helped her up and they continued down the hill. People were beginning to appear on the road, some from over the horizon, some from houses nearby. The sun was getting hotter, the air stickier. She said, "Can we find some shade?"

"Thoughtless of me."

"Now, don't fuss."

"We will stand under that tree for a few minutes, then go back up."

As she leaned against the trunk he stared round. People were passing, mostly in pairs or family groups, mostly silent, all glancing at them, some nodding or smiling. Beyond the road, rolling fields and distant forest had a look of perfect tranquillity.

"Such a pretty place," he said.

"So strange we never came here."

"So long ago."

"But like yesterday."

"Getting very hot."

She nodded.

"We shouldn't have come." He took her hand.

"No, we had to. This heat reminds me . . ."

"I know."

"What?"

"The journey to Albany."

"No, no, I was thinking of the day. . . . Not just the day, the moment . . . I knew, when it happened . . . when he dropped."

Peter put his arms round her. They were silent for a while, till he said, "If only we could have made his death the very last of them."

"But without you and Mister Brattle, particularly that eloquent letter he wrote to Governor Phips, hundreds more might have died."

He let go of her but still stood close. "George's speech was the turning point. But I do not know if he could have made it, with that force and conviction, if he had not just read your letter."

"Do you mean that?"

"Aye. The way his face changed, as he read . . ."

"Perhaps he felt I was there with him."

"I know he did."

"Only eight more. He and you and Brattle saved so many."

"I did very little."

"You kept Brattle informed, particularly about those last hangings, when Nicholas Noyes sneered at the eight dead bodies hanging from the gallows and the crowd rose up against him, and you brought Brattle and John Hale together, after the girls overreached themselves and accused Hale's own wife. What you did was vital."

Neither spoke again for some time. She looked up the hill to see people gathering at the door of the building that crested it, then pushed herself away from the tree trunk. They started walking and when they were abreast again of the space between the houses they heard footsteps behind them and looked round.

"Israel!" Peter said.

Mr. Porter and his wife were with Peter Cloyce and Joseph Putnam and their wives. After warm greetings Peter said, "Let me introduce my wife, Mary, formerly Mrs. George Burroughs."

They all said how pleased and honored they were to meet her.

"Do you know what stood here?" Israel asked, pointing to the space where a building had once been. "The old meetinghouse. They abandoned it after Parris left the village."

"So the meetinghouse we are going to isn't . . . ?"

"No, it's built on the site of the old watchtower, also demolished after Parris left. I hope you will honor me by sitting in our pew."

"Our first time in a Puritan meetinghouse for thirteen years," Mary whispered to Peter as they entered the cool space, already half full.

"You know there is an Anglican church in Salem now, built by Philip English after he came back."

Israel ushered them into the pew nearest the pulpit. The Nurse family's was on the other side of the aisle, the pew beyond it still empty. Israel whispered that Francis had passed away soon after his wife died. He had been buried next to her, on the family property, in the same unmarked grave.

Behind the Porter pew sat a portly man, stroking his white beard, who nodded and smiled at Peter. He had just stabled the horses Captain and Mrs. White had ridden from their house in Roxbury, after giving them the best room in his inn. Next to him was his aging but still handsome wife.

Coming up the aisle together, but then heading, one to a pew, the other to a bench, were a tall, nervous-looking artisan and a floppy-haired younger one, no longer as young as Mary remembered them at Bridget Bishop's hanging.

The pew next to the Nurses' stayed empty.

"The new parson rearranged the pews so old enemies would sit next to one another, to try to make them friends," Israel said, with a small smile.

"Did it work?" Mary asked.

"Not till Thomas Putnam died."

"When was that?"

"Seven years after the trials ended. His wife followed him two weeks later."

"How did they go?"

"He fell from a horse. She hanged herself."

Mary said quietly to Peter, "We'll have to explain all this one day to someone I hope will scarcely be able to believe it . . ." She patted her slightly swollen stomach. "And to the other three. . . . The eldest girl's almost old enough now."

All talking ceased as an amiable-looking young man in clerical garb, followed by a woman who looked much older than her twenty-six years, came up the aisle. The woman's little eyes glanced round as they had when she'd walked up another aisle so many years ago but their expression now was quite different, no longer cunning and bold but frightened and sad. Following her came a procession of young people and children, identifiable as her brothers and sisters by their close-set eyes, tightly curled hair, and prominent noses.

"She raised them herself after her parents died," Israel said.

The pastor, young, round-faced, and smiling, as different in appearance from Samuel Parris as possible, went to the pulpit while the Putnams filed into their pew.

"Brethren." Pastor Green looked up at the galleries and back down. "As you all know, today is a special day for our village. Our sister, Ann Putnam, is to be received into our church. Before we say prayers for her, and give her our blessing, she will read out a statement. Ann, would you stand?"

Ann Putnam did so, turning to face the congregation. Then she lowered her head to read from a paper. She spoke softly, her tone flat. Her voice was familiar though no longer girlish.

"I desire to be humbled before God for that sad providence that befell my father's family in the year about '92, that I, then being in my childhood, should, by such a providence of God, be made an instrument for the accusing of several persons of a grievous crime, whereby their lives were taken away from them, whom now I have just grounds and good reason to believe were innocent persons."

The silence was total. Ann seemed to gain courage, and began to speak with more feeling, though her eyes stayed on the paper.

"It was a great delusion of Satan that deceived me in that sad time, whereby I justly fear I have been instrumental, with others, though ignorantly and unwittingly, to bring upon myself and this land the guilt of innocent blood, through what was said or done by me against any person I can truly and uprightly say, before God and man, I did it not out of anger, malice, or ill will to any person, for I had no such thing against any of them, but what I did was ignorantly being deluded by Satan." She took a breath and this time *did* look up, straight at the people seated in the Nurse family pew. Her expression showed sadness and longing. Mary reflected that anger, malice, and ill will had been exactly what Ann *had* felt, but no doubt she could no longer remember that and believed she spoke honestly. She must have lived in an isolation worse than imprisonment as the village made her their scapegoat after her father and mother died. When Ann began reading again her voice shook.

"And particularly, as I was a chief instrument of accusing of Goodwife Nurse and her two sisters, I desire to lie in the dust, and to be humbled for it, in that I was a cause, with others, of so sad a calamity to them and their families, for which I desire to earnestly beg forgiveness of God, and from all those unto whom I have given just cause of sorrow and offense, whose relations were taken away or accused."

"Ann, do you acknowledge this that you have read out, before the whole congregations, as your true confession?"

"I do." Tears trickled from her eyes.

"Let us pray."

On their journey back home Mary and Peter made a detour. In the woods behind Roxbury, where Peter had gone under cover of darkness with the same band of men who'd reburied Rebecca, they stopped at the tallest pine in the forest. Mary placed a bunch of roses at its foot, and she and Peter knelt and prayed.

Author's Note

SOME OF *DELIVERANCE FROM EVIL* IS FICTION AND OTHER PARTS ARE a mixture of fiction and fact. But I have used the ample historical records as much here as in my nonfiction books to try to reach the essential truths about the causes, development, and effects of the Salem witch hunt.

The hero of my novel, George Burroughs, is based on a man whose life, personality, and even appearance are well documented. We know he was born in England in 1650, was brought to Virginia as a small child, went from there with his mother to Puritan Massachusetts, attended school in Roxbury, and graduated from Harvard in 1670. We also know he worked as pastor in Salem Village in the early 1680s, leaving after disputes with certain villagers to go back to Maine, where he'd lived for several years before. We know he was arrested on a charge of confederacy with the devil, brought to Salem, examined, tried, convicted and hanged. We also know he was brave, strong, and highly intelligent. And that he was short of stature and so dark that people described him as "like an Indian."

In telling his story I have used the known facts but embellished them. Nothing in my depiction of Burroughs contradicts the historical record, but much goes beyond it. Burroughs did not as far as we know go to York in January 1692 to help fight the Indians; he did not, also as far as we know, love his third wife far more than the first two. He is reliably reported as giving a moving last speech on the gallows but the words he uses in *Deliverance from Evil* are ones I have written for him.

Almost all the characters in my novel are, like Burroughs, based on historical persons whose stories and characteristics are well known. This is true for Thomas Putnam, Ann Putnam, Samuel Parris, Betty Parris, Abigail Williams, John Hathorne, Samuel Sewall, William Stoughton, Increase Mather, Cotton Mather, Deodat Lawson, Thomas

Brattle, Elizar Keyser and his daughter, and all the accusers and victims
of the witch scare. The character of Mary Burroughs is unique in that
virtually all we know of the real woman is her name. I have invented her
story, personality, and appearance. The part of the novel concerning
her journey from Salem to Albany is pure fiction, as is the relationship
between her and Peter White. With Alice Perkins, Peter is one of the
only two significant characters created from whole cloth. The other
purely fictional persons are minor, such as the one eyed jailer and the
servant in Beadle's tavern.

For readers wishing to explore the nonfiction history of the Salem
witch trials and the lives and fates of the historical characters, I attach
a short bibliography. I have included John Putnam Demos's *The Unredeemed Captive*, which is not directly about the witch trials, since it is
wonderfully illuminating on the relationship between the Massachusetts
Puritans and the native Americans. My thanks to all the authors other
than myself listed here, who have given me inspiration and deepened
my knowledge.

BOYER, PAUL, AND STEPHEN NISSENBAUM. *Salem Possessed: The Social Origins of Witchcraft*. Cambridge University Press, 1974.

DEMOS, JOHN PUTNAM. *The Unredeemed Captive: A Family Story from Early America*. Vintage, 1995.

HILL, FRANCES. *A Delusion of Satan: The Full Story of the Salem Witch Trials*. Doubleday, 1995.

HILL, FRANCES. *The Salem Witch Trials Reader*. Da Capo, 2000.

HILL, FRANCES. *Hunting for Witches: A Visitor's Guide to the Salem Witch Trials*. Commonwealth Editions, 2002.

HILL, FRANCES. *Such Men Are Dangerous: The Fanatics of 1692 and 2004*. Upper Access, 2004.

ROACH, MARILYNNE K. *The Salem Witch Trials: A Day-by-Day Chronicle of a Community Under Siege*. Taylor Trade Publishing, 2004.

ROSENTHAL, BERNARD. *Salem Story*. Cambridge University Press, 1993.

UPTON, GILBERT. *The Devil and George Burroughs: A Study in Seventeenth Century Justice*. Enfield Books, 1997.